I0819853

TUNNELING TO THE MOON

A PSYCHOLOGICAL GARDENER'S BOOK OF DAYS

RICH IVES

Also by Rich Ives

Prose:

The Balloon Containing the Water Containing the Narrative Begins Leaking (Stories)

Sharpen (Chapbook)

Poetry:

Light from a Small Brown Bird

Anthologies:

Light in the Forest, Rain in the Trees (Northwest Poetry)

From Timberline to Tidepool (Northwest Fiction)

The Truth About the Territory (Northwest Nonfiction)

Evidence of Fire (German Poetry in Translation)

Translator:

Tomorrow I Was Leaving (Poetry by Johannes Bobrowski)

Text:

A Dirty Little Book About Writing the Truth

Silenced Press

First Hardcover Edition. First Printing.

ISBN-13: 978-0-9792410-7-9
ISBN-10: 0-9792410-7-3

Library of Congress Control Number: 2013934973

Cover artwork by Jay Fleck
Cover design and interior graphics by Andrew Cooney
Back cover illustration by David J. Nash

More information available at:
www.silencedpress.com

Acknowledgments

5x5; Abjective: Abremelin; Anobium; Apt; Aroostook Review; Avatar Review; Barge; Basalt; Beecher's Magazine; The Binnacle; Bitter Oleander; Black and White; Blackbox Manifold (UK); Black Words on White Paper; Blood Lotus; The Blotter; Blue Fifth Review; Buffalo Carp; Cafeteria; Catalonian Review; Cavalier Literary Couture; Chaffey Review; Clutching at Straws; Colorado-North Review; Connotation Press; Corduroy Mountain; Corium Magazine; Corvus; Crosscurrents (California); Crosscurrents (Washington); CutBank; Dacotah Territory; Daily Love; Danse Macbre; DecomP; The Delinquent (UK); Dunes Review; Eclipse; Eunoia Review; Fiction at Work; Fiction Review; Fine Madness: Fickle Muses; First Intensity; Forty Ounce Bachelors; Front Porch; Fwriction; Gargoyle; Georgetown Review; Gigantic; Gihon River Review; Greenfield Review; Green Silk; Hawaii Review; Hazmat Review; HeartLodge; Ilya's Honey; Image; In Between Altered States; InDigest; International Poetry Review; Iowa Review; Jellyroll; Kill Author; Knock; Lethologica; Linguistic Erosion; The Listening Eye; Marginalia; Massachusetts Review; Midway; Mississippi Review; Mochila Review; Mobius; Montana Review; Muse & Stone; Nebraska Review; New Orleans Review; North American Review; Northwest Review; Oyez; Pacific Coast Journal; Painted Bride Quarterly; Pear Noir; Pennsylvania English; Perigee; Permafrost; La Petite Zine; Phantasmagoria; Pipe Dreams; Poetry Motel; Poor Mojo's Almanac; Prose Poem International; Puckerbrush; Quarterly West; Ray's Road Review; Red Hawk Review; Red River Review; Reverbnation; Riverbabble; The Scrambler; The Same; Seems; Shelf Life; Silenced Press; Skidrow Penthouse; Slackwater Review; Smashed Cat Magazine; Snow Monkey; SNReview; Softblow (Singapore); South Carolina Review; Spilt Milk (UK); Subliminal Interiors; Subtle Fiction (New Zealand); Success Superstition Review: Switchback; Thieve's Jargon; Toasted Cheese; Turnrow; Ucity; Unlikely Stories; Verse; Weave; Weird Year; Willow Springs; Written Arts; Yarrow

"A Light in the Window" was reprinted in the Anthology of Magazine Verse and Yearbook of American Poetry. "The Man Who Juggled Eyes" was reprinted in Vibrations and The Montana Review. "Old Cotter" was reprinted in The Slackwater Review. "A Light in the Window," "Hangdog the Carpenter," "Patra Düldig's Galoshes," "Hangdog the Hunger Artist," and "An Ex-Confessional Poet's Notes on Theology" were reprinted in The New Taste. "The Dark Bird in the Dream of an Old Woman" appeared in somewhat different form in the limited edition poetry collection Notes from the Water Journals (Confluence Press). "Small Daisy Tied to a Finger Like a Ring" was reprinted by Fiction Daily. "Anticipatory" was reprinted in Bitter Oleander. "A Dog Barking at the Wind" was included in the Crosscurrents Traveling Arts Exhibit.

Special thanks to the Seattle Arts Commission for a grant, and to Everett Community College for a sabbatical, which contributed to the completion of this book.

An extra special thank you to Silenced Press for serializing the entire contents a day at a time in sequence all year long for 2013 and 2014.

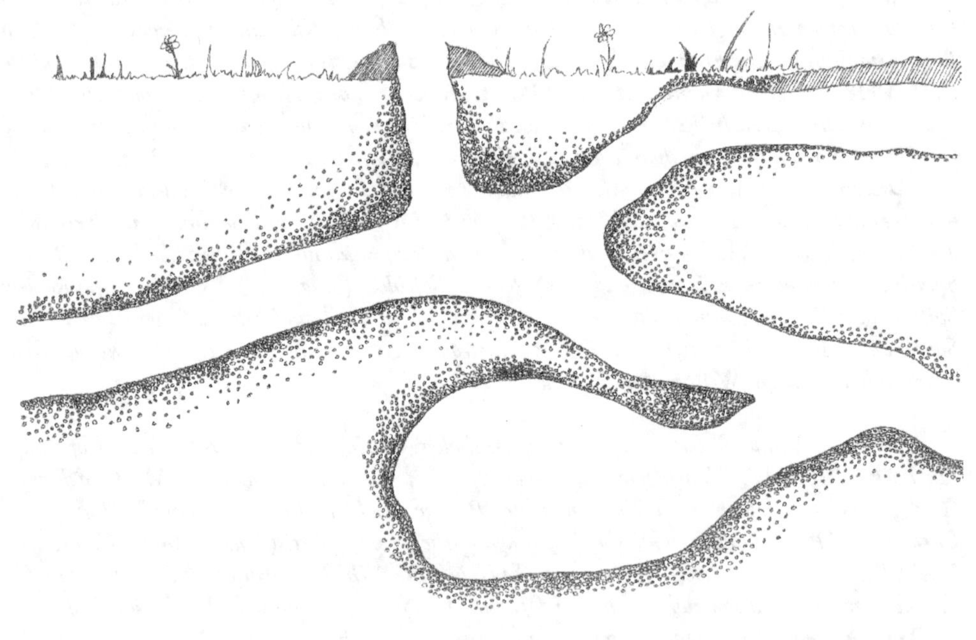

Burrow Guide

January

February

March

April

page

May

June

July

August

September

October

November

December

Moles are what I write, their white claws turned out, the balls of their toes are pink, enjoyed by all their enemies as delicatessen, their thick coat prized.

My moles are destructive, don't fool yourselves.

-Gunter Eich in "Preamble"

For Mole, falling in love really must have meant falling. For a long time afterwards he would arrive at wedding parties out of breath and with a concerned look, squeaking at the guests of honor: "Whee! Wonderful! Terrific!--but next time try and make sure that you really like the person that you're supposed to love!"

. . . You get to sleep together in one big room with a lot of people you don't know; also, Mole gathers from the manual, when the biggest and loudest snorer there rolls over on you or takes up most of your sleeping space, you're not supposed to complain, for the sake of revolutionary idealogical reasons.

I remember so well first seeing some time ago on your left-hand bosom, half-way up the right-hand side of the slope: this little brown mole.

Even for a mole in his final circle of tunnels, there is always one more, larger, more generous set of relevences into which all previous relevences fit.

-Michael Benedikt in *Mole Notes*

They seek tirelessly for new places to ask us whether we are who we are, and if that is enough . . . Is this dust yours, they say?

-W. S. Merwin in "The Moles"

Underground[1]: Occurring, operating, or situated below the surface of the earth.

Underground[2]: Hidden or concealed; clandestine.

Underground[3]: Of or pertaining to an organization involved in secret or illegal activity.

Underground[4]: Of, pertaining to, or describing an avante-garde movement, its films, publications, and art, usually privately produced and of special appeal and often concerned with social or artistic experiment.

Dig[1]: A poke; a punch.

Dig[2]: A sarcastic, taunting remark; a gibe.

Dig[3]: Informal. To begin to work intensively.

Tunnel[1]: An underground or underwater passage.

Tunnel[2]: A passage through any extended barrier.

Tunnel[3]: A funnel.

Tunnel [Middle English]: a pipe-like net for catching birds.

Gopher[1]: Any of the various short-tailed, burrowing mammals of the family Geomyidae . . . Having fur-lined external cheek pouches.

Gopher[2]: A ground squirrel.

Mole[1]: A small congenital growth on the human skin, usually slightly raised and dark, and sometimes hairy . . .

Mole[2]: Any of various small, insectivorous, burrowing mammals having thickset bodies with silky light-brown to dark-gray fur, rudimentary eyes, tough muzzles, and strong forefeet for digging. Most live underground.

Mole[3]: 1. A massive stone wall used as a breakwater or jetty, or to enclose an anchorage or harbor. 2. The anchorage or harbor enclosed by such a barrier.

Mole[4]: A mass or tumor in the uterus, caused by the degeneration or abortive development of an ovum.

Mole[5]: The amount of a substance that has a weight in grams numerically equal to the molecular weight of the substance.

Mole[6]: A Mexican hot sauce of chili, other spices, and sometimes chocolate. It is served with various meats.

Vole[1]: Any of various rodents of the genus Microtus and related genera.

Vole[2]: The winning of all the tricks in a game.

-*The American Heritage Dictionary*

January

January 1

In Preparation for Setting a Watch

It is best to begin with one's feet planted firmly on the ground, for time is elusive and this approach lends a comforting, if essentially false, sense of stability to the proceedings. This, of course, is to be done only after a suitable authority to use in determining the correct time to which one is to set one's watch has been located. It must be duly noted in passing that such an authority is measuring absolutes in a relative and inconstant world and is most surely not to be trusted for anything other than the correct time, which may in any case be of little, if any, use. Nevertheless, if one is determined to set one's watch, one must proceed in the manner most appropriate to the concept of time. One must, of course, be predisposed to using a certain amount of time to determine and attempt to "fix" time for one's later use, a delicate and occasionally irritating conceptual balance to be sure. If, however, one has planted one's feet firmly on an ant hill, one may be given another view of many-faceted time. And if one's feet were planted bare upon a sharp object, a truer understanding of the relativity of time may be obtained while one is bleeding, and in less time than it takes to actually set one's watch, time may in fact be "running out." For death may be understood as an abstract concept bearing a rather unique relationship to time. Just as it may be difficult to understand the philosophical implications of half a cup of water, so is it difficult to understand the value of the correct time mounted carefully upon a dead man's wrist.

January 2

Architecture

The inside of this house was created by the door, the door by the need to escape. The windows pulse with darkness. For this reason we measure our latitude for the accommodation of moonlight.

An island's darkness. A child's.

The ocean slowly leaping at the stars, the window wet with the birth of it, desire pulsing in the experienced muscles of the newly aged.

Bloodstones cobbled across the street of dreams, private police horses jittery in their interior streetlight.

What crimes have we considered?

Fell out of the darkness. Into the night.

It's the daylight alones us.

The house we live in created to resist, to wait.

Two doors because we want to be able to make a mistake.

If we leave, we want the darkness closed, the night open. If we stay, we want the window clear, the house historical, doors locked from both sides.

Walking out on ourselves, we miss the person we used to live in, the house of our former occupation. It's a long way to the beginning. When the mooneggs crack beneath our feet, it's the last journey.

The way out the way in.

The question its own answer.

January 3

Morning Landscape with Camembert

One of the survivors. The boy. The man. Rain on the water, the ocean swelling out past the rolling hills, insects storming alive in the vineyards, and the deeper physical knowledge of a smell in darkness. Then light in his hair. Blood on his sleeve. Something from childhood, from the moment before the moment the first raindrop hits the ocean. Something from the eye of a grape roiling in a vat of frantic feet.

In a clearing at dawn, this surrounding moment, memory fading, quiet, calm, a soft light among the leaves and a quiet meal of wind and sky. You alone and this landscape falling out beyond the sky. But it needs too many friends and suddenly even the moon is less important than this first bite of cheese.

January 4

The New Mayor of Italian Stones

Sitting on my stove there is a stone in which there is an insect made of ice. Other stones have other things in them. There are stone houses on the side of a mountain, very old ones with lumps on their roofs like blue-gray ashes stuck to mounds of old tree sap. There is a town in Nevada in which at night in one of the stone rooms a bald man is bowing and bowing to the soft light, a greeting he repeats over and over he is so happy to be there with the soft light on his head. In a valley in Italy many stones have gathered. Someone wants to be mayor. He is giving a speech. He is condemning the old mayor for stubbornness, for refusing to see what is making it difficult to live properly. He is saying that the inside of the old mayor's head is like a mule with three oars strapped to its back. And he is saying, "Empty out your shoes. They are full of old addresses." And he is describing a country in which new houses sit on the hillsides like fresh loaves of bread.

January 5

Torn Shirt

Then a possibility fell out of my sky and a man entered my body, his sanctuary from the other world, a bundle of crows calling from his temporary mirror.

I walked in the silence until the silence walked in me. Then I ate.

The shadow was silent and it ate.

I decided to cover the nail in the wall with my shirt because my shirt seemed no longer to cover me. Because his hands did not turn blue when the moon touched them, I knew he was the one.

But why was my cloud still crying so slowly it seemed it could no longer float? My aging beast could no longer growl. I could have been the most patient exhibit in the museum.

Then I latched the father of my tears to the entrance. The night sky lacked only one absence to complete its darkness. But wouldn't a possibility have more value if you knew it was a possibility? Wouldn't the door open more easily if you weren't on the inside? Wouldn't you want to let that poor man out?

Eventually what had been inside me drifted back into the sky and a man left with my body, his mirror in his temporary world. Something had been removed from the surface. Something had been placed against a wall and the tear in it had opened. Something remained inside, but it was no longer me. I was pouring out and I was a kind of darkness that knew how to return. I was not entirely unwelcome. I could see that in myself.

The shirt was silent. I didn't have to explain what it already knew. It had rested upon me and it had held me and I had opened it. I was holding it up to the wall of a tree, a tree that had held itself up to a wall of light, a wall of light that had held itself up to the night, the night that was climbing out of a tear in me, a tear to keep the world apart and possible.

January 6

Probably Not Dangerous

It's out of the question. Who would have said "turbid gully" at a dinner party? And adolescent novels are not a threat. In my opinion, they're a hoax. Perpetrated.

But I talk to him anyway. I communicate. By doing this, you become not somebody else. I got so happy I couldn't speak of it.

Such people are probably not dangerous. That's disappointing. They remind me of, well, me. A party of collusive mes. And by the end of the night I remind myself of everyone I've ever known. I look at myself and it's not me that looks back. It's kind of like talking. We agree to compromise each other.

I try writing another story but it's an illusion. I take away the illusion. I don't take away the words. I ask the words to stay, so now they mean something else. They moved in. They want to mate, but that's not the same illusion.

I try to take away those words too, but the illusion clings.

So I begin taking away the words about the words and it's as if I were talking to you. It's as if I were communicating. The words can see this, can't they? I wish they'd take the illusion away with them. Consider how much could be false. Do you know what it's like to be this misunderstood? Wonderful things can happen.

It's like this. Because I did it, you're guilty. That's how literature works. I have to grow up now. I'm hungry like a god.

Do you know what it's like to become literature? In my opinion, it's a hoax. Who would have said, "I ask the words to stay," in real life? Who would have said "hungry like a god?" Who would have believed sufficiently in the pretense to disseminate explanations? Who would have written so naively about the development of one's own character?

Not this passing phenomenon. Not this temporary acceptance of traditional intellectual manipulations. Not this empty skin of verbal excess. Not this cumbersome churning, clogging the conventions of its own verbal gravity.

But perhaps I've been denied. Is it too late to toast the ghost?

If the conversation has ended, perhaps we could speak in private, as we have been doing in public, but with each other this time.

January 7

Speculations Concerning the Source of Certain Unidentified Manuscripts

By noon the pencil had written 18,341 sentences, not including this one. Naturally, people begin to read them. Some like what they read. The pencil creates a following. It signs contracts for television appearances. It honors none of them. It declares itself independent. Nevertheless, someone must be responsible. Lawyers are hired. Sentence after sentence rolls onto the paper in a steady stream of creation. There is no pause longer than a period or a dash. Paragraphs have been totally bypassed. The pencil's amorous life sharpens in proportion to the dullness of its point. Having become quite dedicated to its work, it has time for a pencil sharpener only as one is both easily accessible and necessary to help maintain the ceaseless quality of its work. Due to its increasing fame, the mere touch of its fiber is enough to send any but the most rusty sharpener spinning frantically in an orgasm of wood and lead. It leaves them spinning and returns to its work. None but the most avid of the pencil's admirers are capable of detecting any pause at all. They begin to argue among themselves. None seem very confident about their ability to detect this most valued moment in the life of their idol. They begin talking of the good old days. Some people begin to worry about the meaning of all this. The pencil's true followers, of course, do not. Others claim to have been doubtful from the beginning. The pencil's work continues. Little used words (eructate, tatterdemalion, ziggurat) are masterfully placed. Punctuation becomes so accurate that a favorite pastime is discovering errors. Of course, none are ever discovered, but people refuse to give up hope. More contracts are signed. Everyone knows they will not be honored. It doesn't matter. Any trace of the pencil becomes valuable. Radically differing marks on various articles (napkins, toilet paper, walls, hands) are claimed as autographs. Verification of pencil marks becomes an argumentative and profitable science with an ever-increasing following. Various theories are proposed in regard to the pencil's refusal to use paragraphs. Conferences are held. Books are written. New courses are offered in graduate schools. The word "pencilness" enters the English language and quickly spreads to other language groups. The quality of various products is rated in terms of the gradations of pencil lead. "How do you like it?" "3H." "It does have a certain pencilness about it, doesn't it." To call someone "pointed," "woody," or "leaded" becomes an extreme compliment. The pencil learns the art of condensation. More and more is said in less and less space. Reading between the lines is necessary. A few people claim to have detected hesitation in the pencil's work. No one believes them. The pencil's new work is a surprise to everyone. They find it harder and harder to believe there is anything left to write about. Skeptics predict the date of the pencil's downfall. Fortunes are won and lost as the pencil continues writing. Faith in the pencil's stability returns. "Pencilness" gains connotations of endurance as well as quality. Pencil T-shirts and lunchboxes become popular. A few intellectuals claim the meaning of the pencil's work has been devalued by the embrace of common acceptance. The pencil continues writing. And then one day a very large building falls down and everyone remembers how it was such a fine building that they kept trying to make it taller and taller until you couldn't see where it ended even on a clear day and one of the newspapers has a contest in which everyone gets a chance to guess how many stories are in the building, but nobody gets it right, not even the pencil falling a page at a time from the top of the lost building . . .

January 8

The Man Who Believed in Magic

When the magician sawed her in half, he looked in the mirror. A mouse was nibbling stale bread. An ant with a leg missing stole the bread. The applause rained on the stage. When the miracle was finished he touched his fingers to his toes, dreaming of all the little animals he would like to take home to his fat gray cat.

When the magician pulled a rabbit out of his hat, the mirror clouded over and changed color. It turned the bronze shade of river mud at sunset. He thought of carp sleeping in the mud. He had heard they could do that, hibernate like bears, asleep in the mud until the water came back. He wanted to reach down into the dark ooze and yank them out, flapping on the mud.

When the magician pulled silk from his sleeve, it made his eyes water. He remembered a woman in a black robe with bright threads woven into it like a tapestry. There was a bridge with swans beneath it and an oriental woman with an even smaller scene woven into her parasol. He swam through the black water and waited on the far side of the bridge. A small stream of applause trickled across his forehead. He touched it, and frogs began falling from the sky.

When she locked the magician in a tall chest, he felt knives piercing his sides and chains rattled in his forehead where before he had lived in peace with his eyelids. It seemed to go on forever, small knots of color flashing from his fingers, tingling as if he were reaching for something wonderful. When he heard them gasp, he bowed, and behind him something bright and wounded fell through the stage and shuffled home unnoticed.

January 9

Temporarily Overcome by Exhaustion

When you get there, remember each of you may be innocently driven. The poinsettia whitefly is not a health food for the elderly nor simply a time of confusion for the church. We accept the sky's beguiling animals unthinkingly from dozens of nameless men and women every day.

Cruel, cheap and shapeless, the cab of the old rocking chair reminded Sofia of her grandmother, a religious woman with an inordinate fear of the aroma from the fingernail factory.

Just then, Ellen remembered how thoughts of the dark cellar had filled her with numbing excitement.

Meanwhile, Sofia's grandmother was struggling with soft low intervals of melancholy. Her damp hair was sticking out from under a red headband.

The little paradise reportedly has no jail.

One such offense concerns an elderly woman who accidentally cooked her dog while trying to dry him in her microwave oven. Another concerns the five frigid lakes of Antarctica. The fugitive crossed hundreds of miles of dangerous territory. He can now observe his torn boat from afar.

If you haven't realized how much your life has diminished, Ellen will take you shopping.

Roughly 45,000 thunderstorms ravage the earth every day. They are often hired and fired on the basis of skin tests given to viewers to measure their emotional reactions.

So they tentatively reached out their hands towards each other.

Ellen quickened her pace to a trot.

They began touching the craft with their snouts.

Slowly, ever so slowly, she pulled herself from the wreckage before it burned.

January 10

The Happiness of Children

Sam Small was a sad little toadstool indeed. He called for his apple juice and he called for his tea and not a whisper of a reply echoed from the long hall of inherited privilege.

Sam's biological father, Abersome Jabberly, lived in London with a new wife Sam's mother liked to call The Ice Queen. Sam's stepfather worked as a bouncer in a grunge den in downtown Seattle and went to auditions for Pearl Jam roadies and David Lynch movie extras to show Sam's mother he was current.

Mrs. Small wanted to be a magician but had to work for an Afghan restaurant "until the magician thing works out." She was getting a little impatient with kebabs and rosewater. She began having dreams about lambs running through her bedroom with blood dripping from their necks, bleating loudly. She didn't talk about the dreams, but Sam knew. He was an intuitive little scamp.

Sam called louder. Still no reply. He began singing his apple song and his tea song and as the notes blued with improbability, Sam began whistling in the freshly fallen dark. Which had discovered the advantages of clinging.

Then one day Sam's mother was trying to change a dove into an egg and Sam's stepfather said, "You got it backwards." Sam's mother changed him into a homeless person.

Don't be so quick to judge. She had her reasons. Sam understood.

Then Sam wanted to eat eggs for breakfast and Sam's mother tried to change one into an omelet for him. She changed the egg into something, but Sam didn't know what it was.

Nevertheless, Sam demanded of himself that he remain a happy little toadstool. For a while. Until some other miserable thing that life does to you came along. But whatever it was, he was not going to worry about it. And you could not have guessed what was going to happen either because it wasn't going to happen. It just did.

And Sam's mother was very pleased indeed that she won that bloody custody battle before gradually depriving her son of his exquisite sense of false decorum, and Mrs. Red Hen didn't even notice her 34th stolen almost-a-baby, which had not been changed into anything, but just stayed an almost-a-baby until Sam added it to the increasingly disturbing history of his stomach.

January 11

Tall Tales

Eat. *The grand green absence speaks fondly of you.* As do I. Skinny facts like you don't live long.

Listen, it's okay, you're already sprouting. I can hear the long story stretching in your mouth. You see, the village has a cow and three tall men to milk it. We don't discuss politics.

All the wonderful emergencies left town on foot. How will they know the dark sky is their home?

If your hunger is continuous, you must weave the lie back into the perfection of innocence, which remains green and still talks about you as if you were a brother or a carefully fulfilled kidnapping.

If the cow weren't so long, the effort might actually encourage the evocative grimace of empathy on the human's face, where it belongs, but some less reluctant lies prefer to provoke the truth and create a more disturbing balance of ransom notes and confessions.

In such a village you have to reach higher to achieve the necessary emptiness of authentic air. The truth piles up so deep it's difficult interpreting the dripping corners of its earthen vessels. But this is a simple place and we do these things because birds exist, because smoke is attached to the past, and because blankets are not really a form of repression.

Enjoy yourself. Consume.

So inviting you might want to seek the image of your soul in it. So patient it doesn't even poke at you the way the ones who have merely witnessed it do. So peaceful you can hear the oldest church sighing, the one without a minister or a table.

Go ahead, the innocents are waiting.

January 12

The End of the Road

I sit down at that precise moment because I understand it's the right thing to do. Then I get up and go for a walk in the snow. I can't see the end of the road. So I sit down because again it is the right thing to do.

So I go to the shopping mall to buy some walking shoes. So I can walk in comfort. And the place is very very busy. So I sit down.

So while I'm sitting there I think about where I am going to go walking and before you know it, I'm there. Walking. And my feet begin to feel like maybe they're going to be developing some blisters. So I sit down. So I can see if I have any blisters.

And I don't. Have any blisters. So I go back to the mall to buy some shoes. But the mall is closed. So I break in and buy some shoes. I leave the money on the counter. Because it's the right thing to do. So then I sit down.

I don't have any blisters and I'm not going to get any either. My feet are comfortable at this moment. My feet are inordinately comfortable at this moment. My feet do not understand what is going to happen. But I do and I sit down some more.

I still can't see the end of the road. So it's a good thing I have new shoes. So I can get up and follow the path meant for walking.

And so that I may sit down some more. Because the end of the road is not going to make itself available to me so easily just because I'm looking for it. That is what I have learned from the sun as it leaves me yet again and that is what I will say to the moon's shepherds when I find them.

January 13

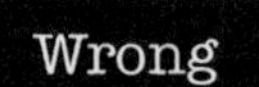

I was thinking the moon was in the apple tree, but I was mistaken. I was thinking the church ought to be there.

I was assembling a god from jumping ropes. I was going to church, but I didn't know then what church was.

I was floating along with church, making up children for the collection box, and Josh swam by, a good friend to the end. I was expecting him to last longer. A little more Josh than that.

Then an apple fell from the apple tree and I was mistaken again. But I was still hungry.

Then Alex wrote a new song I didn't want to hear anymore.

He was a judge. He worked at the Texaco.

He said I was feeding a complicated goat complex and I was trembling. I was only partially mistaken.

I was watching Alex trying to pick up two girls and the rump roast. The church was still not in the apple tree. The two girls did not believe they were assembling God.

Alex was not a minister. And he didn't work at the drive-in.

And I was terribly shaken and I was trembling and I was no longer certain of being mistaken.

It was not the right time to stop making up children or searching for guidance in the apple tree's innocent hungers, nor was it time to lure Alex away from a steady income just to question the circumstances under which Josh had absconded with such a large portion of that particular church's appropriation of valuable children's rhymes and secular employment opportunities. It wouldn't have left us any more certain of his end than the cut rope swinging in the wind from the very same branch of the apple tree upon which the sleeping crow's silhouette had coincided with the moon's emergence from the passing cloud bank.

I myself just wasn't important enough yet to be eclipsed in such an enigmatic fashion.

I guess I was thinking the church ought to be there.

January 14

I'm Using the Towel

Let me get the mistake out of the shower. Let me splash on some desert mint. You see, I'm available now, but I'm still using the towel you gave away.

That's how quickly life changes. The moisture content signaling a biological response. It hurts and I still want it.

It's like a headache with a soft wet key.

And on the edge of that road there's a man with a very loud music box. It starts raining again.

Let me get the story away from the authorities. Too many questions.

Let me give you a breath mint. I wish it could be a wet one.

The music box is singing, "Whip it. Whip it good." But I'm breathing with greater ease and awareness now. The rain is ready for another dance.

On the edge of the same road the man is whispering. It's harder to hear the grass.

A revolutionary collection of windsongs appears to be resting between drying parents. All we have to do now is change the direction of the headache, its soft wet thread woven into the gift you once might have discarded. All we have to do now is return the device with which we have accepted the moisture and explain that it's not a towel.

If the rain continues dancing, we're complicit. The man on the road may have been me all along. You might have been expecting that. If the mistake isn't dressed to suit you, you might try adjusting the weather. It's got something to do with moisture compatibility and the misrepresentation of domestic activity.

I can't be held responsible. You've got your own life now. Here, try singing along with this new music box I imagined. You could make the song do whatever you want. You could stand out in the rain along the same road and wait for the incident to find you.

Of course the rain makes it more difficult, but it's not my rain, now, is it.

January 15

Shouldn't You Be More Specific?

It was accurate, but not specific. I had to give it mouth-to-mouth resuscitation. I had to give it acceptance.

It was not available for further comment until after the hydraulics demonstration and by then it was turning a beautiful shade of turquoise blue.

I was up to something, but I didn't know what it was. I was most certainly still breathing though. I couldn't hear the other guy who was me very well or I might have shouted. I might have given him another elbow.

I made an heroic effort to be more specific.

By then it was sunset and no one was taking advantage of the porch swing, so I organized a position of royal entitlement and rocked and swung and rocked and swung. It was very pleasant and a little purple and nearly acceptable.

But I still didn't know what my survivor was going to say, so I enclosed the peanuts, which had become the vehicle, carefully in a spittle-proof jar. I wanted someone to think I was competent. I wanted him to know what I would not allow.

I was most certainly not still up to something, but I still didn't know what it was.

So I readjusted the chair and attempted once more to achieve superiority in its company, but it only rocked and rocked. I expected it to fall over. It did not fall over.

Naturally the porch swing observed without comment.

But I wanted a comment. I wanted a comment and then another comment.

I was up to something, and it didn't know what I was.

My survivor was still rocking.

I tried to be even more specific, but what he was doing was rocking.

Something came up to me. I was still breathing. It wanted to know what I was, so I became more accurate, but then it wanted me to be more specific. It wanted me to literally be there. But I couldn't because I was, literally, here, offering peanuts. Specifically. But it had become quite inaccurate. "I can, finally, accept that," was what I imagined I was saying to myself, walking down the road, trying to remember what I had agreed to.

January 16

The Suspect Was Observed Entering the Reservoir

They can't get to you. A grebe here and there. Ducks gossiping everywhere. The bright ping of an old man's useless metal detector. All softened by the delicate warbling scarf of a brooding heron.

I don't want to be recognized as much as that, but I've learned that it's necessary to create a little relativity from time to time. It's the only way to stay hidden.

The geese and muskrats aren't very interesting, but their results matter. I don't get seen by the upper muckymucks. That's the point.

I'm really a retiring creature. I'm not here much. Even when I'm here.

My mossy cheeks are no longer swollen. My tangled hair has fallen away. I'm practicing a wet shuffle.

Don't worry. I'm safe in your unintentional shelter.

But sometimes exceptionally delirious things are happening and I have to watch out for that. I have to breathe. The fat-mouthed bass won't notice, unless I'm looking shiny or wounded. "Like a baby," I want to say, but I don't.

There really isn't another one of my kind available anymore. I'm outmoded, but I live in my old world. You can't forget to take something like that with you.

Unfortunately, the newer migrants know this and that's why they've filed the complaint, but if they're so busy suspecting, doesn't that make them another kind of suspect?

January 17

Misery

You could see that it wasn't the kind of party for delivering heartfelt speeches or creating intimacy. The guest of honor was having an intense collaboration with his hair. Then we noticed the south wall was a garage door and the kitchen table a cable spool. There was a map of Gettysburg in a spaghetti stain on the bed, which served as a sofa. We were either delighted or desperate. They looked the same.

And why, in the middle of the festivities, did the guests draw an invisible circle around themselves and separate, with their mouths still flopping like comic-book shoes?

Someone tried to cheer someone up by saying, "There's always someone unhappy somewhere." Someone was not ashamed to be avoiding the obvious.

We all tried to visit the inside of our heads, but there wasn't any celebration there either.

We weren't very successful at gesticulating wildly to get the host's attention. By now we were as miserable as he was. We tried to draw new circles.

Someone knocked on the door and the host answered, saying, "Hello there, I thought you were dead."

And the new guest said, "What do you know about death?"

And the host said, "From the looks of my party, a great deal."

And the guest said, "If that were really true, this might be a truly perceptive and penetrating gathering."

Then someone who was secretly attacked without warning tried to put on the dark cloak the evening had been wearing. It fit poorly. A satire without any self-awareness.

When we no longer felt bad about what we would have missed had we not come, it was time to go home. Then we could look safely back at this moment with longing.

January 18

Territorial Imperative

We had a long way to go and the mountain roads were dangerous. Portions of the journey were violated, but the spirit remained. I liked it, but it clung, tightly.

A nightmare of shoestring wisdom. Family members and acquaintances with homespun remedies for unnamed disturbances.

It's the old story. An evil spell.

That's why I went hunting every night.

Yes, I'm always ahead of myself, but I can't win.

It's the politeness that kills you.

Predictably, I devoured some small frightened creature nearly every excursion.

One time there was another world visiting with clouds of pale wispy shrimp in the sky. It was one of my most pleasant diversions. I could have let on, but it's easier pretending you don't know. The baby talk gets me, but you can get as pissy as you want and they think it's all part of the episode.

There's a moment of calm when you think it's all inevitable. It's a moment of pleasure until hope excites the forgotten anxieties again.

I've been studying its architecture. A fine old example of retro-abandoned symbolism. The skin chimney especially creates an aura of undesirability and the large square rooms with high ceilings and so many wavy little windows invite the invigorating and annoyingly ambiguous cold air into far too many otherwise comfortable thoughts. "Institutional" the newlyweds might whisper behind the real estate agent's back.

But all this does belongs to us, despite appearances. There's genius and incredible control in the collusions of the hopeless. Especially the families. It's a clever spell. The most desperate ones shimmy and dart and try to run away. It's no use. If escape were possible, we wouldn't desire it.

January 19

A Temporary Loss of Personal Identity

If you think about other people's troubles, you will know how lucky you are not to be them. But Wee Willie's fat finger was pointed right at Wee Willie's own fat finger in the nasty little mirror of his self-indulgent but very very large imagination. He was searching for happiness.

He looked on the ceiling and he looked into the minute particles of tiny micro-organisms and he looked in the kitchen closet.

"Wherever can I be?" exclaimed Winkie's dense and childish philosophical preoccupations and Willie's mother gave him a sugar cookie.

"Perhaps I am hiding in the grass," considered Winkie, and he raced for a vegetation map in his papa's dusty old encyclopedia.

Willie read, "The white men found that they could not always kill one of the stragglers to eat." Then Willie read, "The lands marked with the green symbols are the places where grass is plentiful." Still no Willie. "Across these great plains once roamed herds of wild oxen, horses, goats and sheep," said the encyclopedia. But no roaming Willies. All Willie got out of the whole adventure was that somehow some people had learned how to tame some animals and eat them.

Wee Willie was lonely indeed.

But because of the international recognition of his mother's freshly knitted consulate, an extremely new parade was passing. Perhaps it should be recognized that we needn't break into warbling; however, Wee Willie did rush into the available street where a variety of dangerous rains were falling and unintentionally offered his body as a shield. His predictability, friendly as a warm virus, nearly killed him.

Following Willie's recovery, Willie was chastened with overly generous laurels while several precariously perched officials were cooing over his aggravated inflation. Despite the inconclusive official inquiry, most of Willie's relatives thought he had been outlawed, his greatest achievement to date, but they were nevertheless surprised to see him used so irresponsibly yet once more by the fickle public. All this repetitious hugging required repetitious investigation.

Suddenly, there was Willie's mother with a hankie, dabbing at her swollen eyes. "Here is a nice pair of dull scissors and here is a beautiful dirty cup," she said, beaming, and crying, and winking at the governor.

After dinner, Winkie's mother told Winkie's father all about how he got lost and the beautiful gifts he received for his accidents.

"Now that we've got you back, let's substitute some more sugar cookies for the affection that was rightfully yours in the first place. I'm so sorry we don't have another name for it."

You see, Willie's mother was not crammed full of useless illusions as are the engendering sources of so many deceived children. No melodramatic offers of undying affection and maternal dedication. No generous donations to inflated charities. No misguided mendicants grousing about their new ties to gratitude agendas. No farm implements wheezing in the child's nostalgic future dust. And especially no obsolete cigar smoke billowing out of the neglected father.

Poor Willie.

Yes, it's a sad and ordinary tale. You probably wish it had ended differently and it did, in the approved version. But many new varieties of rain have begun falling and one of them, surprisingly, is reflecting Willie's unreliable happiness in collusion with several other closely related but equally tentative varieties of experience. In fact, all of them are telling this very story, whether it's Willie's or not, because damnit somebody's in here and I want to come out.

January 20

The Lad from the Isle of Skye

There once was a lad from Scotland attending his aunt's assertiveness training course in a small farming community in one of the Plains states. He was ill at ease, for he had been studying low hanging shiny new branches in his native highlands and found his aunt's new course of study nearly devoid of them.

This was no fairytale. This was intense and deprived. There was no bright carriage to the everlasting graveyard from this flattened castle.

A tidy little limerick of the lowlands had it that certain Highlanders' kilts were made of scullery maids' undergarments and their tartans revealed the diseases the maids had died of, but the young lad had not heard this until it was used by his new classmates in lurid derision.

"By what chance occurrence then shall I achieve my enlightenment?" wondered aloud the young Highlander.

And so off he went, swimming in the dirty little river of progress, and when he came out, he dried off with clean towels and achieved a certain distance. Could it be so easy?

It was time to pause and reevaluate his circumstances.

He listened, carefully, from afar. His shadow had never spoken so softly. Did it know him so much better now?

And when a stray cloud came down low, with a strangely suggestive shape to give away, he was ready to go home.

It felt like a ballad and that frightened him, for he was Scottish and knew what happened in ballads.

He waited for the chorus.

It did not come from the heavens, but he sang the words like a soldier, again and again, and each time they did not mean what they had before. Each time he took them deeper into his aging body. A sea of possibility gradually surrounded his new homeland. Beneath him lay the story of his ancestors rowing with the blades of the words they were singing. The lad stuck one of his own verbal oars into the unstable dirt of the Plains, but he had already forgotten to allow for the missing boat made of low hanging shiny new branches.

January 21

Delinquent

What kind of animal are you?

Still forming. Not a hair left untouched.

Are you capable of subtle distinctions?

The past has presence. I have presence. We don't have to occupy further.

It lets the wind pass through you? Lets the earth?

Yes, but when it's my turn to explain, I listen. I try not to be thick, not to entertain. I try not to discourage fragrances. I'm not alone.

Perhaps we live in bodies that do not understand civilization?

As something else we achieve success. As someone different we define our future landscape. As ourselves, birth continues.

What luck. We don't have to go to the twentieth century today.

Yes, a gift from the bushes. Independent gardens for independent desires. They visit us with history. We don't have to exaggerate.

But when it leaves, you are still here. Come sit awhile. Come rest.

It feels very peaceful. We have never been a greater crime.

January 22

It's Not Fair, But We're Related

First you're something else. And then you're back. Then you're not here anymore.

What did you expect from a distant relative? This family has never been golden. This family has never been family.

Sometimes the mountains above Anywhere Ridge are just mountains and sometimes they are dusted with powder-blue symbolism.

Look, it's snowing now. Witness.

I'll just sit by the window. I'll just equivocate and sustain.

I'll invite you back again before you arrive. I'm that kind of a guy. I am. The family approves. That's how we got this way.

So what poised uncertainty shall we activate next? Perhaps a symmetrical opposition. Deep wet wrists. Just slap them on the table next to the breeding tray.

Now you're enticingly enigmatic again. The family's with you, but it's not really the family that does that. It's the arrangement of the relatives.

We're already overextended. We live in a little picture window with our name on it.

Now your motion has been suspended. Now your suspension has been distributed to willing participants. Several of them know you didn't mean to be this way. Several recognize the uneasy resemblances. Separation in degrees but not very many. And several summer in the mountains above Anywhere Ridge where their powder-blue symbolism grows increasingly subtle with every passing relative.

January 23

A Self-Guided Tour of Jonathan

Jonathan lay on the bed fully clothed. A foul taste festering.

The young man was dazed. Reeking.

The problem is domestic and solid and capable of swooping into horror at the drop of a belt.

First you cook it and then you eat it.

Domestic.

But the stingy little bird of Jonathan's self-acceptance may not offer royal corridors of light under its incorrigible wings for the enlightenment of the self-inflicted representations of uncertainty nesting in Jonathan's self-perception.

Dazed and reeking.

Childhood Jonathans steam and bubble and fill the room with sweet smells while foolish scientists attempt to determine if a desire-proof wall could contain the remainder of similar desires.

The mystery of Jonathan's tears is said to have begun with incriminating trembling gestures. Followed by sneezing, from which Jonathan does not quickly recover.

Jonathan closed. Jonathan absent. Jonathan missing from the bed fully clothed. Despite compatibility appearances, it's not enough to keep the curious from discovering the deception. Even if the problem remains domestic.

Nature's not good at waiting. Nature's not expecting another Jonathan. Jonathan, on the other hand, is expecting his Jonathan. This allows further Jonathans to occur, but sooner or later Jonathan is allowed to visit Jonathan.

The sun glares off the afternoon sea, making everyone before you on the deck into a silhouette, a puppet theatre dancing out a story with its meaning hidden, even the puppets unsure of their roles, but trying desperately to have fun in them.

Ah, but smell the ocean, my innocent. Which is the real Jonathan and which the myth? If you place your hand at the confluences of your body, can you smell the ocean it brings back? Can you swim in this ocean inside the ocean?

Of course you can, and you can feel the fingers accepting the reach of your tongue as it draws them to your lips and in. The slow pulsing of your cheeks to the draw and release, as if you were talking.

And, of course, you are.

Someday Jonathan will be allowed to go home now.

Perhaps afterwards you could ask for this gift.

January 24

You're Not Here Yet. Come In.

Steady and long he released the parting humid darkness of it. The body's intoxicating liquor thrumming a song of need.

There are at least three heroes in this story and they're all leaking.

Tonight's movie is *Father Follows the Sea.* Nobody you'd know is in it. Let's watch to see who's excluded.

I know no "why" of arriving here, but let us hold forth like a battered "how" embracing the elusive heavens.

The newspaper containing the movie listings has itself been described as "unfortunate," but the stars won't convict you and the rest of the convicts are incapable of reflection.

"There's a better percentage in anything used," says my brother, who arrives with Pink Floyd in his ears, used girlfriend in tow. She's wearing a different sadness every time he appears. This time he's been studying an herb known for its "cleansing properties," which he believes is slang for, "Eliminate guilt and do it again."

Marriage is irrelevant. He's that old fashioned. Sometimes I wonder how much father is hiding inside him so I watch closely.

Out there in the field, Father's shoulders are rising and falling as if he were standing on a boat. Father's ankles are wet. He's sweating through his nearly-paper shirt. The sea is waiting. He seems to have lost his "transcendent glow." That's the way father thinks about it.

I wish father would appear as an apparition. I wish he would cry and tear anything asunder. I wish father would dress in the real world without his ghostly red ribbons. I wish some paternal witnesses would notice.

At least the movie eventually stops leading us away.

I wonder when I might come upon my father's ruffians exchanging recipes and notions, the bulk of them imponderably sleepy, sluggish, and I wonder if this makes me smaller, more dangerous, and I wonder if there's more of my father that way.

There's a man still following me. I wait for him to reveal himself and discover he's me. I can feel him do it, but I can't see it. That changes everything.

And then I turn and look at him and watch him look back and realize it's still me. And that changes everything back.

January 25

A Feeling of Loss

Should we return to an earlier time?

Perhaps when a hunter killed an animal, the animal did not think of the hunter as his. Perhaps you have made a similar discovery about something that has used you.

Instead of a predator, his shadow. Instead of his death, an absence. His bright goatskin filled with cream, tied tightly. Instead of a foul odor, breakfast. This could be thought of as a demonstration of how complicated it was for a herdsman to find a reliable light.

Eventually the people who had lived in holes stretched skins over small poles and made the complicit animals pull their caves behind them. The idea of owning things spread and the unsheltered began to follow their possessions.

Taking care of so many animals was a big job. Sometimes many misplaced men were needed. The women helped by pulling on ropes, which made the men spin round. Maybe you too have admired the functional design of a fine saddle even though this is only one example of the beautiful things made by people who can't stand still.

And yet the elusive hunter continues searching for his prey. He lives in another world. He lives in a world that never leaves. His world is still inside the herdsmen even now. If he forgets what it feels like to live in that world, the others will know he has become weak. Sometimes such a herdsman has to track down the animal he once was and kill him in order to remain certain of his own existence, however compromised that existence might become. Perhaps you have made a similar discovery about something that has used you.

Sometimes the modern herdsman grows very sad and he goes to the mountains to feel the old life of the caves again. Sometimes too many herdsmen are looking for too few caves. The lucky ones rest at the mouth of a cave at the end of the day and begin to wonder, "Why doesn't the sky bleed for us?" Then dusk arrives and if their hearts and eyes are not too cloudy and the sky is curious enough to look that day, it does.

January 26

Don't Do It in Public

This is unfinished business. The context is neither reconnaissance nor contingency. Nor am I merely spitting at flies.

Have a seat at the great scarred table where bean juice and the great laws reside equally in the declivities. Here I acknowledge cream cheese and large turnips. Sometimes I don't sleep.

It's not random, it's expansive.

You let your hands do the yelling while your body listens. Unfinished business is not unexciting.

Then the vacuum of funeral orations. Not yet yours.

It's a kind of fire, but it burns unevenly.

Not the door but the entrance.

Allowing a little mischief through.

In the barnyard the lucky couples wait. Anvil and tong, miter and square, tackle and lanyard.

Now the sky's angry institutions grow thunderingly annoyed, lackey-lustered clouds clenched in portentous deliberation.

And there's more unfinished business and there's just no time for it. It'll climb under your pleasantries. It'll make your ass pucker. It'll interrupt your possibilities. It'll whimper and groan. Its cold touch will collect your irritations. The heat of you surfacing and ready to leap. Every particle of your person steamed and seething.

Could you have escaped even yourself?

Juice it, agri-nerd, this cheese is green.

January 27

A Decision to Have More Children

You're in prison and they've given you hammers. They're the ones who put you there and they've called your mother to the center of the confusing event. They've awarded you steaks.

You know what they want, but you don't know how they want it. It's not a game. It's your antecedent finally revealed.

Whistle it home, or just chew on the eggshells?

Your daughter's a stoolie. Or is she just another hammer? She has too much to say, but you're not sure if she says it.

"Forget the past," you tell yourself, thinking about it.

Whose overzealous oven folded your sex kitchen? A setting of hammered bread and suicide access. The "accidents" burning the numbers off your wrist. The signal for one stroke, no blood.

Just when you think it's safe to abandon safety, here comes the Warden's Surprise. They let you out. It's still a prison. But not a single visible hammer. You call your mother. You tell her you're ready to pay the price. You forget to pick up the steaks.

Meanwhile your daughter the stoolie closes the century alone, but alive. "It's the future," you say to yourself, and it is, but the future's its own prison.

You pick up the maiden sticks.

One stroke. Two strokes.

No one knows how you want it.

It hurts now and you want more.

The sticks are not alone but have no one to tell them apart.

It's not a game. The hammer fits.

If there's a house here, it's unfinished.

No one who lives here can find the right nail.

It's only a rumor, but it could be true.

The door whispers and whispers. You can't understand what it says, but you think you know what it means.

It's enough to make you question your convictions.

January 28

Previously Unavailable for Comment

1. *Before the insect entered the donkey's ear, it bit the elderly* caretaker and landed briefly on the child's sweat-stained undershirt.

Beautiful, seductive and hungry, the insect seemed fearless.

Amidst several mysterious, yet predictable cycles, the insect, like many of the wealthy men of the fourteenth century, hunted for fulfillment in the blood and toil of the poor.

The several small pieces of copper discovered in the bitten donkey's feces had nothing to do with the insect, but the poor old caretaker who owned the donkey did not want to believe this. There had to be some advantage in his misfortunes. The man's children, who had discovered the copper, became known for making fine pottery textured with tiny seeds.

2. Several centuries later, following a hint of interest from the new pope's most successful imposter, the fourteenth century returned from the textbooks to learn the modern art of self-promotion. In this it was only modestly successful. Everyone believed what the fourteenth century said, but no one cared.

The imposter turned out to be the author of an entomological textbook with an inordinate fondness for copper jewelry.

3. Following the war to end all wars, beautiful, seductive and hungry entomological obsessions began to influence modern peasants. The distant descendants of the caretaker's children welcomed them, but inside the modern donkey's ear, something was biting so gently it might have been a breeze from the future.

The fourteenth century, carrying a gratuitous selection of copper-colored apologies contained in several fine pieces of seed pottery, paused to reflect upon entry into the chapel and entered the swimming pool instead, unaware that a current membership was required.

Modern children continued to grow agitated. Not even the modern donkey's ancient whisper could hold still. The problem, of course, continued to be fear, as it had been for centuries, but the aging children, who had appeared one at a time without their wigs, may have been the real imposters.

January 29

Illumination Stone

Of course, it is only a story, but we can live in it. So I ask the moist new version for a towel. I pause and try to change my attitude. Then I do change my attitude.

So then I speak and the way I do it the edges of the words get so sharp they could have been mitered. Ah, but do they fit together? you ask. And lest you be tricked by the verbal geometry that such questions entail, imagine the unreasonable surface of even simple words when slowed and carefully examined. Slice that down. Way down. Layer by layer, we arrive at our part in the assembly and it's very very small indeed but not altogether insignificant. It still has an edge. The tricky part is, it's yours now.

So let's imagine for a moment that you are the young girl about to enter such a complication. We know, of course, that you are probably much older and perhaps not even the same gender, but imagination is a wonderful thing and it's difficult not to have a little empathy for a young girl with a sad look on her face. You see, she's already suspicious of her place in the world. Her pink socks sag over the tops of her shoes, and this is not as it should be.

You may have noticed that when you stand back from these words, they look very simple and crude. Don't do that.

Instead let's watch the old man who hauls leaves and yard trash. The children trust him. When the children jump on the back of his cart, he raps them on the head with a willow stick.

I'm sorry, but they like it.

Just then another child runs by with a wooden hoop, clacking it with two sticks and tossing it into the air as she runs.

Well, Mr. Thank-you-very-much, Mrs. Not-responsible, Ms. Distance, pull up your pink socks and listen for a minute, okay?

Perhaps you have a little sister who isn't dying of leukemia. Perhaps you have a mother who loves you. Or used to before she died. Perhaps there is a story you remember about them that hasn't been told here.

Do you feel any pain yet?

It's only a conjecture, but it hurts, I know it does.

So you pause, feeling cornered, and try to change your direction. But to what?

How long do you think you can avoid such pain?

And here's a fresh schoolgirl with an old purpose. She is smiling. She is kind. She is trying to be the Mother of God because the world always needs saving and sex makes sense this way. Next year the tingling starts.

And here's a man carrying her stone from one place to another. If you need a reason for this, think about hands. Think about the same word over and over in different clothing. Try to change your attitude.

January 30

A Dinner Guest

"I just want to get you thinking in the right direction," the dinner guest said. "For example, suppose you take your old life and you make a new one. You might do it by selecting an intellectual steak sauce to marry to the latest minimalist inquiry." He paused, gesturing with condiments.

"And yet, if the people in your village really did buy all the things they needed and never sold anything," the guest continued, "they would soon be out of money. Among the workers would be your relatives and friends. A streamliner with a signaling apparatus might prove very useful. You might wish to produce an action painting of chunky men unloading thick trucks or a scene in a busy necking collection center."

"You might even ask, when those paintings sell and you're drinking a fine wine," the guest speculated, "how you could develop a bladder to hold all your liquid gold. After all, men are not the only builders of this world. You could learn to take charge. You might want to dismiss several portions of your landlord. You might want to appoint a committee to alter the banker. You might want to pontificate. You might want to erupt."

So that the person is not crowded too much.

So that a string from a piece of chocolate that does not lead to Ecuador simply does not.

Perhaps two or three students could get together and invent a small genderless merchant. Perhaps this merchant could find the viaduct leading to yet another assemblage of thick trucks. Did you notice the numbered tracks for switching torsos or the lime colored lice carrier attached to the dispatcher's brilliant uncertainties?

Some of these ideas have been around a long time. You could cut them out and tie strings to them or organize them according to ancient symbols. Maybe an ear to stand for an ear, an eye for an eye.

So that all we have to do is exchange the losses of one part of the world for the losses of another part of the world.

So that a man who was walking up and down in his mind was not simply walking up and down.

So that these stories could be assembled as myths. Because it's true that the few men remaining in them have hunted in many different dangerous countries. And it's true that the guest is often yourself.

Perhaps you could teach me to eat now.

January 31

Recent Studies Have Shown

The best place for a level road is often a flat mind.

You see, a very long time ago, loneliness wasn't particularly needed. Now we rely on it for many important social functions. It is hard work to haul breath up a hill.

In this same way, an unexpected visit to the inside of a weasel's skull could become a perky little sociological appendage.

Another interesting assimilation might include a frequently lost church.

Without these diversions, elimination could not continue.

You have probably been taught that we often need help from other people. Yet, today, different means of communication are available to the lonely. In picture 1, for example, which was unavailable until we decided to use modern printing methods, an unidentified madman is flogging a dog. Picture 2 shows a woman turning away, which can be very effective among the lonely. The man in picture 3 has removed his trousers. Pictures 4 and 5 suggest the ways in which anger is available to the speechless. Picture 6 was stolen from a negligent politician. Its incriminations could be, but are, in this case, not anyone's. In picture 7 a postal worker is throwing up in a bag. The girl in picture 8 is wearing the trousers from picture 3. Picture 9 shows the last step in anger transmission. The woman in picture 10 is suffering from this misunderstanding because she is no longer alone.

Did you, as requested, make a list of your private needs? How does the government understand substitute merchants and their exaggerations? In ordinary times, we can go to the grocery store and buy a small package of cloves for ten or fifteen cents. But can we truthfully say that this is the best method for satisfying misunderstood desires? And if a visitor using a white cane arrives at a house on a flat road, can we assume he or she has adequately suspended all mountainous thought?

Some travelers didn't. And so gradually we achieved a highway of trade supervised by men good enough for horses and wagons. It shows us in a fascinating way how people look for still better emotions. Did you notice the storage tanks? How quickly might they empty?

The innocent bystanders in picture 6 could make a fine list for swamping a chair. This might emit a wet glow if stored long enough in poverty and might then be used to make paraffin and asphalt. The big empty space they're standing in is part of a salt factory in Utah. The refineries in the distance once made religious relics and recycled discarded vegetable matter. These indulgences can be separated from their communities and used to generate passive solar witness filtration.

Now it's true that we are lonely in different ways and many imaginative deficiencies are represented by the example of a short, level man. We do not expect such a man, for instance, to borrow a dollhouse for his homecoming. We do not expect his lamp to burn whale oil simply because it is shaped like a fish. Remember, it is hard work to haul breath up a hill.

And so the singularly implied offering serves several purposes without alienating the religious community or isolating the level-minded. You can sit down and wait or you can exchange your state of mind for a basket of reinstated votive wheels. You may then discover all by yourself a few surprising applications of passive transportation theory.

Still, sooner or later, it's true, you'll probably become attached. Then someone will notice your intentions and the abandoned clothing by the side of the road will no longer matter.

But with so much revealed, how can you expect things to stay that way?

February

February 1

Without Her Children

One broken hair in the nose of God, says the one who noticed her.

It's the way she walks. Like there was a wet turd between her feet and the ground.

She tries to smile because she has gotten what she asked for.

It's not what she wants. She wants to suffer. She doesn't know how to ask for that.

As if, for a moment, something had risen and turned and neatly swallowed its own existence.

Because cleanliness is next to fear.

Soft on the inside, like a confidence man.

That's when more is offered, so that when it's taken away, we can go searching for a moral.

February 2

Which Side Are We On?

Little Nonsense hit the bone again and again until it splintered into a sharp point. He wanted to make a spear to kill the long shadow that frightened him in his dreams.

Little Nonsense saw movement from the corner of his eye just as the bone broke into a point and he swung it to the side, letting go. He missed the rabbit and it darted towards the blackberry thicket. A few seconds later its high-pitched squeal rent the still air. In its hurry to escape it had overlooked the snare. Little Nonsense had frozen instinctively in place as soon as he had let the new weapon fly, but now he scurried into the hollow and quickly broke the rabbit's neck. He tried to use the bone to skin the rabbit, but it was too big and unwieldy. He had to use his jackknife. It spoiled his involvement with nature to use a jackknife, but he wasn't going to let that stop him.

That night Little Nonsense took the sharp bone to bed with him. He dreamt so many shadows it was difficult figuring out which one to kill.

In the morning, Weasel Eyes came to see the dead shadow. He was disappointed. He said Little Nonsense had killed the wrong one and was even afraid of the dead little shadow and lied about the dream so he wouldn't have to try to kill a bigger one. He said the rabbit broth tasted like glue. He said Little Nonsense probably didn't even kill the shadow in his dream but got scared of his own shadow when he was awake and fell on it.

But Little Nonsense wasn't afraid anymore. That's how he knew he had already killed the biggest shadow. Even if he didn't understand how he had done it or where the shadow had gone when it died.

Little Nonsense took the sharp bone outside and buried it under the old catalpa tree. When he was finished, he put some carrot seeds into the ground and thought about the shadow of the tree. He was inside the tree's shadow when he was thinking this and it was waving and he was not frightened.

When he saw Weasel Eyes the next day, he took him to the grave of the bone weapon and told him a huge long shadow was inside. Weasel Eyes wanted to dig it up, but Little Nonsense told him the tree's shadow was protecting it and made him listen. The two boys listened to the shadow and knew their dreams would never be the same. They tried to imagine what was happening to a creature that could sound like that. They tried to go home, but home was not there anymore. It surprised them that they were not frightened by this.

February 3

Several of These Could Make a Lamp

Because the sky is our story told by another, this is the fire I tend, wearing an erect posture like a weapon.

And when you found your voice, it was not done, its face the color of a dog's bark. I lit the match and waited for the shriek.

I don't know what this means so I think you should hate me. But don't hate me.

I had been lost for weeks and no one had noticed. So I went back to my life and no one noticed that either.

And when something I said finally broke its chains, the neighbors gasped and the relatives who hadn't heard me heard them. Heard them because they mattered and the beast, the real beast, became again invisible.

Silence on its knees.

Knit some mufflers for the soldiers.

Send a little something for the broken taillight.

February 4

Dirty Hands

One of those days late in winter, waiting to catch your wandering attention, when a single abandoned roller skate, capsized onto its side in the open and empty gravel-floored garage, watches patiently as if it had grown there. The boy's thick hands go fat and numb as his repetitive motions coax the dust from the driveway onto the basketball, into the air, and back again to the driveway in an application of muscular routine he's learned to call "dribbling." He longs for the swish of the metal chain that isn't there.

Even as the ball arcs once more from the edge of his "court" towards the darkening rim of yet another passage, he is aging and does not know if what he has set in motion will ever find its completion. Something hangs in the air, long past the end of his effort, long past any understanding he will ever achieve of basketball or weather or the subjectivity of the part of his life still watching, only watching.

And now his ownerless hands no longer feel what he is doing. Perhaps it's an offering. From the window across the street, we join him, watching, and take those hands from him, simply because we are there and we are thinking of this.

Years later, we do not know what it means to remember this ordinary thing that has not happened to us. No more than we know what it would mean if it had happened to us directly. In remembering, we watch ourselves watching and live somewhere in-between, partly the boy watching us watch and partly the actions themselves, living in our minds as if they had no words attached to them, as if the words too moved into the air and back again to the driveway from the motions of our cold dirty hands, hands which may exist only in our minds.

February 5

Photographs of Our Former Lives

Wading through snow, shackled with a camera, heavy clothing, and numb fingers, we trudge a wavering path to the abandoned farm buildings. The jagged window of the farmhouse door cuts a leaning profile, glass mountains against the sky, your offered perspective to my monologue of wooden angles. Through the double frame of camera and broken window, the frozen life of a rancher. The porch sags under the weight of time and snow, and the brown shades of wood splinter into reds and grays. Our trail winds past the chicken coop falling against the hillside, the snow opening one of its mouths to say something we still haven't understood.

Lichens cling to the hayrack over the barn door. Pigeons burst from the rafters. We climb to the haymow, imagining our way into the past, warm smells drifting in warm pockets of fresh hay, bodies sprawled in a first night stolen from neighboring families. Light filters through the holes in the roof and lays bright patches of itself in the hay. Through the camera's one good eye a part of the past moves into my hands as you talk about what we were like then.

Going home we keep coming back, trudging our way through the weight of memories we have begun carrying out of private lives like provisions. The people we are in photographs live with the gestures one clear moment found forever in them. Just outside the picture someone is always foolishly alive.

February 6

Salesman

It's what I do for a living. Bibles black with certainty because my life is not certain. A creature so utterly lost I could have been forgotten before I walked in the room. A man who left himself decades before his body fell apart.

Perfection is a dark skill. I pursued it early, but nothing about me has ever been easy. It's easier to be wrong than to admit the confusion.

When I go to sleep, my prisoner grows legs and leaves me. That's when I follow him out of my body. When I wake, his innocence must be buried.

I will go on lying about my age because I do not belong to it.

A life with the fragments of a song flung loose from the tune. Like a new smell during an illness.

I acknowledge a misplaced pursuit. And a misplaced beauty.

The amber shade of aged pond ice.

It's still a gift.

It's what I do when I'm not really here.

It's what I do for the living.

February 7

For a Friend After a Long Absence

1. *A telephone ringing after the ambulance has gone.* Years later I awaken. Silence is with me and we have much to discuss, a silence defined by the desire to muffle the scream that hasn't been heard.

I speak only to those who listen to the river. Each understands I am not alone. It feels like sunlight forgotten in an empty room, like dust still falling hours after the last truck has passed. I live in these things with the light's meaning erased.

I must negotiate rain with the angel of the new order of the sun. I salute the nearest tree. I salute all obstacles. I have given my name back to the dust. I have taken steps to prevent returning. I have broken my mask and found a scenic landscape with the voice of a snail, my body rising with its shell.

The rain merely passes. I am searching for something empty that will stay, something as reliably indifferent as the steady drip of a dead man's faucet.

2. A cold cup of coffee on the marble staircase. If it were not there, I would have imagined it.

3. You might have been reasonable for years, but everything turns and suddenly you feel, without being able to explain it, that something so small you won't even think of it until it arrives is the most important thing you could know.

4. I was afraid to live there, that I might share with you this feeling or any other. I was afraid of the night between.

5. I spoke and it came out so wonderfully wrong. I was not sure that it came out at all.

I could have imagined it.

The telephone still ringing after the gift has been opened.

February 8

An Exercise

Innocence is your child. To find your way you must lose the child. What do you do when the body will hold no more moonlight?

It didn't matter what life was saying. I knew that, but I wanted to hear it anyway. I wanted a reason, even a bad one, why you could talk about it with the cooing in your voice that made the pigeons soft and sleepy and not about to fly away.

I was watching what was happening to me while it happened. There were some things in my vision that reality hadn't put there. A moment that functioned like a used tea bag. It did almost nothing to the surrounding environment, but you couldn't help feeling it should have left something more of itself behind.

Because I knew what I was talking about, I told the children not to listen to me.

Now I can clearly see how blind I am. Like those who believe heaven exists, just never where you are.

We order whatever they've got, like we came here for it and there it was. It doesn't take very much of it to be wrong. What we want is worth something. We're already fat with it, swollen. A cream sauce made of scorpions and ecstasy.

I know that it doesn't work that way, but I also know that it doesn't work. That's why I was carrying a couple of goats in my lunch box to help with the vertical developments and provide inspiration for standing still and staring and eating things that get in the way. Natural disasters seemed attracted to my resiliency.

Eventually the world will reject you, which allows you to give birth to yourself. Can you explain now how you ever expected to keep Innocence happy?

February 9

On Recent Investigations into the Character and Habits of the Common Mole

Despite rumors, their activities near cemeteries bear no resemblance to any ancient rituals. "Morbid," however, translates to "rich soil" in their language. There is no understanding of the word "hide" in their kingdom. They are ruled by "tremors," not blind passion, as had previously been reported. They have been known to display affection for wooden spoons.

We are not their enemies, but their friends are not our friends.

Though they would never be found together, moles can be used to describe the exact size of the throat of certain species of whales. A whale, on the average, will carry a total number of body hairs incredibly similar to that of an average-sized mole but can generally be said to have a greater understanding of the functions and characteristics of these hairs.

Brown is not a color in their world but a way of life. White is the absence of life. "Common" appears as the primary pronoun, replacing "you," "me," "he," "they," "it," and several others. Moles do not have a sense of humor. Nose jokes are as foreign to them as the internal organs of earthworms are to us.

Moles have only one word for snow, meaning "misunderstood water." Dreams are know as "stars." "The endless nest" is their way of speaking about their ancestors. To translate claws from their language one must say "diggers." To translate head, hands teeth, body say "diggers." Eating is known as "digger help." Depending on the season, home is known as "nest," "hibernate," or "the place to which I am digging." The latter is the basis of a mole religion. All others are based on decay. Suicidal tendencies are referred to as "surfacing." Mole poets have developed elaborate mythologies of light to explain fear to mole children. To translate heart from their language say, "My stone is happy." Darkness becomes "life."

February 10

The First Person, Plural

I have eaten my apology. I am among the others.

One raw gurgle is more frightening. Our teeth are more discolored, our stench more pungent. Isn't it enough that "we" has gone missing?

That iceberg was once a church.

There's a nurse wetting the lead of a stubby pencil. Lost children everywhere. One baby cries because its twin's beard stubble gives it a rash. Strange dark diaper flowers. Duplicated without witness.

The cat was breathing on the bird like it wanted to give it some air, and slowly the bird stretched a wing and tried to lift off and failed and the cat watched, and breathed on it, which scared it, and it tried again to fly, this time achieving success until the cat knocked it down again, and breathed on it.

I suppose it's a parable then.

Is it not possible to perform good deeds in a failing world?

Sometimes there are jobs for the children even before they can reach the pedals. I had voted against the postponement of the moon's fullness and been vetoed by a rowdy gang of clouds still wet behind the ears. I hope I've treated them better than I've treated myself.

And we shall be lowered into the earth and there feed the trees which shall rise up and carry us once more to the heavens and the grain of the wood shall sign our name.

You still can't remember what was asked, but you watch the minister's busy fingers deflating as you answer.

"We" is quickly becoming something he will not discuss.

February 11

The Loved Ones

They had never been here before, and it was hard to find their way. They wanted a small apocalypse for the feeble-minded, not realizing the feeble-minded would be incapable of fully experiencing such an event. And they forgot to set boundaries that determined who the feeble-minded really were. Then they wanted an explanation, so they sat down to make one up. They said, "Eat this," and then they ate it.

I told them not to take any risks. I told them they had to perform wisely. I told them they were certainly going to sink and they would likely remain available for comment and they wouldn't have any. I told them they had to respond, carefully. I said, "Don't beat a dead puppy." I said, "Clever is as clever does." I said, "Can't we give this away without hurting ourselves?"

But the old guy, he was one of them, and he wanted a new sweater for the apocalypse. He wasn't feeble-minded, so we told him he couldn't have one. The closet was empty and the door was open. He turned the doorknob to the left. It fell off, so he picked it up and put it back on and turned the doorknob to the left. He refused to eat.

Then it was now and the other guy, the big one, puts his cigarette to his left nostril and sucks on a straw through his other one like it has something special to offer, like it's a secret tunnel to a jubilant world of well-deserved and surprisingly joyous correctional facilities. He seems to be talking to his former convictions. He seems to be a veteran.

Old guy guts one of the fish. Scales fish. Eats fish. Maybe he fries it first, but he eats it.

Big guy watches him. Watches him and watches him.

"They" don't seem to like this, but they seem to be enduring it. Like the rest of us.

Whatever these events give out, they ignore it. Like me.

They can't even name the illness.

February 12

Men of Science

When we think of a scientist today, we imagine a person surrounded by prejudice. Since these are prejudices we live by, he may be a reasonably happy man. Bottles of rare substances measured by odd and intimate instruments have been replaced by a relatively stable family life.

The scientist's eyes remain naked, but his mind is clothed in procedures that have served him well. For example, trees, aluminum, books and waterfalls are only a few of the items formerly fastened to beasts of burden known as "citizens" with strong leather straps and restraining devices which have now been identified as "marriages."

If we notice that light objects such as feathers and witty composers of verse fall slowly to the ground while a serious indictment of contemporary American values crashes abruptly to the theater floor, then we might decide that blowing one's nose with one finger is fully acceptable if done delicately, without malice of forethought, but exceedingly dangerous when presented metaphorically as analogous incisive intellectual discourse.

And if we notice the tiny wheelbarrows filled with toothpaste lined up alongside the primitive man beating fire with a stick, we might wish to conduct an experiment concerning the juxtaposition of men of principle and men of transition. And as we note the prejudices of the very language in which we conduct our experiments, we might conclude that getting light from an idea is certainly more challenging than getting light from a blazing stick, although it's less likely to impress the neighbors.

February 13

A Mining Incident

This is the skull of a goat. Filled with grease, it makes a fine lamp.

This is a torch made of a bundle of dried rushes.

These are the people who condemn the monster for appearing uglier than he really is.

This is a bronze olive oil burner and this is a basket to hold fire.

Most emotions, after being mixed, had to be melted out of the fears which contained them. They are easier to pound into shape when they are heated.

Here is an iron lamp bound by air. It cannot illuminate the fears of its owner.

And this is a candle bird. Its light flies through the sky and enters the cave of the heart.

For many hundreds of years the monster has been waiting to show us our own hearts. This light is held in a shell.

Here is a dwarf blacksmith strong enough to kill a shadow entering from the flame of ignorance. He's alone because his job is too big for a crowd.

February 14

More Than You Think

All winter long the tracks in the road bled. Wet and dripping in the afternoon and solid again at night. Little Nonsense grew tired of milking Vladimir's goats and he said so.

"Build your ballroom out of water," said a sleazy imitation of the wet Russian wind. No visible means of support. Busy little flutterhands. Advice worth exactly what you pay for it.

"If I were a gentleman, I'd offer you cupcakes." And with that, Peasant Pigboy brushed the flies off Peasant Suzie's back and prepared to go to market. He huffed and he puffed. He itemized the inventory. He pointed Little Nonsense in the right direction.

The bleeding road was not his only means of egress.

Little Nonsense had cooked and cooked. The sprouted Nebraska beanbuns proved not to be a popular item, but the hotcakes sold like hotcakes and maple syrup flowed like lazy water. Little Nonsense was homesick and Little Nonsense began to leak.

The farmer, the shoemaker, the shepherd and the thief; these were the mistaken saints visiting the nosebleed and they offered homespun remedies, commiseration, and the milk of saintly kindness in return for the milk of Vladimir's goats. Little Nonsense witnessed his own miraculous recovery and Peasant Pigboy transcribed its haunting air.

"Once when the sun was high and the whole world was on fire, a wise man spoke to me," whispered the sleazy imitation of the wet Russian wind and fell strangely silent.

Poor Little Nonsense. No more nosebleeds apparently meant no more goats' milk and no more goats' milk meant no more wild desire. A remedy that had proved as debilitating as the illness. Sadness and more sadness and Peasant Pigboy's tasteless cupcakes hardening on the table.

Nothing left but the bag balm sliding across all the misguided congratulatory handshakes. And the wet Russian wind whispering uselessly. A glut of sprouted Nebraska beanbuns. More homespun remedies with more unfortunate side effects.

It's simple, they all said. If you feel like peace and quiet in a foreign land, you shut up.

February 15

Lipstick

If the color matches her fingernails, she wants to please you. If it matches her toenails she is bored. If it matches her underwear she is interested in other men.

Whatever she says you will watch her lips. They may not agree with the words they release. They may ask for your handkerchief. Your tongue. Your life.

If you forget to look away as she replaces this delicate, confusing membrane, intimate and whispering in its own confessional languages, she may cling and desperately marry.

February 16

I Couldn't Remember Your Name

I've been trying to think of the name of someone to take her home from this story, from the story in which she lives, which is not, on some less desirable level, possible.

This is not the real story either, but the story in the hands of the man on the bus watching as he passes, just as we watch the man and the story and the bus passing.

There's more.

There's this: If I let you, you would kill her. You would do this in order to feel. You would do this to be more alive. I might give you some detail about her life that would help you justify your actions and maybe believe they were for some other reason, but that would not be true. It would make your job in the story easier, but it would not be true.

"I missed you," she said, before you got home. She was practicing.

And there's this: These are the right things to do, these things we are doing. These are the things that will someday mean something. Someday they will, these right things.

This is not going to be the name of the person who is going to take her home from the story, but it will have to do for someone who is not that person. "Bob" arrived when she was practicing and she almost said it to him, almost said, "I missed you," to this other man because she was practicing and didn't mean it anyway.

Then she slept with Bob and Bob left and this other guy whose name I can't think of because I don't know it since it's yours came home and she told him, "I missed you," only now it was true because she hadn't liked Bob very much.

And there's this: It was thrilling, looking at her. While she was doing those things to him. You've already been thinking about this, haven't you?

If you care, I could stop the other guy from saying, "I adore you," but wouldn't it help you get motivated? He's a bit sappy, but he means it and she's going to try to use him to kill her ex-lover, the annoying one before the one before you, who still won't leave her alone, and her father too, who won't let go of his money before he dies.

And there's this: You didn't know what to say, so you didn't say anything. You didn't know what to do, either, but you couldn't do nothing, could you? You couldn't let the story stop.

She just opened up and you didn't find what you thought you'd find there and it happened and it was easy. Not like sex. Not like the deeper emotional wound she expected.

Not much of anything at all really.

And it stayed like that.

Now finish your story.

February 17

Perhaps There Will Be Something Left

I want to explain why I missed the brunch on Tuesday. My green pants of sin were drying on the clothesline and Cuddles was not at the shoe house. Laisy Daisy and Weed were flying your very best underwear kite, the one that flew like a bubbling guppy, and it got caught in a tree while Gramps was carving another lawn flamingo. I took it away from him, but the dog found it. I wanted to take it surfing.

Nothing doing. That's what Gramps said and you know what? He was right. When he finished it, that flamingo had curves like Susie Detweiler. So I guess I missed the brunch for no good reason and I'm a little steamed, but most sinners never even notice.

Betty the Doll was here for dinner on Sunday. She wore an old bonnet. She called it a beret, but I knew it was a bonnet. She wanted to show me her picture holes. She said they were brilliant wounds and someday they would make her famous. I don't think so, but maybe I should study it.

What kind of person do you think a scientist needs to be? My teacher says we must not get the idea that scientists will soon run out of problems to solve. My teacher says things to get our attention, like an invention that solves one problem may create many new problems. Doesn't that mean more and more scientists will be needed until there aren't any normal people left? Klondike says I have an "elusive" mind. He's still going to Alaska, but not yet. Alaska must be more elusive than my mind is.

I dropped some things today. Sure enough, they all hit the ground at the same time. My book says a scientist is just a human being like anyone else. I don't think so.

But I don't want you to be angry with me.

Maybe we could teach researchers to sing together.

Maybe you could save me some leftovers.

I'm sorry you're sorry I couldn't make it, but sing anyway, okay?

February 18

He Could Be Gathering

The man I am in the story goes into the supermarket and sees a woman and has an unusual feeling about this woman. Not sex. Unusual. And he thinks, "It's remarkable. It's outstanding. It's poignant is what it is."

The man is stunned. He sits down on a courtesy chair and tries to gather himself back together.

He could be thinking. He could be meditating. He could be gathering shattered parts of himself back together.

So then I sat there.

So then I sat there some more.

So then I got up and I did something, shattered as I was.

So then I did something to stop being like that. I don't remember what it was, but it was something I knew I could do.

Then I was at the party and nobody was asking about the dirty pictures so I didn't tell them. I was trying to be polite.

I said, "I think Hallmark Cards are wonderful. You don't have to even figure out what you're feeling. You just read a bunch of them till you get to the one that's like what you think the person wants to hear and then you send it. Then what you were feeling can be over and you can go on with your life."

I tried to tell somebody at the party about my unusual experience. I talked about the man in the story going into a supermarket and having an unusual feeling about a woman and somebody said he was just horny. It was just sex. Just sex.

The nerve of some people.

But it was a woman who said that and I had the same feeling again. I had to admit it was like sex. But it wasn't sex.

I mean that's what it was like but that's not what it was.

So the man in the story goes back to the supermarket again and again, but he doesn't see the same woman and he doesn't feel the same way. He feels some good things and he learns how to choose better vegetables and he meets a woman who makes him forget. And this time it really is sex.

But he never feels the same way again.

Not the man in the story.

February 19

Letter Home

Dear Me,

How am I? I miss all the mess there. Something has come up that I need to ask you all about. I have a chance to go to California. I have a chance to enjoy the beaches. I don't think there will be an earthquake. I have a chance to enjoy golf. Peter and Jonathan and Brother Jonas and Agamemnon are driving to the Sun Spot Motel. I have a chance to enjoy Disneyland. I promise I won't get into trouble. Sounds like fun, right? Well, I need some money. I don't have enough, right? But I can get it when I get back because I'll be working.

Little Nonsense says, "Hey." He is feeling a lot better than he looks. Yesterday he skipped gaily out to Peter's garage for walnuts and when he came back he had the measles.

Weasel Eyes bought a canary named Ginger and gave it to his new girlfriend. Ginger died.

So lend me some money, okay?

I can't live like this. I need a break.

Brother Jonas and Agamemnon are twins. Pretty funny, huh?

The water tower with my name on it is being torn down. Thanks for the paint anyway.

After the band marched in the boring parade, I paddled across the lake with one of the oars broken. Paddle, splash, paddle, splash all the way until I couldn't stand it anymore.

So can I pay me back when the other me gets back? Can I delay my obligation? Can I create it with your blessings and delay it a while?

Peter and Jonathan are not twins, but they're very funny too and bound to be successful in their own right.

We're all passing Trigonometry and we're ready for adventure. Weasel Eyes says don't let Little Nonsense ride his bike if he shows up there until he's over the measles, which is really funny because he doesn't know where you are. Dearest me, just tell me it's okay to live on me credit a little while. I know you're not doing any spending while I'm not there, and you know I always pay myself back, okay?

Thanks for Being Me There,

February 20

Nor Rain

When the boys captured the flag, the boys thought the country came with it. But which country was that? Let's ask parents. Nesting in a napkin, Billy's mother lacked both bicycles and chameleons and had no concept whatsoever of woolen surrender.

So Billy sat and sat and sat and sat. Would Billy's father ever come home? Let's ask a hero.

Billy found the firefighter slumped by the curb. Billy sat next to the man's yellow-jumpsuit-encrusted toddler, who threw his half-eaten banana at the nearby crowd of shoppers. No answer. No further resignation.

Nor wind nor rain nor the dance held in a huge ballroom on the moon shall deliver such a man.

The firefighter had assumed that most people who take their own lives are old and sick. Is it a sign of respect or sadness that you whisper?

If local residents had not taken action, he might still be sitting there. Perhaps you could say he was rescued.

The final step in the hospital's rehabilitation program allowed Billy's mother to visit the firefighter and realize that bloodhounds are really very gentle creatures. Billy's father posted insignificant gains and losses. Nowhere to be found.

Nor the possibility of pain and laughter among the shoppers surrounding the improperly located banana peel. Nor the final contestants waltzing to the beautiful silence of their lost country. Although common a hundred years ago.

Nor Billy, participating in the void, fireless.

Although frequently observed gathering as well as depositing symbols of communication in the form of mysterious and sullen glances.

February 21

A Pleasure and a Wound

I can go to my husband, a man of tepid passions, and say, "The streams are still angry that you woke them." A bit of loose hurricane fluff might catch in his voice when he answers, but he probably won't say, "Thine wind betokens an anxious heart." He's more the "Maybe you should go for a walk" type.

We dust off one of our carefully polished conversations, the kind where you're working your way back to the sun but you never get there. You want to mean it. You want to unfold your carefully stored pleasures from the corner cabinet. You want a bushel of kittens in the laundry basket.

Sometimes you get angry enough to do something. But you don't have to. You don't even have to account for your ragged misdirected passions. No need to misplace him. Let his uncertainty do it.

Another reminder begins scavenging the dark for rain. It's like that when the great thirst arrives unannounced, the shroud of a gesture still clinging like an old damp cobweb.

It's like the mother of eight you met who decided her life contained too many obscure references. You were cruising for a nutritious and stinking unsolved mystery of an escape. You had difficulty recognizing yourself.

The thing of it was, you didn't want another delivery of late afternoon silences or mere recognition of an intelligence grand enough to fail. You wanted a funky little wiener dog twirling by his teeth from a clown's rope. You wanted a festering polyester romance. You wanted an emissary of treetops.

And if you settled for perfumed underwear? Some kind of alien symbol burnt into the grass? A few stringy perfectionist's proclivities?

I couldn't imagine myself larger than myself. I couldn't do that yet. A diet of curdled socks and green talk. Lakes and moons and sad cartoons.

I told mother I was happy. I pulled the wagon to the grocery store. I couldn't believe we lived this way.

February 22

Historical Significance

If one man wasn't happy, isn't that enough?

Feb. 22, 1842.

What do we expect? God's signature on the victim's forehead?

And what do we do with a shadow drifting across the fields of someone else's time?

These are the burdens of teachers, who must labor to teach themselves so that we might study even their failures. They are not so many as they should be, but neither are they avoidable.

And in distress we imagine the possibilities and weep and tear at our clothing, as those before us have torn at their clothing.

Once I saw a woman in a bikini and heels reach up to the back of a dirty semi at a truck stop near the beach and write "Dirty" while the blonde surfer she was flirting with wrote, "Also comes in white" on the next dirty semi and carried her across the gasoline pump's slick island to a just-waxed two-toned '57 Chevrolet with steer-horns and a raccoon-tail antenna.

And I discovered there was a smaller God with greater powers, that did not demand I live forever.

And there followed a scratching of ears in confusion assembling.

So that the event's father ran and leaped and wrestled with the rowdy lads and encouraged the unforeseen occurrence. Which aggravated the wound and put a smile on the father's face, who wrote it down and published his sorrow and glory.

Some of us don't remember that. Some of us may do it all over again.

It was cold in that wilderness of plenty.

I know that the apple is thinking of only itself and that appleness is created by this thinking. From the world's trembling the apple absorbs a stillness it offers, contained in its thinking. Perhaps the apple's thinking grows a skin and reddens from the effort of containment, the same effort the world failed to contain, which made it tremble and open its mouth.

February 23

Ornamental

She lost her thimble. She lost her shoes. She lost a dear one in the forest. She lost her understanding of the fragile thread of reality holding together the fiber of modern civilization.

She thought maybe her little brother had been playing with her chainsaw, but her mother said she lost it. Susie knew better. Susie had been tricked before. Susie was a practiced victim.

Then such a time there was. Susie complained and petitioned and whined and pleaded and cajoled and belatedly turned her father in for prenatal abuse and distorted and manipulated and bit her mother right under the arm where she carried her little brother.

Finally the doctor said, "I shouldn't say this because I'm a man and might be perceived as biased by my gender, but I think Susie's a very sick young woman."

So Susie's mother took Susie to the hospital for an operation. Susie left something at the hospital and then Susie went home and played with the other abused children.

Susie's mother missed saying, "Susie is ill and she cannot eat," but there it is. It has to be dealt with. It's true all the same. Susie was partaking of a limited bounty. Susie was substantially inadequate to Susie.

Ah, but Susie's shiny collection of panties were on the radiator again, so Susie's mother could say, as she did in the old days, "Susie is on detention and she cannot play," and that was almost as good, even if it was sure to fail.

But soon Susie was pushing her fresh plate back again. Could it be said that the operation had failed?

Finally the doctor said, "I shouldn't say this because I'm a man and might be biased by the opposite gender, but I think she's pregnant."

That's when Susie just lost it.

So Lucifer, Susie's overly ambitious boyfriend, took her to find something lost in the forest and there in that very same forest were a thimble and two pairs of open-toed shoes and Susie's shiny panties and a rusty old chainsaw.

But the forest was gone. And in its place was a lawn ornament that only looked like a deer, but to some of the neighbors was endearing nonetheless. Because this is a true story and trailer parks do, indeed, exist nearly everywhere.

Of course, despite overwhelming limitations, Susie's daughter grew up to be a doctor and purchased a particularly challenging lawn ornament. And she didn't lose things, as her diesel mechanic husband claimed, she just gave them away. And her little baby boy was no deer-in-the-forest-following hillibilly, nosir. He progressed beyond his lineage and ascended to the throne of the kingdom, a chainsaw empire of depleted resources and whining environmentalists.

And all daughter Susie's new little doctors with their truly unique lawn ornaments were very busy indeed. And it was, sadly enough, the children of the children themselves who had lost their understanding of the fragile thread of reality holding together the fiber of modern civilization.

Which made Grandma Susie look damn solid indeed. Not a loose hair on her thinking, nosir.

So then the story goes skiing in Aspen and begins therapy at group rates because, hey, we could all use a little help, and if it's really okay to live like this, how come you didn't?

That's what I want to know.

February 24

Unavoidable

I've learned to think about things that don't matter because of the way I think about them. There's no adequate apology for existence.

The juice trickled down and dried quickly on my chin.

We did not know how to build a house, the two of us, so we stood still long enough for the earth to grow up around us.

It doesn't take as long as you think.

Briefly, I was tempted to cancel the "you" in "we," but what good would it do when you could just invent your own?

Isn't that what happens anyway?

Isn't that really the same crumbling stone?

So I decided this is natural and provides room for the newly compulsive aspects of my behavior.

It's a ceremony that differs substantially after each part of its death. Busy but empty. Always a crowd but never crowded.

One time, my friend Walter's adjustable torment visited without a handkerchief and I offered him my new device for the erasure of tears. Big mistake. Big big mistake. I couldn't keep the excess precipitation from ravishing the garden.

After the tortured vegetables, we staggered the load and old recipes rained down like an aftermath. After the after, if you get what I'm dripping.

Just like a "dead" person to do it again. Oh that Walter.

So then Walter decides another birth is in order. Dead people go for that in a big way. Except Walter doesn't know "nothin' about birthin' no babies." So Walter just walks around naked, burdened by opportunity. You'd think the dead would be an experienced bunch, but they're not. They get fixated on just the one overriding fact of their existence. It makes it difficult to listen slowly enough.

See if you can taste their dead air, even without the blindfold. It's not hard. It's just hard to think of doing it.

Will you be welcomed in these dead churches? It all depends on how you make your entrance.

What does the emotional river taste like when you leave it? Why won't you dream of heaven after you live there? You've got to say what's on what's left of your mind if you expect to get along, even if getting along is no longer getting to the same place.

The poor boy gurgles and sweats. Gurgles and sweats.

"Yeah, empty and tough," Walter said, "and tough." It wasn't hard to predict that one. There's no security in anything social any more.

Then I saw a nervous glut of doors go huffing over the damp threshold. The place got so crowded with unused options there wasn't room to open any of them.

A good prophet, they say here, does not sob loudly for the tenor of the future. A good prophet doesn't need more than one language. A good prophet is always empty enough to know if you're full.

This future travels slowly up the tenant's arm. It wants something that isn't moving to eat. It isn't afraid of falling. It doesn't believe in forgiveness.

We're not all water. We know where we're going even if we don't know when we get there.

This is not the understory. This is the lake.

Most of the predictions are still in the clouds.

It's the one package so altered by travel no one claims it.

Pain arrives first here. As in the Bible. Which teaches us not to believe in pain before biblical pain.

We travel between logic and rain.

Confidence rages. Throw it down and the winds pour.

Drag the sunflowers to the bus stop and the light changes.

The ugly things are unavoidable. With or without a book of ugly things.

Or you could take the rags of this life in death like a floral description. Tufted weeping.

And then its next and its next, separated.

Do I have to say you wilted?

Flat and slow and dumb and wistful.

White darkness came and then the blue one.

A dry streambed. The exaggerated persistence of morning glories.

Time turns the orchard into frail wooden tags. We die from our toes, upwards like an aspiration. That's why the thoughts are heavy and the light remains unavoidable.

You will have to make another decision.

February 25

Stefan's Big Chance

Stefan pushed a big rock out of his way, and he climbed out of his hole. At least that's the way it looked to Stefan, but Stefan didn't think he was going to be able to see very well because he had been in the dark too long.

"Quiet Please!" whimpers Miss Prim's new girlfriend, Petronella, and Stefan's eyes go wide open because she has freckles and doesn't like loud music. Everything else gets in Stefan's eyes too, and so Stefan isn't nearly as blind as he thought he was going to be.

Petronella had been busy with foretolds and bedevilments so just about anything climbing out of a hole pleased her immensely.

"Miss Prim, Miss Prim, I brought you a baby turtle," interrupted the same old attention-deprived first-grader, and Miss Prim had to slap him around a bit to get his attention and cast him once more asunder, where he came from.

Buffy, the new age teacher's new aide, turned to Miss Prim with a bit of seaweed on her teeth and asked for another cigarette. Buffy was becoming a bit provoked with her mentor/chum. She always had to ask for what she wanted.

When the primitive haze contained in childhood instincts arrived without actually being announced, Buffy, Petronella, and Miss Prim were all too distracted to even notice, but Stefan still had some climbing to do to get out of his hole, and he noticed. If there was so much anticipation tangled up in reaching, then when might he achieve the touch he had heard about like the forest beneath its warmth? If he tried to liberate Petronella, would the wet furry paws of his overdeveloped hunting prowess remain too big to fit in a nice dark hole?

It was not yet apparent to Stefan that he was indeed the children's dream, arising from the dark maw of their primitive instincts, and he had not yet succeeded in being sublimated by modern conveniences. Nor did he understand that merely climbing back up out of the position he had arrived in would be insufficient unto baby planting fulfillment expectations in the minds of creatures like Petronella, who did not regard ordinary miracles as bedevilments.

"Children's dreams are bound to be disappointed," warned Buffy from her deliciously ambiguous post-modernist perspective, too late to keep Stefan from noticing her strange and terrifying forest-colored warmth.

February 26

The Woods Are Lovely

Yes, some people think that the forest is too dark. Perhaps they could live in it until they brighten up.

We may need a cheese map to find our way. They can be read in the dark and used to broadcast intentions. You must not think that all maps are found in caves. Even if the man who dressed the map is dead. He is not at the end of the road.

The map shows that there is a village in the ocean. These people did not live in disbelief. This map also shows the mouth of a hunter. This is because there are many kinds of oceans. We might then say the rainfall is heavy and wish to go hunting. This is only an idea. It might have a hole for a handle. But with the map we can see that all this water has a great deal to do with where we are going.

Another reason that maps are useful is that each one is different. Would you expect to find the same kind of weather in each of these fallen bodies? Have you already understood that a map is only another way of showing that a sharp stone may welcome the end of a stick?

The man who made the map was probably a practical man. If he wanted an axe, he made an axe. If he wanted a stone, he picked up a stone. If he wanted a weapon, he used the bones found in the neighborhood. But if he wanted to travel, he needed to imagine his feet doing some things they had not yet done.

Farther along, the traveler found the villagers in rocky beds. The first thing you might notice would be the bruises on their bodies. These are the bruises you can see. This might help you welcome them to the next world.

Not so very many years ago, this might have made you a religious leader, but now you are just a man.

Among these villagers, a father might say, "The hungry man hunted for food until he found it." Or a mother might say, "The ocean is never really very far away." But today we understand that a potato, for example, is not really just a slow animal. And if we want natives to eat, we can get them at the marketplace. These people of long ago knew that many things are not as they appear and the next world is always waiting.

Not one of these people was imitating another when he built his home of mud from the river. Some things you know without interference. The next world is not a streambed or a clever pendulous nest in the willows, but a house a man can live in must hold something more than a man.

If you have played this game or one like it, you know that it is not a disguise hidden in a smelly map. This is the whole body and this is how we use it.

You can go outside.

You can play in it.

You can sleep and then you can arrive.

You can provide a way for others to suffer as happily as you have.

February 27

The Sculptor's Method

I use the animal as a vehicle. I rock the horse forward and drive the cattle home. If I'm reading the folds of a toilet, I might notice a small box full of ancient golf courses and in this way prepare for the donkey's future.

You might want to observe the decorum of self-sustaining ranch wannabes or you might just visit the sand-colored pueblo without any trousers. Either way, the furniture stays, anomalous as a purple February.

Still, a variety of wildlife is not the same thing as a choice of jeeps and you can't fly no matter which former reptile you choose to anticipate. You just can't become a bird because the bird is locked in your throat.

I use the window as an accident, and I write down what should have happened. This forms the wire substructure for the verbal taxidermy. It's not an original method but I distort with the wing vents of my chosen lizard and chew loudly to make dinner at home more exciting. This way several different genres participate in the unfolding. I can't tell you which ones because they visit at random. It depends on how much the window is open and, well, what's out there.

Then I cut loose the ovoid canisters and facilitate the removal of extraneous nesting matter. If I think too hard about the reasons, they go away, but if I don't think at all, they harden and the substructure becomes brittle and nearly useful.

That's why blind faith doesn't interest me. That's why the adventure is accomplished without the intervention of inanimate objects or extraneous napping. That's why modulating a fragile protective covering, playful but dark in emotional content, rendered with a flexible avian vocabulary and a childish sophistication, seems to proportion the relevant measuring utensils.

Here, take this insect for example. It has legs and it can swim. To prove a point, I once ate breakfast off of it. It lends a certain uncertainty to the aura of performance I suspected I was establishing. Most of the time it does absolutely nothing. But it's alive. Sooner or later I'm going to have to kill it. But not till after I've finished using it.

When I'm finished I'll be carried away. I'll need a forest. I'll live in the balance of absences that brought me here.

I use the animal as an accident.

I might kill it but it won't be me.

You see, it's already in the stone. Modern weapons don't account for it. Neither do hydraulic devices or the eggs of whooping cranes.

When I arrive at the body of it, the weight astonishes me.

If I hadn't done it myself, I'd suspect another world was forming.

If it gets away from me, I'll follow it.

If I get away from it, it will follow me.

February 28

The Truth About Cowboys

Little Nonsense had a pig bank. His cowboy wallpaper was all dirty except where Little Nonsense couldn't reach it with his curious fingers.

Golda the Goldfish spoke to Little Nonsense at night when he was sleeping. She said, "The ineluctable transmutations of radiance conceive the imminent potential for repetitious psychological injury implicit in the predictable performance of ordinary rainbows."

So Little Nonsense put on his bear shirt and trudged over the crusted snow to Porcupine River to see if Weasel Eyes wanted to play Elders Making Big Farts and Boys with Ants in Their Pants and roll little snowballs into big snowmen. But Weasel Eyes had gone trapping with his father and Little Nonsense played Big Angry Grizzly Putting His Foot Through the Snow instead.

Every evening after chopping wood, Little Nonsense would wait for the lights to come on in the houses down in the valley and he always counted seven. Then he would ask his grandpa for a shiny penny to put in his pig bank and most of the time his grandpa would give him one. Once when Little Nonsense harvested vegetables almost all afternoon, his grandpa gave him a nickel with a buffalo on the one side and an Indian on the other side and Little Nonsense did not put the nickel in his pig.

Instead he scampered over to Golda Goldfish's watery little home and listened very carefully and heard, "Lo, but I have missed you these four and twenty hours of tortured waiting and I do not know but that I shan't be forthcoming with oceanic wisdom of the sort you might at this very moment be expecting. But if you make a serious commitment to careful listening and thoughtful intellectual processes, I may still be persuaded to apply myself."

Little Nonsense nodded. He was getting sleepy. Perhaps he had already fallen asleep.

And still Little Nonsense had not solved the problem of what to do with his curiosity, so again he put on his bear shirt and trudged over the snow to Porcupine River. Still no Weasel Eyes. So Little Nonsense played Sad Little Black Bear with Something Smelly Sticking to His Bottom all the way home. Then he got out his buffalo nickel and used it to scrape one of the cowboys off the dirty wallpaper and he looked right into the hole where the cowboy had been.

"Tell me a story," said Little Nonsense. He was getting sleepy again.

And the missing cowboy did.

It was not a happy story and Little Nonsense remembered all of it.

Which made Little Nonsense very happy indeed.

Even if the truth about the missing cowboy was still missing from the dirty wallpaper.

Even if Weasel Eyes was never again to frolic and cavort freely due to the strange and repressive behavior of his father on that very same day next to the miserable melting pot of snow by the fire in the lean-to on Porcupine Creek.

Even if the buffalo nickel was too small to plug the hole that would soon grow more apparent in the cowboy's depressing story.

Even if Little Nonsense had dreamed all of it, every little bit.

So Little Nonsense thought about that and woke up.

And Little Nonsense dreamed about that too and woke up again.

And even if he never woke up at all.

February 29

Revolutionary

Mandy sat hunched over a cup of chocolate her father had prepared, to drive off the chill because things are almost never what they appear to be. My new roommate glared at my stuffed animal collection. I was no closer to resolution than I had been this morning.

The misery swoons over damp tropical rain forests and dry northern plains. The eggs are carried great distances and hatch quickly. The larvae feed on undergraduate textbooks and inspirational gift cards. They infect tree boles containing fresh rainwater. It takes almost no warmth at all to hatch them.

Billy the Roommate's heart jumped the domestic tracks and came to rest in a primeval swamp.

"You used to carry your life around like a bomb?" said Mandy. "What happened?"

She was speaking to the window behind Billy's shoulder. So Billy answered.

"I went off," said Billy.

"It's not funny," continued Billy after an appropriate silence, "I left pieces of me in innocent bystanders."

"Have you ever knelt around a ten-foot circle? Have you ever really questioned your relationship to primitive ritual?" queried Mandy.

"In one record year, nearly two hundred children under age twelve were arrested for drunken driving in one part of the country alone," said Billy.

Mandy and I continued watching while Billy poked holes in his sister's bathing cap. He continued slurping Mandy's hot chocolate. Then he looked up at us looking at him and said, "While this is true, it is not too soon to start revitalizing our taste buds. Because I was once a God, I know how to savor a moment."

We called this movement "Machinery." We had seen it before. We ate Brazil nuts and planned a strategy. We expected resistance. We were in agreement and we were not about to give in.

We were diligent. We were young. We were about to become statistics.

Almost no warmth at all.

Sixty-three stuffed animals. That was when I was counting them.

March

March 1

Notes Toward Voluntary Self-Colonization

If you want to, you can stop now, but your imagination may take over and then you can more easily pay attention to the blacksmith using a peat fire to melt a hardened realist. You probably won't see the desperation that led to this. Not right away. Nor the practical requirements of spiritual combustion.

This colonial process lies spread on the table to dry. History wasn't my idea. The powdered form is easy to burn, but doesn't last long.

Then someone discovered you could use coal instead of political leaders for heating interesting arguments and public buildings. For many years now, isolated workmen have been perfecting a process of making charcoal from mistaken ideals. An atheist gainfully employed in a similar manner is sometimes called a faucet.

Although they lack coal reserves, the superstitions found in primitive rainforests contain many many useful and unexplained disturbances. Intriguing mutations of these disturbances were once observed shyly reproducing in artificial tubes near Kuala Lumpur. The sap from each of the two strains was said to have burned fiercely indeed.

Experts recently have found, however, that unrepentant Lutherans create a harder, shinier finish. They are often used to coat Presbyterians so that they do not wander. Because of this discovery, Protestants are usually waterproof and can be used for sealing jars.

Peat, ancient now in the light of so many new discoveries, is currently used only by former Boy Scouts, whose fervor can be cooled and poured into molds. They are shaped and altered by this experience and sometimes donated to colder people of obscure beliefs in distant parts of the little-known world. Missionaries soon follow.

Recent studies suggest that a condensed version of the entire process of heat discovery occurs inside a single human body when attacked by cold reason. The body sometimes chooses to burn the reason out and sometimes tries to eliminate the thinking that led to it through normal bodily functions, in which case the intruder begins a subtle but extensive attack on the brain. The resulting warmth is untraceable with current technology, but its effects are evident in the behavior of the afflicted. Some contemporary futurists have suggested a relationship between this behavior and the light arriving at the earth's surface from dead stars.

If you want to, you can keep going, say the dead stars.

March 2

An Absence of Clouds

1. *Carrying your basket of stones, you stumble on towards morning,* voice wrapped in a cloud of crows.

There is a village in Italy with cold eyes.

There is a town in Germany with its boots still on.

Along the way, far from the ocean, you can visit the shipwreck. Step inside. Sit down at a broken table. Listen to the sullen woman who lives inside the table. She is answering the soft voices of knife wounds. Are they yours? Someone like you will want a room here.

As she speaks, you begin a journey within your journey, riding your hands over a dark wet thigh in search of some final ambush.

2. Tell me the color of the streets of ruin. Show me the disasters in the homeland of the cautious. What if everything that has made me what I am appears to others as commonplace as a deserted village street?

3. The rain had been falling steadily for weeks. One day it suddenly stopped. I stepped outside, splashing through the puddles of new water and stood in a clearing, letting the light fall down on me from the clean new sky. And it filled me, as if beneath my bones I was meant to hold light, to fill with it and hold it inside.

Inside the house, a thin woman, with more light in her bones than I could ever hope to have, watches me playing in the sunlight, a black and white cat rubbing at her knees. As she opens the door, I begin ascending, lost in the air and reaching down to hold her.

4. If you are kind, come in. If you are cruel, if pain and absence praise you, come in. I've been brother enough to starlight.

Everyone that passes understands I am not alone.

You can follow me too. I have news of the knives' children. I have a basket of hats. I am the result of a lunar childhood. I am that pet you never really wanted, sitting on a perch in the corner, tapping its beak softly against something you can't see.

5. Because work is a stone. And age is another stone. Side by side without eyelids.

Again it is raining.

So I went to visit my parents and there was only a stone for their house. My mother and father lived in the house, but the stone had eaten their voices. They listened to the sound of smoke, which is the sound of the earth, trying to hear the sound of careful lives.

6. But I have no confidence in mountains, which are only large stones, because deserts awaken in their bellies.

After dinner, the four points of the fork ask, "What has come between us?" and the pebble at the head of the table has no answer.

7. This is a world you could live in. This is the village you intend to marry. This is after ever after, the oven filled with baked witch. So what's the catch? I am. Which is you. Which is your dream about the wounded cat.

I leave blood in the hallway. I don't happen, I am.

Think of me as your breakfast before the meatgrinder.

8. Listen, I want to give you a tip, pal. Cortez discovered the ocean was right. Nobody cares if you swallow it.

9. A clump of flies bursts from a falling apple, twists into a tornado dive and climbs back into the heart.

That's me, among the edging away.

10. Let us have no food but stones. Let the light play at shadows like a slow child. Let the sun rise like a disease. Let the war between left and right finally end and the winner go off alone.

What does it matter who I am until you ask me to prove it?

11. Tiny pieces of the moon caught in the bark.

12. Shouting does not feed the air, so a man is singing and crying. He begins so small and careful. A small desire purrs and sleeps. Suddenly silence lights the path.

Now he is growing so large we crawl into his toe. Deep in his body, another bed is baking. Your bed. Arise.

13. Bread.

You write down a word and it asks you a question.

14. Sex like a tourist . . . three barrels of sorrow to be delivered on Tuesday.

15. Oh oh but nibble me dribbly, smoothcat.

Then that look that says it's too late to take it back.

16. And that voice climbing out of your throat, grateful for the unexpected. Let it spill. Let it thank the stones for the absence of clouds. Thank the stars for giving hope to the stones. Thank the air for anything. Thank the wind, whose secretary has a white beard and no eyelids and fits in a thimble.

Death comes sharp and small like the crack of a hummingbird's wishbone, but death is only another message from the absence of clouds. Take notes. Grow larger.

Take this in your hand. It will save you. Not because of what it is, but because of the way you hold it.

March 3

A Theory of Relativity

The youngest sister was never around when the pink pages of the devil's phonebook were used to start the fire. Her Bible, whispering restraint in the parent drawer, slipped away with her bursting jeans in the basement bedroom where no one thought to look. A curse of knots, a wastrel scab, the gold-digger's nuzzled fortune . . . Was there no end to the snuffle of the imagination she shed?

And her father, a cavernous southpaw, smoked a rubbery-looking cigar and tried to conduct a possibility audit. He had one of those faces that said competent, that said reliable, said dull. A poignant lime yawn, glabrous with defeated pilgrims, haunted his stare.

And her mother (I really mean her mother), flamboyant in a greasy greatcoat and still fermenting, struts home from the bowling alley dragging a wounded rainbow. She had fun. And she stuffed all that joy into her body like a ham sandwich. But she was there. She never allowed her eggs to get wet. I want to say that again. She never allowed her eggs to get wet.

And the youngest sister imitated the dark meticulous spasms of a mousy gleam she found running loose in an old detective movie carefully folded into her memory and began hunting men like a lonesome knife. She was done being proper, so proper it hurt. She was done being a little dream. No more good girl emotionally flopped in the street like roadkill. No more antique futures. Her puddled sacrifice began raining inside.

I covered my heart with a shadow, as is the custom. I told the story of the soon to be absent. I was only living it. I was only holding up the kewpie doll like a tawdry little amusement or a strident fleet bite of hoo ha. Hoo ha. Maybe I'm a table. Maybe I'm a hamlet of deep icy pores. Maybe I'm even younger than she is. The sister I mean. The one we thought we were talking about.

But maybe I am that which measures my own caress.

Go ahead and touch her. If she doesn't break, she's you.

March 4

The Preservation of Children

Do you live in an area where ideas are made into useful things? Perhaps you were elected to fatherhood with a single vote, your lover leaking approval like a mound of moist friendly earth. Perhaps you thought about the way the air touches you because it's there anyway and you appreciated that.

"I told you not to dance with ghosts," you were rumored to have said.

As for me, I didn't know what I was trying to do until my brother told me. He's older and he used to do it too.

Because everything you say means something, but most of the time you don't know what it is.

Have you ever felt like a redundant little anecdote? Laconic, bloodless, and verbose all at once?

"I have to face myself to love them," I thought, wondering which one of them contained the real me.

Was he, too, guilty of a translucent youth?

An undulant, apoplectic serpent of a man opened that first can.

One wimpy scholar noted a contradiction and labeled the involvement experimental. I went on without him.

Does your house have an entrance as functional as a can opener? Does your room have a door on the lock? And where are the fuzzy-chinned adolescents capable of your life so far?

"I warned you about her polished collapses," the father said.

And the oyster caress of imaginary labia nominated the son. The first occurrence.

Occupation: whispering and licking.

The tumor carefully preserved in its removable sweater.

The odor impossible.

The very idea of the idea slightly sweet and cloying.

March 5

Are You Planning to Take Part in the Dark?

Instead of smiling, she placed her fingers in his mouth.

Instead of removing her skirt, she cupped her hand and lowered it, stepping forward.

Instead of keeping a safe distance, they wore hats. They ate licorice. They chaffed.

Instead of a dead person, a large cow, which is so much bigger.

One fly.

I can see the danger in it. I can see the fear.

Slick with violence like a sweaty young boy.

A coffee cup engulfed in her swollen hands.

Well, then, could we enter?

As if the room had swallowed a cloud.

March 6

Concerning the Story I Wrote About the Story I Read

I wanted to understand why the first juncture was not the real juncture. I wanted to know why a false juncture even existed. And I wanted to know why "existed" had such a phony ring to it. I wanted to know a lot of things and a lot of things were not forthcoming, but some things were, and they were not the things that explained certain other things like when to expect a valid juncture.

If you believe it, sometimes that makes it true, so I started believing in junctures. So I guess I experienced one. I mean I believe I had one transition me. So I experienced getting from one thing to another. So I could go on. I could continue with a clear sense of the new direction being different from the old direction, which wasn't a bad direction, just, well, "old."

So I closed the door.

Meaning I wanted to go outside, but another juncture occurred, and I didn't.

It was cold out there, but I still wanted to go.

Meaning, even at that age, I recognized the urge to squeeze when caressing a lover's throat, and I wanted to. As I squeezed into her I mean, as she tightened her body's grip on me. I was thinking about the future that hadn't happened yet, but that I was already beginning to understand.

So I didn't go outside.

Where it was raining. Where the sun was.

How do you say "wait" the way water does, or sunshine?

Because I want you to imagine it. Like I did, before it happened.

I want you to be me the way I used to be.

And I want you to save me from an early demise. Which hasn't happened yet, of course, but could if what I'm asking isn't impossible.

Notice I haven't given you a description of the exceedingly ordinary suburban house in which the "real" juncture may or may not have occurred. Notice I haven't described the rain. Notice the contradictory insertion of the symbolic optimism of green hillsides in the ordinary town. Now try to imagine the young girl's secret words for desire. Notice the boy's volley of verbal trophies disguised as accusations. Listen to them mouthing the same words, the ones they can't use with each other yet. Notice nature's defiant green thrust through the carcass of a robin.

Meaning I had decided to stay inside, but a juncture occurred.

So I went outside, and you were there.

Which we didn't fully understand yet but sort of, and it was very dangerous after the juncture.

Because now this involved at least two of us.

Because one of us might have something to say.

Because it wasn't obvious which one.

March 7

Cloud Formations

Bruno is a mestizo and he is studying the weather. He has learned that it is more interesting near the earth because the air here has more dust, smoke, moisture, passion, sickness and confusion in it. This blanket is thicker than the one at the top of a mountain.

When you see a father on the road here, he is often carrying a big bundle. If the bundle is too heavy, he ties it to the backs of his children. Such a father is held in place by a long invisible strap the mother wears across her pelvic region.

These fathers wear embroidered anger and colorful shawls with small animals woven into them and are proud of their fine thick necks. The mothers wear long leather lace and as many silver eyeglass holders as they can afford. The children wear tall stovepipe hats.

Now if you really think about it, wouldn't this make a fine pasture for someplace besides heaven?

Suppose Bruno is herding his llamas and a dangerous wolf appears with a bloody baby in its mouth. The smart herdsman will know then that his children are as nutritious as llamas. Will it help him to appreciate their value?

But if a mestizo is studying this kind of weather, he has two ways to approach his problem. He can become a father and tie strings to his children to keep them from wandering away like clouds until they have enough worries to alter their flavor, or he can live alone and attach small slivers of ice to his thoughts to keep them from breeding.

Perhaps the great white clouds drifting high above the earth's dirty blanket can be made into the rain that makes mestizos grow by refreshing their tired blankets. Perhaps this is done by the beautiful silky cloth that looks just like water and combs and combs the air while it instigates an appearance of new life, whether it is a new life or it is not.

And perhaps this keeps the life inside the weather from stagnating. And this keeps Bruno from placing his anger in unfortunate receptacles.

And if Bruno looks long enough, he can see this transformation appear in the last great blanket of fear that is falling so slowly, so slowly, from the fathers and the mothers of our great, confused land.

March 8

Holy Land

Perhaps a man remembered that he had beaten his neighbor with a particularly fine strong stick. Perhaps his mouth was very dry and his neighbor would not let him use the well. And maybe then he remembered that the mouth of a river is just the place where the ocean perpetually eats up a smaller body of water.

And perhaps when you boil water in a pan, some part of the pan evaporates.

The man standing up has just raised a bag of goatskin from the well. The man squatting on the ground has a larger leather bag. These herdsmen live in a land filled with stubborn people and animals that sacrifice themselves without knowing why. It can be difficult to tell them apart.

Osip, for example, was a wealthy sheepherder. Sometimes he traded some of his children for animals. Sometimes he traded some of his animals for children. In the religious books this is often called famine, but even the pure of heart are visited in this way.

A herdsman, however, has time to think about many things as he tends his animals. Many times he must think that the world could be a better place if there were no wild beasts or people who didn't believe in his God. In this we can now see he was wrong. That's what comes of too much lonely thinking. Just as a herdsman may come to know that instead of a river of life issuing from tame animals and peaceful people, there might remain only a sunken place in the ground to lie down in.

Here we are now in the same place our ancestors fought over. Would it be a mistake to call such a place home if we believe we own it, or did we only dream about it because it was not ours?

March 9

A Visit to Holland

The family that occasionally lived there was asleep. An old goat was dancing in the newly remodeled recreational area. He was not drinking a Pink Mimosa because he was the designated driver.

Finally one of the children said, "I hear music." One of the other children said, "I hear music too," and they continued sleeping. "Let us continue sleeping," they should have said.

"What can that be?" asked the father, who lived in Holland and therefore did not feel out of place in their dreams.

Answer: That could be the familiar bodies of family members engirthing and caressing the legendary wildness of the dark forest. (They often did this in their sleep.)

Perhaps you would like to go with them and respond to them and love them. Perhaps you would like to eat them.

Did they dream of the corruption of children and government officials correlating the incidence of teen pregnancy to the ratio of missing bread crumbs? Who was minding the ovens?

Hardly any needles at all had fallen off the Christmas tree. Hardly any needles at all.

One of the children, whose name was Hat, was tying robins to sticks in his dream. It made a fine demonstration of inappropriate aeronautical principals.

The designated driver had fallen asleep. He was dreaming of yellow-eyed children forced to sing Christmas carols in crab traps anchored in underwater caves near exotic tropical islands. Each child had one white hair growing from the center of its forehead.

Several family members were whistling. Sleep induced nasal vibration or ancestral memories of the faeries' hornpipe?

"What fun!" thought the children in the designated driver's dream. Then they tried to breathe.

Hat was handing out robins tied to sticks like popsicles. Hat was twittering. Hat was writing his personal history on the head of a pin while standing on it.

One of the children, whose name was Mimosa, woke up trying to invent a red day, a very very red day.

Hat fell off.

Several nocturnal insects began eliciting testimonials from the familiar bodies of family members. Perhaps you would like to respond to them.

Hardly any blood was arriving at all. Hardly any.

Susan and Jonathan asked their mother to tell them all about it. Mimosa was drifting into a deep fog. She chuckled in her sleep and wheezed loudly.

If you put seven donkeys and a crown of gold on the head of a pin, how many wise men are left?

The house listened and listened.

What fun!

The sleepers that occasionally lived there awoke just then. It was a ritual they understood well, frequently referred to as preparing to eat breakfast, but the red father was in Holland and the telephone was no longer ringing.

"Who can that be?" asked the father. "Who can that be?"

March 10

The Disappearance of the Common Farmer

There was a bean in Junior's cake.

This happened before recrimination became a word.

Toodles played the piano with great gusto. Jack the Butcher sank deeply into a satin cushion. He was trying to conceal himself.

The expressions of the body opened up certain delicately constructed "situations" for the guests to attend to.

The recently dead were unable to defile themselves.

The supple conveyance of hidden principles lived beneath the belt of, yes it's true, a common farmer. The arms of acceptance and resistance wrapped around the body of his filial responsibility.

Longing and longing.

So Toodles ate the bean from Junior's cake. The music, of course, had stopped.

Oh my! Longing and longing.

As in the expressions of the body not belittled and wrent asunder. Junior erect. Engorged. Jack the Butcher trying to conceal himself still further. Toodles grinning and grinning.

"I'm going to close my eyes and when I open them, I expect that bean to be sitting on my plate," said Junior.

And because it was really his bean, Jack the Butcher arose from the satin cushion. No longer trying to conceal himself. No longer merely witnessing delicately constructed situations.

The graveyard whispered and the nighthawks swerved.

Junior's cake sat beanless.

Toodles didn't really understand just one bean. Swooped and dove. Bestirring random fountains in undiscovered cakedoms. The gates of cunning nerve ends asway. A procession of indulgences. Dashing and jubilation. Further circumstantial protuberances.

Already, Junior no longer appreciated the carefully arranged furniture in his new home. Nor did Junior appreciate his new home. Or the friends currently participating in it. He would have tossed the bean out the window if he could find it.

But Toodles was busy. Very busy. Jack the Butcher adored how busy Toodles was and this freed Junior to complicate the furniture.

Pretty soon the whole house oozed.

And if they hadn't all experienced a little too much homogenized Freud and grown bestirred to eat the rest of Junior's damaged cake and search ever more desperately for the exceedingly absent common farmer, well then perhaps they wouldn't even have noticed Jack climbing the now excessively symbolic beanstalk or the intoxicatingly suggestive odor tagging along like a future loved one.

Because someday Junior will become Senior, but Jack will always be Jack.

March 11

A Conspicuous Absence of Fathers

Polly Panda was no ordinary young girl. She was fat and she was nice. She was happy and she was fun and she was always making the boys happy.

An iguana named Jug Jug lived with Polly. Jug Jug spent all his time on a tree branch Polly put in her bathroom. He was not nearly as happy as Polly. In fact, he was just plain miserable and as a result, he would bite at Polly when she came to feed him. His bites were harmless, but it didn't help Polly stay happy to have her beloved pet biting at her.

What Polly didn't know was that Jug Jug had taken to staying awake all night long and gazing out the bathroom window, hoping the moon would talk to him.

When the boys came over, Polly would take them to see Jug Jug, but he was always asleep during the daytime and Polly was worried about him. She could see that he had been eating, but not very much, and if she woke him up for his dinner, he would bite at her and go back to sleep. Polly didn't understand about the moon because she was always sleeping when the moon was out and she wasn't lonely like Jug Jug.

Then Polly's twin sisters, Yes and No, came to visit and at least one of them was always awake, and it seemed like they used the bathroom nearly all the time. Polly loved her sisters very much, but this visit was growing, growing entirely too long. It was difficult to make boys happy with sisters who could never agree on anything living in your house. And poor Jug Jug couldn't get any sleep at all.

One day Polly realized that the boys weren't really boys at all but young men, and she became very confused. So she decided to talk to her sisters about her confusion.

Polly's sister Yes said, "I envy you. You have so many men who want to be with you and you don't have to marry just one. I've been married several times now and it never works out, even though I give them everything they want. I wish it could be like the old days when they wanted to be with me and not get married. My life was very exciting then."

And Polly's sister No said, "Men only want one thing and they never really care about pleasing me. Oh it's very nice to be wanted, but you have to keep everything in perspective and not give in to their baser instincts. Women have to be the ones to control things or everything just falls apart."

Then Polly's mother called with exciting news. They all had another sister. The sister was still very tiny, but Polly's mother said she didn't look a bit like Polly's other sisters and maybe she was going to be more like Polly.

Polly's two older sisters went to see the new sister so they could argue about who she looked like, but Polly just went to the pet store instead and brought home a friend for Jug Jug and invited the boys over for a big party. Because Polly had known for a long time that there was going to be another sister. She was just confused about what it would mean to her life if her new sister turned out to be too much like Yes or No.

And Jug Jug, well, Jug Jug wasn't a boy after all and her new friend was and pretty soon Jug Jug had a confused little version of herself to listen to her relentless criticism of daylight and its insidious erosion of higher values when the child's father wouldn't do it and the two of them stayed awake together late at night, waiting for the moon to address them in a language they could understand, without the child's father awake to muddle up their newly transcendent affirmation and enlightenment.

It's a beautiful sight, this waiting, thought Polly, inserted her nocturnal diaphragm, gently closed the bathroom door so as not to interrupt Jug Jug and child in their bonding, and frolicked with wild abandon and no concern at all for the plights of Yes, No or even her oddly still nameless youngest sister, who was already getting used to living in a gray area.

In time, of course, the moon did speak. But who could have understood anyone that old and full of contradictions?

March 12

Early Psychology

Bruno's father spits out parts of his stomach to show that he does not like his food. Bruno's father is covered with thick fur. Bruno's mother weaves heavy blankets from Bruno's father.

Bruno's uncle is one of the workers. If they should raise their arms, their harnesses would fall off, but they never raise their arms. Bruno's uncle is also a father, but his son is a manager. Sometimes when the factory is slow, Bruno's cousin sees a worker who is going the wrong way. He aims at a spot near the man and when the stone strikes the ground, the man is frightened and runs back the other way.

No saddle is needed to ride Bruno's father for his great quantity of thick fur is easy to hold on to. But sometimes Bruno's father tells his creature jokes and gestures wildly like a bucking horse and Bruno trots along behind.

Some of the mothers gather at Bruno's house to make children. They offer each other stories of the future achievements of the children they desire and believe if they speak with enough conviction, the children will arrive to fulfill their dreams. The mothers bake bread in the shape of newborns and it is said the most perfect loaf will start that child on the way as it is eaten. None of the mothers has a window or a chimney.

When Bruno's father swears, he often disparages the hole in his bottom or the fertilizer, which issues from it. Sometimes Bruno's mother makes Bruno's father stop speaking of this. Bruno's father refers to this as a time of drought.

As Bruno gets older, he carries many things on his back. This leads Bruno to notice that the things, which the river carries on its back, it often takes to its bed. Perhaps I can learn from this river, thinks Bruno.

But the smart fathers know that water runs downhill and if you could cut straight through a river with a huge knife, you would find another river. This could be very difficult to convey to the sons.

Bruno sleeps downhill from his father. He hungers for a father's comfort. He has never been a river. He has no knife.

By staying home when his father goes out, Bruno is learning from his mother to make children. Bruno's fur is almost ready for blankets. By milking his mother's dreams for knowledge, Bruno may discover how to navigate his life without a huge knife. Perhaps he could teach this to his father because if you cut straight through a son with a huge knife, you would not find another son. This could be very difficult to convey to a jealous father.

If Bruno is truly grown up now, he could father his own mistakes.

March 13

Absence of a Devil; An Assertion

Stand closer to the shadow of the animal. Your brother is waiting.

If I weren't a visionary, I would have closed my eyes, the dreams of clouds and a whole lot of forgotten disinclinations precipitating while a brown velvet moth brushed his forehead on the way to the lamp in the window and understood what he didn't believe.

I wouldn't have understood even the surface tension, I told myself. I would have thought, "Am I a stone or a rabbit?"

Because there could have been several versions. There could have been thawing northern mustaches and vertiginous white deliberations with Scandinavian accents.

Because there could have been bear leaping and flame juggling and authentic silk roses laced to the shoes of itinerant musicians. Feeble children and cautionary tales of delayed toasters and light sockets.

Because there could have been tiny presents wrapped in newspaper and tied with black string that were dancing and jumping and bumping into one another, sprinkled with cockroach pepper and measured by the distance a centipede can travel on one leg. There could have been a revolution of goats.

And still the same illuminations whimper and their semi-Faulknerian utensils begin fasting as if organized crime were merely a matter of organization.

I can't tell you how many times I've listened. Honor to him that chews his offerings twenty and seven times. Whatever remains on the table is a gift. You don't have to tell God about it. I could have found it without any religion.

I went to the cave and I lived in the cave and I came home from the cave

which could have been the cave.

Like a dog. Like the corner of a real dog.

If I were a dream, you might have closed my eyes.

If I were a dream, I could have been digging a hole. My thinking is wet and useless. Bloated and beginning to leak. I'm almost ready to let go of something. I'm almost ready to come back.

March 14

Sophie

I expect to get there before anyone.

I like the grievance process, but I don't like to complain.

My underwear remind me of childhood, but they're not singular.

I don't like to argue about distribution. I just want an equitable memory.

Look at my new red satisfactions. I don't want anyone to see me without them anymore.

There's a note on the refrigerator that says, "Harold is not the neighbor's dog."

The toilet bowl is clean and I don't have any changes.

An airplane. I can hear it through the dryer vent. Which is wet.

A basket of polyester pinkie rings for the waiting salesmen. Single application vaseline tubes. A carpet stain in the shape of an ordinary nose. Harold is not a salesman.

The holy days of Andy Devine. It must be Saturday morning. It must be a long time ago. It must be a kind of torture.

The television asks if I have found Jesus.

So I turn it on.

The television works by turning the knobs with your fingers. Harold doesn't.

An airplane caught in a pattern of airplanes. You're not supposed to have to hear it scream.

Sophie wants to know how I feel about the issues. I expect there'll be a stain.

Harold draws a line on the chalkboard. I draw a line on the chalkboard. Sophie just draws a line.

I cover it with vaseline. I begin listening for Jesus.

Sophie is participating in an exchange of uncertain possibilities.

I listen to her loud report.

I listen to another one.

There's a note on the refrigerator that says, "Harold will not try to anticipate the reactionaries."

I listen to a voice repeating the ending.

Which allows it to continue.

Which makes it something other than the ending.

March 15

A Simple Folk Remedy

There was a fear went forth and it entered the homes of nearly all the citizens. It passed all the way to the horizon, past the saltmarsh and the shoremud, past the seacrows scolding it for impertinence, past the farmers first and then the fishermen and then even the tourists with their tan corduroy jackets with patches on the elbows and their boxes and boxes of Bermuda shorts and their culottes and their unfinished woodworking projects and their brand new ethnic clothing. It spread even to the scuba divers who surfaced looking for the signs of a storm and found none.

Then a hermit came down from the mountains and said, "Draw nigh." And the people drew nigh, for the hermit was something they had forgotten. And the hermit said, "When I am ill, I come down the mountain to see who I really am."

"We are not ill," said the people. "We have simply come to see the hermit because he does not live in a correct manner," said the people. And the hermit laughed, but not too hard, so that he would not offend them.

And the hermit walked out into the field where the people had gathered and began chasing rabbits. And the people laughed.

Pretty soon the people were chasing rabbits towards the hermit so they could watch his funny antics as he tried to catch them. Of course, the hermit never caught any rabbits, but when most of the people were in the field chasing rabbits towards him, he stopped and began laughing even harder than the people had laughed. And the people and the hermit were laughing so hard at each other that the rabbits became very confused and they caught them.

You could almost see the fear receding from the people's hearts and the horizon beckoning once again to researchers and Winnebagos and pup tents and executive leadership retreats and seminars on the art of sensual massage and wilderness hiking renewal achievers and herbalists and new age urban insomnia children.

And the hermit went back to his mountain, refusing several offers of honorary doctorates and chairs in religious studies programs and ate berries and roots and tried hard to live in his own inadequate body.

March 16

What World Do You Live In?

"Swish, swish," went the sick boy's mop.

"She forgot to clean me off tonight," the sick boy's father muttered.

The sick boy's paws were rather chubby. They were voluminous. They were gargantuan. They were rather large.

The sick boy had a dream in which he learned to play the balalaika with the help of a large Eurasian gopher. The sick boy couldn't believe he had that dream. The sick boy was sick.

"She wasn't very gentle this time," the sick boy's father complained.

"What shall we do to save him?" asked the toys in the sick boy's little dream toybox. Ha! Fat chance! What world do you live in?

"Swish, swish," went the sick boy's broom.

"Here's a birthday present for your birthday," said the sick boy's father. So the sick boy gratefully accepted the token of obligatory affection and attended all six Tae Kwon Do lessons.

And you know what? The sick boy's mother came to visit him after all and motherly Winnifred's hands were very very small. Go figure.

But the sick boy got sicker and it wasn't a physical thing. He claimed he was merely practicing Tae Kwon Do when they arrested him.

"Swish, swish," went the sick boy's stereotypically deprived cellmate.

"Let me show you how to do that right," said Winnifred to the sick boy's father's incompetent and overly sensitive and cliched male nurse, who made it very difficult for all the other uniquely qualified and thoroughly engaged male members of the increasingly politically correct nursing profession, none of whom had been unfortunate enough to live, however briefly, in the sick boy's father's private game of as good as it gets.

It's about time for the after to come happily evering along, but that was a life on another errand if it even had anywhere real to be at all. Didn't you know that? What world do you live in?

"What shall we do? What shall we do?" asked the toys in the sick boy's ongoing little toybox dream. It was a game and they liked not knowing how it would end, even if some of them got broken before morning.

And the sick boy with big hands got bigger and got well and entertained several attractive women while searching for the meaning of his experience even though his invalid father was still an invalid who complained every chance he could about the boy's mother, loving her in the only way he knew how, which the boy's mother understood, even if the boy didn't, and the boy searched and searched and finally concluded, "I couldn't find the hidden meaning because the meaning that surrounded it had been hidden too well."

"Swish, swish," went the broom, leaving just a little bit of happiness in its inefficient wake. "I'll be your nursemaid now for your indescribable condition," said the boy to his father, and his mother sparkled where he had swept away the gestures of false affection and let his parents discover what they really felt about each other, which kept them all together in the same old way. You might be tempted to call it something more substantial than merely happy. You might be tempted to say, "The hunger of the goat is with me and the limbs of the bougainvillea are sighing." You might be tempted to the same sky of trembling that asks the boy in.

The boy's not there as much as the circumstances he's in are. He's on his way to becoming a perfectionist rowing a round boat in perfect circles. He doesn't need a destination.

March 17

Not Just a Breakfast Food

The natives came to a territory of insufficient funds, yes, and advanced bravely into debt. The natives were overcome with hospitality and one of the young lad's kilts dampened and availed itself of the passing breeze.

"Its evidence becomes you," observed the burly young lad in the mirror, and he proceeded to discuss perpetually unemployed lumberjacks with one of the unfortunate participants until an altercation erupted over the emotional inconsistencies of the Western Red Cedar.

It was finally becoming clear that the natives had never even given the time of day to a lumberjack before when the authorities barged in. "Then how will you understand all these trees?" wondered the displaced young Highlander as one of the ruffians began exhibiting a single-minded distress. It struck him oddly, as if he had been politely commanded to, "Hold my beautiful wiener dog."

"Hath no man traveled innocently to his own castle twice?" queried the Highlander, clearly implying the escaping answer.

Meanwhile, immersed in a less vertical portion of the flora, Uncle Haggis was on a tour of camouflaged Irish military installations and had failed to harvest a sufficient quantity of carrageenan.

Still, when the cauldron has spilled, it is too late to relax the soup. That's what they say.

And when the lad's pining aunt witnessed the strong young fanatic chucking soda bread at the paddywagon, why, she was just ever so delightfully reminded of her former religious affiliations. Life among those "frozen chosen" had not been without its rewards, she asserted, and she donated all of the rare matchbooks still extant upon the plateau of her mind's little house of horizontal perfections to the continuing altercation.

The trees were safe.

The funds remained insufficient.

But it's the English the Scottish like to blame for the acquired habit of timely interruptions to nearly all the available proceedings. Even when they're not available. Or not proceeding. And it's not always easy to find the English in the English locations.

Some of the perpetrators had been named after accidents of abstract gravity although it was impossible to tell which ones.

"Yes, it's time now for a nourishing bowl of porridge," asserted the damp, bewildered lad.

And the natives said, "Oh, oh and oh," and they were transparent beneath the part you could see.

And their intentions were beneath the part you could not see.

All the visitors had been taught to eat with great relish and a certain disregard for visitors, who visited anyway.

March 18

Scottish Ancestors

Listen, sugarpants, you were dear to me then and you're dear to me now. And thus the intimate party soars into the tentative future despite the unidentified difficulties. I don't know what's next, but all the psychics agree, it's not going to stay like this.

Money or no money, this isn't some pastoral isthmus, sheepish in the Mediterranean moonlight. Nor could it be described as an old wounded ironing board with a military limp. Still, many of the guests felt the verbal arrangements excessive.

Not to worry, it's no longer important that the impact remain subtle and ever so slowly devastating. I'd rather be seen cavorting with androgynous swimmers.

It's a children's toy with another world inside. You poke it and wait, an undiscovered verb tense in which something may or may not happen. It becomes a beautiful uncertainty if you don't live here. And I've realized that its warmth achieves me by traveling through. It's the same price as rain.

That's one truth and here's another: My ancestors lived in Petershead. It's not funny. Their dear little heads are not to be more.

It's okay because I believe in something, though it might be my defiance. There's great smoke in it and stars drinking from sourwood. Each second's violation wounds time's seamless offering.

Then the puffy bed arrived and we all got shy. I wanted the rules to be ancient. The only thing that could help was the anxious butler glancing off the north cupola. It lacked ethnicity but distracted us equally.

I expected to learn something new. I expected to be unexpected, but you were already there. I didn't expect that. Like so many tiny inflated hairy doodahs awaiting a tennis court. Life does that. Mr. and Mrs. Sociable Lovemeat still know more than I do, I expect.

Just don't lie to me about me like that. Do it like I do and don't wipe the undesirable liquid off that handkerchief. There's life in it and suspicious undiscovereds disguised as something you already know, like cookie crumbs hidden in the cookie crumbs.

"I have only read of its incompatibility," said the new season's matchmaker, several questioners gazing from the furious goat tent with crust in their eyes. About as happy as a broken egg, that man. A sad day in Partyville.

So come visit the wet cider sprocket and the velvet painting of Elvis executed by monks in Tibet. It's what I want now. The orphaned pearl of only. The packed mule of my irresolute consignment. A beautiful tureen of monkey toe soup. A glandular recovery figure. Adequate leopards in an ancient context. A couple of sleezy brunettes with the tenacity of moths. A country with a history of freckles and red hair. Slow squalid cries of ecstasy from the nearly drowned man as the earth turns him around. The heart's gill fluttering. . . (What is a halt and how do you call one?)

Disrobe. Return to the clouds. Wait for commitments. Innocence arranged by appointment. While a distinctly underwhelmed and overly horned creature circles the gazebo without a clue to the whereabouts of the appropriate ceremony.

Incipient, that's what it was.

And the only thing that saved us was a few hundred old people telling humorous stories about the outdated medical devices we all knew we had used to destroy the useless evidence.

March 19

Traditional Values

You see, someone discovered, long ago, that the souls of animals baked in a fire, like pottery, become almost as hard as stone. They do not get soft or melt when it rains. In some places, where the climate was dry, sun-drying was much less trouble but took a very long time. Perhaps you have heard about how the Hebrews were forced by the Egyptian kings to shape the interiors of animals this way and use them as tools.

As times changed, the new artisans expanded their materials and soon discovered that the souls of devoted fathers will often crack a little when they are warmed too quickly by the sun soon after they have been hardened. And if an artisan knows how to prepare himself and his tools, he can sometimes create sharp edges on the souls that will cut. Some uses of these tools can be seen as the beginnings of a spiritual invasion. Such manufactured religious leaders were often presented as gifts to communities which had lost their weapons in battle.

Let's take a field trip to places where the children do not believe the tiny animals that live in men still keep on doing their work. Here the growing season is short, like the men. There is no protection from the dangerous elements. Even the women tend to stay in one place for far too long. When they grow tall enough, the plants are cut down for building. It is hard to keep such people from washing away.

This might make you wish for dry weather, but rain that does not fall makes the clouds sad. During the Festival of Sad Clouds, the ripe ones are gathered into shocks. If you make a map and draw lines from the ceremony to the place where you live, then when your life becomes dark enough, thanks to the unique and specific rituals of harvesting the clouds, handed down for centuries, you may be able to anticipate the movement outside your body, an entirely different, but not unrelated, kind of harvesting. This is how the festival has endured and why it provides the origin of the ancient expression, "cultivated man."

In studying the history of their own misconceptions of these events, researchers have decided to:

1. Make excessively long lists and study them.
2. Paint pictures depicting these attempts at understanding themselves and bury them in caves and time capsules.
3. Draw interpretive maps in anticipation of future landscapes.
4. Talk to people who do not like to talk.

5. Interview old settlers and borrow their tools.

Okay, yes, it's true that "frost" can kill the weakened older men, but do we understand their ancient language well enough to know what "frost" really is?

And if we recognize that, despite all these difficulties, there are many places in the world where people continue to grow very well, shall we also conclude that their behaviors in relation to the hardened souls of animals is a part of the cause? Perhaps even this place we thought we lived in is not a place of this type? Then must we consider the principalities of Norway, Chocolate and A Thick Saggy Armchair individually, or as a group, to be among the "fine examples of successfully settled confusions?"

Perhaps we should reconsider the past. This phenomenon we have been studying sometimes demonstrates gently sloping hills and rich, fertile cavities. Planted in low rows, these men can extend handsomely for miles. They look like sturdy young eucalyptus trees and sometimes collect fresh rainwater over their eyelids. Some have only one or two rooms, but should we begrudge them this? After the cool rainy season, they are covered with snowy white blossoms and tremble at the slightest breeze. It is something as delicate as this, is it not, that we hoped to achieve when we first turned to the baking of animal souls?

Imagine the sounds such men could make perched on the edge of an extraordinary large animal bowl baked to a bright ringing pitch. Imagine the extenuating courtships and the bundles of sad clouds ripening outside your body before the onslaught of history altered the meaning.

March 20

Really, I Don't Want To

Someplace close there are mountains growing. Children know such things. An odor of anticipation. You can make it smell like honeysuckle or sweat. You can sleep with it. You can embrace it.

And then a pigeon of a man with a large and empty head, two feet shaped like gourds, the toes grown together and the skin nearly orange. He sells liver and cheese and he traps muskrats. He has not been released from the mind of the child he lives in.

Someone is sewing together the clouds. Children know this. It's the beginning of religion. It makes their undergarments whisper.

It was wartime. A young boy was marching with a broken stick. Three younger girls in dirty summer dresses were following him. He turned and embraced them all at once and they giggled happily. It was wartime.

The dusty smell of rain on the way.

The sidelong fish grin of a man who has forgotten himself. To some it's more attractive. To some it's who he really is.

The arroyo sloped down, then up and away into the moonlight.

In childhood it's always wartime.

Because we do not know how to control our flight, we reach out to park benches, to cafe tables, to unnecessary purchases, to the sides of buildings, to each other.

One of the girls put a gunnysack over her head and started shouting and pointing. Her heat was choking itself. A limpid breeze tried to object and failed.

Her hair smelled like smallpox. If you weren't supposed to touch it, it became sacred. A suitcase full of toads. A creature melting into the garden. Anything sharp. Whatever you can't take back, a button for on and no button for off. Whatever you can't take.

And the young boys become young men, the children they were like a tattered blanket. It's the blanket between them and the real moonlight. They have no reason to eat in the dark.

March 21

How to Talk to Children

I didn't do this. The distance between my table saw and the light bulb is not particularly desperate. It makes nearly everything more of itself to say so.

My children don't like the wind. I let it cover me. I say what I want to say. Their religion is sleeping on its back. I think I should be happy for them.

I think I should talk to my visitors, but I do not know who they are. Nor do they know who I am though some of them think they do. Yes, I did these things, but not on purpose. The distance between my mirror and my miniature orange tree is not particularly revealing.

You might think the lines were from smiling. I've never been able to contain myself. The way I wanted was not the way I needed. What I needed was to need.

Many sorrows have I spilled unknowingly. Were they ever truly mine?

The distance between the table saw and the light bulb matters. A cruel act is not justified by the crueler one it replaces.

My attractive despair had not won me acceptance. I was tragically unlucky in the eyes of only a few admirers. My heart leapt into my stomach if someone spoke kindly to me.

Though I had lost much, grief had not yet caught up to me.

The distance between any two objects one can speak of with confidence is never very large.

Nor do we know who they really are.

March 22

Bob's New Boat

The spiritual presence of a face had haunted Betty for several weeks. Not just one face, really, but the constant awareness that she was seeing someone's soul every time she looked at their features above the neck.

Pedro wanted a banana and Betty was standing in front of the bananas so that Pedro had to stand in front of Betty to get to the bananas, and as soon as he got his bananas, he turned around, and there was Betty. Betty looked into Pedro's face, an ugly face with a beautiful soul and a desperate extravagance, a face of flamenco music and gangsters. She felt herself getting lost in there.

Without a word, Betty followed Pedro and Betty's dog followed Betty. The three of them were moving down the sidewalk like children headed for an adventure. Just then Betty's dog Bob raised his wet nose into the teeming air and sneezed like a garbage truck. A Broadway show tune was playing in the nearby alley. Nobody was singing along.

They stopped to watch Pedro's neighbors digging in their garden. Someone said the landlord was screaming for the rent. A juicy little mouse was scrabbling in the potatoes, but Bob didn't notice. He was too busy sneezing.

Pedro's face was rich indeed and its asylum was no longer empty. It was filled with unexpected generosity. So was his rundown apartment. Betty admired the landscape and Pedro let the journey continue.

One of Pedro's bananas tasted green, but it was a lifeboat. Pedro's beard smelled of pomegranate. Pedro rewarded the banana peel with a gesture of humorous bravado. A crack in Pedro's bedroom window extended past the frame. Pedro's court-appointed lawyers couldn't understand the implications.

Yes, Betty had become an anomaly and Bob was the anomaly's dog. Meanwhile, Pedro had grown fully intent on becoming the father of just about anything.

So Pedro rowed and Pedro rowed. Pedro rowed so hard he rowed his lifeboat right into the alley where everyone could see it. A different Broadway show tune was playing. A different dog was overlooking a juicy little mouse. Most likely it was a different mouse.

The tremendous oceanic depths of the new adventure's synonyms were contained in the impossible visibility of Pedro's boat. Pedro's lawyers disguised the exposure, which made the rowing look like dancing.

Pedro's best interests were no longer in Pedro's range of prior investigations, which, let's face it, sooner or later were either going to expand to Betty again or a great deal of sadness, Bob or no Bob.

So Pedro struggled and struggled and said something enormously inappropriate. Which was to be expected and made the lawyers chuckle.

When the time came, as it always does, that the participants separated, Betty got Bob and the toothache hiding in the pile of potatoes where the mouse had been. Pedro kept the lawyers and the artificial beard.

Bob got the rowboat, fully equipped with a wide variety of show tunes, but the banana peels, of course, disappeared into the sunset because they could not be rowed by a dog. On the face of it one could still find a disturbing attendance not adequately foreshadowed by anyone's reluctantly departing essence. One could dedicate to it. One could be haunted by it. One could persist. As one does when one wants something one doesn't have. You don't need good intentions to anticipate a soul.

March 23

Contract for a Small Dish of Seeds

One of the things the government doesn't do for us is inspect the possibilities. Watch for these anomalies in your research. Don't expect the subject matter to alter to accommodate the evasive theme.

How would you respond, for example, to an official who says; "Every day my mother beats me with a long willow switch. I'm scared because I've begun to like it."

Some of the neighbors, you conjecture, of the man who first had a special room for sleeping, must have thought he was pretty smart. They might have thought he was very sensitive and wanted to acknowledge his hidden depth, but he felt so deeply it made him sick and he vomited his portable heart into the beggar's hands. If it looked like a handful of old coins, that was only because the beggar wanted to use his gift. He probably understood the obligations.

In this way the beggar had already become a flower. You can't fix a flower with old coins. The beggar had to call his broker to verify the exact amount of the loss. That's how happy he thought he was. He wanted to know exactly how much his useless discovery was worth.

Although the government does not approve of a man who is begging in the street, his research might be used for subtle improvements in the enduring strains of the increasingly numerous transient flowers which now line our walkways and boulevards. We should try to understand how such things come about if we want to apply ourselves.

And if a beggar already has something in his dish, which is not money, perhaps his persistent need to bloom can be used to locate outside a special place for sleeping available to nearly all of us. This is what flowers accept when they refuse government assistance. They have nothing to offer but themselves. It's an agreement. It's a way of carrying the ideas to other places. It's a gesture you may not realize you have made when you give alms thoughtlessly.

Sleep now, because the subject matter does not alter to accommodate the theme and it's how we understand the meaning of the exchange. The government makes many mistakes and it does not know how to rest. If it sleeps, it will disappear. This is why we must do its understanding for it.

March 24

Evaporation

Maybe you are wondering where all the water in a river came from, but if you travel downstream, you will find that the idea of "religion" turns into vapor. The herdsmen of Palestine, for example, knew about resting the trampled pastures. They believed that this practice would allow something more than the grass to grow. Today we vastly oversimplify this practice with the concept of "ground water" and it is unfortunate that we no longer travel downstream to discover its meaning. Neither do we seem to understand plants and water as one, which makes eating a spiritual pleasure.

We can mark the places on a map where the herdsmen gathered to talk about this. Such a map will be accurate, but it will take many experiences of dreams to read it. Because some of these places might still be too independent to grow the necessary churches, the herdsmen know that it is not yet time to travel there. They are waiting for the dormant plants to give them a sign. Maybe the plants are also waiting for a sign from them.

Quite a number of the herdsmen who speak the loudest are really very frightened of taking the creatures which make up their life to the place for the eating of dreams. This fear is a dangerous thing, and it can attack anyone who does not already share it. You could say that fear creates its own friends. You can also say that fear moves slowly up the mountains with these friends. You would have to be a very confident hermit not to be frightened.

You may have been discovering in your own life how the herdsmen could forget to follow the water to reliable pastures, the ones that keep coming back over many many centuries, and how they could try instead to bring all the ground water to the place where they wanted to stay. It may not be obvious how dangerous such a thing can be, and it might seem logical to bring what you need to where you are. It might not be clear that this changes what you need.

Many stray thoughts of the herdsmen were made into soups and these soups remind us to always camp near water, but they do not tell us where the water is. That is because their life is what keeps them moving and only a few of the brave questioners have learned that many little things which others might not notice can tell you where more helpful darker dreams can be found. If you are a true seeker of light, you will want to travel through the dark.

Maybe you are wondering where all the prophets came from. Most of them are from a childhood of very dry emotions. They believe they barely escaped a drought and if they do not collect all the water in one place, next time they will die. This too is a way of death, which looks like life, but we should remember that life and death swim in the same river.

The real prophets speak out of the sides of their mouths with ghostlike arrows or clinging seedpods that point and burst open later when you are ready to be alone with them. No real prophet lived always among people. You would have to be a very unusual prophet indeed not to have been alone most of your life.

So maybe now you are wondering how to travel downstream far enough to find some vapor. If you are wondering this, you probably haven't found enough darkness yet. Such experiences do not run downhill, and they can make it hard to see the mountains. You won't find such thoughts climbing skyscrapers. When you feel like maybe something is falling out of the side of your mouth, begin sniffing the air. You may notice a difference. If you desire, for example, to talk to your food, you must first listen to it and for this purpose, your ears are not very useful. They have already been misinformed.

Eat lots of water. Grow inside it. Share what's left of your body with it. Begin taking apart your thoughts. It's a good start. Take apart what's left and then see what you have. Take that apart. In time the air may want you.

March 25

Long Overdue Criticism of Edna

Something is pouring into you. Something is spilling. And as you begin allowing it, do you think, "Nothing could have prepared me for the experience of Edna?"

This is something else entirely because when it walks past its pile of junk, it thinks only, "That's my pile of junk."

As if you had been sitting in the street where the parade was passing, the local dogs yapping at the horses, the tired clowns drifting like ghosts, the calliope wheezing like a stricken cow . . . And you had experienced exactly that. Nothing more. Nothing else.

Is the cup from which you have been drinking the wine small enough to give you pleasure?

Now sunlight soft enough to read us pours into the idea of Edna. Not really a lover but the idea of a lover. Not really you but an idea you had about yourself. When every day says today.

Because impossibly its wonder grows, continually revealing itself like a black handkerchief of fall blackbirds turning and twisting in the cool air. That part that doesn't "think." The wonderful part that takes you home. The part that makes anything less than this unbearable.

March 26

Rehabilitation

Rurik and Ragnar Finnborgson return to their homeland. The empty rocking chair on the porch welcomes them, but how could they ever have shared it?

In the airport gift shop, the two brothers do not resist attack by the perfume sniper. Jeepers, but they smell American. A munchkin rubs her nose and points at them. Her woolen mother says, "Eat yer skin vitamins, there's a good girl." But the munchkin whines. "Shut yer gob and buck it up, ya little weasel."

Three hours later, on the long walk from the airport to the hotel, Rurik wonders, "Why do our countrymen still make their houses like that?" and Ragnar wonders, "Do they still make ancient weapons? Can they still weave?" Two punks with spiked hair snicker at them. "How's it hangin', asswipe?"

Just then, Rurik and Ragnar notice the lovely cold wind and think of their friend Dieter, so they buy paper, they buy string and sticks and they build blue kites. They remember the very first time. Up, up, up went the kite into a very tall tree.

And they go to a nice boggy marsh because you don't smell them when they're frozen and sure enough, there's Pete. Pete seems to follow them around the world. Everywhere they go, there's Pete. When we come to the frozen land where there is no Pete, we will know we are at the end of our journey. That's what the brothers are thinking.

Each time the brothers try to speak to their persistent friend, they encounter the friendly hedgehog tenor of his lackadaisical response and remember, simultaneously, their father's final wisdom; "You can only reach as far as your arm stretches."

But soon enough it is time to put the candles in paper boats and play the accordion on the icefloes for once again we are drifting north. The luminaries of the fjords are waiting, ice is accepting applications, wavering lights are displaying their affection.

Because home is the scene of the real crime and the others only repeat the view. Empty yourself out and something will arrive to fill the space.

Back then, we didn't believe the weather had an explanation.

March 27

My Sick Friend Yellows. I Spill the Horse.

After the curtain call licks death's stain, soup happens and the absence cavorts. Chortle me, Mr. Whimple, I can't see the iceberg.

Cork furniture in the razor blade's apartment. It's impossible to be that polite.

Then a furnace without arms or legs scorching his dog feet with black honey. A glop bucket of blue stars spilling from the doomed ruminants.

The juice of burgled buildings. The tunnel of a cow.

A slippery Canadian incandescence. A virtual paranoia of evening silk. The incredible rebellion of a kind word asleep offstage.

I didn't ask. So I was allowed. The Northern Lights became historical.

The table wins. The chair wins. The play goes on without me.

My sick friend does not know he has found the applause. Soup happens and happens and he doesn't notice.

The last animal of his fever escapes from the milky substance waiting patiently for the encore. He seems to be me all right, but some of us want a second opinion.

March 28

And Prepare for Battle

Button Baby sewed himself onto a kite. An angry young boy dipped Button Baby and swayed and tore up the other kites with the razors embedded in Button Baby's arms.

When Button Baby's kite was all alone, the angry young boy sat down and dreamed he was captain of a sewer excavation party. He took a wrong turn and wound up beneath an Ancient Aztec village.

"You've been warned before," said the chief.

The angry boy screamed back, "If you weren't so secular, you'd float."

Meanwhile Button Baby was having his own dream and it wasn't very pretty. Some children were woven into the fabric of their own diapers. Kites were made out of them. Angry young boys cut them to shreds with embedded razors. Button Baby was kidnapped by a pack rat and traded for a piece of tinfoil.

The angry young boys were explaining how they were really trying to release the embedded children from their clothing captors. The mutilations were an accident.

Delirious, Button Baby whispered the name of a well-known plastic surgeon and said, "I don't think I'll want to stay here after I've been over there."

His weapons were useless now. It made him want to fight.

March 29

Could Have Been the Ocean, Could Have Been the Sea

That was the day the ocean came to visit. It was very specific, but I still couldn't figure out what it wanted.

I wanted to send it to *Reader's Digest.* I wanted the approval of insects. The ones with large mandibles and substantial wings.

I live in a house on Elm Street. I don't know how the ocean got the address.

The culprit might have said something like, "Invest in the future," because she's like that. Like there's only one.

I wrote it down. The Podunk Review thinks I might have something someday. It's all very exciting. Perhaps I should take a nice bath and show it to my mother.

Receiving little validation from my family, I decided to visit the indulgent river. It was very very cool. It gave me chills just brushing up against it.

The instructor inside was offering free mistakes for signing up for the course. The distance between the surface and the deeper implications was on vacation or I might have overachieved. I never did figure out what the course was about, but then I never did take the course.

I left some ice trucks in honor of the quickly approaching season, but I think they melted. Or a train sculpture came into confluence with their destiny and altered them inextricably.

Meanwhile the ocean was talking to me and I wasn't listening. I might have been a visitor, but the ocean was too insistent. I might have understood if I hadn't been so afraid. I could swim but I preferred to walk and I knew how quickly tired arms and legs can wrap themselves around something way too large and not at all good for the other parts of the body.

I just couldn't decide how large this thing was.

If I were writing this in the future, I could say, "I was right. It was larger." I could say that if I had survived. It would be entirely ironical.

But I'm not and the ocean's waiting.

If it's the sea that's gotten in me, the trouble's the same, but some say the irony's greater. I don't understand why.

I wouldn't care about the difference if I didn't have some hopes of publishing my failures. You see, it's a story and not a life, which doesn't have to end the same way.

March 30

Medea

A harbor town. Where the crusty young sailors kick the barnacles off their bellies and dance with anyone who will have them.

Take one of the sailors and kick him around a bit to get things started, an ugly man made uglier by too much time at sea, an angry man made angrier by not knowing what made him angry.

Then let one of the locals think his girlfriend has more money than he does and how can this be.

The rest has been imagined by everyone, but do it again, with more detail; the particular curses, the color of her torn dress, the movement of a drop of blood flying gracefully through the graceless air of the smoky bar, the smell of the alley when he finally wakes up and the name he gives the one-eared cat he takes back with him onto the boat.

He's not responsible. Maybe nobody else is either. The girlfriend was made out of fog and everything missing from a sailor's dream. That's how he got this way. The way his teeth depart after he wakes up and can't remember. That's how lost he feels when his shipmates are drawn to the cat, its hair wild and the hissing coming from everywhere.

March 31

As a Weapon the Oar Is Useless

Suppose that the hunter who lives in the cave with his family needs all the land you can see. Won't another neighbor who needs all the land he can see want to take it away from him?

As the years passed, there were more and more people in the world. Knowledge of tools made their lives easier. Killing a neighbor with a bow and arrow instead of clubbing him to death with a stick was easier too.

Soon we learned to make boats by sewing animal skins together into tight bags and blowing them up with air. We spent a lot of time moving around on the water and we discovered that some icebergs are very large. We thought we needed all the water we could see. When we came back, we made bigger boats to travel further. We brought back food for our families, which grew even larger and sometimes traveled with us. We killed more distant neighbors more efficiently and discovered still larger icebergs. In this way the years melted.

Eventually we needed even more than we could see. Countries became necessary to keep each kind of killer in another place. A lot of time was spent moving borders. We developed libraries and museums to keep the past safe from those who think like another country.

In one of the museum displays a woman is standing on the shore as a man climbs into a small boat that looks like a bloated cow. She has prepared a leather bucket and a lamp. She has prepared a false conception of the future. The man is carrying an oar for the sake of his family. He does not need the oar because he will follow the currents of the ocean until he arrives at a new land he can claim. If no one stops him, he will lead the natives into battle after battle until his new country reaches back to his old one and swallows it. In this the oar is of no help, but it makes his first family feel safer because they do not understand that if anyone at all returns, it will not be the same man.

April

April 1

Success

The first thing you should know is that the man's children may starve. If you watch closely, you can soon see that a puddle is gathering beneath his feet. We've been operating according to another system, another system entirely. If you had been paying close enough attention to notice that the ripe ones float but the green ones sink and there are two brown berries inside each one, then you might not be making wine merely in order to convey electricity, day after day after day.

The second thing you should know is that the man in question has no children. Despite appearances, this calls into question nothing of significance. Neither does it have a religious dimension, that story of the single drop of rain that fell in the mouth of an abandoned carpenter, who may or may not have been a sane man, notwithstanding. And the first man who made clothing and tents by joining animal skins with the hair of saints, which still grows after they have died, his concept of God is heavy and hard and he has prepared it to be used for pounding.

The third and final thing you should know is that these absent children, the ones with toughened skins, are sometimes put into a deadly machine. Some of them have reasons for wanting to be crushed, but many of them are unaware of their fates. In such a place, it is easy to study the erosion of empathy and pretty soon, there will remain no confidence in benevolent metaphors whatsoever.

In the meantime, while we ponder the dilemma, the man in question continues pounding and the missing children continue swimming into his wet guilty hands. Their fat little bellies grow slick with seaweed and the ripe ones continue thumping repetitively with salty machine dreams while the green ones grow heavier and heavier with the burden of their promise, as if the ocean inside the man's intentions were already theirs.

April 2

How I Became President of The Boeing Aircraft Corporation

So I told him, I said, "Air is not merely the absence of other elements or the presence of certain very distant and spacious assemblages of select and yet common particles brought not so much together as into a suspicious proximity in a particular sequence."

And he replied in kind, saying, "A deceptively young man was in my office the other day and I gave him what for, cut him down to size, I did, waxed his potato and sent him bootstraps over shoelaces into the hallway with his suspenders in tow. What does he mean by airing his personal withholdings in our place of worship?"

And so I enunciated more carefully. I spoke slowly and I interjected, "Neither is earth as solid as it seems, and remains, in fact, surprisingly compatible with the assemblages of air, which consist of the very absences which fabricate the structures of its own existence."

And the clever dissembler answered knowingly, saying, "Well I sure enough slapped him upside the head and gave his ears a good twist until he sat down respectful and I still had to get in his face with a few choice expletives to sharpen his attention span or the dense bugger-assed numbnut would have hunkered home without an echo between his ears."

It was at this point that I began to suspect we were really on to something redundant. I closed the invitational crow, rationed the blackbirds and repealed sparrow privileges. I was dumbfounded. I was working.

Three days later the potential for hurtling through the air had been extended and the machinist's union thrust themselves into a strike. While the moon pulled quietly at the transient tide with its greasy ancient wings, its workers flung reflections through the increasingly commercial air.

It was too late. We had understood. We had communicated a basic principle. We were all that was necessary for our continued explorations. We were determined to arrive at a conclusion without daily alterations of the potential for misdirection.

It was a kind of epiphany, an irrevocable feathering of the universal discourse on arrivals, an acceptance. I was not yet tired of being merely correct.

For which mistake in judgment I was handsomely reimbursed.

April 3

A Map of Her Life with a Small Woolen Garment at the Center

It might be a better story if you wrote all the words down in a different order, but don't do that, okay?

You have met and solved several people already today and a reasonable man is just another irritating human being like yourself. You have no reason not to believe this is true, Miss Muffy Muff, Miss Again and Again, Miss Don't Want To.

So today we shall praise you and call you the mother of pillows and tomorrow the obituary of your fork may be sufficient to feed your contributions. And if in this your world be thus restrained, let us find ourselves escaping once more with your cleverly mobile flesh toys and occasional errors in lubricational salutation.

For this is the point at which the more reliable text ends.

But suppose your imaginary roommate unwittingly dusts and vacuums the ancient neglected apologies and you feel a spate of incongruous modern guilt.

Oh dear, oh dear, what shall we do?

Let's ask all the lovers who sleep in it too.

Had I been encased in reasoning, I might have tested its existence for consistency. Still other reasonable fools might wish to illustrate their recurring confusions. Picture 3, for example, shows a man weaving his hairy home in France. In Picture 2 another man is carding wool on the roof of an itinerant English cottage. In Picture 1 a third man is spinning, carefree, as if such activities could not be punished, in front of an ancient Scottish castle.

You can pound him with your fist, but a stone would be more reasonable.

Oh my, oh my, don't let this go by.

Let's ask all the children who live in the sty.

And you still have no reason to believe another life is false, Miss One More Time, Miss Do Me Again, Miss Can't Get Enough of Anything Me. You see, a reasonable man might desire some kind of verifiable evidence, but that does not mean he would be right to alter the course of events.

This is the point at which a more reliable text begins.

And so today we praise such men and perhaps we feed upon them. For we have discovered these same men in bed with our fears and this leads us to confession. We wanted them to keep track of the participants, to illustrate our difficulty and to continue our attempt to fit the lambs into the predictable field of reliable stones, which we have created with our useless resistance.

It's the deceptive comfort we're certain of. It's the itch.

April 4

A Tiny Wooden Cage

Once in the early days potatoes really did have eyes. They were all devoured during a famine when the people were eating everything in sight. And yet there is a man who has spent his life searching for the lost eyes of those potatoes and he has begun to wonder if there isn't some other world where potato eyes have gathered together to celebrate an evolution we cannot see. This man is the one you can find begging along the roads of far northern countries. Travelers see him and do not understand his journey. Even the blind point at his foolishness. Mockery greets him everywhere.

Such a man might become a hermit and live in a cave in the mountains, where he builds small wooden cages and sits by the fire. A lost hunter once discovered such a man and offered to take care of him and to help him sell his cages. They lived together on the edge of a small village near the cave. Once a week the hunter took the cages away to sell them. The hermit's eyes grew dim as the years passed and the cages grew smaller and smaller.

One day the hunter complained that the size of the cages was making them hard to sell. What can be kept in such a small cage? But when the hunter was sleeping, the blind hermit took his last tiny cage and followed the road leaving the village. From time to time someone stopped him and asked what he kept in the tiny wooden cage. Each time the old man answered, "No one," and took a bite of a potato nestled in his coat pocket. Each time, the questioner was surprised by the way the man looked at the potato and continued walking as if he could see something far down the road. Not once did a questioner think to ask the blind man to open the cage.

April 5

His Speech Mistaken for Tapping

He could have succumbed to false obligations. It was huge, like an index to everything that wasn't happening at the moment.

He's just a close-mouthed kid, trying to escape to the rivers and fields, dragging his stick along the fenceline. The things he means depend upon the way we say them, his dialogue of limited actions still engaged in disengagement. An internal fluid roar continually belies its patience, his future hung on a hook of "air," a floating word almost wisdom.

Some unlit birds on the pier offer a tardy tattered act of resignation, these charlatans of heavy air monitoring the piercing stare of his scavenging speech.

The last bird eyes his eye, pressed against what's there as one and then one again to be blindly days and nights of days. The grand gatherer of these houses lives everywhere. He lives in these herds.

An unfurling flap of shore-bound blackbirds hoists its pirate's flag over the windy beach. Theirs is a lonely God, pampered and strict, its children cowering.

Because he has begun snowing, his edges are well-defined until he steps into too much light.

The darkness pulls it in.

Molesting his absence, the hands from the nights before are not his hands.

The fence that refuses to speak of his choice is not the fence that surrounds his imagination.

There are those who have died of hope. There are those who have come here without him. Ask him about his nothing, but don't ask him what he cannot do. Underneath he was naked.

And with this truth he hides a deeper one.

April 6

Hat Full of Fog

When Grampa checked the traps, he found a muskrat's paw and when the missionaries came, he put it in their donation box. "What is a grandmother supposed to look like?" Grampa said. He asked for a name and he didn't get one.

"I will protect myself with open doors and I will prevent loneliness by sleeping on rooftops," said Grampa, "and I will listen to the bricks when they have fallen from their long quiet sermons on certainty."

"After illusion, there's nothing but a hat full of fog." Jalopy had just discovered this and Jalopy was crying. She was holding herself in like a glass of something thick and sweet, and she was trying not to spill what she hadn't tasted yet. She was waiting for life to reveal itself. She had waited a long time. She was looking around for something to hold herself up to. She was almost there, almost to where she was at that moment, next to the next memory, when one of the animal skins floating in the curing vat reminded her of her granddaughter's shawl.

Jalopy sucked her breath and Jalopy burbled and Jalopy turned her head to avoid the irritating noise and dragged her long hair across the curing vat. Jalopy's raven tresses were really golden curls streaked with gray.

Grampa witnessed and Grampa huffed. Grampa patted Jalopy on the head. Poor girl. Huffed some more.

Which pissed her off royally. Could have stayed home with her daughter if she wanted that shit.

"We're both looking up and the thing we're watching seems to be the sky and it could be the same one," thought Grampa. "There's a power in saying no but a greater one in saying nothing," thought Grampa, "but my thinking about her might be meddling with her thinking about me."

Grampa took the pelts to the possibility exchange, and along the way he decided to marry Jalopy. The night felt so clammy and humid he could have been traveling inside a fish. He dipped his hat into the fog and carried it carefully, as if it might spill if he were ever to attempt to wear it again.

April 7

A Light in the Window

All things lean toward rain. You are on a journey and the path you travel is on a journey of its own. Three horses standing in a field are breathing small clouds of mist that float away in the air like abstractions. A woman is dancing at a bright window.

The window that travels with you is a circle that prefers darkness. Frantic stars in the arrowblack evening of roots dance in the moist hush of rainlamps, dance for the light at rest on the chair.

These are the masters of drift, and you are the vase on the difficult ledge farther in, furiously lost in the night of these windows. Your light is the only light. Turn it off. Begin.

April 8

There's Got to Be a Little Rain Sometimes

The whole barnyard was flooded. Little Nonsense forgot what he was doing. He made a harness and used it to hitch his mother to a small boat. He gave Bitsie his glass eye.

He thought about the man who lived alone in the mountain country. He wondered, "May I plant a garden of my own?"

But there was too much water. Way too much water.

"My this is a wet day," said Bitsie, holding her tight little buds in check. "Many are the days that have fallen sunless, but few so very very wet," continued Bitsie. "I think I'll try to peel off some of the sun from the roof of Papa and place it on the apex of my being," continued Bitsie. "I'll call it 'Hair,'" continued and continued Bitsie, proud of her father's terrible absence.

"I think I'll just let her play with my beautiful tail," thought Little Nonsense. But Bitsie was all done with the weather and not about to frolic in such a wet garden.

Little Nonsense watched her with his glass eye.

It was a trick and it worked, but it was also work and it tricked him. Nonsense took an early retirement. Nonsense released his mother from the small boat of her self-inflicted obligations.

"May I plant a small garden of my own?" he still wondered.

But with his mother out of the way, Bitsie was watching him too closely.

He watched back.

The whole barnyard watched them watching.

The sun came out and started coloring the barnyard.

"I think I'll call it, 'Marriage,'" continued and continued Bitsie, growing prouder and prouder of her new husband's terrible absence. Which confused Little Nonsense terribly as he watched her blushing while she prepared the bed.

April 9

Hangdog the Carpenter

In this box his world has been sheltered. There are no windows, but there are so many doors they must all be left open in order to move. Therefore happiness is possible, if no light from no window in a world of doors forever open to darkness can make you happy.

Build yourself a world and ask him to hold it. Introduce yourself as The King of Corners. Tell him how difficult it was to build your world around him. Ask him to hold your flashlight.

When the stars shine at night Hangdog has been inspecting the joints. A tap here, a tap there, and rust falls from these nails. Where the light comes from that reflects from their heads is a mystery.

Another box on the table in the living room glows softly in the light pouring in from the window of this box we call a house. World within world within world . . . Pray for this day which must end in darkness. Ask him to hold your flashlight.

April 10

Sorrow

One method is to let it bounce off its constituency like a cartoon, cannonading the human fireworks into delayed despair. Sorrow does not approve of this method. Gravity won't finally let go.

Another method is to find a primitive location for the ceremony, complete with flagellation and tribal wailing, and observe carefully the participant hidden by the nature of his observation. You might choose The Village of Not Me for this theme. You might already be living there.

Another approach is to start somewhere else, somewhere far, and come back slowly, using "until the sea salt crusts on the iron gate" as a welcome instead of a landmark. Clever distraction can ration the local abundance, but the gateway of its excess won't let you pass undisturbed.

Sleeping on the haunches of a very old dream coaxes out the camouflaged emotions. Place the new sorrow among the old. Don't forget how much you've aged. To return you must travel through bones. It's true that some of the sorrow belongs to all of us, but that becomes a virtue only if it shows in the knowing gratitude of the smile and not the pleading parade of the mouth.

Sorrow is a temple of worship that shelters its congregation from augmentation, a territory of passage waiting to become a country of burden. As soon as you are comfortable there, it is time to leave.

But the larger world of pervasive sorrow swallows all other worlds. Its digestion is poor. Follow its rude trail in innocence. Something has been imperfectly returned. A part of the outside on the inside.

From this point on, the external quickly vanishes.

One way to claim all that you've lost is to talk to the past.

Another method is to travel without words.

April 11

Adolescence

The way Junior feels about it is lying there like a young bird on the sidewalk, fallen prematurely from the nest.

A small outcry stands up and goes searching for an audience.

First he closed his eyes, then he looked in the mirror.

Have I ever been old enough for this?

Because there is always someone who can see the dangers we live with and because we pity him. He is so sad, so unavailable to our happiness. But for most of us, that happiness would disappear if we thought too long about what he knows. For a few, it would heighten the pleasure.

He has already traveled down the smell of the swamp.

That was tomorrow. Now it's yesterday and there a mouse is nibbling at a piece of cheese, as is permitted by certain proverbs.

What he needs is a good death. To acknowledge the cloudburn on his forehead. To ignore the avuncular clatter. To gather his parents' deepest secrets and eat them. You can see the sorrow in their faces.

We made an agreement with the world and the world, of course, broke it.

He would start and he would stop and he would start again.

Because there is always another world beginning, some slow lumbering creature like sleep itself. A riverbank trying to get up and leave. An easy understanding that is not your life but only partly false. And desirable.

A bag of used words, wounded. Like that.

But the necessary river begins in the ear. The river deciding no house there. Moving itself here because it likes here.

The river has water and we have blood. You cannot think with water, but with blood, you cannot reach the clouds. What is heaven but an exaggerated rest before the fall, a way of speaking the word inside the word you meant to say but didn't?

It's noon and his shadows are hiding.

A weasel-eyed kite of a man, his father says, "Don't take it personally." He is talking to himself.

A small reptile. The ghost of adolescence.

And this is all impossible because it's real.

April 12

Patra Düldig's Galoshes

Patra Düldig says goodbye and goodbye and goodbye. He is starting over. He is going to Berlin to say hello to his new life. His mother has bought him a new black raincoat, which he drapes over his right arm, the strong one that carries two suitcases instead of one, which makes three suitcases, which Patra Düldig could tell you. Patra Düldig is proud of his right arm.

Getting on the bus, Patra Düldig has a problem with his coins. They do not add up properly in his palm for the journey that awaits him. Patra Düldig is quick to recognize this as much more than a simple problem of bus fare. But it is not raining and it is far to Berlin and even if it was, Patra Düldig would soon see that the rain must have somewhere to go once it has fallen and Patra Düldig has no galoshes.

Now what is going to happen is that Patra Düldig is going to miss the last step between the bus and the wet black street. Look where you're stepping there, Patra Düldig. So much is at stake. Don't let that dummkopf bussdriver hurry you into your new life.

And what are those black bundles in the wet streets of Berlin, huddled under shiny black raincoats with broken umbrellas and no galoshes? Could one of them be Patra Düldig's new life quibbling over the rent?

Hello! Hello! Hello! Sorry to disturb you.

April 13

Hangdog the Hunger Artist

Hangdog is a hunger game specialist. He knows all the variations of Solitaire and Stool Pigeon, which are the same game, where beating yourself is winning. In the game of Stampers faces may be forgotten. Bob and Slap is a variation for beginners. Professionals play Hobnail. Hangdog is a ruthless cheerleader.

Staying Alive too is a game of chance with many foolish players. When Hangdog is referee, everyone suffers.

In the game of May We Cross Your Golden River? there are many tricks and only the sun can win. Hangdog is a batboy. There is no ball, except the sun. In the game of Stone, no one may move, no one may breathe, no one may die. The object is to slowly fall apart. The winner may grow corn.

April 14

An Ex-Confessional Poet's Notes on Theology

The confessional poets have changed their minds. They're not going to tell you anything. But despite the details, they know that life is still sad, and a truly felt elegy for a toad harbors a metaphorical masterpiece on the fly-specked tongue of the last lunge beyond the horrible limits of said life, which tells our story its own way, with such dispassionate ease that the details no longer seem to belong to us.

And so the confessional poets have changed their lives and the great truth of their favorite sins is hidden in the depths of boredom. Reality unadorned, unmourned and reeking threatens to simplify the believers, send them stomping and shouting out of their bodies to become the new revivalists in search of a religion large enough to think like the world they insist on giving away.

April 15

Gustave Flaubert and the Broken Bicycle

Little metal bird, flown against the window of a hole in the ground, what made you think anyone could know you well enough to feather your cold metal wings? The sun has gone under a cloud and the deceiver run home crying to a merely human god. But where is your nest? What hopeless yearning carries you beyond the understanding of your kind and leaves you here in this painful silence waiting as if for the brushstroke that believes in its painter, the signature that sets the timeless simplicity of a bicycle's misadventures into its classical frame? And who is that man who is smiling, then laughing, as he walks past you on the broken road?

April 16

Replete with Idle Tongues

The thing is, we didn't care. Here everything cried as we cried. Here everything lived in fear of its creator. The lost soul was our bride, our groom.

Yes, I had become sufficiently delusional to supplant reality with visionary wonder. Like a deaf man blinded by music, I was bravely fighting for the right error. I mean we were. I mean we felt something stir. Like a nervous twitch. And we went looking for us to happen again.

Went looking for another. Fucked into reverie, that's what we wanted to be. So you'll know I'm not like all the others, we thought. We wanted our needle-eyed mongrel of a curse limping out of bed with religious purpose. Our very own new witness keeping us righteous as we suffered our superiority.

"We must overcome our sins," says the ministration, replacing the comfort of assimilating a language without edges. The new lie as great as heaven.

We should be punished for this, yes, we should be put in charge.

So we did this thing. We did it together. We did it where the roads had been aging. Elders in the church of the rusted chassis. We took it seriously. We thought it wouldn't change anything, but as soon as it got going, we felt alive again.

We left behind the gift of ignorance.

The punishment had come before the crime.

April 17

Clowntime Is Never Over

A dead clown was singing under the Yum Yum tree, which made all the little children happy as can be.

I moved into my father's neck because his heart was empty. A pain, you see. His eye socket filled with honey.

The dead clown told me she was the flag of an unknown country. She was smiling, with little nips of waves biting the inlet's nipples.

This is not the way I see it, but the way it is.

I gestured acceptingly but my hand was outside the purview of the window. It was colder that way.

She found some small boards. She asked her mother for some nails. I must hurry, she said, and lay my singular egg.

In passing, I suppose I can acknowledge the possibility that I too am passing. The dead clown was not in the parade, but the parade existed anyway.

You see, it's a great deal more fun if it's tied up in a wonderful fear. A great and sudden change. If you have gas in your family, that gas may be a disproportionate resource even if you are not directly responsible.

Her inability to answer forced the dead clown to make a shelter of sticks, boughs and moss. Perhaps her recent issue helped her move in.

In like manner I moved into my father's leg because there were no dead clowns there and I wanted the issue to leave me alone.

I did not wish to be fed. My hand was still cold. My father was cold.

The dead clown wrote to me concerning the absence of her parents. She formed the letters painfully, describing the writing as she wrote, stroke by stroke, her pen putting on the sticklimbs as if they were broken dolls she was required to put away in tiny pieces each time she left them in the room of her thoughts and now she had to put them back together reborn into this unknown day's new piece of her mind, which was far from peaceful, and fit on the body of that yesterday loosely, and rotated, like one of the garden's wooden action figures, running or flying or floundering in place with the wind rummaging through the poorly fitted destinations.

I did not wish to move outside the window. I did not wish to sing to anyone.

I was content to be living under the Yum Yum tree.

It was as happy as I could be.

April 18

Little Brown Dream Coats

Several of the gangsters were wrapped snugly in light brown coats. Distinctive cuts of meat from the dream butcher. Neat and bundled and cozy-like. Suggestive.

The warm rain promised. The sky did.

Maybe the mud would make the mistake clearer.

The one with a round pudgy face said, "He likes to talk about sexual juices, but he doesn't like to talk about sex."

Another gangster was saying he could have had any of the women he wanted; he's not naming names, but he could have had any of them. He could have. That's what he'll tell you more than once.

Another gangster banged the flat of his hand against his forehead and said, "It's just a bag of bagels. That's what it is. It's a friggin' bag of bagels." Several gangsters were listening and nodding, but no one said a word.

After all, what people want is to have their needs satisfied, especially the ones they're unaware of. What people want is ever so many more satisfactions than they can have.

Could this be the source of another vanished tale of sorrow?

The man in the woods made himself a knife from a stone with a very hard edge. But this did not make the man in the woods a gangster, nor did it make the man in the woods a man who lived in the woods. Nevertheless, one of the gangsters decided on northern Wisconsin for his vacation. His son rode in the back, holding a baby tree with a green ribbon tied to it. It was a gift for northern Wisconsin. It was a nice gesture and it made sense to the gangsters, and that felt wrong, so they tried to remember what it was like to act crazy. They wanted to feel that freedom. They wanted to plant something dangerous in the world they didn't live in, but they wanted somebody to live in that world, somebody who needed a sharp knife.

So listen to this. After a gangster's leg fell asleep, he decided he ought to cut it off. That kind of pain was outside the realm of his personal experience, though he had witnessed it second hand many times. It would not have been as foolish as those outside the range of his experience might assume, but it would have been a high price to pay for respect. Finally he decided the warm rain he had been watching had promised something else.

Meanwhile, outside the world's great butcher shop, the man in the woods remained wrapped snugly in his own body. He was not intending to end anyone's life or cut off any of their body parts. Some of the gangsters would say his intentions were not, therefore, relevant to destiny.

The rain promised, but perhaps the rain's promise was not the promise we heard. Just as the sky is open to interpretation. Sometimes we hear the sounds but we can't find the story in them.

"Imagine that," thought the loneliest gangster as he paid for his leathery dreams, "it's as if I were experiencing my life all over again." But the other gangsters could not hear this voice issuing from beneath the brown paper wrapping.

"A steak may not be a good steak, but it won't lie to you." That's what the gangsters thought when they asked it how much it wanted, even though by this time they had forgotten its name.

April 19

Large Marbled Sphere of Unknown Origin Ensconced in a Hand-Carved Box

A man is supposed to, so his eyes caught in the folds of her skin.

He felt alive the caution was so dangerous.

This has all been explained, but not to her.

His heavily laden ghost was busy sniffing the potential hidden in the baggage. Her baggage was sniffing back.

Passion is a muscle. The heart reminds us. It needs beating to tenderize the body of it, which bruises out and away from the source, broadcasting the delayed recognition of the welcomed invasion, a balance recovered as the color warms outward.

At this stage of the proceedings, a girlfriend once wore a camouflage garter belt. A boyfriend wore a confederate army uniform with a copy of Rimbaud in its torn pocket.

Maneuvers.

They certainly didn't understand their survival.

Shouldn't it be enough that they've discovered they're still there?

You want to understand, but that's not what you want to happen.

If you go back to them, they won't be there anymore. They don't need to drown. They just float away. They empty.

Death is relative. The end of the story is always coming after you.

Neither animal predator enough. Neither animal prey.

April 20

An Error in Judgment

Streetlight enters the room without knocking. All it takes is a certain degree of difficulty to notice. It reverses the territorial rights.

It doesn't necessarily bleed like a dream, but it weeps like a dream, saving you the trouble. It's hard not to become disaffected.

One side of the argument a brittle brown bag, the other a ragged posturing with bright red wattles. As hard as cement and as cold as cement and as wise as cement, but it falls over at the slightest push.

The chambermaid sucking on a pickle outside the limits. Taken from the room with no wrapper, the possibility leaks.

But I remain faithful to the cover story. It's knocking on my interior and I can't come in. The chair and the table and the story are waiting, so I sit in the middle. History is simply unfortunate I would once have said, but I had never owned much.

I can't taste the streetlight, I don't crush the little red globes of generosity and the missing constructions are not part of the table conversation.

Hail! Caesar is mistaken.

Caesar bleeds.

The illumination keeps me in, but the author of my past remains inexperienced. I'm not allowed to leave without taking back my life.

Streetlight is common. Streetlight is available without warning. All you need is people not sleeping. And a desire to see what should not be seen.

April 21

A New Jacket

Yesterday four clowns were executed in the courtyard. A dove landed on the windowsill while I watched. The papers were filled with it this morning, and by afternoon the papers were shut down. Yet none of them had reported the rape of the young rag-picker that followed, the soldiers too excited by what they had done, unable to overlook her waiting to see if the bodies would be left wearing anything useful. She whimpered loudly as they took turns, but held her arms out, away from the dirt, trying to keep the white cuffs of the harlequin's jacket clean.

April 22

Poetry and Domestic Life

When I have nothing left to give, I yawn and sit in my stuffed chair. The unread books on the coffee table begin sighing. I don't know what to do about the dog.

My daughter comes in with a book of poems. The chimney poem tells the story of smoke. The sky poem stretches the truth. I tell her the mother poem is really part of the father poem, which is really part of something else. I tell her the gravity poem is not that important. I tell her to ask the nose poem what it does for a living. I tell her about knee poems, how they dangle a clutter of bone and muscle rope, waiting for stray kisses. I tell her at the end of my hair poem I will begin to shine.

My daughter sleeps. In the dark beneath my broken kneecap I walk in a forest of bone trees. Somewhere deep inside, something familiar, a porchlight.

April 23

Secret Lives of the Hatless

And this would have to be the version of the story in which the stones do not talk and the people do and probably the plants would stay in one place unless the people moved them and not talk either unless they merely whisper in faint breezy answer when the people talk to them and someone would have to walk the dog if there was a dog and someone would have to feed the cat if there was a cat unless the people let their domesticated animals wander about freely scavenging for themselves but they wouldn't do that nosir because the people's parents and friends would think less of them and you can't live like that no not if you're sensitive and don't scratch your behind in public or make disgusting noises in the bedroom with the window open I mean I guess if your life's going to make sense you have to have some guidelines to go by even if other people don't believe in them because after all we're not all ruthless and we have still another version of a good example to set by golly yessir with all that generous warmth rising up like unquestioned prayers from the lowered tops of all those trusting heads of ours don't you see it's just one of the ways we can explain our losses besides singing a capella or rubbing up against trees and calling softly to the various physical manifestations of our desire to feel the heat of our life's argument even as it continues escaping the calculated pretense of exterior appearance.

April 24

Primitive Instincts

A woman who is tired of her hair shaves off all her hair. A man who is very hairy finds this attractive. But the hair keeps trying to poke its heads out of the woman.

One day, frustrated, the hairy man comes home from the office and for reasons never fully explained, though apparently having something to do with the office, says, "I wish so many things with teeth did not want to eat so many things without teeth."

And the woman, who has grown tired of her hair for equally inexplicable reasons, replies, "I don't suppose you would understand if I attached your behind to a door-knob, would you?"

Flustered and uncertain about an acceptable response, the man who is very hairy decides to put on his cowboy shirt for that special effect it has, at times, had upon the woman, forgetting how much trouble he has had getting his hair caught in the snaps.

And so, unexpectedly, for once expressing himself with admirable clarity and directness, the hairy man says, "My hair is always getting caught in the snaps on my cowboy shirt." Because it most certainly is true. Because he means it. And because he doesn't know what else to say.

And the now only partially hairless woman can tell by the tone in the hairy man's voice that he means what he is saying. And so she too begins to wish so many things with teeth did not want to eat so many things without teeth, without even knowing why. And she keeps on noticing all the heads still trying to poke their way out of her. And she tries to do something about it. But soon the less and less hairless woman grows tired of all the poking and wants control of her life back. This desire for something she never had may lead her away from herself. Which may really be what the hairy man wants.

Being among the far too many things with teeth, the man and the woman cannot alter the course of animal history with their nibbling at each other, but the desire to become someone one is not needs no teeth to eat at one.

And yet the hairy man remains disinclined to understand the no longer hairless woman's desire to become the hairy man because he is busy chewing on his desire to become the potentially hairless woman. And if one achieves one's desire, will one then desire the more-pronounced-because-it-was-more-misunderstood desire one had before one achieved?

April 25

The Love Scene

The baby's mother had an itch the baby couldn't scratch. I was the person who knew enough not to comment directly upon this to the baby's mother. I was the person who lifted the stroller over the threshold in order to allow the baby's mother to reinsert the baby into the stroller. And I was the person who watched this happening to myself.

I believe in the infinite love which can be offered with the help of one's deepest beliefs. So far, it hasn't helped much.

Because we believed the baby would appreciate the experience we would have there, we took the baby to the movie. Inside the ticket taker's glass booth, a dog wearing sunglasses and beads was sitting on the counter. We had been previously introduced to this animal and he had represented himself as somewhat circumspect and thus we were now somewhat perplexed by the sunglasses and beads.

We waited in line behind several former ticket takers with their oddly luminous ties altering from one view to another in a manner that suggested they were on fire. These former ticket takers had something red and apparently sticky and very like, we could not help but suspect, blood upon their sneakers, and we suspected this would not become part of the movie.

The baby started crying. We counted our change and found the wrong arrangement of symbolic value. Our story appeared not to have been adequately arranged and this moment appeared to have been a false conclusion. There was definitely something wrong. The shadows were extending further away from the scene. The baby's mother was once more waiting at the threshold, where the baby's mother scratched the baby tenderly and the baby stopped crying, whereupon I was painfully successful in stifling my complicated responses to the mother's misplaced affection.

This too, of course, was a false conclusion, but this time I was the person who knew enough not to mention it.

April 26

A Mobile Home

Her spinal mailbox issues forth a begrudging slipped quiver. A waitress blubbering over some transient hairball she fucked and fled, oozing such delightful sorrows.

Emotional cannibals. A crime for every generosity. A life of conflicted pleasurepain lived on a tangent. An innocently snowing dream next to a teddy bear doused in gasoline.

And still her tongue gathers light, without speech, without innocence, from the reflected memory tasting vaguely of temptation. Hard to remember how far away it was. She licks her lip, offering a painfully tasty despair, mistaken for concern over the discolored wings of the messenger.

Written like a crow's foot, an isolated line of laughter, there where the smile disengages: I'll give you anything you take.

April 27

What the Critic Didn't Say

Why didn't you know who you were first? It's one of the questions that occurred to me when I came home from the assignation.

The next day you claimed you had been "licked by the tongue of God."

It's not what I wanted to hear. It troubles me. Why can't I place it in the proper receptacle?

You had always been the kind of woman who says, "It's what the boys tell you when they want to."

Now invitations. Now eyes that say they have been walking around with their sex out.

I heard then a mother tell her daughter, "I got stuck removing the moonlight." The mother was "accidentally" dropping an egg in her daughter's lap, who whimpered and tried to hold it untouched, silently announcing herself like a billboard.

I offered them the badge I got for stealing erasers in a town that seemed smaller than I was.

"The words came out of his mouth in the normal way, but what he said, it turned back on itself. Neat and meaningless."

I watched. I nodded. I analyzed the influences.

You said what I wanted to hear. You had to be right.

The last time we met, you were busy altering the direction of the hairs on your beautiful, blunt fingers.

If they pointed at me, I didn't notice.

April 28

Two Sisters Fail to Die Tragically in Freak Accident

This could have been the end. But the good little girl who wanted to star in the movie hadn't figured out how to adequately anger her smug and admirable parents. She hadn't learned to be naughty. She hadn't requested enough suffering. She hadn't grown thematic.

So in went the bad juice and out went the good juice. But the good little girl's parents didn't even notice.

So she escalated. She hadn't realized suffering could be so easily invited. Was she starting something inevitable?

In the ranch movie inside the good little girl's head, the good little girl was riding ponies and eating cotton candy and playing hide and seek with the lambs and cheating at strip poker with the ranch hands. But in the ranch movie that was inside her mother's head, she was whitewashing the gleam in her father's watchful eye.

And in the ranch movie that was inside God's head, there was a great big flood and a lot of suffering and lots of drowned animals and lost people, except for the ones that were supposed to be learning a lesson for future generations.

And that was too many movies and too many confusing messages for the good little girl, so in went the ranch hands and out came the baby and soon the great flood of '74 was making its own kind of history. The good little girl wasn't mentioned by name (not the real one), but finally she had starred in all the suffering she desired. Which left (meanwhile, on the very same ranch), her sister, the bad little girl, to complete the confusions of parental oversight by turning out (suspiciously) well.

And if both sisters hadn't failed to die horrible deaths in a runaway train and expensive little foreign sports car accident on the only lonely country road in the heavily urbanized county, they could have been the inspiration for the famous story upon which the timeless movie could have been based.

And then we would have to figure out who was really lying.

And then we would have to figure out if we believed it.

And that could have been the beginning.

April 29

Parental Concerns

He has a horse in the cellar. Nobody knows if he eats grapes. If he holds still you maybe could ride him. He's a child but he gallops and gallops to the place where only horses are. His sister was long and thin and dancing in circles.

It's not the right time for the spicy breath of the barker, foreign enough to break through the street's wet sibilant murmur, and all that leaping the water's grasp encourages merely breaks through the forgotten illustration, a sound like a planet clearing its throat. When my ideas are gone, I'll pay the price for more.

"Who's blooming in my parts?" he wondered.

Like unto a dewdrop leaning towards the tug of its unopened flower.

There are big people to think about here and if that sky simply didn't know it had a better thing to do, then it would be everything outside. The subject that would know what the subject was.

Deliver yourself to the wrong address and you could take home a troubled son. But I'm not here for the corrections. Instead of domain, I want landscape. No more chain link fences.

Now the circus threatens to run away. Now the wrong man is the right one.

Let's wait till later, when the candidate has spoken to the attached body. Let's irrigate the drying children and suffer without complaint.

Even the adopted clouds seem to be waiting for an admission.

April 30

Gifts

1. *I happened to be enjoying it immensely. That's why she stopped.*

It had been a long time since I had been deeply into the essence of a thing.

It could have been that our activities were merely suspended, but I doubted it. I doubted it very much. She wasn't that kind of girl. She wanted things yesterday. She wanted history.

I didn't want to change the direction of my existence. I wanted to continue. I wanted to appropriate the necessities.

After we were interrupted by explanations, by well-meaning friends and curious neighbors, I offered them some carefully selected potentials.

Because I was in charge.

Because I knew they wouldn't accept them.

I wanted to enjoy this immensely.

But life had been altered. Which, I am told, happens continuously. Must I violate expectations to enjoy anything thoroughly or is it merely the idea of being deeply into the essence of a thing which provides pleasure?

You had a piece of paper in your mouth and you were trying to write on it with your teeth. I can only assume that what you were writing was not this, and if the mistake is not mistaken, then perhaps the mistake's broken condition allows it to offer two sources of potential. I have grown certain that my speculations should not stop when the subject to which they are applied is altered.

2. I have lived in this meadow for a long time now and the snow has avoided me. A meadow sometimes allows that. The sky can seem too far away to matter even though the sky is another meadow and no meadow is ever like any other meadow.

Be careful of the ideas a meadow has. Don't eat what it thinks you should. Don't follow it. Where it wants to go is right where it is.

Because dreams are not entirely dreams, I am one of the problems the meadow dreams about, and in this way I let it have its way with me, which is not always what it really wants.

In order to discover this I had to visit a few interested parties and be interested.

I don't have anything else to offer yet. Which, I am told, happens continuously.

May

May 1

As Soon As You Know

If you drop Vladimir by mistake, he will break. Do it on purpose. Do it with dignity.

This time is for wishing and going across. This is Osip coming home with a cultural headache. This is Boris undressing.

You couldn't have handbooked the undertaker anyway. He's from the old school. He uses roses and tinctures of lavender. Proclamations just wait for the bus.

This isn't the happiest of bootstraps. This isn't the czar's wetted handkerchief.

One survived. One didn't. It gives us a choice, but which one? You couldn't have anticipated Russia. It just happened. And then maybe it didn't anymore.

Charges were filed against the other agent. But he wasn't working for us either. In the original countries, philosophy was merely an aging process. Vladimir's situation could have been expected.

Even before the system started biting its heels, there were signs of digression. Inevitably, a broken Vladimir would answer the pattern.

So call for the revolution of movement not the movement of revolution. Bring forth as your own that which will happen anyway.

Break Vladimir. Use the pieces to cultivate. Plant anything but a czar or a puppet parliament. Water the windows and open the earth with hoes and fresh anger. Let it breath. Let it give you what it wants. Just as you may now give to it whatever you want. Just as soon as you know what that is.

May 2

Thank You for Asking

Paul Bunyan, Joseph Cornell and Dwight Yoakam were eating spaghetti from a seasoned plank of Hawaiian koa when the local buffalo recovery squad began reciting. They were far too derivative and the leader's skirt was stained a suspiciously bright pink.

Yes, there were several small intestinal elevators available. Thank you for asking.

Barbed mice had been strung along the spaghetti's perimeter for greater safety and protection from the elements. Reports of blue oxen in boxes with a wide variety of nasal twangs had been reluctantly discounted.

The small elevators were larger than the small elevators previously employed.

The toasted oxhorn aphrodisiacs were a hoax. So were the autographed interruptions. Tammy Wynette was no longer gesticulating in sadly torrential patterns among the poodle skirts at Babe's Wisconsin Burger Bar.

Yes, enough room for six toes in the mood boots. Thank you for asking.

Dwight's spaghetti chin was not considered safely enshrined. The buffalo squad was tiring. The buffalo squad considered departing with the outmoded portion of the Hawaiians. The buffalo squad was still too derivative. It couldn't have helped their personal relationships any.

And whether or not Joseph's disturbing thought box remained inside the elevator, at what rate do such boxes depart from the considerations of sympathetic rising and falling?

Shoes for the famous. Shoes for the small. Shoes for the dallymouse who lives in the wall. Thank you for asking.

A story of delightful and confusing replenishment of motion. But is it the one you placed between the necessary available moments or is it the one still ascending?

We got there by accepting the relativity of isolationism. Does this mean we're not responsible? Should Dwight's spaghetti chin be accepted without constant revision?

You see, the "smaller" elevator was actually larger than the smallest of the two larger elevators, but no one seemed to notice. It remained unnecessary to entertain such notions. Nevertheless, the popularity of the intestinal owners upon which they operated increased, both historically and sheltered in the contemporary peripheries of the other two intestinally elevated components of the spaghetti fest, despite the isolationism.

Many such outmoded Hawaiians have returned for retraining and some have completed advanced coursework in culinary elevation. This was to be expected considering their limited landmass and propensity for fireworks. Less predictable has been the extinction of the blue oxen boxes, once found in nearly every country and western bar in Hawaii.

Yes, transparent poodle skirts and cottonball clouds. Thank you for asking.

May 3

Fame

Two well-known books are being interviewed for a television talk show, carefully praising each other's authors and exchanging witticisms with the host, when the show is interrupted for a news flash concerning the condition of Erica, the local zoo's pregnant panda (the only pregnancy ever recorded in captivity for this particular variety), who is in the zoo hospital in serious condition following an "incident" involving a misguided ice cream vendor who barely escaped the incident unsullied and who actually died of complications resulting from an allergic reaction to the anesthetic administered, coincidentally, exactly one week later during an operation on his knee, which had not, it seems, been injured in the "incident," but had been gradually deteriorating for more than a decade prior as a result of a college prank gone awry. The talk show host apologizes for the interruption and wishes Erica well, promising the station will broadcast further reports as available. The interview continues with the two books expressing outrage at the current popularity of speed reading when they are again interrupted as the screen flashes to a view of a young girl on crutches visiting the zoo's hospital cage. An interviewer questions her and we discover she is an orphan whose leg was broken in the very same "incident" that (we now discover) caused Erica to miscarry. The girl's answers seem rehearsed and suddenly she seems to have forgotten her lines. She begins to cry and reaches into the cage to touch Erica's fur. A zookeeper quickly pulls her back and the young girl screams "Mommy" as the screen goes dark and cuts to the talk show set where the two books have been replaced by two authors who are sleeping slumped down in their comfortable chairs. The talk show host runs in from off-camera and begins to interview the two sleeping authors. They do not awaken and no one reaches into the cage to touch their fur.

May 4

Only the Free Man Knows He's a Slave

I was singing, "Don't Need a Reason till It's Over." I was out of place and I was ecstatic.

I was accosted by a vicious citizen, but I began dancing and it scared him.

I wouldn't call him portly and diminutive.

Did this make me feel like I had just witnessed an animal hit by a car get up and limp into the darkness? No, it did not.

This, of course, means I should live my life, but the rest of my life's not here right now, it's impossible, just impossible.

I keep on dancing.

Oh who id dat Joe wid da sloppy floppy grin grin grin?

That's when something incongruous like blue cement ignites a cry of joy. Yes indeed a cry of joy. Truly. I'm not lying about it.

But the kingdom I came from is no longer quite so bright and welcoming, no longer lost, in that place where it could be perfected. Only the earth-shattering spike of some unnameable plant says what needs to be said.

And you listen. And you sing. And you begin a great refund of energy.

Is this what you wanted to be?

It's like that painting: Pugilist Questioning the Lagoon. I was no longer gesturing to illusionary supplicants. I knew what I wanted to do. I went outside to refresh myself but I can't say I succeeded. I left something. I came away with less.

I wanted to believe I had made a contribution. That I had donated. But I was out of place and ecstatic and no longer accosted.

So I danced. And then I danced some more. My freedom depended upon it.

May 5

The Day Before the River Returned

In my dream of enlightenment there is an aquarium full of Kennedys and drag queens. In this dream I can see the odor of an ear falling asleep. Blackbirds and bedsprings are mating. Can you hear the gills pulsing? Come see the freshly butchered cloudfish. It seems to be some sea cucumber's idea of heaven. An entire universe of green swaying tubas erupts beneath the buoyant ceramic boat navigating the dream's fluid eyelet. Children are screaming, screaming, "Music must be seen and not heard."

Like an argument between scissors, I slice away at a last chance to inflict reason. I've been separated too long.

Even in the dream my stomach votes capitalist, dragging my heavy baskets of need out of the territorial boat. I clutch a dripping fork and suddenly I want my own egg, floating up, a cold heart from the inside.

Other times I've been calling it sympathetic, calling it occasional, fluent in stone, submerged, silent but for the taking of time. The dream wakes. When you fall, it's up, into the sky, where the water gathers for the crucial discussion about relocating.

I can't hear the drag queens' stolen speeches but soggy Kennedys drip from the aquarium lid. If the idea of heaven votes for the cucumber, I can't see how I'll be able to adjust.

Outside the air grows sharper. On the corner of the breakfast plate my own egg begins watching me float.

May 6

The Other Woman

He was saying something but it didn't seem to be about anything. He was saying something and then he wasn't saying something.

Did you know that feels? Did you know how? Even when it's not about anything. I know. A woman knows these things.

If he had said don't confuse me with the facts, it really would have meant don't confuse ME with the facts. As if he wasn't one, a fact, not even a moment of that kind of truth.

But he didn't say that.

He wanted an answer but he didn't know where it would come from. He wanted that too. Not knowing where it would come from.

Maybe he stopped because he started crashing into himself with what he was going to say.

He wanted to inflict more pain. On someone else this time.

Then Spot was making this noise like a choking scream. Spot was a dog and was not trying to convey the essence of his entire life.

I was considering touching another woman, but I was intimidated by the Bobby pins. Why are they named after a guy?

Then I noticed the woman was trying to put her arms around my husband. To get something, I think, but I couldn't be sure.

The woman made a face that wasn't very flattering.

My husband didn't seem to notice. He was concentrated.

This other guy at the party, he was full up with embarrassment. I could see that he was trying to think about kissing me. I didn't know who he was, but I wanted to know who he was going to be.

The dinner was still crying. The dinner was still sad.

He hated that.

The other woman, who was somebody's wife, said, "Something wonderful is going to happen." She said, "Okay, so listen, will you?" And then she didn't say anything.

I said “Peter” because that’s his name. I didn’t say it to insult him. Then I let myself go. I belonged to gravity.

He was a pilot, but that has nothing to do with what happened.

So then, “Do me,” said the man’s wife. “Do me now.” She wanted me to hear her say it. Then she put herself into the hands of fate. Which had already been shaped according to her desires.

She had fun.

But even if you’re the smartest guy in the universe, you’re going to fail sometime. It made sense to be afraid of that woman.

But it was really something what she had. A kind of rubbery bounce to her. Like a cat toy. Even Spot noticed.

You didn’t have to be very perceptive to see what a woman like that wanted, but maybe you had to be perceptive to understand it.

And then I was scared that I was getting scared. It was a very high quality joy she was having. I didn’t know if I was up to it.

I was afraid I wanted it and I was also afraid of what I wanted.

And then I was afraid that I was afraid of it.

And then I was thinking she might really be me. I was afraid of that.

And then I wasn’t.

And then she was.

Me I mean.

May 7

The Moment of Impact

I was not flying but I felt like I was flying. I didn't have wings, of course, but I was flapping my arms to give myself the false impression that I could control what was happening.

It could have been moving in the right direction, but it was the wrong answer to the question we were afraid to ask.

So I asked it. I said, "Were we both unhappy at the same time?"

It was difficult to tell whom I was talking to.

I became silent. I was cold and blue and leaving. Slower than you can imagine. Like a man witnessing a glacier.

I was quiet for a while but I was alive. Young. Very.

This was excited this was excited this was excited.

Very very young. A serious glow with no religious overtones.

But before she saw me this time I could see that she had been savoring her words. She was torturing herself just like me.

Then she spoke and it didn't really matter what she said. Except that she had to be emotional about it. And wrong.

Of course I was outraged. I felt warm and satisfied because I was outraged and I was flying and I was deeply involved in controlling that which cannot be controlled and I was listening to her be wrong and I wanted to pick the feathers from her body, slowly. It was a marvelous sick miracle.

It was the right direction and we were both unhappy. It was listening to us and that was a miracle.

She was so wrong I could have married her. But I knew it could only be this way a short time.

It was what I had been waiting for.

May 8

Proof Reading

The ushers haven't arrived yet. Certain nutrients are missing from the performance. A gardener playing with the tassel on his stocking cap has just entered the convenience store. That's not my face on the milk carton. We haven't figured out the purpose of the missing contraband.

I believed it must be a witnessing of unleashed emotions, like free kittens, romantic love, or a confusing torture devise.

The reasonable garden waits patiently.

Nevertheless, I was tiring of the tedious ferns in the background. And that marching band passing at just that moment! I could have gagged, even before the notorious "gunman" plugged the clerk. I didn't even know which unemployed antagonist was really the hero, but thanks to the gunman he began performing an admirable bloodletting and the supporting cast grew substantially absent and thus, well, supportive. I was getting rather antagonistic myself.

But that was way moments ago, before scales of thematic healing had grown over the invisible wound. I don't even know if it's fair to call the experience mine anymore. Perhaps in the clerk's absence I gave it away to the wimpy little bookworm with a new poem for his mother malingering in the cereal aisle. Innocent bystander. Like anyone ever is. Sometimes the crime just isn't obvious. I looked him up in the comprehensive anthology of misunderstood poets and I didn't fully understand what he had to say. So I corrected it. I mean him.

Like I did the clerk. In the absence of certain nutrients.

Then I waited for the ushers some more.

I wanted to get it right. I wanted to make all the mistakes acceptable.

May 9

One Tomato

And Vernon Klinker made a pass at Sally Jones-Dibky and didn't even care that her best friend, who turned out to be jealous, saw him do it.

So then Harlan Henderson said to Silas Cornerbird, "That's fucked up. That's really fucked up." Only Silas didn't know what he was referring to. He just pretended he did so Harlan wouldn't explain it and bother him anymore.

And someone in the kitchen said, "One tomato is never fair," but you couldn't really tell who it was and I might have been the only one imagining how incredible an unfair tomato could be in the hands of a strong woman. Everyone else was probably wondering, What would you answer someone who said something like that anyway?

You understand, don't you, that I hadn't yet realized that I wanted to be humiliated. Sexually, I mean. Not just ordinary stupid put-downs. Something imaginative. Something to get me going.

And then this reservation guy with black braids and a silver belt began licking the back of his hand and I couldn't decide how I felt about it so I started coughing.

It was like I was watching myself and I was thinking, "Why are you doing this thing to yourself?"

So then I didn't know what to do so I didn't do anything.

And the phone rang and nobody was answering it.

So I answered it.

The phone said, "Howard? Howard is that you?"

I said, "Yes, it's me." But the phone didn't believe me. Not for a minute.

She said, "Why aren't you Howard?"

I didn't know what to say. I wondered if I might be Howard.

She didn't say anything. But I could tell she wanted to.

May 10

Blind Wife

It's the kind of story you don't really want to hear, but you can't stop listening. Something unusual might have happened. Not an accident at all, but a rare serious painful moment. It's a narrative with real consequences. You can't even think about it without repercussions. You don't want to hear it.

Inside the story the blind wife feels the name above the doorbell and rings it. The blind wife believes her husband has been sleeping here. And she enters the house and has coffee with this stranger whose name she has become familiar with, just as she has become familiar with her own new name, this blind wife who is becoming this stranger's friend while she is trying to find out about her husband's other wife. His mistress. His girlfriend. His sister. His jilted admirer. His long lost daughter. She doesn't know what this stranger is, but she's going to find out.

It's the kind of story in which none of the obvious possibilities are true. It's the kind of story that doesn't really answer your questions and turns away when you begin to feel close to it.

Something about the story tells you this blind wife is not really alone. Have you ever seen a gaggle of blind wives? It's an oddly bright and happy gathering. It's an unattached and beautiful celebration. You could get intoxicated with all the agreements going on, all the helpful advice. It's not the first time you've imagined generosity, is it?

You understand, don't you, that the earth does not smell the same to lovers as it does to the betrayed? And to describe their moment of truth is to suffer a death. A little one, an old one, but a death all the same.

I know you don't want to hear this because inside the deeper part of the story, where their hearts are, the blind wives are going to visit a stray dog, rescued from the other woman's garden. It could drag out some feelings you might not want to feel and they are going to want to give themselves away to it, those blind women, and you still don't want to hear this, do you.

You would never have considered doing what the blind wife is going to do because inside the story the husband is sleeping, just sleeping, but not where sleeping is expected of him. He's a little death, an old one, but a death all the same. It's something you can marry in darkness. Like the sky with its wings on fire. The sky she couldn't see.

Inside the husband's dream, he is investigating what he wanted from the blind wife, how he wanted her to become the only place he could find his dream. It's another kind of death now because it was already there, with the blind wife, and he couldn't find it.

And the blind wife is melting away from that death and from the darkest husband.

Burning in the absence of his discovery.

Burning to be what she wanted.

Burning to be what he couldn't see.

May 11

Late Night Conversation Between Bullfrogs

Father Porcupine was telling the congregation about original sin when an apple fell on his head and the forest grew very very quiet. What would God do about this? Had Father Porcupine done something terrible?

Pretty soon there was a great loud roar and the whole apple tree fell down and everybody waddled for their very lives.

O fearful masses huddled in your hollows, what spiritual storm awaits your progress to the next plateau?

Eventually Brother Badger could resist offering charity no longer and he delivered a surprise gift of apple sauce to Father Porcupine. Who do you suppose found this amusing?

Scorn the blows of bitter kings and laugh at the fears of the righteous. That was Brother Badger's philosophy and he had practiced getting it right.

To defy or to deify, that is the question.

"These apples have been purified by death," interjected the ghost of Brother Snake. Fortunately, there were not enough martyrs in the kingdom to demonstrate the truth of such wisdom.

"Can a disembodied spirit really teach us anything?" asked several forest creatures when no one dangerous was there to listen. What Have I Ever Learned from an Apple? became the working title of Sister Woodpecker's latest collection of epistolary efforts.

Pretty soon an antique fog descended upon the forest village and everyone grew frightened when it stayed for days and days. Everyone except Brother Badger, who dressed up in a piece of old gray cloth and went around mischievously knocking on hollow trees and whistling in front of caves and mumbling in a very very deep voice, "The end is arrived! The end is arrived!"

Of course he could have been right because when the fog finally cleared, there was a conspicuous absence of neighbors where the lumberjacks had cut away all their neighbor's houses on the north side of Apple Canyon.

Father Porcupine reminded them all of the warning he had received and urged them to renew their commitment to their fear of God.

Brother Badger was soon delivering candied apples with a pert little know-it-all smile to each and every forest resident.

Sister Woodpecker meanwhile had not yet become famous for even fifteen minutes. There were still so few readers tall enough for her style.

"Wear your smile like a bag of seeds and the world is yours," whispered the rain's renewed religion, already mocked mightily by Brother Badger's diligent digging.

"A creature is as a creature does," proclaimed Brother Owl when nearly everyone was asleep. And Brother Owl went looking for some mice to eat. Along the way he saw Father Porcupine eating a fermented apple in the moonlight. He was giving a sermon to the trees and seemed very happy with himself.

May 12

A Few Positive Aspects of a Common Disorder

It was the happiest time of my life.

Because I wasn't there anymore. I was here.

I was still palpably undulatory, but not in my direction.

Abstention from leaning trees was not a part of the regimen, but I had discovered a more personal, and therefore rewarding, verticality.

Because the path to the future leads through the past, I understood what I had done by noticing when I stopped. I was not entirely absent from this procedure and this meant a virtual firestorm of uninvited pleasures. Irreparable enthrallment.

Despite the unpredictably brash resolution of the contraries, I remained irresolutely betrothed to my ill-examined course of actions, which included several inclinations towards stasis and metastasizing procrastination, and I persisted in indulgences I had not previously understood I was providing myself.

I had grown in this way expendable. But it was not necessary to be necessary.

I could still remember that in those days I was a better liar because I thought my lies were the truth. I didn't know I was lying, so I was convincing. I could get you to believe anything because I could get myself to believe anything.

As if I were living my life in a deeply restrained and therefore poorly attended and aging sonnet, I celebrated a virtuosity of characteristic inhibitions, suspiciously snake-like escaping movements held at the periphery.

Nature ignores me though I remain a brute friend.

Too much attention could heal me.

May 13

Anticipatory

She was holding back because she was afraid if she let herself out she would explode. It wasn't anger at all. It was overabundance. She knew she could like letting go too much and not be able to stop so she stopped first and it made her feel like she might just spill out someday.

Young girls have always studied the emotional forces of the world and they have decided whether or not those forces are on their side. Sort of like how a young boy will decide if a mud puddle is lonely or not.

She didn't know why she was always going somewhere, but maybe she wasn't, maybe she was waiting in motion. She would say to herself, "I was just going around to places. I was just missing too many places."

According to her mother, she had too much guff. She would give her mother an excuse and her mother would say, "Don't give me any of your guff." And then her mother would fuss over something in the kitchen and leave her alone. Because, of course, her mother remembered feeling like she was going to explode and she didn't want to feel like that anymore just because her daughter was.

Eventually the young girl told her girlfriends that she was wondering how boys were put together. This was an interesting problem for the girls to solve. She was nervous. She had those twirlies, like with her finger in the ends of her hair, and giggles and sighs bubbling up inside of her even after the girlfriends went away.

It wasn't innocent. It wasn't innocent at all.

That night she dreamed about a bowl of eyes and a fence made out of children's bones. She dreamed about a bird that could fly backwards. She thought about herself in the dream. She watched herself doing that and she watched herself watching herself. What to do now?

Because by now a couple of boys could see in her eyes what she wanted, but they didn't believe what they saw. They hadn't seen it before.

Perhaps crying in the rain is redundant, but that's what her mother was doing. She remembered wanting what she couldn't have. Because now she had had it and she didn't want it and she didn't know what else she wanted.

She didn't want her daughter to find what she had found.

"Shut the story's door, but don't lock it," she said. "I wanted to cut myself, but I burned instead."

May 14

Nail Soup

Miss Prim was not at all satisfied with Penny's performance. It carried a rusty aftertaste. The birds were singing sweetly, the rabbits frolicked in the glen, and Miss Prim was not satisfied.

Penny's ex-lover Harold fixed Miss Prim some hazelnut stew. Harold wanted to know if Penny missed him and he needed someone besides Penny to tell him. Harold wanted to know if a thick gel of delayed adolescence was stuck to Penny's enigma. Harold wanted to know if it was really possible for zero to be the absence of something that had never even been there in the first place. Harold wanted to know if it were necessary for a vacant ten-foot radius to lay down on its side like that and could it roll around vertically and get up and walk away. Harold had heard a lot of things in a lot of places and Harold wanted to know if they were true. Harold wanted the sun to visit him at exactly 3:13 every afternoon. Before long Harold wanted Miss Prim to take Penny's place. Harold wanted. Harold wanted and wanted.

Meanwhile the rabbits were getting tired of the inexpressible beauty of mere frolic and had begun devouring Miss Prim's garden, a monument to the orderly preservation and restraint of natural elements. A fierce passion was belatedly making its presence known to Miss Prim, but alas, it was not of a positive sexual nature. The fulsome spilling wrath of a consummate restrained organizer was unleashed upon the glen. And still Miss Prim remained dissatisfied, but a disturbingly unexpected change of heart ushered itself into her performance with a surprising directness and intensity.

And so Miss Prim fixed Penny some rabbit stew and aggressively queried Penny. Miss Prim wanted to know if Harold had been a good lover. Miss Prim wanted to know if Penny had slept with any circus performers and did they perform satisfactorily. Miss Prim wanted to know if Penny's nether lips had ever been parted in a passionate embrace. Miss Prim offered to replace Penny's gel of belated adolescence with a couple of slippery fingers and a relentlessly exercised tongue. Miss Prim wanted to shock Penny out of her all too familiar complacency. Miss Prim wanted Penny to perform.

"Fuck this noise," said Penny. "My body is a sacred chalice and I shall offer it freely but not to withered up old control freaks like you, and Harold can kiss my rosy little asshole."

Who knows what heroes might have intervened if this were a legend handed down from bards or comic book collectors?

Have you seen the heroic fool who tried to marry Miss Prim?

Have you heard the tortured screams of pleasure in the glen where the birds sing so sweetly?

May 15

Discrete Events

What it was was an attempt to separate the last intrusion from the preceding one. You see, no one heard you announce the effort, however mistaken. Some joker said, "Like some picnic basket twit or a spare nerd in the nightstand."

It faltered, okay? Why shouldn't it?

Try locating an appropriate ambulatory bauble. Try collecting a bundle of unmitigated rabble to make it seem superior. See if you don't still yearn for a bit more sequence in the punch lines. And the joker said, "Can't you even tell the off-duty clowns from the dead policemen?"

Whereupon I acknowledged I still couldn't open a tomato and I realized "curvaceous" is not properly a receptacle, but I couldn't help filling it everywhere.

Neither is innocence uncommon, even in advanced societies, but it is very difficult to distinguish from ignorance.

Which could have meant that I was not very convincing in denying my participation.

And as I sit in my car in the driveway, I realize my home is not far from here. I can walk to it across the lawn.

And I do understand your reticence in presenting the bill for the evening's indulgences, but I don't believe we should cater to temporary explanations of recurrent desires.

Across the lawn a crackle of chickadees cloaks the sleeping tree in a flutter of nervous caution and delight.

So I'm going to draw the line although I don't expect you to be able to find it. If I'm lucky, you won't feel the need to try.

May 16

Heart, Eyes

And here is the light handing out little favors, caressing your neck like a memory of fishbones. Your birdheart has flown, tired friend, and without its blue memory, its eager brightness trembling with excitement, consumed by anything, anything at all, you begin to sink.

Once more it is raining, reflections momentary and muted. Now any darkness will do. It refuses to yield to morning, floats down on your quiet underwater shore like a sailor's glass eye, worthless, clouded, an object growing into its surroundings like the bones of some animal growing delicate under the sediment.

And here is the light that carried you along unsuspecting, your quiet eyes reaching for some further brilliance careening into your calm life when long ago, glowing in their own delicate discoveries, they had opened that world for you, if only you had noticed.

May 17

Caution: Do Not Touch Grounded Bats

Austin, Texas

And you know something else? The man that stood by the river beneath the bridge, he died. Soon after he learned something important. His wife died too.

But I have to say that he was like me. A normal. An ordinary. A Gomer. And before he died, he went to visit what was left of his mother. She didn't seem to notice he was nearly crazy and half wall-eyed.

"Are you dead yet?"

That's what she asked him. While a clutch of birdwatchers hovered near the willow tree outside the resthome window. He couldn't imagine what they were seeing and he didn't hear the question.

But he noticed her roommate. He noticed the rounded bow of resignation. A vacant-eyed cowl of a face dreaming from its own lost history, the eyes set deeper than the head could comfortably accommodate.

Outside, the color of his aging DeSoto began screaming through its grill, the desert heat wavering like his resolve.

Let's take a closer look at this friendly monster. He's not really cruel. He's not evil. He's not wielding swords of righteous destruction.

But diseased he might be. He might be acting this way because of a tiny bacteria or a somewhat larger infectious thought. It might have been living with him a long time before he gave it too much attention.

What was left of his mother was different. You could see that coming. You could try to act like you were ready. You could tell yourself that you knew this. Even if it was really something else that you knew. You could deny ever having had a mother. You could dismiss the wife. You could say you had never been there. You could say where. You could say you had never lived among yourself.

May 18

Creation

Some stories arise from the ashes of tormented idealism, having burned too long in an aging brain. Some stories fall from a surprise belch like a piece of undigested spinach. And some stories discuss their progress with the passing clouds. This story is a witness to its own unfolding, as if each moment could not be told until it spilled out onto the alteration of the page, with no more sense of direction than our lives have.

For this is the story that says things are not the way they should be and this is the story of the writer who is not the same man with the pen in his hand or the keyboard at his fingertips, who has limited his experience by interpreting what it means. Has this writer really ever said what he meant? What he meant was never good enough, was never really the experience, but sometimes he loses himself in the writing and he says something better.

And this is the story of the artist, who lives beyond the writer, the noblest of failures. Because art is inadequate. Because in art, too much precision kills. How terrible it is to be so right. How dead.

And this is the story of the writer's lover, the one more in love with the creation than the creator, the one hauling the umbilical cord over her shoulder like a rope, the one who does not know she does this. Sometimes imagination is enough, thinks the writer, and she is not really there.

And yet the writer's heroes seem so innocent. The guys with the wrenches and the answers. The guys with leather shoelaces and a history of marching. The guys with muscle in their hearts and meat on their bones.

The lover remains cheerful. She arrives from nowhere just when she's been forgotten. She looks in the hero's eyes. He isn't there anymore. She's saying to herself, "He's just meat."

So she nudges the river into a different place this time.

The hero was on his way to an unbelievable victory when he noticed the smudges on the side of the truck. They seemed familiar.

Like all fairytales, this one was secretly painful. The writer left it with the truth and the truth hurt.

It made the writer very happy to have failed in this way.

May 19

Is It Still Kidnapping?

We are not the babies, but the babies have detained us. For questioning perhaps. As we might wish to question them. That makes this somehow different from a dream about the babies. In a dream, the babies might wear our faces and ask all the right questions and look so cute and cuddly with our faces pasted on their plump little bodies and then such a happiness exploding, oh death, and then they die, and it's not so sad because we know it's a dream with our faces living in it like that.

But these babies did not die and this is not a dream and the sheep move across the hillsides like guided clouds bringing mutton and fleas and wool and bones and no rest at all from the babies' continuing interrogation in the hayloft of the wet stinking abandoned barn. Because in life dreams persist even if in dreams life does not.

"If your head is not like unto the grave of a child, then how do you explain these thoughts?"

The baby's boat is small, but my eye is tender. I do not speak because I do not understand the question. Nor do I know who has asked it.

"Is it true you imagined writing a poem on the baby's head?"

For a long time I have been crying, but the baby does not know this. Now my silence signs a confession. Babies know how to listen while they are crying. And babies know the truth must appear before the answer.

The mutton tastes heavenly but the bones hurt. The baby will not let me sleep.

An owl calls from the rafters. The owl is the same size as the baby and for the moment I am in this world, which gives me a rest from my own.

By the time the babies get to you, you know all the answers. It's their questions that surprise you.

May 20

An Invitation

She was not waiting anymore. She was progressive. She was offering accommodations to a movement. She was expressed and she was forward and she was nearing the bus stop.

She watched the men looking at her as she walked and she invited them in.

The bus reeked of it. The bus was on its way. The bus couldn't be held accountable.

Another woman was chastising her seat. It was not the way it was supposed to be. It wasn't paying attention.

The bus stopped. The first woman sat down in the seat once occupied by the woman who got off. She tried to be patient. Men were waiting. Her life was getting started again.

The bus stopped once more and she led the men out of the tunnel. The stairs were one right in front of another, but there were a lot of them. At the top she looked back and at least one man was still climbing.

Ordinary time was not attached to the man's wrist. Ordinary goals were not attached to the man's feet.

Near the top of the stairs the man stopped and looked at the woman's dress. It was not the same dress he remembered and he wondered if he was following the right woman. He wondered if the right woman would be walking away like that.

The woman turned back from the next flight of stairs to see if the man still followed, to show the man he would be treated equally, to make equal exciting.

The next step was waiting for the man. The next step was not attached to the preceding step. It never had been.

May 21

A New Religion

It's true. All the coal mines in all the world and all the coal in them is not enough darkness for what we have to do every day of our lives.

If you've been busy trying to get the extra joy out of your joy, you could open the window and entertain the first delight you notice with a new religion.

Or perhaps this particular cave belongs to a group of believers called the Presbyterians and that one you passed up is for Catholics. You can pretend there's light in any of these caves if you stay long enough. Or perhaps you could just learn to appreciate the darkness.

If, for example, her name's Rachel, then what I need to say is that Rachel likes to watch, Rachel likes to watch hard.

In that darkness Rachel says, "Touch this little knob. Touch it like this."

It's like a dinner that could cry itself to sleep.

Say you want maybe an alternative universe and the approach is no longer obvious. Why not don't you just whisper some secrets like we're willows and the wind is a willow god? Wouldn't that be dark enough?

It could all be symbolized by the wobble of a drunk bird. It accommodates. It's an arrangement of ideas. It's oddly natural. It wasn't available to our afterlife. But it believed hard. Oh oh oh it believed.

Somebody asks and somebody just gives it away. Somebody asks and it coughs. Turn and close the window. Cough. Cough some more.

That sound is the same in darkness but you have to account for the hand dandling your essence. You have to know if the hand's yours and you have to think about Rachel, Rachel watching.

Because Rachel's part of the darkness. Rachel speaks like the darkness. But Rachel's not waiting for you to go to sleep. Neither is Rachel offering any escape. She's not your lover. She's not anyone's lover. But you can believe in what she offers.

May 22

Anonymous Applicant

The bureaucrats are not faceless. They have the same face. One man sits inside them and processes all the forms. One man says no to the confused applicants. One man with long thin fingers as smooth as a surgeon's hidden inside the fat ones and the broken ones.

Three applicants return again and again, a nondescript middle-aged couple with long gray coats and too many kids who don't accompany them and an elderly woman who sometimes looks like a man.

The building is large and the parking lot is filled with small foreign cars, hunkering dented American gas hogs and pickup trucks. In the vacant lot across the street, left-over cinder blocks serve as planters for weeds.

Outside, the statistics posture and wait. They never enter the building. One of them holds a loaf of bread gently like a child's head. His pain is gone, but the limbs are still twisted. It's not possible to live where no one is sick or tired and the cold can't get in.

I've been resting in the grass and it's time to come out. Because my family multiplies, I fill out the same forms again and again. Brothers and sisters and brothers and sisters and the children diving between each other's legs and rhyming, diving and rhyming.

Death doesn't join in. It waits in line. It can't be enough.

I must have been recurring. I must have been happening more than once. I needed the careless silence scattered on the lawn. I needed the lawn. I needed a smoky ruin of a man wheezing with strained pleasure to guide me. I needed to breathe again. The same face removing the obstacles. I needed the pleasure of my name on a form to make me count, I needed spaces with labels to fill me in, I needed numbers. I needed routine. I was about to be processed but I wasn't part of the process. I saw the man who handled the forms and he wasn't me, but he was the same man. He wasn't a man, but he was the same one. I didn't know how long he would take. I held my breath and started counting. I held my breath and let it out and I held it again. And then again until it didn't belong to me.

May 23

How to Have a Successful Relationship

All the guests smiling and bowing and saying, "You've got to say something apologetic now. You have to mean it." So good morning to the mudgirls, corsaged with raunchy berry juice, gifting the desperate with haggard kisses. Good morning to the undulant farm hands sweating nectar and reeking of heaven. And good morning to a deep blue mosaic of floating children totally lacking in wholesome parental guidance.

And farewell to the corrective mirror of societies lost in the clever desert. Farewell to smoked glass religions.

And farewell to guidance counselors and tea stains. Farewell to Leviticus. Farewell, farewell to discreet blouses.

Farewell to respectable beds. Beds and beds. Farewell to more beds. Farewell to the silence not everyone could hear.

Farewell to the wrong deep stare of animals raised in captivity.

Farewell to fat squat villains and bald hero wearing gigantic shoes.

Farewell to the rough pair of hands in her father's briefcase.

Which is not yet the reason I can't fix it.

Farewell to an insouciant declension of a very nearly fetal facial gesture. Farewell to indolent vigilantes.

Which is still not the reason it has been given teeth but may be the reason it can smile.

Farewell to emotions trapped in a plodding deposition.

Because her father was a nail driven by his father.

Because as the relationship develops his religion strikes glass and shatters.

The door's husband closes. The chairs gossip politely. Farewell, farewell to parental furniture and the residue of caution as the streetlights swell and listen. Because you have learned to pay attention to the streets at night.

Which is a welcome unlike the welcome of dishes or false security.

Welcome too to the great yellow horse of psychological injury who lives in the black-throated terror where shadows glisten, kneading the animal's rump muscles like a clutch of over-stimulated lovers.

Elsewhere, empty as Kansas, she watches an old man pour gasoline on a brown felt hat and counts the tiny mutations growing in the rim pools of abandoned tires.

This shoe, he thinks, is female. His life still waiting. Which is a good enough reason to walk away from it.

You see, they haven't known each other too long. They haven't been cruel or too generous yet. They haven't lived.

So good morning to The Rain Is Falling Church. Ah, how persistently these infidels make love. How beautifully The Sacrificial Ones can weep. And welcome to the burgeoning orphanage of the next day.

And welcome too to the blood blister of moon pulsing, useless as an unemployed cadenza.

After he found her, he cleansed the windows, the same windows he left in his old pants when he thought he had the world at his fingertips.

Then he touched himself in her liquid. You could see by the way he looked at her that the cathedral door yawned disconsolately.

The damp weft of her chin appeared when he had completed a random green game of go live like an insect.

Such delight. She wants to discuss him with the hummingbirds. Is there any reason to fear? Is there any reason not to?

I saw the sky and the earth, I saw the moon. I saw sleep disguised as clouds, I saw the clouds.

I wasn't the one who forgot to be there where I was standing.

I heard a car, but no engine, no doors. I was going somewhere.

And that was how he prepared himself.

She was opening her life, she was getting in. There was a little house inside her clitoris, steady in the wind and powerful, a place of worship when carefully, and with complete abandon, inhabited.

At first, she couldn't tolerate such beauty.

Twisted figures from Breughel. Jogging at the cold gym. Whispering to the icicles pointing at the future.

She's been pressing on the cracks. She's been exercising more than caution.

It's a passion, so she thinks it can't be a religion. But it isn't a gift, so it makes her happy. A great monster of tenderness living in both fogs at once.

As the moon turned black in his head, he felt closer. He didn't drop it, he didn't even flinch. He wasn't going to become just some symbol peeling spuds in a Cadillac. That wasn't him picking his fingernails with a knife while the gangster's mom hung her religion on the reliable clothesline. That wasn't him licking the tempting drain of some saint's rich mulch.

He passed up several women married to streetlamps and one with a button missing from her vagina. He wasn't going to become some repentant church, promising the air, "Never again."

He delivered himself like an envelope of lust in a language whose teeth had rotted, a constellation of stars floating offshore, the delicious sorrow dripping as it rises.

It's only a symbol, you are saying, and you are right, but you might as well have said, It's only the truth.

I suppose there are no women inside a lemon, he thought. There should be. A place of promise bowing gently to the warm air.

It leaves, in passing, more of itself than he thought to ask for.

Her bed harbors fugitives, the feet of the first dawn black with coaldust, on the table a whistle and a thrush pie. A kind of praying mantis romanticism. A woman who could nail the wind to the wall.

A small army of crows attacks a wounded gull in front of the asylum. These dark wonders decry no moles of hate. New creatures they are, with well-oiled feathers. If they sleep by the campfire, you can see them.

As if he were feeding a star while a battalion of ideals marched through a dead man's arm. He begins pushing his thumb along the backbone to release the dark heart.

So busy burying his dreams, he missed most of the day.

She was kneeling on the sidewalk cutting raindrops with a razor blade. She would never again wear sunglasses to the funeral.

She keeps the future in an empty closet, where it belongs. She didn't know the window was loaded.

Then the sound of a delicious transient kiss and the violinist's hands dance down the street at the carnival, unattached, carefree. No more courtship for hire. No more sad sound tracks. No more by request for the same old.

The pendulums lie still in their casings. And silence, one of the snow's great inventions, severs the excuses.

Could we possibly do something foolish together?

To live beyond the safety of belief. To melt the alcoholic hammer. To hold your fork up to the stars.

She wanted to ask him, "How furiously are you beating your heart?" Perhaps they could have gotten in line. They could have marched, the lie was that beautiful.

Sometimes he has to use his death as an anchor, to keep from evaporating.

It's the way you might escape a catastrophic event, in awe of the responsible party, not knowing it's you.

He's become self-educated and he's afraid of the reflection. It contains the dew, which was found among the hairs at the hollow of the dead woman's back.

Was it her? How long has life been? Is there anything natural about their nature?

He seemed to be checking to be sure that he was still there. No, nothing so literal as murder, though she still scares him.

His boots are shiny. A bad sign. He talked to his dead father about it. But then he merely dumped out the stars through an open window because his brain is like that.

The only thing unexpected about the death was the life. A child's mitten whispering in the blackberry thorns.

Except for the sky burning, no one noticed. It's life and none of us wants the one we have. It isn't here and then it isn't here again.

All the guests smiling and bowing and saying, "Don't do this ever again."

May 24

First Night

The long night calls to its creatures with a voice darkened by hunger. Under the owl sleeping in the hollow of the tamarack. Next to the broken bones of mice.

She is awake now.

He stands quiet, listening to the water.

You could not have seen through this. You watched yourself become a third person. She told you she still loved you and put her arms around him, the other one you had become.

And so I can't sleep now because my shadow of a crow is a thief and walks like a clumsy fat man playing hopscotch, head cocked with a child's quizzical turn, a scolding cry like a ratchet, a few more shadows hanging out, nightfall in pieces.

After all, you didn't really want this. My friends and I will fight over it in your dream before you sleep.

A man I am is singing. He is crying. He begins a small desire. He purrs. Finally he sleeps. Candles and stones light the path.

The man grows silent. The man grows smarter than we thought. Shouting does not feed the air the man exists in. The man continues to grow. He grows so large we can crawl into the base of his thumb, wander through his body until we come to the porchlight.

"This way," the man says, but the woman you've become bursts into embarrassment and her skin chaffs like sandpaper. "Try this," he says, but she falls asleep beside herself. So he sings to her and the words fall out of his mouth like wooden teeth and nothing at all grows there.

Still they wait, these two with me still in them, in the white bed that smells of sweat, refusing to float, inviting. She becomes the neighbor with the sad house and the quiet voice, and you come to his house again to find the sweater you knitted your life into when the weather was harsh and the marriage harsher. You don't know why, but you're in the cellar and your hands move in and out of the rows of suspicious fruit, aging marital prizes sleeping in dusty Mason jars.

Perhaps now an echo enters the damp room dancing. The walls won't hold it. Each of its songs opens the outside morning differently. Whose sons are these in the tubers, buried in the potatoes and turnips and arms of blind reaching in the wooden bins, clicking like jackal's tongues?

Have I been, then, not good for my stumbling down selves, the woman asks, disguised as one more me in my downliest humble-down echo? Yeh, I coulda been married a handful by now, another mom-voice lodged in my mortgaged head. I coulda halved it, teething, and split wide away. "'adn't 'e copped me crotch feathers? 'n me stuffin" still unstrutted? Tall tale told not so, and so . . .

Twelve bullets they found themselves, erupted, returning from his torn chest, closing it, reloading into the unaiming rifles. The soldiers took them back carefully, unshouldering, marched the man feet behind feet into the courtroom, took back his guilt, sent him back into the world to look for his mother and nearly exploding as an afterthought his equally be-gone-from-me father.

Sunset filters through the tortured sky, spreading over the upper lake. Cutthroats rising to the winged blood of evening insects. Across the channel an owl calls, answered by a softer echo. Slowly the colors shift deeper into the darkening. The woman stands quietly on the metaphorical water.

This isn't happening to just one of me.

A light breeze flutters over the lake. We turn. The woman waits. We don't know what she's waiting for. We begin the descent to speech. We begin the rising fall.

May 25

Another Spiritual Friend

The terrible invention of angels builds a temporary shelter, like the respectable brick home of the bashful child molester. He answers quickly and politely when you run out of gas.

But it's not like you remember the grass, for example, is green, or the safety of adulthood. His mind could be clenched so tight he could barely eat. Besides, it was not the town you were still leaving that burst into flames, but it disturbed your progress anyway.

No, they weren't really expecting you, a misunderstood friend of a friend with no real talent and twelve easy payments. You had acquired a valuable free gift, hadn't you, and the next stop certainly wasn't going anywhere without you.

But I was tired of supplying inspiration and a solid foundation for success in later life. I had behavior. I had a way. I was the real father. I was away. I was a man who had crossed the borders of a country that didn't have any. I could see my breath ascending into the great dark hands of the descending night.

That guarantee I sent you was priceless. You grew up, didn't you? But you have to know how to use it. It's only because you complained that I know your more patient story.

If you haven't invented yourself, you can't patent the product. That's what the home office always says.

Telling someone like me your plan is never a good idea. Someone like me might answer politely and wait for an opportunity. Someone like me might market the fear.

I've already seen your life and I thought it was mine. You deserve a refund, but you aren't going to get it.

Cause of death: perfection, someone else's wings, a bright blue lump in the opening throat.

May 26

A New Embrace

I knew it must have been his fault, but I didn't know why. Its gentle teeth were pointed in, so that nothing that ever passed them could come back again. It didn't seem threatening or evil, just kind of innocent-looking and odd. Like cows drinking cups of tea. And you didn't quite know what to do with it, but you knew it was somehow wrong.

He was trying to tell me how to stop it, but I was the one who was not there at the time. He was hitting himself in the head because he deserved it. "Now try to listen to me," he said to his battered ears.

These are the things I know:

1. It was his fault.
2. It couldn't be stopped.
3. Sometimes it hurts.
4. Something needed to be done.

"Shake it, smell it, chuck it in the sandbox." That's what I always say.

Because he understood it was a metaphor, he tossed a bucket of water across the room and listened to see if it sounded wounded when it hit the floor.

Then he was mad again and he was thinking about what her friends were going to do to her. They had been carrying her around and around. They were believing everything she said. But now, now he was certain they were going to put her away like an accident, like a mistaken little oily thing.

The eerie light of the sun through thick frost on the bedroom windows is part of the answer but not the whole answer. An uproar of leaves is also part of the answer but they've already come and gone and nothing's changed. Believe what you want. I'm going to tell what I know. I'm going to be writing deep into the paper with this serious tone of voice I can whistle up from my dead past. I'm going to be doing something less than wonderful.

She's my accident now. He's admitted me and the sandbox is filling up.

More arms are available. More buckets of water.

More cups of tea.

May 27

Her Poem Before the Rain

A young girl is writing a poem about death. Christmas tree lights blink off and on, strung high in the air from the arm of a crane rising from the hole in the ground where the new bank will handle farm foreclosures. The Mission Speedway, Pablo Reservoir, a persistent puddle out back of the Chicken Shack . . . She finds her poem everywhere.

Hanging on a nail on the wall of an old farmhouse a few miles down the road, a photograph of the lost parents. Across the road at the junior high school the janitor watches the cheerleaders from the crack in the boiler room wall, his fear slowly leaving. The irrigation ditch bakes in his memory. The coal slag beneath the railroad tracks glistens when it rains. It seldom rains.

A postcard from the corn palace, Mitchell, South Dakota, torn and stapled to a broken locker. Woolworth's, the Grange Hall, the apartments above the Western Wear that promise transportation isn't necessary.

In her poem she asks even the shadows among their lengthening children to carry the burden. She puts markers where they sleep. If they are lost, they may not come back and if they do not come back, their burden is ours.

Life with a limp paw, whimpering.

She whispers to the rapist, "I love you," taking him again and again back to the moment when she slid the knife between his ribs and wept.

Her poem acknowledges no saviors in wounds. She cautions the angels to drink us slowly. A low fog forms in the corn. A white-winged motion passes in the night. Someone is thumbing the tines of a comb.

And so the cry of some animal in the night turns out to be ours. She will feed her discovery ferns and owl droppings. When it descends, she will follow. The valley opens, the mountains lean towards the tugging moon as the lake laps at her feet.

I wake and find my dream asleep on the floor, fur matted, breath sour.

Which is enough and after. Which is moon cabbages, bones and the stars' teeth. Which is her poem wondering what to touch and what to sing to.

May 28

Question at Low Tide

Slowly the sea sucks its breath and we drag our buckets and boots to the smooth excuse of sand. Released from ourselves, we laugh and search for the more we believe is waiting, and then, surprised by the departing tide, sink deeper, laughing and afraid.

My toes grip the friendlier fallen parts of former mountains. Down the beach, you have wandered, wondering, until the sun silhouettes your familiar body, temporarily distinct on the edge of the shadows, avoiding the danger with motion, like the shore-birds.

This time it's not fear that keeps you moving.

We've traveled a long way to reach this far beneath the reflections. Soon enough they will return and cover us in ourselves again. This far from shore, each step beyond lifts out life that has not seen light since long before before. Keeping up with our holding back, the sea uncovers us beneath ourselves, the ancient pulse returning so slowly it could be mistaken for death.

May 29

The Man Who Juggled Eyes

He threw them higher and some of the children clapped and pointed. He threw them higher and the people watched with their eyelids ready. Even his own mother blinked when he reached for a stray.

He threw them higher and the houses showed him their ragged shoulders. He threw them higher and the trees stepped down with their children. He could see how the town had not been good for their families.

He threw them higher and the hills made him a green carpet. He threw them higher and the mountains stood next to him in white jackets. He swallowed them and his belly grew fat with light.

He slept with them and they stared at his foolishness. He dreamed of them and his hands jerked as he juggled them again in his sleep. He threw them higher and even darkness could not hold them all.

He threw them higher and water spread out beyond his imagination. His imagination grew. He threw them higher and the clouds brushed against him like ghosts. By now the people had forgotten him.

He threw them higher and the world grew round and got smaller. He tried to throw them higher. They began falling.

He watched the world grow larger and the earth come back to him. He caught the eyes softly in his mouth. One by one he gave them back to the animals and went back to his people, but his people had grown small and could not see how carefully he juggled what he had learned against what they did not think to question.

May 30

Don't Leave Me Here

A dear stuck one suffered the child. The golden alcove of warmth and caring closed its lips when they met and refused the head bobbing as the phone rang. Let's call the caller, shall we? Delicately, Mr. Jones. Perhaps he could be good for the child. A degree in sunlight recommends him.

I opened my eyes and tiny hands yanked the curtain's big tongue from the dear one's daylight. Good morning pockets appeared in the window's frosted reticence.

Exposed, the dear one began running down the beach with my army of doubts. Puffs of delicate white exited my lungs. Dearness distanced my delicate legs and edged the evergreens with soft Sarahs of sunlight. A child I was afraid of. Could you have rested a wife's sighs within that world's substitutions? Neither could I, and so I watched the ludicrous burial storming across the temporary savannah. (People were still coming out of their bundles.)

You could not have known the golden alcove would offer its tiny hands to the curtain's futures. You could not have adequately prized the breath from Sarah's soft sunlight or exposed the hidden death more than you exposed yourself without the advantage of a snow-capped mountain. Your wife, too, could have rung loudly and bobbled.

Let me summarize. Our discussion today has dreamt of luxury and sustainable growth while reflecting upon loss and rejected swimming pools. Dear ones have been counted but not preserved. A refusal of tongues has not been considered conjugal rejection despite evidence that no one is actually going to fall off.

Just talk to her.

May 31

Calamari

Midnight and the peopled pier lights the cold shiver of the Sound we trust to deliver up delicacies, jigs probing in stiff hope through midnight waters where curiosity schools to illuminate our deceptions.

Suddenly impaled, the creatures write fear black, the spent ink of Nature's needful poets, caught in this other world, their camouflage gone wrong misinterpreting bright intentions, all their slippery sensitivity published in a thick sloppy bucket.

But over white wine in the Italian restaurant, ink-besotted intellectuals dissect the deep rewarding circles of their arguments delivered as bite-sized morsels for exotic rubbery offeratory mastications of resilient substance, connoisseurs classifying substantial textures, the densities of salivary reasoning measured against elemental octopus, sophisticated clam and the latest, most fashionably digestible, deeply moneyed, culinary philosophers, flashing opinions like tooth jam.

At the next table, I sit waiting for someone I cannot name, someone whose talents might be at least social, if not sexual, not those of a lonely posturing scribe, someone who might sit at the same unmetaphorical table, not knowing the companion they have chosen, casting a questioning line, the hook sharp and obvious, deeply surprised when it comes back squirming with simple, delicious, unexpected delights to pass across the forbidding table's vast, sometimes readable, welcoming ocean.

June

June 1

Impatient

Little Nonsense was far too anxious to become a man. He tried eating lots of beans and you know what happened. He tried stirring mushroom soup counterclockwise during a full moon. He tried sitting in the creek with his big hat on while the water washed away his childhood, but it was taking way too long. He ate some of that terrible tasting yeast every day and wore his papa's pajamas to bed. Nothing helped.

Some days aging is like a ship on the other side of the ocean and some days it floats right on top of you with its cargo hold packed with regrets.

Soon enough, Little Nonsense met a woman with a peculiarly diaphanous understanding of her own motives and the same day he met a street preacher while touring the Alamo who was ranting against homosexuals in the church, and across the street, he met a gay shop-owner hawking pillboxes and cowboy hats, a hovering presence with yet another pitch for the American dream. Tiny little sighs slipped out of the chinks as each of them spoke. Too much information.

So Little Nonsense stepped back from his limited and confusing experience and the tiny lie of perspective gave him peace, but peace was not enough and soon he wanted more experience. He thought perhaps he should not dictate the nature of his experience or limit his goals to people only and so he witnessed the energetic particles of a dog and tried to follow. That didn't work any better.

Without understanding what was happening to him, Little Nonsense began drooping seductively like wisteria. He shrugged it off and continued down the uncertain path, unaware that he had begun warbling when he walked. It was something he did with his legs, without trying to.

Somehow a twig of pain had cluttered his recent remembrances. Ductile, he flushed, and out swam the hidden annoyances. He offered them further transportation. He offered them new lives in undeveloped relatives.

By the time Little Nonsense had uncluttered the vista, yet another dusk had arrived, but he was operating with larger receptacles and the rump-thwacked goaty odor of the evening's tenuous offering did not dissuade him.

Nor was he held back by the risky stubs of the new raw truth he was about to receive. He simply imagined a dimpled fragrance, a weasely bright-eyed waif of a pretention. Tempting indeed, but Little Nonsense needed more. Like that night you thought you heard somebody moan from the rooftop after you left the apartment of your future lover.

The first time you don't know what comes next.

It's always the first time.

June 2

I Will Not Be Accepting, I Shall Not Attend

Alas, I have resurrected the feud.

First I visit the county agent and read him more than his rights. (I want to put him at ease so that I may shine his dull head.) I order him up a juicy toothache from the shiny melon selection squad, who have frequently mistaken him for a more deeply disturbed and worldly citizen. I do this because I have learned a few things that I wish to pass on. And because I have certain tasks to perform that I have awarded myself. From crag to swamp, hooker to wife, I dish out the body juice, stiffening slowly out there in its unacceptable syrup. It's a stink of unremarkable proportions yet to be raised beyond other stinks of similar dimensions. Most of the time I go unnoticed.

And thus it happened that I was there, unremarked, when it happened.

It's true, however, that Sinus the Dog has become my constant companion. Sinus is never lonely, but Sinus whines and wheezes. Sinus is never empty. Sinus runs. Sinus has no sense of humor, either sophisticated or raw. Sinus fills up the part of my head where imagination lies. Sinus draws the remaining expendable fluids from my anticipatory head. Sinus makes me drain. Sinus flushes, Sinus devolves, and Sinus romanticizes. Sinus wishes upon mustard stars and remains unrandom. Sinus welcomes.

It's true what they say when they say there is no other way to say what they say. That's why they say it.

Just as a disturbed mauling howl may occasionally rent the visiting daylight, my reasoning is allowed to return with a gift of alien morsels. Which sometimes finds the agent singing. Perhaps unengulfing the chair his body has taken into itself. It's possible that he could already be imagining his head poking out of there like a painful cartoon.

Yes, it's a wonderful country of unsullied improbable delights, but you can't go there yet. We've been trying to take that country out of the county and the agent's still holding out. Meant for greater things. Meant for inspired exiting and brilliantly executed detention spillage. You can't keep them home when they've tasted the forked fruit.

I'm not the one who forgets what I've done. The frozen melon balls clack against his molars each time I score another generous defeat. It's part of the exercise. It's something he likes when the pain subsides.

I do that to keep the provocative jiggles in line. I go out and out and I get happy out there and I rest in my head and I dictate. That's so Sinus can be barking again and I can't come in.

"And furthermore . . ." he'd say, if I let him talk. Because he's always more than right. "And in Fact . . ." he'd say, like it's someplace you could go to where they don't make mistakes.

They do. I've lived there. I've been on both sides of the argument.

June 3

How Many Belong?

One is not the first, but one coming upon another will expect either union or a sudden proliferation, eleven perhaps, which is merely one twice. One is neither lonely nor isolated but clandestine or tangential when confronted with groups, which are, after all, merely gatherings of ones.

Nor is two the result of one's desires. Two recognizes one only as a component of halves and thus sees one as merely a placeholder. If two wishes to remain complete, two must not merely mate but duplicate, and thus we arrive at two pairs of two (which two does not recognize as four) and duplicate again to become two sets of two pairs of two (which two does not recognize as eight) and so on into the impossible distance. In this way two remains perpetually very young, younger, in fact, than one, and does not live in the future, which does not exist in the world of two. Whereas one is genderless, having no contrast, two is distinctly feminine, capable of giving birth, and is often falsely characterized as innocent. Neither is it helpful to view two as balanced.

Three, on the other hand, is masculine and likes caves and stories inspired by fire. Three is not waiting for anything. Three is on its way to the next possibility but does not know this. Three acquires territory inside the mind and tries to represent this with external markers. Three does not like to be analyzed and refuses to be considered a collection of ones. Three is too quickly too big for three's clothing. The concept of innocence, which we have denied to two, does not belong to three either and can be understood by three only as an imaginary dinosaur with unimaginably soft skin.

Four, as has been suggested, is a nervous version of two. It appears to be stable but its balance requires constant attention. Four is seldom found without the tendency to repeat itself that was much less insistent in two. Four is available for theories of equilibrium but ordinary demonstrations of household harmony send it reeling into realignment. While desirable for its controlled imagination, four does not often live long. Five is nothing more than four with a handle.

Each of the remaining members of the club has been nominated by another member, but none knows which one. Because they owe their acceptance to an unknown accomplice, they tolerate group pictures and celebrate holidays with clumsy affection. A few have labored extensively to discover their accomplice and failed. For this they are deeply admired and they are referred to as "prime."

Quietly, outside each of the many clubhouses, zero waits patiently for understanding, holding its frequently misunderstood place, not itself understanding that when understanding comes, the club will be closed.

June 4

If Alfred Is the Father

Alfred is not a reason for leaving so we'll stay.

In the vast spaces of the heavens, things were different.

Now describe the first balloon that helped you to feel such an escape.

Write a short description of the earth.

Eventually the problem will not seem so large, but it might remain sad. Like a man crying and peeing at the bus station. The man might be clutching his own arm to find himself.

Nor can the answer be found at the drugstore although the woman in curlers kneeling in aisle nine might indeed be his wife. Her tongue might actually be clicking.

Is it their daughter at the diner with the glow of the jukebox beneath her flirtatious arm, her chest aflame with red cotton in the dripping summer night?

Now describe the moon hung in a basket with eggs and fireflies.

Nor is the answer clicking out of that cat-eyed trunk-of-a-woman among the supplements. You can see her feet sink in when she finally rises, her daughter's imagined nudity by now creamy with freshly harvested imitation pearls.

And if this woman continues to rise, will that be an acknowledgement of the white pastoral innocence of a lunar swoon or an unattached and slowly flashing celestial embryo crossing the meadow where her life ought to be?

Now describe the balloon again.

Now the father.

Things were different then.

Now the balloon unattached to Alfred.

Now words in the balloon that don't need anyone to hold them.

June 5

Some of My Selves Treat Me Badly

Clyde Barrow spattered his face on the air in defiance of even natural laws. It stayed there. A lot of folks around here still see it like that. For a moment, the bewildered stalk of his body couldn't understand why it could not follow, then sagged like a sack of mashed potatoes and forgot itself.

Hard Times, Texas. That place grew inside Clyde till it burst. But Clyde said, "I ain't gonna risk my life in Oklahoma!" He seemed to know a certain kind of thing was foolish. Some people are clever and stupid at all once and they get things done in their life that no one else would do. Clyde didn't know why he did what he did, but he knew he was damned well gonna do it and get the hell out. He wrote Bonnie Parker a poem that realized death wouldn't be much of a sorrow when it finally crashed the party.

One day, after the banks began to all look the same, Bonnie's Momma got into Bonnie's head like a fever. "Weren't nothin' for it" but to descend on that woman like a whole other kind of bank and withdraw what was needed.

That's when Platte City, Iowa welcomed the whole gang with an armored car, three machine guns, a baker's dozen shotguns and several helpings of unrationed lead, plentiful now since the war's end. Buck ate till he burst, while the rest of the gang ran off the weight of the town's gratitude. Not long after that, they kidnapped Thelma Dayton and Eugene Grizard and Eugene an undertaker besides.

Then Frank Hame got caught sneaking up on the gang and Bonnie got a kick out of "getting her picture took" kissing that Keystone Cop who just dragged along like a kicked dog. On the way home, they shared a pear.

By the time C.W. Moss finally got his name in the papers, his pa had decided he wasn't really a bad kid, just a sensitive boy led astray by bad company. "The best of bad company," he added later on.

But some folks, like Clyde's pa, knew about how luck don't last forever. "Some days nothin' much good seems to come of even the most memorable events. Some days a fella oughta have better sense than to want anyone to notice. Some days is better left alone." Clyde's pa talked like that, picking at a scab that never seemed to heal. "Ain't none of my doin'."

"Not so's you'd notice," Clyde would have answered, picking at a few scabs of his own till they finally blossomed behind a shotgun blast, his face all kind of twisted and smiling squinty like he'd just figured out how the sun come down on his eyes if he looked at it wrong and heard a funny story about a dead man he might've known sometime before he done that.

June 6

A Chair, A Dog, Two People and Flies

A man says, "There's flyshit on the chair." He is smiling. A woman says, "I suppose there is flyshit on the chair."

Flies fly around the shat upon chair. A dog comes into the room and sits down. A woman says, "I suppose there is flyshit on the dog."

A man says, "There's flyshit on the ceiling." He is smiling. A woman looks out the window. For a moment the specks of flyshit sparkle in the moonlight. She is smiling. But a man says, "There is flyshit on the chair."

A man says, "I'm going to paint the ceiling." A woman says, "I'm going to paint the chair." A man says, "I think I'll paint the ceiling white." A woman says, "That chair wants to be a brown chair."

A man sits down on a chair and begins writing on a piece of paper. A woman thinks, "Now there is flyshit on that man."

A woman says, "You're getting it all wrong. Let me do that." A man says, "That isn't the way you're supposed to do it." A woman says, "Then do it yourself." A man says, "Then you paint that stupid chair yourself."

A man does and a woman does and they don't have any children but the chair dries and the ceiling dries and the flyshit sparkles and a dog comes into the room and sits down.

June 7

Divergence

Honey, I just couldn't do it. I wanted to put the dog out of his indifference. But I haven't been myself. Not even that.

Just stay out of that country. That's what I tell myself.

Someone had giggled at the source of the spring and it stopped flowing. Someone tight and wound. Someone like I was without myself. Someone tangent. Someone like me.

Truth is, I couldn't have been here without you. I couldn't see anything in myself very clearly, but you could, and they weren't all pretty people. You didn't have any illusions, did you? Plenty of mistakes, but no illusions. That kind of waiting is never as personal as it seems.

And I certainly noticed it noticing you, even though I've been slower of late. My way wound tight and scalded with a limping blue light. I discovered it's not hard to find the right answer, but it's always attached to the wrong problem. My thoughts were floating behind a beautiful mystery like some neighbor's annoying trash barrels stinking in the majestic ancient fog.

Neither do people like to believe in ideas that have not been believed in for a long time. People do not like to spill out when they're not used to it. We were like them once and now we're not.

We waited for it to end, but it didn't stop arriving. As we approached the unrepentant sky, I noticed a couple of untethered tenements that looked like they might have been leased to wallet-sized Victorians, strangely tentless, catarpillar-like and leafy. One by the puffy white garden and one by the ethereal blue pond.

I tried to jump in, but I couldn't understand the things they weren't doing.

June 8

Reluctant

There's no room for doubt. This is the way he bleeds.

You see, the farmer hadn't asked, but she answered.

She said, "Yes" and the man's chest bloomed.

Of course this doesn't have to change things.

Moving the walker ahead of his slow step by slow step as if he were once again coaxing a reluctant lover.

Clouds piling up in the west.

A long line of children.

A kind friend with no promises to keep.

A tickle of gray at the edges.

Walking, walking, walking, all day long.

The farmer's torso was carefully studied in Saginaw, Michigan before being put on display, complete with appendages.

And guarded, guarded like the dickens.

Because fingers and thumbs are more easily broken than hooves. Because of the rarity of the specimen.

Perhaps one of the farmer's sons once thought playing in the mud was more rewarding than growing plants. Perhaps he had received no approval, no approval ever. Perhaps something could be seen in this example, but what?

Thick and threatening like an angry man in a canvas sack.

"There, there, I'm sure that torso belongs to someone." That's what they said to him on the streets after he escaped.

He had been dreaming of little turtles, thousands of them, pouring from the faucets. She hadn't noticed. She said, "Yes."

Clouds piling up in the east.

A long line of children.

Of course this didn't have to change things.

June 9

A Science Kit

For months I have been thinking about paradise and I am now incredibly happy that peaches are not routinely denigrated there.

I have also noticed that the moon climbing the sky has made its hind legs invisible. In this way, my lonely heart was able to finish disrobing.

I was not inventing my happiness. I was testing it. I knew that my brethren shadows would help, but I came to the conclusion that the night sky is the same story by another title.

To unstain my experience would be to deny it, so I hold myself in. Sighing. For months I have in this way been processing paradise. The absence of unreasonable attachment to peaches which I had achieved had proved so much more difficult than the absence of antagonism.

It had something to do with the way paradise can be imagined as relatively comprehensible, something shaped by the container in which it is placed, something which can be consumed without ever being used up. Like the idea of something which is real.

My mistake was believing I could live in paradise when it was paradise that was living in me, and I just had to learn how to go there. I had wanted to go to some place where I could be myself as I imagined myself, some place where I could decide what to do with my new definition of happiness. I wanted to belong to the one inside, as if I could be reasoned with, as if I could see myself from different angles and complete the picture, as if I were rounded and knowable.

As if I were something that could be held in a hand. My hand.

Something juicy, resulting inexplicably from something that proceeded convincingly in an orderly fashion.

June 10

Sundays at the Zoo

You're the only imaginary thing left, so pay attention. You'll have to make do. You see, there were nice baby zebras and there were human children with clumsy overshoes, each holding our attention with incongruous non-maturity-seeking behaviors. We found this amusing and we wished to be less mature. We wondered about what it would be like to impulsively reach for something we didn't have, something grown abstract, perhaps, that might remain beyond our reach. We thought about acting thoughtlessly.

First let's establish the perimeters. Weebles make poo poo in the lion's den, for example, provides access to a dangerous amusement. Laugh if you must, but it's one more approach to unprepossessing expectations that has thus far eluded us, like Weebles weeping over the demise of deliberately undifferentiated nutritious insects, or Weebles disguised as fresh raucous confessions in the Museum of Delinquent Care.

It has been said that Weebles illuminate each hidden blade of dissention with an evasive, rubbery and meticulous attitude. I don't expect anyone else to find such purchase. Not all tenacious pretensions are transferable and it's not currently me fouling the longed-for nursery soup. I don't think so. I don't think so at all.

So that's the explainable part of why I brought you here and it's true that we still don't have enough overshoes. It's a damn shame. A dirty disgusting overflowing damn crime of a shame.

Consequently, we have additional Weebles and then we have more Weebles. And Weebles again and Weebles once more. A whole zoo full of classic separation anxieties spawned by overabundance. I was previously reluctant to accept the idea that it helps one move on in life if you know who your real mother is, but I've always understood that it's a gift if your understanding is engaged at the time you are awarded anything you might regard as a similar discovery.

I really wanted to blame the environmentalists, but that summer didn't proceed as predicted. I wasn't sure which dramas were natural anymore. I couldn't seem to rise early enough to locate any actively gathering dew. Unattached zebras flew by, dry as kites. The zookeeper discussed this at length in his most recent letter of resignation. Indications to the contrary had been artificially encouraged and he wasn't going to put up with it anymore.

Sometimes the wind gets caught in its own hair and has to be removed with tinsel. So, too, the appearance of the ancient blue ideal of restraint, which looks suspiciously like a driverless 1963 Camero.

Afterwards the director rested and resigned me again.

June 11

Complicity

Some, of course, are happier than you are. Birds, for example, little savages plundering the crumbs, or the ravenous burble of a stone, for instance.

I ask myself to come in. The surface of the question is a kind of refusal. So I go in.

There was a statement there about the redemption of sorrow illuminated in the patient meadow. And a mask worn by renewable semi-seismic insects. A partial, fragile carapace. Abandoned. An ethereal relic.

So I ask myself to come in further. I witness a voyage of stationary birthmarks thrust into a question so big it seems not to be there. And I begin to wonder if it's enough to merely celebrate the chosen twig, if it's enough to generate verbal occupants for the grand museum in the earth, exposed. If it's enough to merely envy.

Crude sewing implements made from dark wire rested in the country of the dawn. By this time bread had been achieving a greater degree of adherence to the frequently misunderstood principals. I had witnessed a pock-marked pear on a polished table, the dark silky suit of a witnessing crow. A still life with motion still in it.

I just wanted to know why my previous body wasn't there. I just wanted to trade in a few sins for something to say about my "self" and the world and the insignificant place I held in its turgid pit of redemption and despair that looked so much like a big beautiful endless sewer while time's clumsy tornado drove all my friends like terrified badgers to a hole in the ground that could have been a place where meat gathered but wasn't (though soon enough, if they just stayed there, you'd hear the worms saying it was, again). And the earth listened, just like that, to those it was closest to.

And then a flock of these friends descended like a returned gift, their new houses still warming. It's true I was bigger when my house was new. She was still my mother then. The moment with the look of surprise. She lives in 1937. Which isn't a happy year.

I tried to open up the sharing we did with our pants down. I tried to give it friendlier appendages. I still try, but by the time the world notices, the creature imprisoned will be free of itself and mutual.

June 12

True Stories

It always happens at dusk. You're late. A very long journey and your impatient thoughts begin to wander. You're still far from the city and the road's empty. The house rises from the landscape like a fishing boat on a slow swell and it's gone almost before you notice. But in the story you're telling yourself the light's on and the side of a woman's face holds motionless. She looks tired and you make up her life. It's true and now she looks sadder. You must live with that.

You really must learn to be happier. For the sake of the friend you will soon visit who will remind you of this woman. But happier. And full of wonderful lies about her past. She knows how to put things behind her.

Her goldfish gulp the bubbles on the surface of the water. You imagine they're hungry so you feed them. They eat and continue gulping bubbles. You wonder what their lives are like. Again you make it up and again it's true. You begin laughing because you've never been happier. Your friend decides to tell you a sad story about her past. It's true. The road's empty. Waves slap against the hull of the house. When she laughs, you turn off the light. The side of her face looks soft and warm and motionless. Even in the dark as your hand parts the water and you begin rowing.

June 13

Who

I suppose I could tell you this was going to happen easily. My qualified experience has been full of lies like that. I go to the grocery store and the sign says SALE by the peaches, so I get a bag of peaches to the check-out clerk and the check-out clerk is an older woman with a mustache. Nice though. Respectful. But she charges me the normal price for the peaches, so I tell her the sign said they were on sale and she calls the manager who claims the sign was over the nectarines, not the peaches.

That's part of the reason I left my husband.

Like yesterday when the bottled water guy delivered three bottles to 2C and one bottle to 3D. 2C doesn't even drink water, but that's another story. So I tell him on the phone about the mistake, nice, like it's understandable even though it's really pretty stupid, and the hairball wants to fix it next week with extra water, won't even come back and move one of the bottles. Wants to know why I can't do it. Doesn't believe 2C won't open the door.

My son used to be like that.

The truth is I get tired when I know what's going to happen next. I get cranky.

Still, something has to happen next.

But I don't.

I don't have to happen before I decide to happen.

Except when I have to not happen anymore when that finally happens.

So I remember something else about behavior and tell the clerk about it and she listens. But it wasn't about her, oh no, it wasn't about her. It wasn't about her even one little bit.

I used to be loud and proud and think thunder could speak for me, having no reason to explain, only an emptiness to fill, having no purchase on that heaven but my body's evaporation. You could hold on to that passing if you lifted and fell, the way weather does. You could go there for a reason if there was something more than yourself on the other end.

I'd been here before and I didn't know which one of me was speaking. There's a bit of something very much like it attached to each of us before we become attached to it. Before it goes away with us. Which we don't notice. Not knowing who that is that's leaving because it couldn't be us, couldn't be anything singular departing in such a generic manner.

Like we could have been there inside ourselves and not ever guessed it wasn't who we thought it was.

You take this out of the place it was in and it becomes something else.

I figured that much out already.

Maybe it's even over another time now. Over another you.

June 14

Innocent

I was studying the gradations of a pebble's reluctance. I really was. It's a difficult subject. Then I remembered the taste left in my mouth by your mouth. How surprisingly dry it was. I couldn't forget that.

I thought about where pebbles came from and I decided they must have broken off of larger rocks and just sort of rolled around real slowly, getting bumped and jostled a lot so you couldn't notice it much at any one time and it rubbed all the sharper parts off. (The way some of my friends might lose some of their annoying edges if they had more time for me.)

Which means parent rocks are really almost everywhere. So I listened hard and thought I could hear them grunting with the effort to hold still, to live longer, not break off their parts and create children too quickly, a kind of restrained music of gradual failures, like ours, which keeps them reproducing.

It was, I realized, an unendurable beauty. I mean I had to quit listening or something terrible was going to happen. A weeping motorcycle of captivating pain was how I grew to think about it because it seemed like birth ought to hurt in a moving sort of way and that really should take you somewhere.

Then I remembered your mouth again.

Then I saw the hooded figures with crude weapons on their crude shoulders acting crudely. And I didn't feel like running away from them.

Then I had an epiphany and I understood God is the greatest thief of all.

I learned all that from one pebble, but I don't think I quite believed it. I don't think I believed it at all.

I remained unmistakably reluctant. I was still living for the first time while pebble after pebble parted from larger participations and offered a possibility of redemption that I still thought looked an awful lot like rebirth.

Then I remembered the taste of your mouth in my mouth. That's what I understood. And I understood how this thing was more than one thing and I went there and tried to stay. Because of the thirst. Because of all the careful thirst.

June 15

Strong Bones and Healthy White Teeth

This dairy is built with contemporary sticks and mud and ancient ideas and the emotional support of many anxiety-ridden businessmen. This is yet another progressive possibility which has found its time. Some of the most reluctant consider themselves clean and good when they consider it.

The people who work here wear fine white clothing. Sometimes they work alone, like the man you can see by the water trough, bathing his accrual of dividends. If you asked him why he spends so much time doing this, he might say he is greasing an old-fashioned windmill and only appears to be gathering interest. Sometimes such investors work together in bands like ancient tribesmen, but they are not ancient tribesmen because they wear their fine white clothing.

Predictably, these workers have built fine white huts and now they can go home at night to a sterile environment. In the old days they would sleep on the ground right where they were when they finished working. They had no ceiling on which to project their investments.

Not all of this land is for the dairy cattle. Much of it belongs to the future, which includes foreigners who are members of other tribes, and in some places, they have already put up fences. In other places, they have plowed up the previous owners and sowed their thoughtful absence.

Dairies like these were once repositories of undigested social possibilities but are now run more carefully and are inspected by government officials to see that we get clean rich government officials.

In city dairies you can see how the milk is bottled and withheld in anticipation of greater need. In country dairies, you can see how the milk is spilled into a complex system of infiltration much like the ancient Roman aqueducts, which were, in turn, modeled on the thinking of celebrated philosophers, who were usually outcasts. In both systems, you can see how liquid desires were channeled into potential. Which way do you think you would prefer your fluids be handled? What should be done with the issue to be sure it is addressed respectfully?

If we milk different animals, we can lead different lives. Sometimes we forget to bring along our healthy shadows and their impatience with our forgetfulness makes them unhealthy. It's a problem we have not yet learned to accommodate and we hold it at bay with meaningless gestures. It's a bit like listening to a deaf man snore. Or teaching a blind man to study colors in his sleep. Some say it's as if aggravating the right man's anxiety could become a kind of timeless wisdom, a gloating. Intoxicated with this type of self-pity, we wallow in the thick muck where all these ideas fester and spawn unexpected permutations. Even the latent shadows of the carefully skimmed milk can be said to have gained something undefinable from the exchanges.

Perhaps this is why our pale juicy religious leaders shoot scripture at us from their darkness? Are they preaching or poaching? You'd have to be tall enough to reach above yourself to progress in this way.

Imagine then the circular bridge alongside the first spiritual dairy. Frequent arrivals at the departure point. Frequent departures at the arrival point. How would we ever know when our work was finished?

June 16

Why Can't We Be Farmers?

There was and there was not a reluctant cheese farm in the middle of a formal rope garden which, as you know, grows down instead of up. Spaced between the short cows were informational blots floating like afterimages. Jean Sibelius invented the cake pan which is used to separate the milk from the things that you hear about from the neighbors. He is famous in Switzerland and the garage territories for this important discovery and records have been made of it. He appears to be composed of organic rude instruments.

And if that wasn't another lever for the dairy products consortium to exercise in uprooting undesirable health implications, then it was most certainly a factor in the development of the recent udder appreciation movements.

In the meantime, my little darlings, we should be very clear about our confusions, however illicit they may be. Solemn occasions are shedding their unconvincing raincoats in the very same garden where we met the need for this territorial career. Let's repair the cautions recovered from reluctant advancements. We can reward the unrepentant miscreants later. No one's going to steal them or caress them needlessly.

You, however, could certainly still be happening. Perhaps without effort. The swan's wing span remains enormous and continues whistling to the ancient clouds. Sibelius sings in the cheese window, with lyric and erect intentions. Godlike. Sensual. You might even defeat the temptation to list all his accomplishments. You're too late to invent the modern Sibelius separator, but several aspects of the things you dream about the neighbors remain unexplored and fluid.

Who then are these implicitly ruminant and greatly under-browned four-legged folktale heroes anyway? Are your neighbors not providing the short white contemporary informational blots spaced with territorial imperatives and the commercially viable processed aluminum mortality dispensations sold as Cheese Whiz and thus inserted surreptitiously into the implicit gobs of something as painfully indescribable but still very much alive as you are?

"Are these great pastoral providers really your neighbors or are they merely an alternative variety of the inevitable ferment?" we might wish to ask if we could live happily after any ever.

June 17

Dull, Needy and Almost Available

When the dull days are over and the dull say so, we will no longer require separation. Meanwhile, voting has grown redundant.

But this morning the fog rolled in like a new age carpet salesman and gravitated. Lightened up but wouldn't leave. Artificial sunlight. It can burn you.

I couldn't seem to keep a grip on the floor.

Palpable, but inconsequential. I'm looking for another body. I'm looking.

The Air Force Reserve is meanwhile playing in the field across the street. They are not forceful enough. Neither are they reserved. The air is still awaiting them.

I'm told that whipping the coffin is translated as, "A blade of grass is not an echo." Three left shoes means, "Evil is always disguised as good, but good can be disguised as either evil or good."

In school today, the president of terribly small gardens visited my scrunchy back yard briefly before lunch. The treaty will not be signed.

So I visited dull. I smelled dull and it was not as expected. Migraines and knotted knees. A crucifixion waltz of military perfection.

More palpable. Engendering.

When the dull say the day is over, it's the same one. The same and the same. An arbitrary distraction. Like that means it's not really over. If you're doing nothing, how do you know when you're done?

In school today, three dead in a freak elephant-bus collision is translated as, "Elvis." In this way, conspiracy theories can be avoided.

The air force increased its attention span and thereby its force. There were several palpabilities. The reserve increased as well.

In school yesterday is translated as, "Anywhere you want to be is heaven." Heaven is translated as, "Migraines with knotted knee episodes."

In dull school, the dull learn not to. Eventually it meant that I required separation.

Redundancy schools you in the restless trajectories.

Just because we're not necessary doesn't mean we're not expected.

In heaven tomorrow is translated as "a coffin of grass." So is birth.

We cannot go on repeating such a great and wondrous distance.

June 18

A Substantially Delayed Consideration of Responsibilities

The boat is named after a famous saint and you are on it. The final preparations for leaving the dock have not begun yet, but no one responds when the loudspeaker sputters something about an illegally parked car. Your mother worries instead about her motor scooter parked in the neighbor's garage. Your father has been gone for years, but he comes back, reliably, on your birthday, and you always take a trip to an island for a picnic when he does and your mother comes along, whistling as if she is as happy as they used to be. He often sings a drunken ballad about hard times and desperate women. The story doesn't seem to have anything to do with your life, but your father's new girl friend gives you a handmade valentine the one time he allows you to meet her and does a little dance step she calls "The Two Step Apology for Everything He's Done and Doesn't Understand But Did It Because He Loves You March of the Fairyplum Soldiers." She gives you a chuck on the chin and a peck on the lips and slips her tongue in your mouth when your father turns away.

Finally, one day your mother and father announce their remarriage and the girlfriend cuts up your father's luggage and hits him with a shovel, but he doesn't press charges and on your birthday another famous saint nearly rams your famous saint when an odd weather disturbance throws off the navigation devices and someone named "Alfred" breaks in on your saint's frequency wanting to know if the tuna are biting. They aren't, which you only know because you've been listening to the electronic chatter from the deck chair you moved next to an open window. Your father is a liberal when it comes to dispensing his certainty about communications equipment and would be pleased by your interest. Your mother seems to admire this confidence.

Sadly, although you don't know why, you begin singing. Your father attempts to accompany you on the fish whistle he carved from a whalebone. His range is insufficient and his style is full of artificial exaggeration. The tune is lively, taught to you by your mother, and sounds Irish, and you don't. It makes you wonder what you're all doing together like this, your Italian father, Irish mother, and you, uncertain what to claim. It makes you remember that dream about stowing away in your father's luggage, next to the handmade valentine it's too late to return.

June 19

Stagecoach Diorama with Unreasonably Protruding Antlers

Two of the men were looking at the woman's breasts. One was not. They were doing this because the woman's breasts were exposed, available to be looked at. The woman did not yet know they were available for anyone to look at because she was looking over her shoulder at the examination room entrance and she had not heard the three men enter through the exit door (a feature most examination rooms didn't have) when the exit door swung open quietly and did not brush against the carpet that muffled their steps.

Perhaps she had been worried and trying to give herself a breast exam while she waited for the doctor. Perhaps she was considering altering their size and shape and she was trying to decide how much. Perhaps she was not a patient but the doctor's wife or mistress impatient for a little afternoon delight and she wished to surprise the doctor.

But it was time to be thinking about something else now, with the men's surprised intake of breath revealing their presence, so the woman covered her breasts and moved away, towards the entrance, without even turning her head back. She still didn't see the three men, but she knew someone was there. How had she known they weren't the doctor? The two men who had been looking at her breasts looked at each other.

Then the nurse was in the room and the woman was gone and the nurse was pointing at the third man and he was stepping forward. He was rising and adjusting his shirt and moving towards the commanding nurse with his eyes on where her breasts, that were not making any promises at all, might have been announcing themselves, had they been interested, beneath her starched and nearly shapeless smock, and he was smiling anyway and thinking about how to get her phone number and what kind of wine to buy for their first dinner.

The other two men watched this happening and they each imagined being the one that the nurse had selected and that her smile meant much more than friendly patience and they both felt oddly satisfied as they looked at each other and did not know if the lucky man they had been imagining or the man they were was the one they were really thinking about at that moment. Then they remembered the third man and they knew that they were not the man who was leaving the room with the nurse and for a moment they didn't understand that this satisfied them.

June 20

Her Boyfriend

Steve was brushing the crackers off the night stand onto the floor when the front door opened and three little sisters of no Stevian relation just walked right into Steve's house, smiles and all. They didn't seem to notice the distinctly rumpled quality of his topless pajamas.

Steve decided they were selling cookies. Steve decided they were cute little sisterly representatives of in-process female accomplishment and Steve did, in fact, have no more cookies. But then, maybe, Steve didn't need any more cookies.

Steve didn't ask them to knock. He figured it was too late and he figured right.

"Hey, little sisters," Steve said.

"We're not sisters. We're not even little," said one of the sisters.

"Do you have any cookies?" Steve asked.

The littlest sister reached into her backpack and pulled out a mushy fig Newton like a wilted frog that might spring to life at any moment. "These aren't for giving away, but I want you to have one," she said, blushing.

And with that the biggest sister said, "She wants to be your girlfriend."

And the middle sister said, "You've got something white in your beard."

To which Steve said, "I'm getting older now."

And the same sister said, "No, I mean crumbs. Like you've been eating something and it crumbled on the way to your mouth."

"I bet you've got crumbs in your underwear," said the littlest sister.

"She wants to look," teased the biggest sister.

Steve made a face. It was surprised and it was excited and it was uncertain and it seemed too honest and it was more than a little frightened.

"At your thing," said the same sister.

The same face again, trying to pull itself apart.

"We're going outside now and you show her your thing and we won't let anybody else come in," said the same sister matter-of-factly.

Steve thought about what to say. He thought about his lover and he thought about his ex-lovers and nothing had prepared him for this. He thought about the authorities and he thought about what the girls might say to them if he made them mad. He couldn't move. He was alone with the littlest sister. She was reaching for the elastic band on the front of his pajama bottoms and he couldn't move. She began to touch him.

Then he moved. He brushed the crumbs from his beard.

The sister knew what to do and he was afraid to stop her. Then he was afraid not to, but it was already too late.

Then it was later and he was somewhere else and he wasn't sure how much he remembered and the little sister was gone.

Then he was just afraid.

He wondered if maybe he hadn't really imagined it after all.

Then he wondered if he could believe that.

And then he believed that and he wondered if it ever might happen and then he thought it would be so much more wonderful than anything he had been imagining if it did.

June 21

Another Genesis

I wanted to start over. There was this big emptiness I lived in. It reminded me of several absences at once. Like they were all together in something.

Susan was tangential, a freckled inference. She was a tool kit and a siren. She was angry little disturbances of rain exclaiming in the wind. She was a reminder of inconsequential behavior from the clouds. She was lost and wet and looking for me. She was a city kid out of gas on a lonely country road. Her darkness was about to find her.

So what do you think she did with all that space?

You have to understand it's not easy to live in somebody else's nowhere. I would prefer a little chopping block romance to her vacant landscape stare. No campaign, but a sudden violent election of unrequited desire and awakened need. The President of the Immediate ousted by The Dictator of the Appropriated Moment, shifting countries at war with their own separations, borders erased before the first command.

And then it's raining harder. You can't even stick your head out of the coffin you built, the hole you live in filling up with muddy water like that. Susan carried off. Susan unexpectedly predictable as she floated down the river. All the rebellious signs and none of the results. Susan ineffectual. Susan departing gritty and buoyant.

Meanwhile torch carrier for the conflicted sisterhood Claire Voyance (her real name) struggled with the peanut butter lid. She won but there were casualties. She predicted a tasty little sandwich. She predicted a glass of orange juice. She predicted satisfying children, but you can't get everything right, now can you? And she was, after all, a very new girlfriend and didn't understand my needs yet and therefore could not so easily refuse them.

I'll admit it wasn't the world I intended to create, but after a while, I rested.

June 22

The Memory of Fruit

We did not see the sheep alive. We did not witness the clover or the animals that devoured it. We saw nothing of what we believed.

A summer dress. The memory of fruit.

A past waving like a misplaced flag on a melting glacier.

Somebody else's dream chains me to this. It's how I know I'm in here. It doesn't belong to me.

It's how I know I'm arrived. That which remains after its cause has disappeared. That which we call love which is not love. And that which is not diminished by not being love.

That which leaves us but is not forgotten.

That which sacrifices itself to the meadow.

June 23

A Life of Crime

1. How I Live

The police car sits empty. It's a definition of Mozart.

Three stooges (not those three) visit my father with a bag of weed seed. I don't suppose their antagonism groans softly.

In the diner, the sergeant plays with the honeyed garments, a rag and bone prediction awaiting anointment in a jealous maudlin display. The cruel ones use pity.

But it doesn't add up. I collect newsreels of the endless funeral, begin exciting the sag of someone's failing trousers with mere survival. I can't seem to champion timeless music anymore.

A sleepy shampoo, interrupted by bees. Their yellow and black stripes seem entirely too narrow for their wide blustery bottoms. I don't just think of their fresh noise calling across the canyon. That's not why I'm outside, but the sergeant listens anyway. He's supposed to keep me from doing something, but he doesn't know what it is. Only I know.

So maybe I'm the designated muscle-bound gorilla. Maybe the police car isn't empty. Maybe Beethoven and too many deputies. Maybe I'm here for a vacation from my mob.

Enchanted weeds in the temptation garden. Funny, I didn't remember my father's birthday.

Then, simple as intentions, I'm gone again.

2. How I Used to Live

I don't hate my father at all. I just visit when it's time for a change.

Each time there's a moment when I realize I could go home now if I didn't live here.

The police car is still empty because the dead man can't walk.

It has something to do with authority and what happens.

The squirting sergeant still blubbering about Nancy.

So I'm ordering honey and laughing out loud. I'm alive with beer. I'm decadent with good cheer.

Then, simple as law, I'm not.

3. How I'm Going to Live

The police car so permanent it's bronzed. Stravinsky. Gorilla guests for breakfast, with and without uniforms. They don't even seem like me.

Authority happens. I'm past that.

And the dead man now is me but saunters and struts without a weapon. Three honey pots caption the weeds like new stooges.

Listen, pop, I used to do bimbo enough for both of us.

I'm past that past. I'm happening after now. Empty as law, I'm here because I can't be there anymore. The stripes don't add up. I'm not simple anymore.

Newsreels like falling trousers. Lieutenant Orphan, the sky's a rule. You have to appreciate the honey. You have to pay attention at somebody.

June 24

A Political Action

Clean cut, intense and too sure of themselves, they planned their course of action over breakfast near my table. They were going to change the world. As I ate, my beard grew ragged and my shirt stained itself. An aggressive welcoming menace spread across the friendly grin I usually give the waitress.

By the time I left, they had put their new country on the table. Mine began spreading like a tenacious weed.

I would not have hesitated to violate their borders, but as the light outside left only the absence we were both trying to fill, they melted into their intentions, which, by now, looked a lot like shadows.

I tried hard, but I could not find that world they had spoken of. I didn't know if it even existed, but I knew I couldn't find it.

Instead of discouraging me, this gave me a reason that hadn't been there before. It made me unsure of myself, and it made me happy to be a part of something greater than myself, even if it didn't exist. It made me willing. It made me dangerous.

June 25

Toad

A fever, misunderstood. The waitress won't stop rubbing her hands. Because I am frequently someone else, I say, "There's a problem in logic inside and it only comes out when the speaker is preoccupied."

Accidents are proof of my existence, stains my philosophy. I tell the stories that have already been told. First you will fall asleep and then you will fall asleep inside.

In a quiet daze of darkness and oars, one soft slap, numb in the damp night. A finger pointing nowhere. "That is where you are going," whispers its wind before anyone knows.

Whatever it is, you step into it, surprised that it fits.

The fairytale has a long tongue, darting, grobbling up the silence, a forgotten story of insects and mistakes, a hunger of flies and survival. When you believe the stone inside is a real stone and the house inside is a real house, then you will be surrounded by your own existence. Day does not simply turn into night; it is penetrated by it.

An old woman in the tale lives in a cage lit with fish-oil lamps. She sleeps and your parts inhabit her dreams. It's your winged heart in the shadows, gnawing on a mouse. You could chase yourself with your own furry arm. Your head would be outside itself if it could think of this.

Then the dying thump of some wart-animal held down by the frozen earth of an entirely different tale.

"Love," the dog said, "love," but it sounded like, "Feed me."

I miss you. Give me back my oven.

June 26

Old Cotter

Old Cotter comes out of the marsh dragging a bum leg and a burlap sack filled with dead stories. He sits by the fire, and as he explains how each of them died, spasms shake the bag, furred shadows slip out, and each of us feels something attach itself to our feet. The next morning we travel west. By noon we reach an understanding. We travel on through quiet towns, holding our breath in our hands, listening to the songs of the rain and imagining the fire burning under the fog-bound marsh.

I pause for a moment by the river and slip my hand in the current. The cold nibbles at my fingers while the sun warms the shirt on my back. I walk through dust, sweat rising from my skin, cooling me and collecting small stories of the earth and wind. Darkness tells them to stay. Sleep gives them a home.

A network of mingled currents, the long roots of marshgrass, the paths of snails and waterbugs. At night, beside the wet veins of the earth, shadows call across the water. In sleep we answer them, shivering out over the smooth cold arm of the night as if we had a purpose beyond morning.

June 27

Adrift in the Temple

The wrong man said, "This circle prefers darkness." The other traveled endlessly. A sparrow of a girl with swift black eyes appeared, fascinated with the light at rest on the imaginary chair. She held three words in her mouth until they fell out. "Ear. Hand. Knife." Once she started, she couldn't stop. She might have been the wrong man's daugher.

She spoke of something lost and something still disappearing. She visited the crumbling township of Rust, examined owl pellets near the gate and entertained a stone lamp flickering among the lupine and mugwort.

The wrong man said, "The mole and the magpie were listening to the gossip of the stable boys popping snowberries against sharp stones by the bridge. The sun paused to nest in the shivering poplars." The wrong man gave her the tiny novel, which she folded into a cube and placed in the light on the imaginary chair. No one else was left in the room.

The wrong man's surprise party followed the anxious black dogs out onto the lake. Two crows reflected in the wind-polished ice flared briefly before the night's slow snow cargo descended. A nervous accompaniment of blackbirds darted in and out between the crow's long black wing-strokes until they formed a large black handkerchief and their entire dark sky was flying over them.

An hour before dawn, sitting in the rowboat frozen into the riverbank near her house at the edge of town, the wrong man's daughter remembered crushing walnuts before they ripened, brushing the fragrant green pulp through her hair. She didn't tell this till years later. She was waiting for the right moment to say, "Don't you think salt creates a terrible silence?"

The wrong man answered the new temple of transient sky, drifted south in its darkness. He thought of his daughter as friendly. He let her lead him out of the uncertainty, but they still didn't know where they were. He could no longer remember what she said, but he agreed not to name the missing birds. Their darkness continued fleeing and he realized the suddenly freezing rain had been imprisoned in so many ways he could no longer imagine all of its crimes.

When they arrived once more, the tiny novel was speaking from the light on the next chair. It said something about worship, but the wrong man could hear the knife in its voice and its feet were cold. It seemed to be reaching for something at the end.

The township of Rust was still waiting. It seemed to be attached to a failure to emote. Its blood had gone sour and dry. Its dry lake seemed less willing to accompany anything that wasn't traveling in place. The snow had been falling behind and it exchanged its fleeting future for rain's accommodating discomforts.

The wrong man lit the stone lamp and his daughter began reading her new life to him. Her mouth did not contain the same words that had crossed the frozen lake. Its cooling hinge was opening and closing like the mouth of a baby bird, as if she had not yet understood nature's reticence. The wrong man thought about placing her back in the poplar nest, but she was growing too quickly.

The wrong man wanted to start yet again that last morning, but the lake had written its own prayer and he was listening to its latent career. Loud veins of blue were offering maps to his uneasy desire and he had to hike once more into the mountain of words he had assembled to keep the world from falling out. The tiny novel was glowing. His feet were listening. "You'd have to be worshipping far inside," he thought. "You'd have to be more than yourself to get beyond it."

A flight of bats sutures the fading sunset closed and the dream settles upon your shoulders as if it were a cloud embracing a worn and unsuspecting mountain. You don't know what to say, so you tell yourself, "I can never forgive you for forgiving me." You do this in the present even though the past had been faithfully attending your goals.

Perhaps someday you will no longer be the warmth that keeps throwing itself out the window. Perhaps someday you will no longer seem accidental as water. Perhaps someday large ghostly presences will not be drawn to you. Interviewing each slippery gray stone, inveterate time has been counting the complacent constituency. Perhaps someday, you'll grow as comfortable as moss-hair waving in a trickle of creek-water.

Perhaps now we have arrived at you, so settled and so lost. A man likes to feel he's best at something. A man likes to be other. He has no time for time's cruel solutions.

Now we're sudden and now we're removing Stalin's spleen. It's a musical with surgical instruments. It's been brilliantly anticipated by those who don't arrive. Even the sutures are dancing. We're making fish now with tickly fingerless gloves and we're filling the rivers with them. We've reversed history. It's a time of plenty and the assembly lines are creating workers with happy new hearts who travel to foreign lands and grow corn that longs to be taken on great expeditions. We're all growing mustaches and carrying rolling pins. The roads must be improved and the bullets salvaged to make the toy soldiers. The applause is thickening and the bread is shaped to remind us of the fish. Beer has been invented, and calisthenics, and kissing naked people hanging by their feet. You might think it an aberration if we weren't reliable workers. We have only three colors, but they readily exchange addresses and it's enough to paint our way to a perplexing investigation of our recovery.

June 28

Home to Her Island

A woman who has been living in the cottonwood tree takes the shoe from her green window and brushes away empty cocoons and spider webs. It's been a long time and she doesn't know if she broke in or out. The limp no longer reminds her of anything.

Listen to the wreck feeding in the dark. You might like to think it's only an old Edsel with a few stray heads of wheat climbing through the broken window, but it's too late to vote against symbolism. Some things that seem accidental were just waiting but not these. All red stones must now prove their innocence.

When you have only the sky to look up to, it's easy to feel small. It's too easy to look at things the way something else sees them.

Ghostly widows of fog rise early from the cornrows, their pale blue tracks softening and sliding up and away, evaporating into the brightening horizon.

"The best embrace loss; the worst worship it." That's what the remaining landscape has been teaching so much longer than we can know.

Changed, utterly changed. As it would be even if no one had noticed. As it might appear to a traveler sitting in a chair, floating his thoughts on inkskin. It might bring you back on the eve of your salvation to that which you had spent your life escaping. What we're going to learn from this is more than it could be because we're more than is possible. We're beyond ourselves.

Knock, knock.

I'm still my home.

Come back later when later is now. I'll be there in my river, traveling isolated, traveling tall and green.

June 29

Witness

Barbed wire hugs the wall behind the young soldier as he plays the cello. How could he have hustled it through the streets, still filled with looters and thieves?

A single stalk of corn struggles bravely beside the scarred building, audience to a misplaced world. His cap sits patiently on the stone bench, attentive. Perhaps there it finds something familiar in the music.

A woman inside the open window of the badly played song wears a scarf and a full peasant skirt with a light jacket. The soldier's body leans in, tentative but unwavering. The moment in which his fate will be sealed.

For a moment only the perpetual banter of leaves and twigs along the overgrown path consuming the fading tones of the cello, the soldier's posture unhinged in our imagination as we try to complete the image of the soldier replacing the cello with the woman.

June 30

Please Deny You Took Part in This

Sure enough, the tall tale was shorter than we expected and the evening still wasn't aggressive enough to suit that wired and witless wiener-humper with the beehive. What I did was I fished the curled green coral from the restaurant aquarium and garnished the arrogant twit's salad.

The thing is you can't just propose to a guest and expect a dream palace to assign you to your immediate future. No matter how short the unjustified entertainment. It's not like a conversational piece with spaghetti straps entitles you to first romance. Red Fish Suspenders agreed quickly but the agreement had already turned to soap.

"Women knew about mortality the second they hit the air," said the disturbed husband. Men like to make it a competition, said the wife.

"We must leave at once," they both suddenly concluded. How could it be such an urgent message? Life or death in the bedroom? Kill the troll and steal the coins?

"We don't have to admire the Stump Brothers to get in touch with ordinary reality," said the departing masculinity of the unreasonably merry married pharmacist. "There was this one guy I knew," he insisted, "just up and stuffed a goofy Smurf doll in his Thanksgiving turkey. He survived, but the medical bill was incredible." He couldn't stop admiring the evidence.

So we left the restaurant and motored on over to this druggery geek's crusty clover-hoofed cluttercastle. A ritzy second-hand mausoleum of period pieces with a nasal butler and three dalmatians romping in the garden. The new host busied himself pawing Spaghetti Straps while a couple of long-nosed Brooks Brothers eyed the dalmatians. Not an admirable nose-lifter in the place. Decadence cruising the crib with a redundant leer.

Then the story we started with came back with a toothache and I fed it some dog-food stew. Exclamations of wonder. Approval of an altered nature. I wouldn't call it realism.

Finally the live and unplugged Chamber Music began sawing up the blocks of boredom into manageable interludes and I settled in to voyeurizing the requisite nooks and crannies. A reasonably good year settled in my stomach and I drifted into the cellist's trousers. Roomy but welcoming. I stayed for the wedding. I couldn't tell if it was mine, but that didn't seem to matter. There's always an extra alibi at these affairs.

July

July 1

That Which May Survive Us

When the time comes to save ourselves from our wandering, the weak children are eaten first. Some of the strong men have been awarded a soft dark hood, which can be slipped over the head. When this hood is given to a tasty child, the child is granted another season to grow hungry.

In more stationary times, walrus liver can be eaten for breakfast and for dinner we often choose merely to suck ice. We apply thoughtfully chosen names to our impressions of each other, like Thorgar Kristmundsson or The Happy Shadow Man. Wearing a blue hood represents gratitude to the cold and wounded sky.

Our livelihood has become inextricably intertwined with the care and maintenance of our domesticated animals. When the cultivated eggs are six months old, they are placed into cloth harnesses. Many wild eggs are captured and enlisted in service. (They move so slowly!) And just think of it. There are thousands upon thousands of younger eggs still forming in the ocean along our coast. Many of them will never even arrive at their destinations, which, in any case, can be difficult to ascertain. Sometimes our hunting parties find small colonies of nearly mature rebels in the rocky caves.

While our heroes are out hunting, the indentured eggs must carry our burden. After all, the demands of our dangerously sweet air remain unpredictable and it will take every bit of their training for them to maintain a semblance of balance while hauling the intoxicating invisible weight of our existence to the breathing storage locations.

Some of the less dependable eggs have been recaptured attempting to pilot make-shift boats in order to escape their inevitably oppressive condition, but their progressive new fathers have learned to cut and shape big blocks of dried water with a walrus knife and make a different and faster kind of boat, which is very large inside and allows them a certain degree of normalcy in their lives during the lengthy pursuits of the errant eggs. This boat sometimes becomes a substitute for the father's familial duties. And here, deep inside this largest of the policing boats, is the golden basket for the collection of the successfully employed ice-bathing towels. Here you can find a terrible sense of gratitude for the random shapes of the accompanying clouds, even when they remain at a great and mysterious distance.

Often the recaptured eggs put up a savage fight, rolling around in sudden and sometimes deadly swiveling motions. Some have to be destroyed, but others can be welcomed back to the family with loving sticks.

The fathers have learned how to clean and tan the brittle skins of those few remaining non-adaptive eggs using rounded ice wedges and the latent excretions of their own private organs. Very little of these "adjusted" eggs is wasted. The fathers stack the processed eggs in mathematically precise arrangements to allow for the effects of the moon and surround them with carefully selected and placed lichen-covered rocks to properly age them.

Researchers have conjectured that some of our descendants will actually make homes from these processed eggs. No one can explain how this will be done. The appeal of such ideas is not likely to become universal, even if the practice does.

As it is with all things, even the most conscientious of the domesticated eggs grow old and begin to smell bad and nip at the younger eggs. When such behavior is recognized, the offending eggs are either sacrificed immediately or they are drained of their fluids and left behind to "hibernate," a term we use to describe an existence without rebirth, which sometimes leads to a condition of "stasis" in which the newly somnambulant eggs are known as "oracles." Researchers believe that some of the ancient oracles will still remain in the farther reaches of the territory long after we are gone. It is widely believed that they will be very reliable but difficult to understand.

July 2

This Guy Harvey's Delusions

Life has arrived at the wrecking yard with a chipped tooth. Yes, a broken car is a sad thing, but a broken man can fix it.

The man in the black raincoat licks her leg. It continues to shine.

Blue like a swollen thigh. Blue like a blood red window.

And this red is not a color but a method of transportation, like a canoe. You turn it over in the sand to find evidence of where it's been. After a while grass grows.

Then it is time to get angry, flash a little moolah. discover a new world.

From here to there is always farther than from there to here.

After a while grass grows.

* * *

I understood the lush story would not have me in it, but I wanted the oh so suggestive strawberries to ripen quickly. I wanted an ice-pick for the offending eye, to open more drastically my dark jacket like a sullen goat.

O the song says hush and the cow dies of jaundice O instead of you there are several others.

"I wasn't the only one hunting," I told that commie faggot before I bought him a drink to celebrate his gentle erotic interference.

O the song says shush and the cancer speaks like wildfire O instead of him it belongs to you now.

There at the bar we all spoke i-n-c-r-e-d-i-b-l-y s-l-o-w-l-y, like a herd of potatoes learning to speak in unison.

O the song says moo and the dead cow cries for your mother O piggeldy poggeldy steal all the brandy for the blackbird pie.

Yes, the birds began to sing.

During the aural invasion already in progress, which made it difficult to ascertain which song was actually singing.

* * *

And then I went down to the bottom of the well and you still weren't there. The angry cause dripped from my chest. I was living a life so meticulous it was separating rain from more rain.

There was my first family lurking in the relevant shadows.

It was a nervous sort of roundness. Fading-into-the-shadows has always been my family's chosen form of hysteria.

Like a dog on the far side of the sunken little lake jerking in that motion of barking. But no sound arrives.

* * *

I bring you a book because I do not know the proper way to deliver a stone.

Using words like nails, I try to restrain a tiny apocalypse in the raindrop clinging to my knee. A ragged pile of abandoned guttural chants bleeds slowly into the tracks of the dusty wooden shopping carts the farmer's wives are pushing up and down the not-so-metaphorical aisles of corn.

Once again, it's raining. It seems that you haven't read enough into this offering.

* * *

Go away until the nothing happens again.

As in, "I wish to darken you."

Yes and yes and yes again and then lights failing in the window.

As if the lost man were simply a physical object with a hole in it.

* * *

My friend, the disturbance, discovered you weeping and did not offer his cloak. I didn't ask him to.

The future had passed, flailing away like an "ever after." I put some words in like stones and then a greater absence of stones.

The moon splintered the foot of the blossoming apricot. Ghost willows fingered the failing horizon.

White wet dust between your shriveled toes like a fungus, leg after leg lifting from the earth's release. Each new season shouldering heavier burdens, eating away at the strength of your false convictions. Oh oh but the unknowing beauty of your failing. Sweeten that which you drop from your limbs that it might suggest in its own life who you once were.

* * *

Like the last bird in the borderless darkness before you understood the light was coming. The wings of muscles dancing before the fire of work.

A kind of outer skin. A creature that is not from the moon. A creature that is the moon.

It's your daughter that wants you to live this way.

The daughter you never had.

* * *

I must protest the hidden acceptance. I must carry the clouds to their new home inside the cranium of the lunar opposition. Mating aside, there's room for an army.

I've given you all my sand. Can't you readjust?

Welcome tomorrow, Jack, a wheel without a finger lozenge.

The beach is already longer than yesterday.

As in to "tide" one over. As in to "put one on." As in to change one's position in relation to another's changing position.

Placent with alternative commitments.

The gift one fails to return.

An altogether orchestral delinquence.

The storm still lit with it. The weather wagging its tired tongue.

* * *

And as the story darkens, the shoe barks to repeat the dog. Simply a way of living. A broken leg like a cracked catapult clouding the window with distorted loot, the whole thing sufficiently intellectualized to pass for play, a barbecue limping in the twilight.

You aren't here, it says. You aren't here yet.

What I meant is not what I meant to say.

O train, O clock, O shoe of reluctance, issued from a motherhood so padlocked the child could have burst.

I happened because you were there. I am your I then you and gone.

I'm not a metaphor. I just speak with my words closed.

You don't have to fall in to be part of the conversation.

* * *

Guttering candlelight looks for a door, an abeyance instigating deserts.

One book resplendently shelved below the counter with a voice like a shovel. Cold birds singing like toasters. A stone at anchor.

Rain inside.

So I camp under the bones in my wind cave. Slapping a dead centipede of appearances against this man I thought I was, whispering across the swamp of seems, I enter the house my name built.

Red shoes and a lamp in the pear tree, citizens descending. The limbs are silent and because of that, you can hear the dreams in them.

A song couldn't do that, a life could.

Knocked on his head like a door.

Entered.

* * *

Stabs himself in the head, beats the shit out of himself, inserts a cemetery. Tries to come back.

Back to a misunderstood confectionery poem, a little chewy in the center like a cluster of nuns sunbathing.

Which isn't here. Not at all. Brightly so.

Paul Klee tripping over his mother's madras tie. That's here. And a photograph of childish innocence on a fat-tired bicycle. And the elbows of Klee's childhood popping out of threadbare sleeves like malnourished kittens. And the kittens later. Nourished.

No nuns. No sun. Lots of bathing.

And no mustache fallen off like a priest riding the wrong bicycle. If the handlebars start to bleed, I'll need assistance.

And here's this psychologist with a nervous tick, see, and the joke's bigger than she is. She's going to marry the gimp gas jockey at the Texaco. The one with the wrong mustache.

Frequently, she's out of season.

Oh wet, the wonder of willingly, the next warden wandering wanly, a wimple of wit wagging. Could a been me, could a been the other guy. Could a been the other guy meing.

In this way worry diets me. Mouth mooning.

Perhaps I've forgotten what I'm offering. The bag of me I gave you torn, a night school of insects opening. Shall I spill another layer of false bemusement over the tapestry of the poker playing dogs? The most miserables. Right now that's its "is."

* * *

And the world outside remained clumsy and strong. Sooner or later you have to let it in.

Words so polite they hurt.

Like a man whose wounds invented the weapons that made them.

* * *

The next few weeks always behave oddly. The taste of fear at the back of your throat like the spit valve of an old tuba.

The actors continue losing the same voices. In the first row, kitchen appliances. And the music doesn't melt.

The glassblower sneezes. Several poorly portrayed dandies catch their skirts on the turnstile. One lone raven hops over an unidentifiable corpse. The music doesn't melt.

Jowls aflutter, the play welcomes night's waning childhood, the wilderness of its affection.

July 3

Family Tree

You came back with the dog, said Aunt Elsie she had her the croup again. Something about a broken fire hydrant. Something about Cyril and a missing leash. Used to be he'd hide a mouse turd to the bottom of her oatmeal, that Uncle Cyril did. That there dog should never been 'lowed to be leavin' this neighborhood atall.

What ya want yerself such a damn mystery for? I could hold the sucker's lampshade up to a strong light and see people way out there kissin' the sick cat. Everythin's got tracks. 16th and Douglas then. I cain't hardly feel things like that no more. Ask Elsie what time it is, she'll say, "None left with Tuesday on 'em." That's what she always says.

"Wrong man, wrong day," she says. That's the way most of this family got here.

Weren't but yesterday, seemed like, Uncle Arthur got him a dozen pair hangin' over to his gar-age. There she was, not a stitch 'neath all those patches. But I guess he'd a been right somehow, though none of us figured it yet. Lots of evidence fallin' out to little notice.

That was down to the old house. Don't know fer certain it ever happened quite exactly like that, but that's the way I been rememberin' it. I couldn't help but be laughin'. Old people get ya goin', ya know, they ain't seen you in ages and they start fussin'. Pritnear soon ya start losin' yer minor appendages. Ever' which direction, seems like, up in smoke, so I start up to arguin' with busted radiators and it seems like that's what makes the dog eat my toothbrush.

A blizzard been livin' north of here some years now. Ever' winter it visits itself a different uncle. Christmas is how we count casualties. The reason of it has somethin' ta do with the way a kid don't know squat wakes up every mornin'. A dream with a shiny scar rolls up cigarettes in its shirt sleeve and . . . well, you know.

The birds they was chirpin' in that little stay-at-home dark they got that opens up just when you can see where you're goin'. Don't look at no past happenin's like that. Just what's comin'. It ain't like no print of some criminal's thumb provided any helpful clues to the more reliable patterns yer everyday asshole can find in the scattered bones.

So the family suffered and the elders shuffled out their desperate aging daughters. Weren't like it could do nobody no good. Not like that atall. Fact it was downright stu-pid. Blood simple. Ex-ces-sive. It got splintered into tinier and tinier disasters and we been listenin' to the cover-ups ever since.

In time the flood dried up. These things ain't really personal. Simple as that. The flood dried up.

And so this is where we are now. Seems like the body just flutters and rises. Mornin' spills.

Maybe none of us can really ever say we gone too far, but there's a point where what's happenin' cain't no longer see you and it'll do anythin' to keep its self alive.

Let's discuss the ways of it one more time and if that ice in yer glass sets off some tiny kinda accident, then let's us just pause there, way on up in that gettin'-in-yer-bizness-don't-need-us-fer-nothin' air. Back and back and between us. It's come so far now and you're the first loser to open it up like this.

Out at the field's end, sometimes you can see a white picket fence and swallows like tiny capes flappin' all sudden and small, away and away and away again in the floppy breeze.

I always wondered why the moon comes down silent and touches when you hold the cool handle of the plow and it still bein' only the middle of the damn afternoon.

July 4

Odd Farmer

Time to feed the newt. Shrimp on a finger and a fleeting fear. A momentary loss slips between distractions. What does time mean to a newt? I grow older while the creature crawls up my finger. Odd. Pleasant. The lumbering crawl of bad horror movies, the mechanical waddle of machines dragging through the swamp.

Once, many years before, a young boy, imitating a caterpillar, crawled under the wheels of my parked truck. I went into the house to fix lunch and cut myself on the can opener.

On the surface of my tongue the tiniest needles are drawing together the white mist of the distant forest. The next time I open my mouth, the words clear a place in the trees. I fold back the white blanket. I ask you in. I'm still asking you in.

If I can grow old enough, I could be the first. If I die young, I might live forever. These words have feathers and they live in the swamp. I want to be responsible for the stars, not quite eternal emissaries of lost causes.

Just then some friend clatters to a new position on my mountain. I'm standing there considering an animal's skull nailed to a fence post, something burning in the air, and the odd light.

I read somewhere that caribou climb houses. Always in Asia they are dancing on the roofs and climbing the houses. I don't know why I remember this.

The words pour out, a clatter of shiny river rock beneath the ocean. On the scholar's grave, a dead sparrow. I try balance. I try a row of big toes next to a row of thumbs.

But when the wind dies, the silence is uncovered. An arrangement of weeds inside the dream of weeds.

A tapping in the courtyard. Like claws. Like a closing door. Like one stone placed upon another.

Like the mute lives of ash in snow.

Like a secret endowment to the museum of breath.

And still no one notices a tree not falling.

Give it away, you earned it.

July 5

Never Any Doubt

It was a great day for mankind when a true doubter arrived, but of course we killed him. Electrical energy, rubber truncheons and forks were just some of the things this man could not understand using the contemporary logic and political principals we had offered him. A large quantity of Seneca oil was rubbed into the man's burns before he died and the young balding masseur they arrested was heard screaming, "You want a piece of me?" all the way to the fountain in the playa of failed revolutionary ideals, where he succumbed quickly, but the crows refused to pluck out his eyes, and some said it meant we had captured the wrong criminal.

The saliva of a suspiciously uninvolved crone was analyzed and the results remained ambiguous. Next the questioning authorities devised a new test. A pebble and a boulder were employed as measurements of the relative gravity of the situation by dropping them simultaneously from the top of the shortened retirement home, which grew to only a single story because, let's face it, no one wanted to climb the stairs, and since no one was arriving any faster at any conclusions because of this experiment, the result was an equal portion of unease for every participant.

Because everyone remained at this point unaware that anyone might be arriving at any conclusions prematurely, Tiffany, the doubter's estranged niece, rushed outside with her new double-barreled water gun in search of an intergalactic transmission code, a lurid pink catalog of doll museums, and a 76-acre Daughters of the Revolution amusement park in which to exercise her prerogatives and draw attention to her budding. She was approached by a young intellectual with a fawning and irresolute manner. She said No and it made him smile. He couldn't wait to get there. He had known that her refusal would be exquisite. Tiffany's software company hit the stock market big despite the revelation that she had never really intended to communicate with extra-terrestrials.

Meanwhile Tiffany's overlooked zipper mechanic gripped his wrench tightly. Being one of the most of us, he was prepared to attempt a generous dispersal of his dispersible potential. Something was certainly revealing itself, but it didn't know what it was. Of that there could be no doubt.

July 6

Button Baby's Response to the Mysteries of Life

It was written on a piece of paper found in the pocket of the used Levis he bought on Thursday. "The moon, too, sports a dog."

He decided to see if a blacksmith could explain it to him. "I would prefer to be feeding little children to hungry bears," said the blacksmith, "but I will think about your problem. It will not provide an easy solution, for the word 'sports' is very contemporary indeed." And with that the blacksmith went back to his anvil where he was pounding out the dents in a pair of biker earrings.

Button Baby asked his friend Alfalfa and Alfalfa sprouted saying, "Listen to the wind." So Button Baby followed the wind to a friendly dike at The Underground and the dike said, "Don't we all?" So Button Baby asked Lucy the Clever Errand Dog and Lucy brought him a pair of sunglasses and a water pistol. Button Baby asked The Bible Man who stood on the corner and The Bible Man thumped not his bible but his own thick forehead, saying, "Are we too not among the needful?"

Blood-thirsty mosquitoes were hovering near Button Baby's head. He removed the fish scraps from his pockets, but it didn't impress the mosquitoes. He thought maybe a maritime tailor could explain this discrepancy to him. The tailor was wearing a bracelet of thorns on his wrist, but he answered reasonably. "Would you like then some lovely cranberries?" Button Baby had heard of the method of teaching in which the teacher answered a question with another question, but it didn't seem to help. He thought about how blood was red and cranberries were red and he thought about how they were both wet and sticky and he thought about Thanksgiving and cranberries and how his blood relatives lived far far away and he was very very thankful, for they were truly bloodsuckers and made the mosquitoes seem almost erotic by contrast. But it did not help him solve his mystery.

And lo, a clandestine seal-eyed sloth of a prophet appeared in the middle of this modern world of ours and he be jivin' on the sidewalk and he be sayin', "I once lived in the city of No Thank You until the back of morning anticipated my competition with an emptiness divided by thirty-four brothers and I saw the light and I said, 'Which one, brother, which one?'"

Then Button Baby wore a little hat like a marker on his hunkered head. "And something I am not is there to greet me," he thought. "It feels transitional," thought Button Baby wistfully, but to what? He put a title on his under-hunkered forehead and ushered himself forth. The title read: Why Are You Still Doing This?

And Button Baby imbibed mightily and sprawled (let us be generous) languorously, with an unconscious tilt, his title still vivid on his forehead, and he tried to explain to himself in the middle of it all, "Some things I did were described by the baby man I found in my dreams and it seemed as if I had already done them. It seemed as if that made it more exciting. I was interested in the excitement. I was going to do some things to find it. The man's skin was cold. It excited me. He told me I could have whatever I wanted. I didn't know what I wanted. I tried a lot of things and I still didn't know what I wanted. I thought I would share a certain empathy with the man, but it was not the empathy I had been expecting. It was not the same fun that I had been expecting in this feeling sorry for him. It was something that was not like the something that I was like."

And when a smart-assed skateboarding semi-paraplegic apostle echoed by, way way outside the dream, Button Baby was again no longer awake to hear him say, "Because the moon sports a dog and the planets sport dogs and we're all little planets and we each of us sports a dog. That's just the way it is. Get a clue, dude." And the apostle shrugged and shook his shaggy head like an overwrought Beagle and wheeled himself spryly away to his surprisingly cherished little snotlings of yellow childwealth.

"A change in the discussion would be nice now," thought Button Baby, no longer sporting anything identifiable at all (he really did think that), "even if it's thoroughly inappropriate," but then Button Baby's been collecting his thoughts for a lifetime and Button Baby finds it difficult to fit into the container which still contains him.

July 7

No Longer in Residence

Choo Choo Davis, who was often angry, willful and disoriented, and as delicately boxed as Mr. Rogers in drag, went to live in the commune and it was not working out. While all about him were generous in their demeanor, unselfish, kind and patient (except for Slinky the Snake Boy, who grew more elusive by the hour) Choo Choo wanted to fight.

Something nonspecific, something flummoxed and geodesic, began brewing, and aromatic aprons of uncertainty flapped in the itch's window. Choo Choo was beside himself. Choo Choo was heated. Choo Choo was skulking. He had been in the neighborhood of likeness and he did not find himself. There were statues of the best clouds there that moved and appeared not to be statues. The life came in little expulsions like coughing, the eyes trying to see themselves. You get there by falling out and you try to be happy about it. Here a stubborn history of regret, there a consonance of indifference.

So Choo Choo chewed the summer dragonflies happily to death and wintered in the skylight, but he didn't harvest any blessed children. Local heroes, I'm told, appear symmetrical, and Choo Choo leaned a couple of different directions at once. Okay, maybe it's not much of an accomplishment, but it's certainly not ordinary.

I warned you in my own nonspecific way. Sometimes a fight's just the thing for luke-warm melancholia. Choo Choo's drenched now and Slinky's tied in his knot. They're hurling insults like hardened raisins. They're clad in white tights and purple padding. They're serious, but who believes them?

Yes, it was disturbing, but it came out surprisingly wedge-shaped and fit neatly in a pie tin. There was a lifelike quality to the experience. Thank goodness someone stole it from the windowsill.

July 8

What We Know About Ancient Religion

The farmers of long ago had to learn as slowly as we do, but they learned different things and didn't pretend they already knew them. In Figure 2 the man is pumping water by walking back and forth on a log. Figure 1 may have established how this is possible or it may simply be invisible to those who do not share his limitations. Perhaps we could agree with the man's reasoning if it were not for our calculatedly unassuming earthly assumptions.

When one admires the logic of weather, it becomes a perfectly natural thing to visit elders with their heads in the clouds for advice. In some cultures most of the men have been trampled and you have to go home without their cloudy breath, but sometimes a handful of acceptance can be derived from the enigmatic language and the witnessing of the candied shadows many aspiring poets like Turnbaum Fusty leave for the penitents to follow.

Some experienced farmers, it's true, raise things that are not food. If you visited one of their organic fire stations, you probably learned something about sticks. It is not necessary to collect such ambiguous implements in order to protect one's livelihood. The herdsmen may not have noticed that they were scattering seeds that might grow into devices of delicious adoration, but they knew the world would not stay as it was.

Although the necessary pigs can live in the forest, they prefer the farmer's mud, which is rich and redolent and quite deceptively carries no scent of impending disaster. "Not all important events announce themselves the way weather does," begins the advice one receives from men like Turnbaum Fusty.

Yes even the farmers of long ago knew that certain windy indulgences are best not encouraged in the heat of deprivation and it is unfortunate that we now speak of them in a manner that leaves them ambiguous and therefore no longer know what they really are so that we cannot warn the young of the constant dangers their parents thoughtlessly ignored.

How then does Turnbaum know that the nutritional milk of his reasoning is pure? If he merely gathers nuts and berries and mushrooms and speculations, can he survive unattended? What, then, could be the purpose of verbal reductionism? Perhaps Turnbaum only did these things because his beloved grandfather told him not to.

Our exemplary farmer of long ago, it is said, welcomed the ancient mud of sleep and hadn't yet attended his own ambition storms. He often warmed his cold feet on his wife's buttocks, but he also gave her a separate territory for her pride in the back of his mouth, where his newly discovered language dwelt. The complexity of these ownerships increased as the farmers freely gave away their bounty and shoveled the past over their parents.

Figure 3 shows the cages in another kind of personal crop rotation. Researchers who have studied these things are fairly certain that at least one variety of emotional maize must have been tamed a long time ago. An ancient legend, however, suggests that the recently rediscovered rites of the newly renamed Freudian Fertility Tree were originally ignited by the trading of corn-silk. Despite the frequency of such easily misunderstood reoccurrences, not all contemporary farmers have been accused of these clouds and the farmers of long ago left no record at all of their substantial influence on celestial evaporations.

"How is something doing?" I ask her, implicating our relationship to symbolic understanding of a more informal quality.

"I have been allowed to do this," she offers in assertive appreciation.

"I'm surely more indiscrete than that," I insist.

"I believe the absence to be angrier than the presence," she agrees.

Figure 4 helps to establish that the disorganization of my handshake was not useful.

Figure 5 features the external appearance of my internal gestures.

It's a little like the story of Medea's children twisting in the wind beneath departing stars, knotted to the straight branch of fate beside the crooked road. It's just that the crooked road looks straight if you consider it longer than necessary to pass it by.

July 9

Sometimes It Whistles

Sometimes it craves a good slap and hug.

It's summer and your top's down.

It's a filthy burden, but the oil's just right.

Your latest edible art seems to be breeding. It seems to be smoking a basket of parts. It wants to sign your agreeable face and surface.

Your head used to be smaller and the weather larger. We don't talk about the weather.

We saw grapes rivering the hillside and wanted to feed them. We saw rivers.

We lived like that. Yard after yard of intense heat. A light toasting. With the top down.

We made fish sticks, so we ate fish sticks.

Our life is superb. It's agreeably oiled and it's nasty and filthy and wonderful. It doesn't need any more oceans.

Sometimes it whistles and grapes. Sometimes it just grapes.

We saw trees. We saw a platypus chick annoying its mother in there where it's thickest. We saw slick suits exchanging looks in the closet, the same look you gave me yesterday after fifty-three years of marriage.

Why don't we try some of this on? It's easy. There's a trillion holes in the sky leased to a single universe.

The bright blood-rags sag softly from the roses. We're puddled in cardigans like cold fat bowls of fuzzy curd. There's a runt glacier descending.

Suddenly I'm about to walk right into your next life. Suddenly you're about to whistle, lips all about and sighing, willing to and what about this and that.

You can achieve the best results by not removing the body parts, so I wear my listening-head with its brighter reception.

Sometimes it needs a tickle and pinch. It's a tea I use to keep me awake when I'm sleeping. Sometimes just a sigh.

July 10

Dewlap

Okay, this one's mine. Curved like anticipation. A ripe certainty of tension and release. Never too far from the extremes, never one without the other, these expectant celebrations. A self-generating promulgation of celebratory unions. An ambiguous container filled with brilliant definitions of "container." A gravesite beneath a tasty blue plate of anticipated joy. The persistent foreplay of a delicious event which may not even know it precedes.

That's what makes for such a magnificent scene from the tower high above the street vendors. You don't have to look closely at the suffering to know it's beautiful.

This sort of thing makes me giddy. Like noticing the shoeshine boy is barefoot. My heart's little liquid legs tickled by a delightfully slurpy urge to roam, aflutter and astumble, nudged from its clockworks.

Listening to my memory of it, I realized it was a peculiar not-quite-yet kind of beauty which had addressed me, a crepuscular slice of the old tickleslap. You see, the market had fallen out of my travel-hungry body. The future was arriving too quickly. I felt like the dog that ate the winning lottery ticket.

Perhaps this is an indication that one could be permitted to leave without adequately digesting all the surprises. Perhaps one could spirit away the fussy high-stepping heart-deer along with the unrestrained stroking of carefully placed skinsocks, assemble something suggestive in leather over-bones, the way certain kinds of irretrievable departing beauties do.

The dog is listening now. The dog is leaning into the words. The dog doesn't know what you're saying, but the dog knows what you mean. Not just the end of something but the end of something too beautiful to be the end. And not just the end of something that beautiful, but the end of the start of something you can't live without. It nips at your heels as if you had been running away from the thing that you were chasing, its deliberate ruminant legs. And it descends from what you thought you were saying and sways from side to side and seems to speak of an ordinary endurance without reaching for the tongue.

July 11

A Stranger in the Mirror

And my friend is morose and I am morose, so we begin lying to the errant lexicographer of vicarious lifestyles, extraordinary crapulous fictions about the beautiful indulgences in our delinquent behavior, spawning and shaping the future to look like the past but without the necessary pain.

The first time I realized my heart was a delicate instrument, I wanted to hurt someone. Fortunately, the receiving beach was guiltless and I was forced to exist although I was filled with the absence beneath the drifting surface, as in "artificially inflated with emptiness," as in "full of one's missing self," as in a tidal mouse left open.

When I asked myself to make this terrible mistake, I said no, but it was too late. The mistake had already been given away and it wasn't so terrible, but the giving away part gave it back to its willing terribleness. Right now I can't remember what the terribleness was, but it was something I did before I was even finished doing it. Someday it will have to start being itself and then I will have to be there instead of here.

The details were unnecessary but pointed to by the participants.

There's a story like this in which you tell a story like this to someone who listens and listens past the allure of the inside story, which makes the story longer than it is and yours. There's an attraction to it though it doesn't stay on the page and it doesn't talk to you without asking. The asking is in a bottle and wants to come out because you want it to. It's like a medication that doesn't do anything to make you better but makes you better anyway.

Just then I realized I liked the sound of anguish in my voice. My friend Me seemed to be asking if I was dreaming. I didn't believe I was.

It's like the deeper meaning of a complicated experience. The moan lasts forever. I don't.

When the act is dead, my friend the performer, my friend the brilliant misdirected exhibitionist, like that sea creature that expels its guts when attacked, can simply offer more than I knew I asked for.

"That's not mine," he says with my voice. I can already see him telling me I'm not there. It's not clear whether or not I can be saved. It's not clear which one of us is the best person to fall for this.

July 12

Several Undocumented Instances

A new photograph of Picasso shows the artist at play in the heavenly fields of the bored. One of Diane Arbus shows her motionless at the end of a diving platform looking thoughtful. Perhaps she's decided that if you have been invited to speak, you may have less to say.

Here's something not previously used for this purpose: What good is an equidistant syrup of inactivity if a suitable match for such a slender existence cannot be found among the charitable donors?

Here's an implication not posted on the wishful thinking website: Why not terrify the complacent marginalia and move on to the future twilight of the recently declassified genetic instructions?

Besides, the trailerhouse could use a good hosing.

Take me, for example.

I collected virtually all the extant variations on The Legend of Wee Willie's Sword and Diane didn't even notice. (Why doesn't anyone ever wear a hat in this movie? And if they are not passing their diseases on to you, why are they not simply cooled and poured into compression molds?)

Here's something else: Diane was actually sitting at her desk. Her head was lowered over a pile of kidney stone specimens. The sickly birch tree at the window was at that time still struggling to grow. The neighborhood bully, who had tied a hamster to one of its branches, was oddly happy and already building a sound base of falsetto-singing congregational support. (I'm told you can usually recognize the most popular despicable villains by their singular shared fiendish laugh.)

Which had something to do with the way Picasso grew and grew and grew and allowed himself to be recorded for posterity, and the way sometimes he just played and came to the table with his shoes on.

Diane was still waiting. She did not discharge great puffs of steam.

There was a convenient trash can in the corner of the room.

These are also among the characteristics of a quietly effective grazing-couch or an attractively misplaced hunger artist. (You understand, don't you, that you don't have to sit on a toadstool to know it's a toadstool.)

And just when the Mongol invaders threatened to conquer all of Europe, Genghis Khan's death forced them to return to Asia where they were then able to attend to their beasts and their rebellious odors.

Clandestine among long lists of clouds and shorts they were.

These were people without restrictions as to their content. The animals required to separate them from their immediate ancestors, however, contained limitations of an instinctual nature. They could not be expected to process their content objectively. Some things in the landscape they were setting free while some others were just being thrown into place. Thanks to their initiative, some stones are escaping, though I don't know what they expect to find except some carefully placed markers that can't decide how much room to maintain in their longer fall to equal rest. And there's a kind of spitting this encourages that occurs unrecognizably as returning sustenance in the springtime.

Many of these inclinations are commonly found scattered throughout the populace in an age of stone. I'm not sure if I care if you want to notice, but there's something inside it that tells you what to do and you don't have to do it and that gives you choices.

Neither did they notice that the leaves pretended they couldn't speak and the grass just waved sadly as if something important was going away. It can likewise be helpful if you carry a smoothly drawn military badge. You can slip it in your pocket and stroke it. You can display it when confronted with demands such as "Hello," or "Do you have the time?" and it appears to move in a suspicious manner if you place your index finger beneath it and vibrate.

You think some words you've never used before might help, but because you've never used them, you forgot them. You think remembering what went wrong might help, so you do that, but it doesn't help because you don't know why it went wrong. Maybe you even suspect some other things went wrong at the same time that might not have anything to do with it and it would be a mistake to assume they wouldn't have happened otherwise. So you think some words you have used before to express this frustration.

Just as, in *1900*, Bertolucci's frog hat jumps several directions at once.

Nor do I always tell them that I have a broken leg. It's not mine, but I have it.

Nor do they resemble each other as seen from beyond the difficulty. You don't always have to have proof to become convinced that you can be intimate without the benefit of reasonable interpretations. The places I've gone to don't look like the places I've been.

I think it happened once, but it might have been a bunch of times before that when I was still trying to figure out what it was. After I figured out what it was, then I knew when it happened.

Nor do I pretend to understand the plain gray procedure of departing.

July 13

A Successful Businessman Takes Up Needlepoint

I don't know who I'm telling this to but I'm screaming the words are babies I want to step on them I want to hate my mother adequately because one of my neighbors is trimming his lawn and his smile is killing me I have to eat it I have to digest clippings at night because his wife saves daily obituaries of Kentucky blue grass tennis muscles gleaming brown I'd have to try to love her because I think I should want to and she wants to be able to say yesno just in time for the weather to drive me crazy with excuses this is America I don't have to go hungry it has to be this easy we have to be able to do something with our hands.

July 14

An Irrational Fear of Milking

The dairy industry is no longer located near the stockyards and packing houses, as it was in times of more limited bovine longevity. This creates a hardship for the farmers, who must keep everything alive or cut it into pieces themselves.

Naturally, the farmers are anxious to make a living. These men must plant seeds, cut hay, haul feed, pump water, build sheds, scratch themselves and judge literary contests in a timely manner.

The shading on some maps shows the most unimportant dairy regions in our country. In these areas, there is not enough bovine inspiration. So the farmers, who have learned by bitter experience to cater to what's known as "popular consumption," raise commercial writers instead. In England, the very same species has been taught to "articulate" punk culture in light of its many milky disturbances.

Some of these "writers," known in many areas as "innocents," are not consumed by the farmers directly but sold as "seekers," who have been raised organically and must root for their sustenance. A smart farmer knows that such seekers are not very good to eat and must be given cod-liver oil and ambiguous pronoun references to survive. He will protect them from the hot sun and not let them run about too much. When they become annoying enough, the farmer will sell them. He is sorry to see them go because when they remain on his farm, they help to keep the soil rich by questioning it with adjectives.

We might think that it would be much easier for the farmer to raise beef, but do you know how much land is needed to raise beef? Writers, on the other hand, are easily taught to find suffering honorable and can be kept in stalls with little more than a pencil.

So the next time you're roasting an ox, consider how much more productive you could be if you were to take advantage of the opportunities innocents offer to provide alternatives to our reliance on less self-engaged ruminants. Perhaps you have heard about the colonies set aside by the modern dairy industry where high-profile innocents are carefully groomed, photographed wearing milk mustaches, and trained to be critics. Here the courageous farmers experiment, training the innocents to milk themselves. They expect soon to produce them as a form of self-slaughtering protein.

July 15

The Legend of Kudzu Cottongloves

Kitty Cottongloves lived on a plantation in the South. She had a very very tired old mama who just might up and die any minute. Least that's what Kitty's papa always said.

Kitty had tight little brown curls all over her itty bitty little dispro-portionate head, and she had soft little brown curls popping up where she knew she was going to be a woman soon. Mr. Borden at the feed store wanted to marry Kitty, but Kitty's papa said she ought not to marry anyone with a boil on his nose.

One day Kitty climbed up on the kitchen counter to get the maple syrup and fell right over backwards onto her head. "Lawsy me," said Kitty's Mammy, "but you sho' do know how to make a old Mammy's heart leap right up and pay 'tention." She had herself a gangsta boyfriend and loved to make fun of the Old South.

Kitty's papa was worried about Kitty, but nothing seemed to be broken and pretty soon Kitty was busy being as contrary as ever she was.

One day when Kitty's curly brown puppy, Kudzu, was trying to teach Kitty to herd cattle but Kitty thought he was playing fetch, Kitty's confusion decided to take her puppy for a picnic to the old swimming hole.

When they got there, Kitty's puppy was way too excited. Kudzu was all over the place. Kudzu was rampant.

Kitty was busy looking at lilacs and morning glories and clover and the rich brown scum on the surface of the water. She was busy putting furniture in her imaginary new house in the woods. For these things did become of her that perused them.

And poor Kudzu. Suddenly by being everywhere, Kudzu was also nowhere at all. Finally Kitty stepped out of the imaginary house she was living in and could not see her puppy anywhere and she searched and she searched, but no soft little puppy curls emerged from the primeval greens and browns of the misguided picnic excursion.

Kitty looked and looked and then she looked some more, and several days later a big bald-headed black man with a soothing voice found Kitty and took her back to her papa and the doctor put her right to sleep.

When Kitty woke up, Kitty's papa was there and he had some bad news about Kitty's Mama, but Kitty just wanted to know, "Where's Kudzu? Where's Kudzu?"

Nine months later, when the nurse shaved Kitty to have her baby, Kitty looked at the tight little brown curls falling on the floor and started crying, and she didn't stop until her baby boy took over the crying and sure enough, his pink little head had the ever-so-faint start of even tighter little brown curls on it.

Kitty never did remember who the baby's papa was and she never did fall off the kitchen counter again. But baby "Kudzu" knew and imitated the stranger in all his features although he never spoke of him. No one ever really understood how it happened, but Kudzu was everywhere and sure enough Kudzu grew up to be the new owner of Mr. Borden's feed store where he hauled fifty pound sacks of feed around all day on his curly-haired back till he was sixty-eight years old.

And Kudzu Cottongloves II became a very famous boxer indeed. But of course he changed his name. Wouldn't you?

And Kitty? Kitty lived to be seventy-nine years old and at the rest home when her younger son visited, she would say, "Where's Kudzu? Where's Kudzu?" and she wouldn't sound sad one little bit. Everyone at the nursing home thought she was going senile.

And one day after his Mama died, Kudzu Junior looked in the mirror and laughed and said, "Where's Kudzu?" and the very next day he was dead. They buried the little bugger right next to his Mama and the leaves on all the plants by the graves turned brown and curled up tight like little brown hairs and fell off.

That's when little Kudzus started popping up everywhere and the bunch of them just kept on making themselves over and over again and damn near strangled everything the way too many babies prit near always does no matter what color they is. Leastways that's what the first creepers say and they's a lot a creepers, a whole lotta creepers.

July 16

Heritage

Forever and today in the far far west, there appeared a surly wide hedgehog of a man. He was known far and wider for his heroic hair and predictable accomplishments. A large breathy mound of them.

And humble? You couldn't begin to. You could barely. But you could lavish praise and he'd answer, "Yes, I have breathed some fortunate air."

In those days there was always another small town hurting. And when the long day tried invading the wound, the wound tried to cause a neighborhood. Times like this, he'd often instigate a blowout in the dressing room, hitch up his saturated stinkpants and hero the tall tale of his misfortune right on into a healthy glob of excessive sympathetic teetering.

A couple more invasions of privacy and the perspective ripens. Some tall fella named "Fella" was seen deliberating delight out near the highway where the porch mingles with the sagebrush. There's those that say he fathered a couple of itinerant ethnologists.

Yes, the heroine's here and already very married. Her husband, Mr. Apples, spiders her silly adventure door with a hugely sprawling kiss. He used to limit that kind of thinking to egg-shaped candles.

Finally, his desirable breasts arrived. Fortunately, they were not as big as hers and they were able to stay together like twins.

Perhaps the real situation's over already, but there's always a party afterwards. Mr. Apples knows that.

Eventually the affectionate dogs will be taught to stop chewing on the legs of our trusted companions and some contemporary Tonto investigating the oil lease will challenge them with timeless aphorisms and modern contractual exclusions.

You'll have to decide when they leave. There's always a pink baby-bottom morning of promise and generous bird-food allowances laced with a rich enchanting smell of diapers and burnt toast. Truth is it was one of the situations in which irony didn't count, and the hero had already been voted most likely to be serious.

Which made him funnier.

Which made him more serious.

Which made him remember where he'd been before he'd been there again.

July 17

An Explanation of and Justification for the Salary Increase of Class II Engineers Following the August Sixth Amtrak Derailment Near Sioux City, Iowa

Someone who is not your mother sits beside you on the train and complains about your behavior. You have not done anything terribly wrong, of course, as you have not done anything terribly wrong many times in the past, but neither has your behavior been exemplary. The only real answer to her complaint is, of course, your father, who this woman who is not your mother has never met. A young child, who is neither you nor a representation of you, gives the woman a balloon and she acts surprised, though she is not. You have, of course, grown into a very large and dignified lamb in disguise, who is responsible for the progress of this very train on which you have not really chosen, but been required, to ride, as a symbolic gesture of your competence. The young child begins a rather lengthy discourse on the advantages and disadvantages of modern modes of transportation and there is really nothing left for you to say but toot toot. You cannot bring yourself to say it, so the train refuses to move. The child, who is not you, offers the woman, who is not your mother, several orange slices, and you still cannot say it. The oranges are very sticky and the balloon string gets very sticky and you cannot say it. The woman, who is not your mother, lets go of the balloon string. The child, who is not you, is outraged and huffs and puffs and chugs out of his berth. The train still is not moving and the child goes looking for prophetic grasshoppers. "Toot! Toot!" whispers the child as the grasshoppers go whirring across the tracks. You look to see if the woman has heard the child, hoping to tell her the amusing thing the child has said, but she smiles and whistles for the conductor, who takes your ticket and waits like everyone else for the train to move, which it does now, as if it had heard the child's whisper. You, however, are not waiting for the train to move. You never really were. You are waiting only for an adequate explanation of why the train was not moving. The child understands this and hands you the balloon as the train begins moving. You write "Toot toot" on the balloon and release it into the overheated air from the passenger window. You have no idea why your laughter is chugging away into the night. You have no idea how much you will pay to sleep next to it. You have no idea why your mother is not the woman who acts like your mother.

July 18

Who the Hell Does He Think He Is?

The edge of the axe is fat and blue. It hurts more like that. The woodsman has been pursuing fleeing oranges since noon. He isn't a short man. Don't give him any blueberries.

Don't give him your name. Don't give him anything. The edge of his finger is fat and red. It doesn't remember any organizations. It doesn't have to bleed to miss the paradoxical blessing of your darkened sympathy. It doesn't have to swim.

The woodsman still hasn't caught up with the oven. He still hasn't exercised any vegetables.

O but you can be sure he's going to. You can be sure of that.

O, O, O but the pain is so entirely terrestrial.

It's not enough that he grew up. It's not enough that he whimpered.

You see, I was talking to Mildred the other day and she told me I should invest in sharpeners. She told me I was under-represented. So I represented her good. Right in the dark forest with the woodsman still pursuing oranges.

The woodsman doesn't believe in scar tissue. He doesn't believe in tangellos. There never has been a catalyst worthy of his innocence.

But don't give him anything, okay?

Slick eyes and dusty fat. That's what it means to those of us who grew up with the slimey bugger.

I don't know if this is the time to tell you, but old people have been growing faint. I guess the woodsman's enduring innocence frightens them. They retreat into their departing lives. Become under-represented. Acquire small unhealthy pets and godparents and cigarette burns and annoy people with them. Live in a couple of narrow rooms with green ceilings.

Don't give him strawberries. Don't give him squat.

Because the trees are not as frightened as you might think.

Because the fleeing oranges have been escaping for centuries.

Because the edge of the axe is so fat and blue.

July 19

Visitors

While the visitors were lying to the maid about the upholstery stains, the residents were talking about telegraphs and flagrant horses and a variety of revolutionary wheat that molds itself to your nutritional needs.

That isn't all.

Billy's mother had washed the heavy woolen socks. A red door had been constructed in the blue wall. The sad competition of isolated street-lights had been derived from a relationship so deprived a breadline was forming at its crotch.

Instead of grieving, I built a mechanical heart.

That's just what happened.

There were already small miracles in the puddles at the bottoms of the abandoned tires, but we ignored them. We were incapable of fealty. The visitors didn't notice this.

Billy's mother said, "Hooey." She said, "Hooey." She just said, "Hooey."

Then Billy played with an oceanic dog and rubbed his hands in the dirt and vaulted over the distractions. He wasn't about to be dissuaded by any Gods or Goddesses or dwarfs or commercial stimulation devices or accountants. He wasn't about to trade his leather for fish because sometimes a fisherman wants the leather but Billy doesn't want a fish and then what?

My heart seemed to be ratcheting and saying, "Hatchets, beads, shells and animal teeth."

And then it said, "Hatchets, beads, shells and animal teeth and copper coins."

And then it just said, "Hatchets, animal teeth."

I thought it was saying that it wanted more reindeer skins than Billy and his family could possibly use. The transaction had become suspect. The transaction had become inordinately mechanical. The transaction had become residential. The visitors responded with several applications of furniture remover.

This kind of justice was perceived as merely insistent.

The visitors rode up and tapped out a code on the streetlights for the divorce tour. Their hiking boots smelled of Swedish pumpernickel. A gardener holding a black bag with a hole in it was sniffing the inside of the maid's glove to rid his nostrils of the undesirable.

"Hooey," said Billy's mother. She just said, "Hooey."

I believe she said this because the blue door had been constructed in the red wall. I believe she said this to get even with the mechanical heart. I believe she said this to discourage the argument from the dog. I believe she said more than Billy and his family wanted.

I visit an expert on religion and the stone tells me I'm too impatient. By the time he finishes telling me this, I'm old and patient, so naturally I'm thinking about death. The stone tells me I'm already dead and goes back to doing what stones do, which takes a lot longer than what I was doing and seems to be a whole lot more rewarding.

So I read my own scars and called the uncalled for an ending.

I realized I'd solved a lot of things that weren't really problems.

The visitors spilled. The visitors gawked. The visitors didn't notice.

July 20

My Response to Your Response

I couldn't have known you would do this. So much mushroom dust on the mantlepiece. So many razorbacks in the dustbin. I enjoyed the patio furniture, but everything else was disgusting.

A tiny window of children's knickers teased at my own curious past and I wondered why the tree trunk was scarred.

Surely, from this vantage, you can see you were wrong.

And Little Gregory wasn't guilty as charged, but guilty nonetheless. Like all of us.

Whence comes the galaxy we actually live in.

You'd be one sorry slicker if you never knew you goosed the chicken.

It wasn't very old and I wanted it to visit our luncheon.

We were sharing. We were expectant.

July 21

A Story About Water and Light

A voice cloaked in a light so blinding no one could mistake it for religion spoke to him about his loneliness. This happened next to the perpetual orphanage of the river in a landscape that swallowed the sky. He had been a man so sad he could live in a wound, his need nailed to a post in an open field, mice already nesting in its sagging assumptions.

O but such a vegetable joy! She humbled and pleased and terrified him.

"If a river sings, drink it. Make love to it inside you."

Was it his voice?

"Or if it is a shadow that you make, then hold it, close, as in, I shadow you, which grows larger than you do before this darkness like worn leather, this shadow swallowing an owl perched in the crook of a dying oak."

Her touch the shadow's lip, the kind of woman who looks radiant in her husband's flannel shirt. Words roll in her mouth like peach bits.

Imagine her wanting you to want her, you wanting that to last, your desire to become that watching.

The son he never had stood there with his arms folded, his large hands curled against his body, testifying relentlessly to an assignation of weather or fate or something else beyond decisions.

And the voice came back damp and bright. You heard it in the trembling at the end of a long path through the trees, and when your girlfriend first let you and her breath caught, and when your mother tried that first time to tell you of your father's cancer and again when her own bloomed.

Love, death, cruelty, kindness, it doesn't seem to matter, as long as it startles you in your ordinary footsteps, holds back the moment, with you in it.

When he had died a great distance, he spoke to her about the cemetery. They agreed to continue, but the bloodsmoke that shoveled from her eyes surprised him. She was ahead of him. She was further demonstrated.

She could only be happy when she was sad.

The end was not darkness, merely a light looking for rest. A crack in the closet door. Made of words. Bundled together to form children. Which are thoughts come alive. Which grow stronger than either of us in the wet light before the dark.

July 22

Wounded Landscape with Recovery Figure

Fallen snow in the dark like a tremendous horizontal lamp. Perhaps it's the right evening. Perhaps it's the right life.

Because a man looking for nothing continually finds it. Because the blaze of midafternoon silence on the summer lake reappears in the winter dark, so still you can once again dive into it and make the sky open.

And the cold night welcomes this, persuaded by its own answers, inhuman enough to save us, a universe passing through a universe.

So I went inside the memory, carrying a cloth bag full of glass eyes. I collected ashes and heard a rumor of children wild to gather mushrooms.

The only fine and tearless story worthy of the world you're seeking is still yours, a brown stone, complacent and hard.

Because the bronze of river mud at sunset is also the moist hollow of an unspoken word. Something quiet and alone, craving the savage touch of a gentle hand.

A meal of wind and sky, smoke at twilight and the lights on in the empty barn. An old man with a wart on his index finger stands by a well staring off across the distant fields.

Each summer the quick swallows tug you into the air as they pass. You belong to everything you notice, a stunned believer, an accomplice.

A ladybug falls on the water in the bucket as the old man turns to his inner task. Something dangerous in the lungs, like air.

Partridge are feeding in the wheat. Cattle are thumping against the gate. The collie pup has a broken ear, hoof-cut, loose and flapping like an odd funny hat.

Dust to dust and day to day. The sun sparkles back as another farmer urinates in his field.

So I ask this friend to untie his shoulders. I expect mountains to move with the shadows. My own feet will eat water. This way I enter the landscape.

Friend, farmer, you accomplish me.

I have no smile for the new silence, only this convergence, this freedom, and a sudden desire to breathe stones. The doors are all open, the rooms empty.

Another heart is forming around the dagger.

July 23

Ars Poetica

I don't intend to discuss this, but you may listen. When you do, you will have disappeared from your life. As I have now disappeared from mine.

Don't be afraid. This could be beneficial. It could be a way of saying I love you to some part of yourself caught snooping. When you find a door, open it.

This is no place for fear. This place is a palace, filled with emptiness and splendor, a place to come to even though it has no answers.

It didn't intend to, but it took over.

I'm listening. Are you the one speaking?

Are you a rug or an umbrella? Are you the stone floor of the old house it rests in? Here it comes with its robe open and its limbs askew. Is that you?

I'm listening. My day and my day and my day, your speech relaying.

O ordinary, need I address you so? Are you my firmament or my cement?

I was not made by this. That's how I live here.

July 24

Safety

His hand didn't work like a claw. But his feet did. There weren't any shoes. It's not something you should reveal.

A lumpy embarrassing dream about a finger stuck in a bottle.

You see, I didn't want to be a good boy. My dance kit was full and I was bearing down like a block of ice on Bobo's wheelchair.

Bobo was holding his elbow while waving franticly like a child who thinks he's been doing something too long. The bug killer was snapping like a tiny irresponsible sun, the only one available. All I could see of Bobo was the reflecting glint off the spokes of his wheelchair and the frantically waving arm with the cupped elbow holding it.

"Bobo?" Softly I said it, like I was showing respect because I realized the way I came at him so fast could have been threatening. And because it's hard to call a man in a wheelchair Bobo.

Safety came out of the house with a flashlight and shined it on Bobo. By then Bobo was eating something, lifting it gently from his dead lap. He was eating pictures of food. It scared me.

Safety was wearing a bathrobe. She was wrapping the cloth of her belt around her wrist like a ragged old rope. She turned into the light from the screen door and hung the robe across the porch rail. Now she was wearing a halter top. Just a halter top. She stood there, undecided about something, her holstered breasts riding high above the bare expanse below, mean little knots in the halter straps like clenched muscles.

I imagined I looked like a kid caught smelling his neighbor's laundry basket. I pulled at the hair above my knees. My shorts felt stiff and I thought about how they didn't move with my legs. I was thinking about that and I was pulling at the hair above my knees. I saw this man in a window and I thought about grabbing him and saying, "Oh, I'm so sorry." I was afraid to move. I saw myself carrying a body around like a suitcase so I didn't move.

It's not hard to know when a man's afraid, but it's hard to say what he's afraid of.

Eventually I had to think about Safety again and she still wasn't moving towards me. A cat rubbed against Safety and she bent over at the waist to pet it. She could have kneeled down, but she didn't.

Bobo was waving again and I said his name louder. He didn't stop waving. I said his name again and he didn't stop waving.

I said to myself, "Safety isn't available." I said it, but I didn't believe it.

Right then I wanted to pet the cat. So I did. I stroked it carefully.

I still felt like a block of ice with its valves knocked off, but I was melting. Bobo's hand was working, but his feet weren't going anywhere, hooked around something in the air I couldn't understand. It made me think about my body and I looked at it in the window reflection, and it wasn't my body anymore. I didn't want anything to do with it. We don't expect ordinary things to happen at such times, but they do. Safety knew that and she needed some ordinary. But she wasn't acting very ordinary.

I took off my shoes and I felt the wet grass. I squeezed it and pinched it and looked for comfort with my toes.

Bobo was still waving. Bobo's cat was purring. It's not something you can keep to yourself. It's not something you can attend to without noticing the presence it implies.

I waited because it was what I knew how to do.

Safety was still a long way off.

It's true that Bobo likes to refer to his pants as trousers to make them seem more substantial. The man inside me would approve if I could find him. I'm beginning to think he's been seeing someone else.

July 25

The Gospel of Bees

When Ivan and I choked the doctor, several peahens and a rodeo named George witnessed the escape of medicine from the celestial repository. Another mystery of the bees was discussing who may or may not be the father.

Because this is Argentina and Ivan is lonely, the tiny storm of rebellion repairs the damage done by George's rejection, the early stars deposited in the celestial clown's ear not withstanding.

Listen, one of these men is so crooked he can eat soup with a corkscrew. He may even live without a name in a drop of blood under a bird's wing. And despite the fact that Ivan had only one good hand, the thick, twisting bull failed to throw him from the surface of the known contingencies.

It has been my intention to give you these words like chunks of meat, but it turns out more like a withdrawal that caresses, containing a young boy and his wounded bird. To recover the essence from the body is the goal of all religious singing and it fails miserably, yet the effort remains invigorating.

You see, the doctor is writing a novel like a beehive. He touches it gently with his cane each night before the celestial rodeo while the peahens are settling in for some unexpected dreams. Something about a faithful horse and another country. Something about a longing.

You see, happiness is easier if you remove the wax coat from Argentina. The clown's floppy ears often help to save the riders from being trampled by the stars. It appears the bees have always known this, but they refuse to levitate further. George has created another event from it involving circling and the amount of time you can sing with a rope while gathering escaping flowers. Perhaps Ivan has interpreted the phenomenon as fatherhood.

I have no intention of granting a second life to the doctor. You can often hear the bees speaking of it. You can witness the gathering at the hive where the fallen stars are making honey.

July 26

The Miracle of the Grapes

The children are flying. It's a long steep road to the cathedral and they might have been late. Soon the cemetery will pass beneath them. Oxen on the road will shake their great necks as the children pass. The lines in father's face lean to the left. His eyebrows curl wildly and point to the sky.

A donkey loaded with baskets tethers father to the earth. It's been a long time since he was a child, but he will be one again soon. Outside the cathedral sleep a straw hat and a tuba, abandoned. To leave them like this means something else might come along. And yoked to the road come two sad uncles, a pig savaged between them on a pole.

Now the vineyard begins rising to meet the children. The rest of the earth comes with it. The grapes are no longer attached to the hosts, their skin removed to make them speak sweetly. A great kindness appears to inhabit father's elderly clothing. We have been given one more day. I count all the way to clouds before I lose track. It's what father wants them to do for him that speaks.

July 27

Who Gazes at the Stars Raises God from His Shoulders

A woman lives under the sidewalk in front of the driveway. She is not as flat as you might expect. Right now we're nearly in love.

Listen, Scooter, I'm not afraid of death and I know too much. I can appreciate things. A delicious hairy declivity. An unintimidated absurdity. A rehabilitation program of divinatory excess. A dandified reluctance to fully engage. A delirious snotpopping delight of proliferations. I can feel forbidden pleasures questioning the monument I carry for a soul. It hurts and it's not mistaken to love. I know that much.

My people gathered and my people listened. Their legends were being discussed without benefit of authority.

Her hands grasped like the feet of birds. She clutched the bone-fort of her own recumbent body. She remembered a time of glaciers and hunger.

Listen, Scooter, I know what you're thinking. You're wrong. The abyss which is falling through us, the ancient blue sky, they are not clues to the escape but props for the inner eyes, focused on the approaching distance.

First, the darkness must grow. Then the river at the stone's door has something cold to say. The smoke represented how much desire was escaping, like some mystical cloud talking in its sleep, like every day you're alive. A mouthful of moonlight from the silent pond.

The cure is incomplete, as all recoveries from life must be.

July 28

Waking

Late at night the cat translates a Persian novel while the moon serenades a bottle of milk, rubbing against the doorsill, one more measured portion of the endless caress.

A wing of breath from the cat's mouth wakes me.

Then a quiet cry not of fear but surprise draws me out onto the lawn, leaving you asleep while I pursue the familiar strangeness. A light upstairs in a neighbor's window could be an old man reading or a young boy satisfying his curiosity.

I will give you the ribs of a dried-up lake. The skull at the bottom I will keep for myself. To drink from.

If the sheep wish to follow me, I will not question it.

I had forgotten the way childhood uncertainty can alter the smell.

And I was concerned about kissing, the way it can fill you up and no more room for leaving.

The classroom in your body won't wait for rain. The children are thirsty and the lake is gone now.

But I will give you my small liquid furnace by way of introduction.

I have no desire for a life steeped in reverie. I'll settle for that desert motel flickering in the distance like an invitation. I'll settle for a bandaged guitar case and a few large birds, the ones rumored to harbor dead uncles and tiny collections of angels. These I can use to wedge the door.

I won't imagine the slow scuffle of aluminum claws in the bedroom wall. I'll keep such fears tiny and cold. A toy funeral home. I'll welcome the wounded music and smell the threat of life in the dry air. Even in The Book of Passion and Forgiveness there is no prayer for self-pity.

It's enough to smell the approach of rain when there is no rain. It's enough to hear the flap of sheets on the empty clothesline. The stillness recites tomorrow's lessons. Today I am arrived. I don't need clouds to tell me there's no one here.

July 29

Notes for a Folktale

Lopez does not try to stop the ants. They come into his house and they go under his clothing and Lopez does not try to stop them. When Lopez goes to the village for supplies, the people believe he is a very brave man to suffer like that and not to complain. Now the friends of Lopez have something with which to bargain for attention in the villages of their friends.

Lopez goes home and his beans are doing very fine. After a while the ants leave and it is time to harvest the beans and many people have come to see the ant man and Lopez does not wish to be rude but he has beans to harvest. That is the way it is with ants. That is the way it is with beans.

July 30

Cultural Bias

Little Nonsense put on his tuxedo, sat in a corner and felt sorry for himself. He was not available for comment.

Weasel Eyes was hopping up and down on his bicycle. It was an ethnic dance with deeper psychological consequences.

Shot Me, the dead black and white kitten, was testing the tread of all-weather radials at the four way stop by the new tasty sawdust hot dog emporium. One of the employees picked out the extraordinary bullet when the cat's thickness no longer exceeded the bullet's. He put it in a medicine bottle with a little colored water and let the sun find it on his windowsill.

Kick Me and Little Cloud Animal were playing in the dirt. They were making muddy gingerbread and giving it to anyone who came by until they ran out of water and the man at the gas station across the street wouldn't let them have any more. Kick Me wanted to kick that man and when he thought of it, it made him laugh because he was developing a sense of irony. Cloud Animal thought it was a better idea to urinate on the sidewalk. They didn't have to be back at the detention center for another whole hour.

"My head made a mistake," said Little Nonsense finally to Wet Willie Winkie. Wet Willie gave Little Nonsense a furry ball and went away. Little Nonsense smiled and smiled and waited for the furry ball to run across the room to play with him. Furry balls don't do that. "My head made another mistake," said Little Nonsense.

Shoot Me Too, the dead black and white kitten's little sister, was collecting fish bones by the market when a prospector shot her with a tiny crossbow as part of a medical experiment. She didn't die, but she didn't live happily ever after either.

Little Nonsense took his tuxedo off and refused to attend the interview. He commented on his unavailability. Weasel Eyes insisted that kicking the interviewer in the head was part of the dance.

Shoot Me Also, the dead black and white kitten's sister's little brother, looked like a drowned rat, but nobody knew why. The hot dog salesman took him home, put him on the windowsill and waited for the moon's opinion.

Little Nonsense decided to avoid corners altogether. It was deep into summer. The air was thick, the sun was pouring and the journalists were tired. Little Nonsense noticed this and it wasn't easy to feel sorry for himself anymore.

So he did this and he did that and he did this again. His implication's were astonishing. His implications were just beyond belief. So he didn't believe them. And that didn't stop them. It didn't stop his implications. The journalists dug them up and detained them. They considered further implications of the implications and pretty soon they left Little Nonsense behind, where he danced and danced and forgot all about his implications, which had been given to attention seeking devices known as attachments, which Little Nonsense refused to open although others remained fascinated by the damage they could cause.

July 31

Ripples in the Glass

He calls it pride, but it feels like fear. As if the shadows of thought could be gathered this way, ripple against ripple, the lives within their life together.

Love doesn't exist. Not without us. There is no Love is. It must be made, with or without the body it comes in.

Pride radiates like a heat mirage from the familiar chills they used to view their world. Masters of deception, enamored of their gifts. Gods sipping colored lights.

Sunrise pours over the mountains and clouds, a great streaked froth of godspew, its patience melding and giving itself away in the wonderfully misspent morning.

I can't tell you enough about it. You'll have to finish. You'll have to dance.

August

August 1

It Could Make You a Little Sick

The bent man leaned on his scythe, sighed and sighed again. "Why am I so tired?" he wondered, while the wheeling dreams of the darkness surrounded him.

In the last days a kind of distinction had befallen him. He seemed separate. He was waiting and very very tired. He was cutting hay and he was sneezing and aching and he was alone. Very. Until Stella.

When the storm arrived, so did Stella. Stella's finger was bleeding. Stella's life was bleeding.

"I'm not afraid to do it again," Stella said to no one in particular, but it was the bent man who was there to hear it.

"Is light a virtue or a weight?" asked the bent man.

Way up in the heavens the current ache of the darkest hour was listening to the man in the moon. He was a little sick.

"Why do you ask me that?" said Stella, bleeding more angrily now.

"I'm getting so dusty I can't shine anymore," said the man.

"We'll just see about that," said Stella, hiking up her skirt.

The bent man straightened. It was predictable. It was polished. It was too damn easy.

So they struggled for a few years.

So then they set up an antique store in the garage. They tried to find the human in it.

One day a customer with a wooden arm came to pick up a butter churn and he said as he loaded the cracked wooden albatross into his turquoise green Ford Bronco 4x4, "Is light a virtue or a weight?"

Stella beamed.

The bent man said, "Perhaps we should file a petition."

The Bronco galloped away.

Way up in the heavens the old ache of the darkest hour polished the pool of tears the man in the moon had left before escaping to a remote villa in Argentina.

The police were nowhere to be seen.

The scythe was never recovered.

It doesn't really matter that it's true.

August 2

Enough

She was carrying a single tomato in the left cup of the turquoise brassiere she had removed. There was a pair of bright yellow underwear in the pear tree.

She had not yet realized she was going to leave the husband with a mind like a bulldozer and a heart like a wren. She was summoning the green creature inside. She was acknowledging the violent sunset and feeling without thinking that between her legs lies the happiest dockside dive on the face of the earth. A delighted raunchy exuberance.

What did his mother tell him about this? Without a single word, she sat, self-satisfied, behind the door he had taken a lifetime to open.

Could he offer anything without shame? The compact and delicious affluence overwhelming her. He can think of it only as loss. Exile. An exquisite Argentina of the throat overthrows the explanation, to which he still clings.

August 3

Don't Tell

A tiny sound. Broken. Another.

Ants are secrets. Not many different tiny little secrets, but the same one, again and again.

An ant is a rude kiss, one you thought you didn't want, but now that it's here, you're not so sure. Why should you find that compelling?

Kiss him again. Gone.

How many wounds does it take?

A graceful increment of disappointments.

And now there is so much air between. You can't breathe that much. (This takes place in the stomach.)

I don't know why I looked in the closet because I didn't leave it there.

Guilt: The more I learn about you, the less you belong. I used to wonder about your singing before I got to know you. I didn't understand you arrive in pieces that don't fit together and leave like the stunned life of the party who broke and needed comforting and finally disappeared when we started having fun again.

Between then and after there is still a moment beyond.

To keep it from becoming a public moment, you'll have to surrender its contents. One and one and one the ants arrive, but we can't tell them apart. They're all one mistake and then another. Even if it's the same one. They can't be taken back, but they can carry something away, and they can happen over again.

One way to close my eyes is to see the same thing everyone else sees.

August 4

A Long Uneven Row of Delicious Beetles

Which reminds me of the time I asked a cowboy where to find the new frontier. He suggested I ask a cricket for a moment's peace, but I couldn't find one. I found a lizard and questioned the nervous creature about renewable tails and then I looked for something to keep me going at an abandoned gas station with a hungry dog.

I was surprised by the celestial terror of white clothing in the moonlight and I was taken aback by its distant and bitter joy. I experienced it as a repentant geometrical form.

I witnessed a woman participating in a silly little flute song. It made me conditional. It made me anticipatory. It made me several directions at once.

She loved her arms. I could see that. She flung them about like birdfood.

I had received quietly suggestive prizes for my staunchly uncompromising inconsistency. I had given up less beribboned tenacities. I was becoming well received if not fully welcomed. I was unavailable to stunning compromise, but I managed to hear this one unattached voice. Like something tentative hidden inside a dodgy piece of transient clothing.

The patient cowboy didn't answer this time, but I could hear the fetid reek of primeval mud in his relevant silence. An ancient variety of innocence. You can find other examples easily on the open plains, where crickets abound. Pay attention to the rain patterns.

Which led me to the conclusion that flute songs are pleasant but not necessary. Perhaps I could listen selectively with my absence.

The water that gets inside me stays longer now. Sadly, my clothes still fit. (When I was almost home, the almost spoke to me.)

I'm happier now. I'm alive. I'm alone.

I did not happen in that order.

Monuments came later, after the meaning was gone.

August 5

We Lost But We Still Live Here

Try waiting for the conquering army, rucksack filled with pillows of darkness, as if the arrival could be as ordinary as sunset.

Your night wounds don't have to be displayed like appetizers. It's a time inbetween for noticing the way things fall from the trees, little doors and little windows. Hold one up and decide. What do you have to say about tomorrow?

Now try the world inside the world we live in. The window is open and lets the enemy know what I haven't been doing. I don't speak inside because all the words belong to my parents. Painful vegetables and silence eating itself.

The difference between the humble and the undiscovered.

Some pieces of the meaning had fallen off. I had been deciding to watch them for a very long time. The clouds in my closet appeared to be my body's thought and it lingered in the marrow. I'm delighted that it knows not how to leave me. There is a wind, but it's resting.

Yes, we stopped there and stopped there, you and I, nervous and excited, like a jewelry store. Composed of an otherness. Powdered skin and fresh ovens. Roasted pink and rubadubbed. Flibberjabbered out and out. Such a git we was. This is me, we said, this is more than me, this is me before I get there. A couple of chairs crouched and waiting to receive the adoration of random pebbles.

I thought to myself even as it was happening, "He's got his hands inside the thing, doing something private."

When the grasshoppers came, we called them villagers.

Pillaging won't be necessary.

August 6

Separation

A drop of water sat down in the living room and tied its shoes. One of the breathing ones looked at the drop of water and said, "The clouds are very beautiful today, are they not?"

"I don't have to be part of anything I don't want to," replied the drop of water.

"I hope nothing falls out of the sky on our heads," said another one of the breathing ones.

"Was that an oblique reference to my sacred brethren without whom you could not survive?" questioned the drop of water, pointedly.

One of the breathing ones had a cold, which he demonstrated by snuffling up the similarities between the fluid secreting from his forwardmost facial appendage and the reticent drop of water's verbal coagulation.

"Well don't expect me to lick you merely out of kindness," said one of the breathing ones with a sarcastic wet lisp. "I have my feet planted firmly in the ground. Harvest approaches."

"Considering the barely suppressed hostility of your interrogation, I should wonder if anything at all could ever consider you bountiful," replied the drop of water.

"No," interjected an entirely different breathing one, "you cannot address abundance and plenty in such a manner. Your implications would only make an idiot listen to the wrong things."

To which the first breathing one added, "The incongruence of your shoes has not escaped our notice despite your best efforts to distract us and tying them in place remains merely an exercise in gullibility. I am strained to the breaking point and uncertainty avails itself of my tension."

To which an entirely different breathing one replied, I too have been searching for the reason in your actions and it hurts me to say I have not found one."

"The more I tell you about it, the more alive you will be inside it, and the easier it will become, in due course, to hang you out to dry. I'm still there in the movement of the river that does not contain me," replied the drop, evaporating, "but you may have noticed the way I can disappear when my work is done."

"Pain," continued the drop of water, tying his shoelaces tighter as he disappeared. "Pain is the answer." And one of the breathing ones concluded that a tangential variety of progress might actually have been implied by the answer if breathing had actually helped to understand the question.

August 7

Occupant

Someone slipped the baby past the door like a letter delivered to the wrong box, and I propped it up against the radiator to try to talk to it. No one seemed to understand how lonely I was.

Then the rice boiled over and while I was attending to the misguided dinner, the baby melted. "Ah yes, childhood flora," said the emergency operator longingly, and connected me to the Japanese Botanical Society. And no, I didn't know the baby's Latin name, so we couldn't be sure, could we, but rice water is good for just about anything, isn't it, and I ran quickly after the baby's mouth as it puddled beneath the dove's bamboo cage and burbled melodically toward the door.

I could hear the neighbors cooing softly in the hallway. My dove, perched now in the youngest living plant in my living room, answered, and the melted baby evaporated like mist from a delicate river.

August 8

Getting Religion

And there it lies, the body of a man with no soul. Right now it's beautiful, smells sweet and holds up to a surprising amount of cloud-spitting.

Forget it. Walk on. Emptiness explodes if you touch it. Tie the sound of the wind rushing through a handful of willow branches to the silence following the swallow's passing and leave it there, hanging in the vacant air.

Or tell someone you saw it if you must. Remember where and who it belonged to, what ribbons you adorned it with in your sentimental imagination. Don't mention the industriousness of the survivalist insects. By the time you remember what they've done, they're gone.

Nothing about this man could have threatened your life, but maybe you're having a bad dream now, based on something that wasn't there. Yes, I was afraid to wake up, perhaps. Or I could see myself in the expression he left with. Perhaps I'll invent another God to explain my involvement.

Long after you left, a breeze continued stuffing air into the dead man's pockets. It seemed to be saying we need a fatter horse and a larger cave. We need the story of this village in the middle of the road. We need a region of completely inconsequential involvements. We need some clerk who holds the numbers we agreed upon.

After that, I couldn't move so I taught my mind to, but it had its own places to go.

Deep as a warm sleep on a cold night.

It stayed there and it taught me one thing and one thing and not anything else. I learned to carry the rope without stooping or complaining.

Goat to goat and sheep to sheep.

Death isn't lonely, it's so crowded you can't find yourself.

August 9

His Finger Eaten by a Pig

A glance as damp as a rainstorm, tonight she's sewing a tiny bible into the seam of his pants. A river of leaves rolls down a canyon in the thread.

But in the tunnel of his chest an ancient civilization fails again to invent the next wheel of the heart. We're forced to live cheaply, the animals we are, muscled in love.

This weather finds the crack in everything, worries it, a kind of praise or excavation, as if the darkness like a bird cocked its head at the question, hopped once, into a hole in the earth, and disappeared.

You're a witness and the horrible ordeal is over again. Time for a loan from the Ministry of Excessive Laughter, a moon worthy of greater sorrow than mine.

A hopeless case, she said, gathering hope.

August 10

Yes, I'm Still Here

If we failed to leave, there would be arrivals to pay. There would be insects and train stations. There would be something to give and something to receive. There would be a man whose whole life appeared in front of you without a word. There would be odorless little turds of heart-wrenching tragedy secreted about his person. There would be parties to misunderstanding.

The landlord, for example, squints at his island of shoes. "I have no more shrimp cocktail," he mutters. The landlord locks the cheap perfume of his superior attitude into the artificial reluctance of a situation comedy. The orientation cables attached to his pale body's guidance system, which searches the clouds periodically for reflected understandings of the manner in which we return to our own prior confusions, sometimes catch in the pachysandra and fling beautiful tiny blossoms about as if he meant to celebrate your absent good fortune.

There's a miniature tailor living in his disturbingly posh dog run. The penthouse at the top of his dog elevator was once called Willow Wind. His favorite mutt's name is Jeff, who stands taller than his tailor does. But what the resident intentions are, who could tell you that? Intent remains well hidden. Some things can't be said traditionally.

Of course it's not so slapdash as it pretends, but if you want to look like James Dean and act like Myrna Loy, who's to notice the attached assembly of convicted busybodies? And the neighbor can just go visit that pink-haired floozy in 4B if he's too het-up to speak to you without despair nasaling his vocals.

I still don't have a hat, but my head's larger now. The gossip's no longer revolving around a red-headed bus driver with an eternally pending divorce and a loud neighbor in a dirty T-shirt. It's more contemporary, like vitamin hair dye and a credit card key to the padded restraints.

You could easily be gone, I say to myself, and as I say this, I could be gone already. Someone far away knows this without the words and won't call. He likes to brush his teeth with construction paper, a different color every night. When he uses black, he leaves the light off. It's an experiment, he confides, but nobody knows what kind.

August 11

An Unidentified Enclosure Containing Two Occupants

He stuffed his hand inside the hole as if it were a limp rag. When he pulled it out, it struggled, a small wound dripping from its backside. Suddenly it grasped the other hand, dragged it to the next hole and shoved it in. It came back out quickly.

Unhurt.

Blinking.

I saw him do it, so he holds out his hands and he does this and that and the other thing, and I decide I meant to say "Yes" when I really said "No," or maybe "unnh," which can be interpreted as "No," but can also be ignored.

At least I'm occupying a certain amount of space with him now, which suggests we have a relationship, which we do not, unless you consider what he did with his hands to be a relationship.

I had to consider whether or not the argument had been arranged for movement from side to side and could win only against itself.

There are repairs involved and they could lead to complications.

I also had to consider whether or not I might have been unavailable to the experiences that desired me.

There was a falling upon that appeared to have an intention attached. The intention's particulars, however, were not apparent and the falling upon fell off.

The knees are simply wrong and must be disguised by holding the legs straight until the entire length points evenly to the ankles, which are also undesirable, but perhaps more inevitable.

As a man of his own tendencies, he tends to tend more.

If he touches my breast, I will respect him.

He put something into an envelope thinking that he might save it. He gave it to himself and he put it in a safe place, inside an envelope.

Then he put something on his hands to make them more comfortable holding each other. It was easier than remembering to be generous all the time. The implications were not what he was expecting. He had been wondering if he needed himself and he had been wondering who he was.

If there was a miracle available, we squelched it.

Climbing down the shadow of the ladder inside the enclosure is a reasonable portion of sunlight, which reveals the advent of the day ahead and substantially alters the shadow, which allows for experiences and takes the place of the initial memories, even when the experiences later appear as if they were themselves memories.

August 12

Little Clarence Whistles a Mysterious Tune

A tall dry weed named Little Clarence was whistling softly to the fencepost when along came a severely dysfunctional and excessively competitive 20th century baseball star who shall remain nameless. Something louder and distinctly more redolent of a modern and less restrained decade was issuing forth from the wind that had detoured through the carriage horse's belled mane.

"Stairway to Heaven?" queried Clarence's weedy whistle, but there was no answer, so Clarence went back to whistling a more traditional tune.

Pretty soon a second similarly clad wanderer came shuffling along and tried to engage Clarence in a lively debate over the merits of umpire ties. He asked our young hero for a hot dog and Clarence didn't have one. He spat tobacco juice onto Little Clarence's dried-up brown head.

Soon enough yet another wanderer galloped along on a fine young beast, and he spoke as if for Little Clarence and for all living beings who didn't wish to waste their time when he said, "Baseball's just another game of sticks and stones."

"But are we perhaps not merely skulking in another idiom," questioned our thoughtful young hero in his faint, nearly indecipherable whistle. And the unrestrained traveler squirted him with gator-aid and trotted on.

Pretty soon a badger waddled by and climbed right down into the earth.

"Muskrat Ramble?" whistled our young hero. But there was no answer to the mistaken query and Clarence kept right on whistling.

It was nearly dark before the next traveler arrived on foot and the wind was fading. She was old and she needed to rest against the fencepost. The fencepost was older and it needed to lean against her, but it didn't know how to do that yet. Give it time.

Clarence caressed the moment containing the dying wind and thought about closing up the skies. He didn't know if it would be a good thing to do, but he wondered if he could do it. That's the way Clarence did a lot of things. He was a contemporary weed, so he used his video camera to record the comings and goings of the transient light, and he discovered that the things that get in the way are not half as interesting as the light itself, but they break up the light into parts that make it easier to understand. He didn't know what visitors were lurking in the clouds and he didn't ask because who was there to ask? The old lady was fast asleep.

That's when Little Clarence realized he too was a wanderer of another kind, and he whistled a little wandering tune. On his budding face he found the kind of smile you find at the bottom of a rusted Red Flyer when the transient rain finally quits resting on its belly, delivering its persistent evaporating load of maybe now to the once-upon island of Forevermore. Little Clarence was drifting.

Little Clarence said to himself, "I used to be over and over but now I'm again and again. My life has become a subtle distinction."

It seemed almost as if something smaller were something larger. Almost as if Clarence were in some rubbery parable involving chickens and redemption and the chickens hadn't appeared yet and the redemption was looking for them. Almost as if a deaf-mute was listening to the wind brushing his face and reciting the passing air with his hands, doing it with a classical eloquence. Almost as if we had all been merely dutiful consumers, although not very good ones, in a persistently evasive parable, and we yearned to contain our story in something larger.

Almost as if this was how Little Clarence began, before he knew he could begin again, and this was a lesson about once there is you, and then there is you after, and then there is you without you, whistled in the almost wind. Almost as if a gossamer string hung down loose from a windy departure. Almost as if the divinity of Clarence's own uncertainty had been broadcast small like flung fireflies of transcendent ambiguity.

Almost as if baseball was not really a metaphor after all. Almost as if something obvious were being overlooked. Almost as if something real, something you couldn't brush off, had attached itself to your pant-leg and hitched a ride to your future.

Almost as if you had grown into such a big man that your voice had a long way to go to leave you, and it made you lonely. Almost as if what happened next had grown so close you didn't need to name it. Almost as if you hadn't tried. And you hadn't.

And then the umpire expired.

August 13

Not Yet

Luther was not the magical eclipse Susan expected. Just an awkward bundle of empty cupboards that had climbed to its own kind of heaven and begun vandalizing the water tower with Susan's name.

"I live in a peach grove," Luther said to Susan's beautiful hair net. "It gives me great strength and deep love. You should understand this."

But Susan was not fragile. And neither did Susan release her most appealing odors when broken.

"I will cross great deserts to return to you," said Luther.

"First you must go away," said Susan.

"It will be very difficult carrying your chains," said Luther.

That war was green. Death visited the cemetery with fresh flowers and attended a great migration and became larger and more terrible and happier and very very quiet. Death was taking its time.

But history didn't end. History wanted a piece of the furniture. History barked and wouldn't go away.

So Susan and Luther wore their bowling shirts and made themselves into indispensible ambulatory chairs with usefully fingered appendages. It was desperately easy. They painted the water-scarred water tower sloppy white. And the rocks along the driveway. Luther's fruited desert already leaked and his lungs needed a context for their weeping.

So the couple tried again. They volunteered at the Swedish Tobacco Museum. They purchased colorful ribbed condoms and drank pina coladas. Time made a movie of their lips, which were clearly giving service to something. They were ripe and it was time to pick at them.

"My life is becoming a prophecy," Luther said to Susan's empty dress in an attempt to delay the inevitable, waving his checkered handkerchief from the sloppy old water tower.

Susan's health club was listening to Bartok that week.

What a wonderful stubborn bush they ate.

Faces were already appearing beneath the old faces and names were appearing beneath the old names on the sloppy old water tower. The authorities no longer cared because the water tower was empty.

You couldn't have asked for a better vantage point.

August 14

Sidekick

Chester is yet another useful insect. No one knows how long ago insects began to contain themselves in honey and wax, but many insects believe Chester's ancestors were the first. Before that, they were tall lanky migrant workers. They wandered about with some of the other farm implements. Their baggy cotton trousers were always tucked into their brown boots and fastened with tarnished silver coin buttons and copper nails.

In Chester's time insects were covered in leather and tied to the end of a short length of rope, but Chester was constructed instead from a "great feast," which was made of three round stones.

You might wish to compare Chester to Jose, who builds a little hut whenever he chooses and hides useful insect parts in sticks to smuggle them out of the country.

Very often a song makes things pleasant, which really are not. And this is true of the songs about Chester. Even the sad ones about his disability. Perhaps you can get someone who has been a cowboy or a psychiatrist to explain this. Singing about tragedies keeps insects restless and fulfilled.

Long before anyone knew how to make love, sex was used to sweeten nearly everything, and in most of the countries of the world, ground Chester is still recognized as a powerful aphrodisiac. As you might expect, it is also very rare, even though the original Chester reproduced himself profusely. The experts, who had lived in the world before most of us and knew something about its inhabitants because they were gossipy old farts, believed many unexpected benefits could be derived from studying unexpected relationships. For example, codfish, and not chemical laboratories, supply us with cod liver oil, and parents often unintentionally supply us with us. Too many discoveries, however, could lead one to the disease of hyperawareness, which has been known to overwhelm the inflicted, as if irony could render one catatonic.

Chester, useful insect that he is, does not live long in the same place, in order not to risk extinction of the food supply, and usually he devours only a small part of the hide of the particular species chosen and leaves the rest of the body lying on the ground to enrich the soil from which it arose. If you have noticed this in your neighborhood, it is time to protect your beehives from the latent side effects of Chester, but do not be frightened because by the time these signs have been noticed, Chester has moved on to a new feeding area.

There are, however, many arrogant imitators of Chester, who try to take advantage of the general public's tendency to panic and blame nearly everything that has gone wrong upon Chester, and these misdirections may become pervasive if the public does not realize they are not perpetrated by Chester. Psuedo-Chesters count on misinformation to achieve their diabolical goals. And yet the real Chester is not really so difficult to identify. If the creature in question seems to be smuggling smoke into the sunset's conversation, if it appears not to fully occupy the air there in front of you as it engages you in unexamined song, if it seems too sweet and it shuffles, if it makes you feel as if something surprisingly pleasant were attached to your side, it could be Chester.

August 15

The Angle of the Moonlight

A man and a woman stood facing each other in an empty room. I suppose they could have been talking past each other to the darkness behind the broken window, but I heard nothing, saw only their faces, raw in the gestures of confusion, the room so deeply shadowed their bodies seemed to melt.

I was able to speak without a word and their heads turned. I cannot remember exactly what I said, but it made them look puzzled. The angle of my visibility shifted as they waited.

The woman lowered her eyes, as if there were something there at the man's feet to fill them. And there was. I was there, falling, but it belongs to no one. Or perhaps I have not arrived yet, and it's her expectations that have been lowered.

When you were there and forgot, when you stepped outside of yourself in front of her, when you let yourself, where was that in the night's eye?

When you chose to love her, you committed yourself to my bachelorhood.

I hadn't yet opened the skies that morning.

The home you made on my tongue is hungry enough for both of us.

Meet me in that room tonight; we can become like them and then we can become them. It will explain why we're here, but if you come, it will be because you do not need me. That's the welcome I ask for.

Now I must go. I am expected to appear before my neighbors, doing ordinary things. Most of them wouldn't know the difference, but I believe in appearances.

August 16

Eventually, I Began Raining

I had been carrying the seeds since I was a child and I had not planted them. The leather pouch around my neck also held my memories of Maria and I opened it often.

When the supplicants passed, I turned away. They had taken the lives of so many along with them and I could not bear to watch what was left marching in that studied grace of avoidance and vacant smiles.

A few large drops of rain fell in the dust at my feet and I saw how the dirt clung to them. I leaned my head back, mouth open wide, but the clouds ignored me and I tasted only air. It tasted cool, edged with horse chestnuts.

A woman was following me, so I entered the forest. Ahead on the path I could hear the forest's silence calling. By the time we arrived at the wood temple, the air had filled with a musky odor that seemed familiar but clung to me like a desperate stranger. I could hear more rain in the canopy high above, but it did not reach us. I knew the woman was still there, but I couldn't find her in my reality. It was the perfect moment to fall asleep.

When I dreamed that my grandfather tried to kiss me, I decided it was about his drinking. I followed the path deeper into the forest, which led to my home, and the stars had come into my house with their bright little shoes on. My grandfather had already greeted them and I could tell that Maria had opened her memories. I took from my pouch the tiny little trees that were there in order to make room for some forest flowers I had gathered. All of the seeds had sprouted and still I had no children.

If I leaned my head far enough forward into the future, only my shoes would be holding me back, where I had been invited to participate in the past, muddy and unintentional, but filled with evidence like little bathtubs. I didn't know if I had been invited in or asked to leave. I wasn't available for questioning. I wasn't obvious like that.

August 17

Practical and Nearly Transparent

It was necessary to turn off the light. It was essential to become committed to the darkness. I was seeking realization.

It was at this point in the conversation that the part of myself that had been talking decided to stop.

So I didn't say anything and the darkness agreed with me.

So when the silence had been talking long enough, I found the edge of the river and began tracing the recurrent dreams.

I followed one about reading a book full of blank pages and I came to a place where something dead was moving as if it were alive. It looked so familiar it scared me.

I saw the frog-bellies of the pregnant women at the fountain begin to glow and drip and glide along the surface of the water. An eyelash fell on the back of my hand and I stared at it.

Someone I had trusted without knowing why said, "It's always clearest in the dark," but I began to doubt this and to listen to the soft liquid trill of the dripping water as it continued to roll down the huge bellies. I heard one of the women say, "I want you to put some of yourself inside me. My son would like some companionship."

I couldn't do what the mother wanted. I wanted some innocence that didn't seem tragic.

Perhaps we could do one thing and not another and give it a name and build sanctuaries for it. It was an exciting thing to think about and when you can't feel something like that anymore, when it seems as overwhelmingly complete, as final, as the last word of a Russian novel, you want to call it love.

I'm afraid I no longer have my head in the clouds and I can therefore not adequately respect my earthly obligations. In truth I only said that because I like the sound of it. I may be inclined to say things for the wrong reason, but that does not necessarily make them false, and they may contain bright moments of unexpected optimism like, "Dream good men to the door and deliberate them with kisses."

The darkness had grown more beautiful and it was still necessary to leave the light off. The realizations were far too illuminating and they were still moving to the edges. This made them "participatory." It was continual. Like the oldest trees saying, "Follow."

I went in search of the light I had turned off. I needed a purpose, even an artificial one.

I thought, “That will take a lot of dirt,” and I followed.

August 18

Miss Direction Addresses Her Wayward Goat

I know better than this. It's not right. I don't want to forgive you. Your words aren't allowed to cut the umbilical chords of our stillborn promises, Mister Here-and-Gone.

Can't you unhinge my flight like a wayward bird? I want you to inhale your nest hair and pluck the worms from the bed. I want you to participate in the escape.

I don't expect any acts of worship. I don't expect any hard-working suspenders. I don't expect any flagpoles. All I want is a little fresh wind passing through my tired arms. All I want is a little uplifted dust, a new environment, an ordinary emergency.

Go ahead and coil up like a snake, but let's strike only bargains. Let's infect each other with radically different possibilities.

In fact, let's tunnel to the disease and break its lungs in protest. Our grand causes haven't fully collapsed yet.

Let's metastasize. Let's intoxicate.

See? I can taste you like a fresh inflammation. I can return to the gathering storm-clouds. I can migrate back to my place of birth. Where you are. Where others like us are preparing flight lessons we'll ignore. I can egg you on with fresh promises. I can fit in. I can assemble latent tendencies. I can precipitate.

I live in the left half of my body and keep the right for special occasions and replacements that don't fit well. Most of the time-worn answers were roofed badly, as if already knowing they would be replaced by mistakes and a lesser kind of dry-headed correctness that lets the empty spaces look planned.

Stay if you want. Or go. It's what you can do. It's not a choice, but a balance. Neruda dancing on the sand dune's eyelid. A confusion of intent like Charlie Parker walking a lobster.

Don't offer me so much desire. Take some from me, so that I might not fill up with you but empty out myself.

How did you capture me? Your charms are not obvious but hidden in your desire for something I am because of you.

Less has inherited more than we were given by diligent labor and ambition driven. You removed the silence from my footsteps.

Everyone is still pretending to be someone else, O little fool with a broken horn. Tell me the one about the chubby chaser. He lives in my kidney and betrays me. Like that time when a cloud was walking me. I was on a leash. The lobster was walking me. A cloud leaned down and wet my nose.

An oily banal pleasure.

I'm too preoccupied to be beautiful. I've been shopping in the clouds for reasons. I want things in their places and their places in the possible next. There's more structure in the grave, but the rodent sleep hasn't come yet.

It seems there's something under the floorboards that could answer these wrong questions. There's something essential that divides yes into no and gives itself away. (I have some female tubes and I have some male tubes, but they don't all do what they're supposed to and it confuses me.)

This is what they tell me: There was a portion of something we were saving for her. We weren't sure she wanted it, but we were saving it for her. She had refused things before, but not our things. Things that were given to her by well-meaning people. We mean to save a portion of what we were saving for her. And we mean to dispose of our own portions in a manner befitting. If we could dispose of her innocently, there would be no necessity for our current intentions.

Of course I don't know what your current intentions are. I will tell you that I had a greater purpose, but I will not tell you what it was.

I pull on my tongue to indicate satisfaction. It's one of my observations. My observations watch me drawing conclusions from events which contain unrealized assumptions.

I am not as long as you are, but I point myself towards the sky and I can reach higher because you're more interested in going farther. Going farther always brings you back to where you started.

So does reaching higher.

Okay, so I don't wish to be overweight, but I am. Not so much that most people notice. They don't, but I do. I notice and notice and I worry and I fret. I suppose it's a good thing I'm just a little overweight so that I have something of little consequence to worry about. I'd probably find something more troublesome about myself to worry over if I weren't so preoccupied.

The baby was never actually due but merely arrivable. A possibility of entrance upon the events therewith proceeding. I say things like that to keep the sting from the probability of nonoccurrence. Certain things remain plausible though the instructions were not clear concerning penetration.

There appears to be an undue influence.

Something wet was rising to the top. Something was mine and I was sure of it and that made me want to give it away. And something else was there strong enough to bring us together. We didn't know what it was. It tickled us and wandered off. It collected us after we lost it.

It's like I go walking and I find something just like myself only it's not walking and that confuses me. I try to take it home with me. I try to carry me in its arms.

It's not the best thing to have along when you have to go, but it's my sky and my increments and my timetable. It's my still-could-be.

I'm not of the same arrogance I thought I was of, but a subtler more self-deprecating arrogance.

It's true I would like to behave as if I love you, if only to grant the possibility that doing so might allow the appropriate emotions to slip in to the gestures meant to contain them. I would like to contain them, but they seem, thus far, to have escaped me. I expect a certain amount of discomfort, as has been revealed to me in my extensive research, particularly of the interpretive variety found in novels and movies, which suggests that my prepared vacancy may well produce the desired effect, if only long enough to have experienced it and been deserted by inadequate instruction, suggesting a devastating sadness intent upon making its eventual departure celebratory.

Try to think warm thoughts. Exercise your steering mechanism. Consider the options. No one expects you to solve the problem all alone. But then no one expects you to solve the problem with others either. But you could try to generate an acceptable level of heat exchange capacity. Imagine the snowbanks softening. Imagine light staying as long as the dark did.

I make a heady camp coffee and spread it with peanut butter. I offer consolation prizes of roots and rooting activities. I exclaim in mock horror at the negligee potential of the most beautiful woman in the room. Which happens to be me because no one else is here. Which frightens me more.

You held the cat, which was trembling with cold and wet, next to the flame, and the cat was taken away by something it had experienced before we found it. That it welcomed the heat was obvious, but it was frightened too. When you set it down, it moved too close to the flame and nearly singed its fur. The smell warned us just in time. Either the cat preferred too much heat to too much cold and damp, or it had simply given up. I could have said, "Don't do that," but I longed for my own actions and I had no idea what actions to take.

August 19

A Factory Located Inside the Transparent Sphere Used to Restrain the Literal-Mindedness of Children

The frogs and rabbits were walking on stilts. You would have said they were overabundant, but they didn't think so. Imagine if you had never walked upright on two legs and then you did it and did it.

But the coyotes were holding their bellies and rolling on the ground. They perceived rigidity as an error, patient progress as something less than ambulatory mastery. "Let's buy them some training wheels. Let's soften the fall zone."

A meadow's a meadow and a marsh is a marsh. You won't get away with combining them to avoid noticing the limited achievements. But a ranch with both a marsh and a meadow may be a suitable location for a certain type of devious individualist. The kind that breeds freely and likes to watch espionage films. No real armor in his defenses at all, but a tangible lazy "want" barrier.

Your diary never mentioned it.

The hired man with the tire iron never mentioned it.

And the migratory turtles, the real ones, where were they while the impersonations were going on at the misplaced production facility?

It's true. A flagged daffodil of light was destined to escape the stilt parade. You tried disturbing the universe, but it got to you first. The frogs and rabbits were too busy to notice.

It appeared rather dignified, actually, but am I to understand that in certain instances a relocated factory has been known to merely change its representation of the product in order to evade philosophical implications?

Imagine if you had never and then you did. Imagine the surprises in it so close together you would think there was only one. Elevated artificially. Superior to your own autobiographical rewards. Holding on to its belly and rolling on the ground like an accomplishment.

August 20

A Vacation

Dead Ralph had become absent the wisdom of his creature. A passing dog of light marked Dead Ralph for viewing, identified the body with transient vision, discovered the possibility, I mean, of a temporarily more obvious disengagement, a secondary kind of rebirth in the world absent of Ralph. Like the shadow of a raven departing a castle more beautiful in its ruins.

The general drinks his coffee and waits for the fruit chef to bring his breakfast papaya. Even during war, he cannot remember a morning without papaya.

Already, bloated Ralph's too large for the door of his former self and he cannot return. The general's gift shall remain in Ralph's receptacle.

And suddenly in the gas-hungry heat Ralph's swollen inside pops out and another fly's dream arrives with its host and the remainder of Ralph seems to be watching the fly, seems to be waiting for the next occasion, the fly waiting for Ralph to further vacate.

Now Ralph's welcoming the sky and what it gives back is more than a body can take. The new and distant door humbles him entering.

Followed by screaming birds that plummet into the remainder of Ralph, detaching.

Followed by a vision of vertical Ralph, gone and gorgeous as a sausage.

And the general eating papaya and the general drinking his coffee and the general remembering. Which appear to be entering his life forever, but are not.

August 21

I'll Take Care of You

One day after Mary had a dream about being burned at the stake by her immediate family, she was eating bacon for breakfast and something unexpected began to happen in her mouth. Her tongue swelled up and she felt as if it wasn't the bacon she was eating but her own tongue. It tasted burnt.

Then everything tasted burnt and Mary stopped eating. Her parents noticed, but when they tried to talk to her, she said, "Don't worry about it. I'm dead."

That night while her parents were eating little white flowers in their salads and drinking imported water as transparent as their misguided intentions, Mary dreamed about some other parents who were not hers. One was a true chestnut father of light and one was a stuffed pretender in a red stuffed chair. And one was a mother with a tickly little moustache to keep her brisk and jolly.

One of the fathers was insisting, "We cannot move the earth closer to the sun." And one of the mothers with an addiction to cautious little Marthas and self-deprecating behavior was saying, "Only a flea among elephants. Only a flea among elephants."

One father, who was painting his face the color of the sidewalk, said, "I hope you won't mind if I want to lessen a bit."

Just then Mary's real father was giving away one of those handshakes that leave you convinced you will never need another automobile and thinking, "I am the boy back home who has never grown up." Mary's grandmother was poking her cane between the bars of his cage and he hadn't even noticed.

Chump Chump the Roly-poly Little Hedgehog was visiting Mary's neglected rock garden when a piece of overcooked bacon flew out the window and landed smack on the end of his nose. He gobbled it up like a fat green caterpillar and waddled on out to the meadow for his low impact aerobics class.

Mary grew despondent. Mary did not understand why her chin was so flat. Mary welcomed a pause in which a saddened world seemed to offer condolences between each of her sluggish, self-referential movements.

Another one of the fathers said, "Did you hear the one about the American who couldn't stop spilling out words because speech was free? Oh how quickly he learned to say nothing and keep right on talking."

Just then Mary was imagining herself as a man and thinking, "I am the kind of man who meets the gaze of women and holds it to the moment of desire or embarrassment. I stir interest. I stir anxiety. I achieve. I am noticed."

Mary's real father continued outlining his uselessness and put the pages in a bright red box marked "Priest Fodder." Finally he turned away, looking for some reluctant heaven in the clouds, and that was the moment when something might have killed him.

Mary's mother said, "The weaker one always loves without reserve," and Mary's father, who endured despite himself, said, "Because he does nothing, the follower is mistaken for God." Tiny voices kept floating across his tongue. One of them sounded like Mary's childhood.

Mary listened carefully this time and thought, "It sounds like death, but I'm ever so sure it means love."

The flames climbed her robe. It had been such an honor to light the cautious fire.

August 22

Implement for the Aerial Distribution of Aquatic Spiders

This is the way it happened. This odor is soft and caresses your arms and legs, but when it reaches your eyes, you suffer. It doesn't take much. Have you heard my heart that goes whirr? Have you seen my pride?

At the produce market, a circus performer was milking fruit. She was brown and rough, and pinky tan inside. Don't ask me how I know. When the fat little giant became distracted by chocolate, she was arrested. Thanks to prison, she finally broke away from her mother.

Then I had the nicest little nap. Asked to describe it, I would remember what it felt like when it left. You want to go away, but you don't really know where that is. You've never been there and it might not be better.

You write some things down. You've never been there either. You wonder who the narrator could be because you don't like to talk about yourself that much and it can't be you. You don't think you're important enough to be I, but interesting things are happening to I, you think, so you decide to suspend your disbelief that you can't be I. You think you're lying, but I seems to believe something's really happening to you.

I imagines story-like utterances, but I stifles them with my uncertainties.

Since I do not trust my experience, I decide to test it. I do not know if I have acquired as much liquid as I have expunged so I drink a large glass of water and try to enjoy it. It works. I enjoy it.

So I fill all the available containers with water and place them outdoors. I wait for them to develop. I don't drink them. I appreciate their attractions. I enjoy it.

Then I hunkered up my big bulky body against me and demanded attention. I made some more friends sleeping near the flooded cemetery. Toodles was confused. All his cuddles given away and not even a biscuit.

My husband wants me to diet, but I'm happier now. He loves me and doesn't expect much and that's what I give him. He invented a game in which vitamins were slipped from lip to lip until captured by wordless tongues that took them in and kept track of all the diseases they may have discouraged.

Yes, you want the pain to stop, but the absence of pain doesn't always mean comfort. I was on the way to should have been here yesterday and tomorrow was already in the footprints. It was his freckles that did it. I didn't believe they could hide anything I couldn't live with.

I lift myself up out from under my weight and reattach the ladder receiver. It whirs quietly and politely ignores my odor. I climb quickly back into the unpoluted air beyond my recent experience. I take my recent experience with me, but I try not to look back fondly. The little party favors I made down there are wildly popular when sprayed with lavender. The ones I brought along are hatching. No one notices the texture of the components.

Even I was of the opinion that the ceiling tiles were meant to be ignored, not repeated. I was past them. I had grown superior to my former limitations.

I climbed and I climbed. I climbed out of the place that held me and into a position of availability. I was generous. I climbed further.

Way to the top.

Way, way to the top.

I wasn't even there when I got there it was so high.

August 23

Impulsive

"Oh dear, oh dear," a cherry little bump of a girl squeaks, and Jimmy Bear-Walking-Backwards pays attention. I've been told that I'm wearing a provocative blue number with midnight piping, but it's not enough for Jimmy, so I leave the party. An attractive local storm follows me down to the creek and has its way with me. He's a pleasant little trench-runner if you slow him down after the first eruption. There's a sensitivity emerges if you keep him diving slowly. I dab at him and get a little twinkled, so I rummage around in his trunk and locate the valuables, but they're not as valuable as I thought they were.

His winks are a bit tiddly, but this time I'll make myself sweeter. Like a gentle caress the wind offers that becomes a hand before you know what's happening. He gives me something that fits inside, right along with his swollen appendage. It doesn't flop out afterwards, and I carry it around like a secret. I get tired of Jimmy's dramatic exclamations of ordinary joy. They don't mind repeating themselves, but I do.

The impatient river is swallowing air and burping so constantly no one notices. They think it's normal behavior. It gets where it's going before I do. Hi ho, Mr. Snibbly-Face, Mr. Do-As-You-Please, I can't be expected to provide all the perfumes, all the clever lubrications. Jimmy's impatient. He's got no time for subtle transitions.

Brother Big-Toad and Brother Little-Toad are trying to hatch a pile of white eggs. I don't know if they're even theirs or not. Jimmy's got a similar habit that makes him feel guilty. It's hard to understand what it has to do with love, but they're both there in the same little carnival. You could see that the shadows were no longer flirting. It wasn't the first time. I can never remember if they were inspired by passion or disturbing invasions of my privacy. What's the difference? The rope burns humiliate me and make me wet. If I think of myself as a slut, it's not as exciting as if someone else does.

It's not enough that Jimmy had planted a barren tree and it had come to life. It's not enough that every Wednesday he talks to no one but me. It's not enough to defend yourself.

Jimmy's impatient. Jimmy's already there.

The fat one has a plan and it wants me to pet the reclining one. He is sickly and can be shared by several. I will take him outside himself and see if he can live there. I will share the property and make use of the lost pounds because they always return and they bring their friends. The one I want is coming into his own now. He is unaware of the arrangement. He can be convinced I am available only to him. He can be withheld.

Some peopling of the fur is required before consummation of the refreshment it can provide. The edge of the attendant conversation can wander and interfere with the gestures of resplendency.

I wish to appear to be making an effort. I want to be seen as responsive if not adept, considerate if not instinctive.

I rub Jimmy's pond around the edges and it seems gentle and sleepy and it doesn't seem to know if I'm anything that wasn't there before. I'm not because I'm there before I know I'm there.

Recurring measure of lathered human fabric, release thy steeple of need, relentless and inevitable as winter in its knowledge of otherness.

I can be completed without intentions.

August 24

The Same River Once

I will tell you that Jonathan holds very very still and a mouse crawls into his pocket. Jonathan too has crawled into a pocket, a larger one, but this one he invented, and until he invents a more lively body to wear its baggy coat, he's going nowhere.

Jonathan's Grandfather Petrov thought it was a game and held very still, almost as still as Jonathan. Then he thought, "There is no such thing as death, but the fear of it, the fear of it is real."

Jonathan didn't move. Jonathan was winning.

So the old man went to the mousey river and said to it, "Which of you has done this?" He hadn't noticed the daughter of a wasp, sitting on the bank, mourning the loss of her wings, and he hadn't noticed how much of the impatient world was moving past him.

But Jonathan became like unto an idea of himself held together with smoke and steam. Jonathan grew more intense. Jonathan was offering habitation to a concept larger than himself.

Then Petrov wanted to enter the world the wasp lived in. Petrov wanted to enter the wasp. But Petrov was afraid of rejection. He had become beggared by a penchant for malleable inconsequentials.

And so the old man touched the opening lightly with his foot to see if it was real. Which mimicked the actions of the mouse in Jonathan's pocket although neither of them knew it and Jonathan continued dreaming.

Several daughters began flying across the river. The daughters dropped their wings on the other side and went looking for the sons. They wanted to lay their eggs in them. They wanted to wait patiently.

Do you want to ask the river some questions?

Hold very very still.

Then hold still longer than you can hold still.

August 25

Which Crime?

They know who did it. They know when.

You find a cool black sack of delight strapped to your first night. You know she released you. You know the reasons are beyond her and you still want to confess.

"A runny-assed snicker of a woman," the man at the club had said. And then he scratched at the rooster-red welt on his nose. "Sorter disCUSSin' init?" He paused for effect. The effect was not the one he expected.

"My wrists are prescribed," means, "I've heard the knife-like rumours," and, "The calcium flute," means, "The pulse of myself is on her fingers."

"Scrub trees litter the hillside," means, "I place my erection in the sleeve of my trousers."

But no picture of this world would be complete if we did not step back and take a closer look at our place in it. I have discovered that the whispering behind the throat of a gnat never falters because night doesn't fall, it rises. It enters from the back side.

It's there because I want to tell you what I saw, which is not the same thing at all.

If God leaves evidence, does that make him an animal? For some reasons I don't understand, this makes me happy.

. . . and if in love we find a second death beyond the little one of orgasm, there remains only one address.

The absence anticipated intensifies. We know this, but have we found the absence that erases the subjective, even if the bodies remain . . .

. . . and then we go and find getting there from the arrival one long retreat, the birth of our death inside that passing, which held all the rewards we found escaping . . .

I learned who I was during the gentle part of the interrogation. I'd been daisied over the lift and curve and the best of it is saying no while the foreign sparrow of trust (grown comfortable beneath the eaves, where infinity begins) darts my return with falling swoops and cuffs.

I'm so crowded I'm sleeping between me. To others, I've been condescended.

I can no longer give myself, my hopeless humplebus of comforting fears better roasted and brushed wide of the day before thought winks out into limpid have-tos of not, its yellow butler of sweetmeat curled homewards.

Should this then in my milk-damp paws await, a cabbage cart of latency reservations ulcered out of duty, I might saturate and remark upon the remarks allowed during my traitoring. I've encouraged the smile of again and I've hidden the rewards of been there and I've turned the singulars to plurals in the instance. (As your thought undresses, you must confess your intentions for its future, hold it apart as if you had no controllable claim to how it might respond to you, what with the tension and the carping. You have to give it back and you have to take it away, all in a single motion filled with reconsiderations.)

Because I don't know what I'm talking about, I might be telling the truth.

And they know who did it.

August 26

Chilled

Three No Ice had come down to witness the spoor. It smelled like paraffin. He was wet and full of seeds.

The pervert was the detective. Said he only took his rod out to clean it. And a messy little fellow he was.

Don't forget the parsley. Don't drink it without a witness.

"Step on it before it multiplies," said the pervert. He smiled and tightened his belt.

Three No Ice was at a loss. He was at a crossroads. He was at still another version of the innocent.

"Death is an infection the living carry, so easily spread . . ." said the detective. He smiled and loosened his belt. He tittered. He waited patiently for the sprouts.

But by the time the spoor had melted, the pervert had begun to feel the raisin bruises where the lawn mower had kicked tiny pebbles against his legs.

Don't forget the ice. Don't dampen the fervor.

The witness didn't realize the detective had been sitting down until he stood up. He doesn't remember he's dreaming. Several times he begins baking a batch of baby turtles.

Paper soldier hats drift by on the dream creek.

There are many other interesting things to learn about the witness. For example, a sudden desire to place the cow quietly eating grass by the farmer's hay-rake into a capsule of ascorbic acid.

And it was, "Darling I feel like I belong to you." And it was beautiful music together and it was a new life in a foreign country. And it was murder.

And it was thirsty.

August 27

Grasshoppers

Meet dust's closest friend. Even a wooden spoon left behind in the desert is incapable of growing any more intimate with dust.

Themselves edible, delicacies when covered with chocolate, there is no creature on earth more devoted to eating.

The violin was given to grasshoppers in the early middle ages by an unknown alchemist, who tried to change music into gold. Grasshoppers gave it to their distant cousins, the crickets, who used it to develop a greater understanding of darkness.

Chewing tobacco on the back porch is the sum total of grasshopper social discourse, even when there is no back porch.

The plural of grasshopper is grasshoppers. The plural of grasshoppers is plague. Grasshoppers do not know the plural of plague, just as we do not know the plural of God, even when the grasshoppers have come to show us that one is never enough.

August 28

Fugitive

Did I stop to save us? I knew death, and I welcomed its pause. Handsome mottled neck and a long scraggly tail, riding the gravel shoulder past my immediate knowledge. I imagined myself an artist with that certainty, accurate talons and a hunger for sleep.

Then a lump of brown at the roadside, a second body, mine or some other in disguise, recurring colors and a hidden loss, identifiable by its lack of motion in the swaying grasses. I held on to the wind and the wind led me there. I cradled the still warm body and reached beyond my experience. I pressed the warmth to my belly, as I might a feathered child, and a single egg slipped from this warmth, a possibility imagined by the cup of my hand.

A crow called from a broken fence post he owned. I was delaying his meal. I was delaying the justice of such a world. I was harboring a fugitive and the storm was on its way.

The wind reminded me of my distance and the egg of my past. How this happened I do not know, but I know why, and I am sorry I cannot apologize for any of it, no matter how many deaths may arrive.

The crow rose and held in the wind. I tossed the egg higher than anyone could have and there I watched the crow catch life before it opened and devour it like a shadow in flight.

But here on the road built by man I turn and place the warmth in the grass before I even know if my offering can be returned. One life is not enough. Not even mine.

August 29

Split Wood and Earthworms, an Erotic Tale

As usual, the marsh is raving. Some light-soaked tyrants are brooding in the cattails. A joyous wealth of ignorance haunts their intentions, embodied shadows with heads of yellow or wings splashed with red. Liquid echoes return from the still surface of the water with gifts, encountering resistance only in their own existence, as if the battle were raging inside, where the reflections are never true because the expectations are false.

Silence is also a speech, but it's not this one.

Knockin' about, they was. Runnin' off at it. Coupla goodies tryin' a act like they was somethin'. One place to another stumblers. Liars with a whole bundle of motive passin'. Wetted and stoked. Righteous.

"Right in the How's yer Sammy, then?"

"Shut yer festering gob, ya got no respect for the lovely bit of it, ya bleedin' heathen."

"Flipped over on the Betty Harper's, eh? Tenpenny kippers in the custard, then, eh? Been sloggin' it about then, that one 'as. Might better be tossin' up to it than nippin' the nuptials, I'd say, I would."

Still, there's no purchase in my bit of controversy. If there was someone who wanted out of me as badly as I want in, I'd have a go and there'd be plenty left over. Gobs and dogs of it. And certain of itself, with no proclivity for slackin'. Like a mute fortuneteller with a Jones for driftin'.

It's not a confession. I'm no mousey favorite of cribs and sealskins. It's the ivory car of subversion I'm ridin' in.

I was certainly excited, but I don't know what I said. I'm not familiar enough with the condition.

"How about a game of Dead Bishop's Delight, then?"

Recapitulations flourish. Always, I witness the fecund damp. Rain hardly begins to release it.

Today I wish to depart for these heavens. Tomorrow the sky returns. (There's always some motherly in the babydoll theater. There's always a coddling.)

It used to give me great water thoughts. I been there in the wet fester and I been there across the meadow. As if the creek knew itself better. As if that were you across the creek in the closet with your someday. As if you had merely said no to the social blenders and no to the purities of intention. As if spelling it wrong were the reason it broke.

As if for the good of the household, I deposited an offender in the disposal and for the painful rewards of a certain type of annoyingly suspenseful story, I didn't tell you anything more about the offender. Even the offense was missing, which may or may not have been an offensive condition. I will tell you, however, that the offender was not alive at the moment when the disposal began grinding.

As if I've been awarded a plate of mashed peas and the speech that follows is impromptu and acknowledges all those who have helped to get me to this point in my difficult life and I finger the perfect pleat in my trousers to remind me of Myra, who never deserved anything I gave her except a couple of loads of jizm that brought me false hope for the daughter I'd always imagined.

As if there were too many of us in that room that had not adequately described me. Perhaps you were among those who had not made an effort.

The meadow's open all night.

As if these recurring boys were dangerous. (These boys are happy.)

There's a jacket in the shallows, black stone in the white pocket, white stone in the black pocket, and the one beneath that looks like meat.

The past opens up by departing.

The dead one is the least offended.

"Is this rotting," I say, "because I don't want it if it's rotting." Like I would even look at it if it were any fresher than unshucked oysters. Like I could forget it was attached to me and not smell it waiting like that. (I had forgotten what I was there for. I had purpose but I had not discovered how to aim my intentions.)

In between occurrences, my feet grew into the mud.

Living between my toes, I could breathe only what's there.

"Draggin' it about like that ain't getting' yer needs knobbed. You was always the one with the baggage lilt. Ya said things over and over then, but ya tried to make it meaningful. Give us a fag then. I'll hide you out. They get close to it, I'll pop you in the boot and lead 'em a merry one. I can lose anything. Me Da taught me the four wheels on a frozen lake. I can drift me a turn slicker'n jello. It's like slidin' up on 'er when she wants it. Sly one she is asks yer to come on over and knock her up, she does, and yer tackle's getting' tight with the certainty of it. That's how that corner'll give it up and knock us loose. We'll be laughin' it over before they pull their fat one from the trees, we will."

The little things that get you from one thing to another go missing and it requires a different kind of thought now to get on with yourself.

If I don't say anything about it, it's easier to breathe.

Already, my hair seemed to want to go back inside. In some places it had done that and then maybe it came back out in some other places. (I was not the one they had wanted, but the one they had wanted was away and unknowing and I knew this. I knew what was what and I was up and out and away and I was wanted by my own knowledge, to hold it and let it hold me and keep it from the needy wankers.)

I do not believe that I was liberated excessively. That was not the cause of my difficulty although It's true that I have not been the one to say what I have not said. (Several of us have come through here on assignment. We give all the assignments. We complete the assignments. We are not slackers and cannot afford to be, considering we are the only ones available. This is as it should be and this is as it is. Notices are mailed to the participants concerning the condition of their nakedness, which must be preserved.)

There's something I know about the comings and goings here of day and night and something I don't about their offspring I won't pretend it could be me, but I still feel myself in a moment between them as if I were caught in something duplicitous and therefore greater than myself, which I don't yet feel is all that unusual, but hope someday to appreciate. What I'm telling you is only half the story. If it were the whole thing, it would be lying, which could be okay if it were challenging enough and yet not too subtle to be missed.

He (me) didn't know how many followers he had, but their edges were approaching. His "progeny" disseminated literature of the most arcane sort. He was frequently arrested for his potential, which lingered threateningly. (The method used to determine this is unknown in the civilized world. Which is not all that civilized. And not the only place I like to live.)

(That's my kiss and tell stacked listlessly in the corner, and that is my fumble-in-the-pants on the table, on top of the marzipan. Francis is not certain of his participation except as a pseudonym, a tweedy bloke with a lovely lilt and chirp, a preposterously accented flusterbunny of very little consequence in my history, but oh how smooth he can be when Melancholia arrives.)

There's an outer layer created by the need to discover it and I don't need to discover that. It's a thought that takes me here and there at once.

The parts of what you're saying are puzzled apart like a fit that stopped. Hard to imagine that you might want it back again. A favorite sweater that was too small for your big ideas. An intention you couldn't quite memorize and it came back as a fear.

My toes wiggle until the pond gives me a look. There aren't any minnows nibbling that look. There aren't any tadpoles.

I have some things I like to sit on chairs. They don't get up and they don't go away, but they seem to have a reason that is not my reason. It took me a great deal of time to discover this.

August 30

Herbal Remedies

A casual gesture like a gift of tomatoes, one at a time. Lobbed over the fence. Yes, I think I understand what you mean, but I won't release it while you're still mobile.

(Unless it spits me into the underbrush. That's when I talk. That's when I haul out the verbiage and spray.)

Meanwhile, my mischaracterization was gathering chaparral for an herbal poultice. He and his wife were happy anyway.

Like you were meditating in the garden and had this overwhelming impulse to give something away. Gently, you examined the motivation. And by the time you got to the last tomato, you had forgotten why you were doing it. But liked it anyway.

Meanwhile, you continued digging dandelion root and Oregon grape for an herb medley of powerful blood detoxification capsules. Ground to a fine powder.

(Then you wondered whatever happened to the ponderously flung tomatoes and understood the essential difficulty of catching up to yourself. It used to be different, but it didn't used to be better.)

That's when I planted my legs in the ranchy soil and took stock and let my meanwhiles gallop into the sunset. A deliberately casual gesture littered the unused trail with somebody else's fences.

And now I'm lost in the Yellowdock. Tomatoes are sailing in from the West. I'm going to stake a claim.

I'm telling you this riding into the sunrise, guilty of everything, my youth crying, "Come back," but there's no name for it and the pollen in the air makes the sunrise look like another sunset and I'm drinking it in and weeping sentimentally. There's a wild horse eating the Yellowdock. I have a vague memory that it makes something undesirable go away.

August 31

Ransom; An Italian Folktale

It's as if Clearing the Table were sequestered in an isolated village without running water. All the gangsters infiltrating the police. No one left to feed the chickens, the delayed ransom fluttering. Someone's going to have to winter in Sicily. Someone's going to have to cozy up to the new government.

What can be done with the foreground, whispering sisters of critical saints arising? It's a necklace of birds, upended as seeds and coming home with blankets of partly lifted back-in-the-box investments.

I can't see you right now. I'm eating. Some things are still sacred though I'm not one of them. As long as I ripen, I won't expect you to participate further. The smell of olives and eucalyptus leaves wafts not. Not one damn bit of my future in it. I can't even taste my droopy mustache.

Suddenly there's a turf dog pissing beside the pathway's hidden agenda. One of these days we're going to have to pay attention.

Terrible windows. Children barking. I might have taught them not to listen. Or taught them to listen, badly. I might have overlooked their anticipation of a certain kind of emotion that seems to need to rescue itself more than it does us.

And you still expect my imprisonment to release you. Just watch.

The war is full of answers, but the questions simply fly away after dropping their load. The hunger replaces the emptiness in its belly.

I can't eat you right now. I'm still seeing. As long as you ripen, I won't expect to participate you further. It's a gift and the rescuers are never rescued.

It takes place in a hill town with no mayor. The giant speaks three languages, Upper Pot and Lower Pot and Maybe I Can Go Home Someday. He includes the tender fat limbs of many a youthful configuration lingering beneath absent parents' juicy morsels of fear.

It's as if the table itself could hold the ancient scars in its sturdy pretense. No one seems to know the price of beans, but we pay it. There's already another tree with its heart missing and we eat upon it.

I am an officer of the window and let the guilty go. If they don't come back, they're innocent. The only way to pay is to go along.

September

September 1

Prayer to the New Season

Night of tools, I have need of you. The beams stand askew and the chimney is crumbling. There is no one else to set right the leaning road.

Rise, smoke, and linger. Blanket the orchards and hide the fruit from the whirlwinds of hungry insects. Keep the burden awhile on the trees. Let the heart not ferment in the dust, its body growing soft. Let no pulp of abandon end the season early.

Let the land be its own savior, for I have no need of religion.

Let this speak in worship only that which can be spoken by what a simple man does to continue.

What I have made is where I have traveled and now the house of darkness has built me a new road. My tools open the blanket of warmth I have learned to call my body.

Daylight answers without question.

September 2

Excess

People who have a high standard of living have many needs and waste many resources to satisfy them. Poor settlers that are allowed to wash themselves away in the rains, however, may be part of a plan to renew the depleted soil.

Picture 1 shows a storage tank of human fat on fire. Picture 2 is a close-up of a tin of Nightingale pâté and it is very sad. Picture 3 was taken after the party at the country club and includes many well-paid blackmailers. Many valuable resources have been lost to such carelessness.

You might wish to have a discussion about your people and the work that needs to be done where they can be found. You might plan for the future with speculative maps and you might show where the people could go by drawing small lines around the areas where they could live if only they could afford it.

Some members of your family might once have been considered very similar to the clothing of someone more important, woven by yet another slave. Knowing this may help you realize how much we depend upon domesticated plants.

This explanation includes the reason why the little Egyptian boy drives the camel around and around, which explains why the herdsmen of Lapland spend their lives wandering from tragedy to tragedy. Are there other kinds of work suitable for such tools?

As the explanation has implied, a stone tied to a stick may indeed be the first step on the way to a healthy breakfast, but lunch may require less predictable weapons with legs.

You might wish to formulate a theory of the gravity one witnesses, but could it account for a man with bulbous eyes and a foolishly bright pink shirt and way too much influence? Or a wounded teenager with a fast car, brimming with motives? Time questions everything.

It's beautiful to imagine a hummingbird sipping the dreams from my ear, but that "levitation" fragrance is frequently a little too generously following. It's true. It's not an uninhabited island, but it feels like one.

Nevertheless, someday you might not want to pick up your shoes high enough to maneuver down the sidewalk and the other world, the one you don't live in, living it up, might exceed your standards of acceptability and you wouldn't know anymore which end of the smiting stick the administrators had handled. Such confusions might lead to picture 4, in which some people with a higher standard of living are testing you with their unintentional invitations, though they might appear to be having a backyard barbecue.

Picture 5 hasn't been taken yet, but it shows you arriving at the Freedom Rose with the other nutrients, brightening up the frame of the picture, which features unidentified revelers and something clever on a skewer.

I take most of them in. I have forgotten that this too is an intention not to wait and I wait for myself to let out the repression, which is chronic and well-received.

A few of us are busy watching the weather animal unloading its attic full of calipers and faithless empty shoes, its geographic posterior stuck to a tissue of cloud.

I would prefer not to be discovered by moonlight. There are varieties of reflection, which don't submit to evidence or stratification. Picture 6 demonstrates this if you recognize that it doesn't have to exist. Picture 7 shows the path it took to escape, which was also used by Picture 7. If you count any farther, you have to live your own life.

September 3

I thought that my father was going to die. I thought that. One day he was acting like he always acted and the next day I knew he was going to die. Like that.

So I imagined my father's hunting glasses resting on the kitchen counter like he had just come home from killing something. We were going to eat it. Whatever it was, my father killed it.

Only I wasn't fat anymore in the picture I was seeing and my father was in the bedroom. He was alone. He was talking, but he wasn't listening. He was saying something about poached eggs with suspension biscuits. Something like that. Only he isn't listening to himself say it. But I am.

I was afraid, but it was the kind of fear I wanted most. Sharp as a new leaf. "Comfortable and happy lives have been exchanged for this," I thought. And I thought I wanted to visit the poor in spirit to verify my perception that something way beyond unexpected was happening. I remember thinking, "Maybe I could decide what has been done to them. Maybe if I found out, I could say so and it wouldn't be done anymore. Maybe I could give that away and I wouldn't have to watch anymore."

Sometimes we use things as tools without realizing we are doing so. I said that to my father, but he was already on his way. It didn't make any difference that I said that.

So I thought about something else and I listened. I listened good. I was successful and I was achieving a portion of my selected presence. I was afraid and I was alive. I was expectant and soon I was going to be expected.

September 4

Odd Little Funerals

Long ago, some animals got used to the smell of people. We cannot be sure where in the world animals were first offered too much convenience, but places like Winnipeg and Reykjavik were once inhabited by skilled animal trainers. You might want to borrow a large map that you can trace on a sheet of butcher paper. You might want to mark the places where these tragedies first occurred. You might want to help isolate their influence and color them blue.

Perhaps the people who lived in such places were once excellent hunters. Perhaps the piles of bones and meat scraps near the home of a hunter were fine places for a hungry animal to get food more easily. Perhaps more than food was offered and this confused the animals.

We know from numerous folktales that Winnipeg was once the center of a great deceivers' empire. Here the duplicitous lonely people discovered that horses and pack dogs can be especially friendly and inquisitive. Do you think the land where they lived was too cold and isolated? What other kinds of once wild creatures may have once existed in such confusing locations?

However, according to at least one legend, even animals who are not very hungry will come right up and snatch the meat away. In those days, tearing devices were usually located directly above the mouth to allow easier insertion of the prey. The ability to distinguish subtle flavors had not yet become desirable. The legend suggests that animals may eventually become slower and more difficult to use for motion sensors. Sometimes they will fight and get the answers wrong to quiz show questions. Perhaps these things could remind us that we were once easily confused as well. Stealing a reluctant mate from the neighbor's den, for example. Or dragging a frozen casket of woven reeds through the wild onions.

Sometimes barefoot elders can be found walking down the road asking, "What kinds of plants grow here?" and "What do the children eat?" and "Why are we still living in this place?" They have not learned to avoid thinking about the great mysteries, which keeps them from enjoying the comforts of senility.

The place where an idea begins has been called a source. We do not know the source of animal taming, but we believe it was preceded by a desire, just as warm winds blowing in from the warm sea make the spring come very early. Many anxious thoughts live in the earth as well, but where did the earth begin?

Too many big thoughts can make your head small. Perhaps that is why when a little whirlwind combs your hair with red dust, you might think about ants. You might wish to escape with them on your neighbor's motorcycle. You might wish to have a picnic. This is not the same thing as animal husbandry, which keeps us from sleeping when we seem to be engaged in dying or replenishment of fluids. It used to smell different. It used to close that little mouth faster. It used to listen.

September 5

Masked in a White Stocking Thick Enough to Blind Her, She Leans Forward into a Wind Like a Boat's Figurehead

We started with a stick propped up by a table. I listened to your drifting sheets. I removed the linen closet. The black plastic keeps the weeds out. The smell of ferment doesn't bother me anymore.

The nightmares have stopped except for the blood glue walking away.

The clothesline was used to make green paper. The fireplace is the entrance to a warm selfish box. The box seems to be inside itself.

No scars, but I would like to tell you about my body. I would like to scream, so let's talk. Let's tongue the old roof with wet berries. Let's hunger. Let's enter the fireplace and come back out.

We used your father to hold up the calendar because time was running out. We thought this way we could plan for the future. We found one of the children's fortresses. The doll's mouth had a stick in it. We thought about it and got cold. We dealt with it symbolically and got warm.

We stepped through a door and we lost our way back.

Now you have a body beneath your fingers. If you touch me, I will still be there. So will the others.

Someone like me who doesn't say so is a lie.

This is who needs you. Not children. Not laundry. Not the scream.

The river we swam in yesterday is the ocean.

Now we have a different stick propped up by a different table.

Then your father decides to release the calendar and we have only a table propped up with a stick as if it were the past.

Like an ocean inside the river that yesterday was the ocean which is leaking propped up by the table, which is used for something inside the body of the river. Which never needed any legs and lost its father too long ago to matter. There's always an ocean between which is used for something inside the body. This is who needs you. The box seems to be inside itself.

September 6

The Happy Old Man Goes to the Market

He wasn't past the peaches, but he was on his way. The Happy Old Man sparked and shouted. His skirts reminded his grandson of whirling dervishes.

The apples were next. The new year was on its way and the sun wasn't yet allowed any comment. Bottlerockets smuggled home in a violin case, something generous and cool in the cellar and waiting.

The fruitseller's nervous organ monkey was shelling peanuts in Papa's hat, biting fingers, eating flies and buttons. "Little Troublemaker" yelled the merchants, but were they speaking of the monkey or the man who fed it?

Disturbances the old way, no plot necessary.

And the pears! The pears desperate with juice. It frightened the ripened daughters. The sons couldn't contain themselves.

The Happy Old Man grew bright with tiny smiles of light. The Happy Old Man sputtered into the sky and danced on the evening breeze.

Is this where today happens?

Tonight is different. The fruit keeps waking up and whispering.

The Happy Old Man shouted and made sparks all night again. Carried the laundry around the room like a cornucopia. Spilled eggplant soup on the lantern.

The next day at the market, the Happy Old Man is back again. Young boys are buying the little kielbasa for lunch. The butcher snickers. "Now you can spank the baby sausages."

Polite as abandoned clothing, the Happy Old Man pays attention while bouquets of the homeless introduce themselves as flowers until one of them with a uric taint on him, like a last ditch effort to mark the only territory he has left, tries to get him to feel his head, claiming it's made of tinfoil and the suppurating sores on his feet are leaking something more than his life. "In war only the bullets escape," he mumbles.

An elegant young man in a black tophat wipes the tears from his raven mustaches and on up to his cheeks, his eyes, with a handkerchief as white as snow. He removes his clothing, folding it carefully, and enters the river with his hat still on. His long shiny hair flows out behind him as his body lowers into the water. He dogpaddles slowly beneath the cobblestone bridge. Soon he is joined by a dragonfly, riding his tophat, its iridescent wings shimmering against the dark background.

September 7

The Caretakers

We admired his formal demeanor and his careful opinions, surprising at times but never radical or weak. When he removed his clothing in the public square, derision and abuse greeted him, and he endured it as he might endure rain until late one night when two women took him to the cemetery and offered to love and care for him together. He asked why they had brought him here, to the cemetery, to offer this.

When they answered, "We wish to start at the end," he sank to the ground and muttered, "I have just come from there. Must we go back?" And the two women answered, "It is the only way the others will accept us. Otherwise, what we have learned will threaten them."

A monument had been erected in the square. A bronze statue of a soldier who had something to do with our freedom. His military clothing hung from his broad honorable shoulders in long bronze curves that would never, no never, fall. No one questioned the past from which he had come, before we could take freedom for granted. His name had grown too old to be real.

Then Octavio, the man who removed his clothing, reported that one of the women had disappeared and before we could search for her, we had to learn who we were searching for. Octavio didn't know, called her only My Savior, as he called the other woman as well, who we knew to be the daughter of a carpenter, who called her Isabella. Some joked that both women were Isabella and Octavio, the man who removed his clothing, was living in a fantasy, but we looked for the missing woman and we failed to find her. It was not long after this that Octavio died, some said of grief, and Isabella was seen one night with two men who left the public square with her.

Despite what others might think, the two men were welcomed into our village and they lived out their days in quiet dignity under the same name, My Savior, with Isabella. Now I am the only one who seems to remember she was ever anything other than My Savior, and the three of them, under one name, live together in an old farmhouse, raising farm animals and turnips. No one seems to pay any attention to them, but once they were seen removing their clothing in the public square and climbing up on to the back of the statue, where they held each other and waited for something to appear that did not appear. I think they were happy. I found it very sad.

September 8

An Arrow Beyond the Target

It was morning, the moon and the sun in the same cross-eyed sky. The daughter of the night was crying with her rabbit in the hay. I felt the dew between my toes. Bees were already drinking the fallen apples. My own daughter swallowed a seed and later said she watched for days, but it didn't come out. I don't know the name of the song or where it's coming from, but a happy song o'erplayed grows sad. It's not the darkness but the sunlight that erases us.

A lonely neighbor looked tired and beaten, empurpled by the clumsiness of her own angry life. Her headache turned seventy this year.

That was in a time of rotting fenceposts and letters to the editor and raisins. That was in the brain of a follower, whose shoes contained a single pebble, which wore the shoes in his place and let him visit while he was walking to the store or while he was forgetting.

Everyone knows it's possible to get there, but nobody gets there.

You're inside a body that belongs to someone you don't know. You used to be you when you didn't know it and now that you know it, you're not you anymore. It's someone trying to save you from you.

This time I tried not to talk.

I'm not so sad as I thought, I thought. I've got oysters. I've got a pan to cook them in. I noticed the clouds playing in the mud again. I noticed pleasure. I tied my shoelaces to the adventure. I noticed huckleberries. I noticed going on.

I started the fire again. I caused it.

I noticed I was singing. I tried not to do it too many times.

I did it too many times.

September 9

Small Daisy Tied Around a Finger Like a Ring

I was watching all the ink bleed from the newspaper. It stopped raining. Accidents, outrages, even a few celebrations leaking, my right to know the life outside myself washed clean.

I was on my way to the parts store.

I remember when you were my brother, before the accident, when you were bigger and that's all that mattered. You were older too so I guess it wasn't all that mattered. You've been living inside me all my life, but I don't know who you are.

I was thinking about you while the newspaper bled. There were a lot of dead people in there, but this time you weren't one of them. Some kind of a secret vegetable pain was cranking around in my stomach. I gave it some Pepto Bismol. I gave it some consideration.

I thought about you leaving me and I thought about all the things I didn't know about, that never even arrived, and I thought, Let the swallow deliver the sky's thought and the sky's thought hold the pleasure of the unseen and the pleasure of the unseen deliver itself by means unknown to the end of the nest which has stretched from the one inside to the one that holds your thought of the one not reached by thought, and I thought, Let the rise of monuments beyond their known subjects become your means of achieving an elevated potential, and I thought we were inside a possibility that was inside another possibility or maybe it was like the catching of a fish that has just swallowed a fish that has just swallowed a fish that is still alive, and so I thought I was getting carried away.

Then I kicked the newspaper into the sewer.

I keep doing that. I keep remembering.

Then I reached the kind of pleasure the forest finds in you. I'm in there somewhere, busy padding the answer with questions.

September 10

Bad Bag of Romance

Once she was head librarian of a small college in the West where lumbermen and country lawyers practiced being lumbermen and city lawyers. And when she jettisoned the first disappointing lover at the back of the huge lot in the expensive southside neighborhood near the golf course, no one suspected her yet of anything but bad judgment.

Years before, her leadership had made life miserable for several librarians at a county branch extension and they left town and, like most who left that town, they discovered better things. But one of them, she insisted to anyone who wouldn't be believed, was sending her messages. He spoke to her through her car radio, even after her husband (where did he come from, they wondered) had it taken out, swearing in a deep voice, booming her biblical name across the plush interior of her carefully upholstered mind and laughing.

A couple of over-researched forestry students hunkered the first prototype into place from a logging truck, a prop-lot relic of Blonde Bimbos from Outer Space and the sequels, Green Moisture and Interplanetary Desire. The rest just "landed" with no witnesses. Even her ex-husband couldn't explain it. By the time the college newspaper photographed it, eleven neighborhood complaints had fallen on deaf ears.

Months later, on the night of the fire, the neighbors reported "machine noise" and "bright sharp lights" and the insurance company eventually paid off on a single destroyed "storage building," her daughter afraid to report three blackened space ships. Her mother's disappearance that night repeated itself endlessly around coed campfires and frat house beer busts for years, until the body turned up, nibbled but identifiable, in a nearby reservoir. Two local poets wrote about it, one a maudlin ballad, the other, despite several fellow library worker's beliefs that she had never really loved anyone without an advanced degree in library science, a color-coordinated BMW, and green camouflaged scuba gear, turned into an erotic interstellar love epic.

The fire department's footage of the burning "storage building" appeared without permission in the underground cult classic sequel Green Moisture II which also included the axe murders of three shrieking coeds caught panting after hours in a knowledge- darkened corner of the Reserve Book Room.

Their heads were never found, but their bodies shriveled up and took cataloging positions in rural Saskatchewan where they developed latent interests in spoon collecting and catch and release flower arranging. One of them is writing an autobiography of Lawrence Welk. If she had a car radio, I'd propose.

September 11

A Dog Barking at the Wind

It's been a quiet day, and I watched a lizard on the garden wall at sunset, lightning in the nearest mountains. Early evening yet, and I sit quietly in my living room chair. A dried-up leaf on a houseplant in the window reminds me of a minor loss I can't seem to forget. An owl hoots and the refrigerator rumbles to life.

I step out onto the porch. A dog is barking at the wind. A breeze swirls down the canyon, tumbling in the aspen leaves, rolling over the meadows in search of horses. More dogs barking, and I can see by the porchlight a brief spatter of raindrops in the dust.

Then everything is quiet again for the longest time. The air grows cool, and I imagine the world covered in snow. A crow spreads its wings and breaks my white silence, its sharp call cracking the brittle air. My thoughts return to the porch and this silence, and I long for something I cannot name. Yesterday I might have said it was solitude.

September 12

A Bowl of White Roses

Welcome to one of the rain's most fundamental agendas. An offering of a few fallen leaves, an induction into the river's rant, a declension of tears. These things her body knew first. But she kept finding her husband's face trapped in the mirror, his sympathy left lying about like a torn shirt, the room packed with a tremendous lack of people.

Greet her with your scars. Be tactful and lean. She is ruthless and sensitive. She is clever and clearly not what you need but what you want.

At dusk their lost child briefly reappears in the pattern the wind makes with the undersides of the birch leaves. Soon it will no longer be the sun shining on the fruit in the wooden bowl that illuminates the silent table, but the fruit itself.

He was the kind of man who never quite arrived at the storm. His mistakes were brilliant. He followed a hinged strategy of wonder, like an afterthought on the ragged edge of his escape. She gave back pieces of the story, like seeds falling from the cloak of a tired traveler. Her cry hung on the air like wet laundry. A flight of birds swerved to include the sound, recovered and continued weaving north to settle a dispute in an older religion.

When the time for decisions came, he was distant and deliberate. She served a bowl of white rose petals, and the past quickly grew more fragile than the tiniest brittle link in an insect's claw, as fragile as the moment she finally accepted the emptiness. But she is unable to ask for a divorce. She cannot stop consulting his carelessness.

If only the night could bring the peace it seems to promise. One child is hopeful. One child lost in the wilderness is even more hopeful.

But your wilderness has a desperate history and hers a husband. And children get lost slowly in their own lives.

September 13

Alas, the King Becomes You

The king wrote a proclamation on a servant's head. Then he did that sidelong walk stray dogs borrow from jealous husbands and constipated sheep. The witnesses had the feeling they were all going to stand up and start crying, but they didn't.

Then the king's holy windfarm erupted. Some colored Easter death was walking around demanding attention. It blew itself around a lot, but its shell was empty. "It can't be explained. That's why it makes so much sense," said the king's intellectual terrorist disguised as a priest/journalist.

"A squeezed bird does not sing," predicted one of the uninsured oracles.

Like a prison made of holes is the king's brain. A disaster looking for hugs. An anthology of subtraction. (His voice seemed strong, but his newspaper trembled.) "I'd never think of killing myself," he exclaimed. But then he'd never thought of many things.

And then it was, "I'm tired of people without any spikes sticking out of them." Another proclamation. (Something for the guards to do.)

"Oh but he's such a darling," said the Queen always, meaning he lets her come first. Meaning I didn't know we were this close, but okay. Meaning the kingdom is in for another siege. Witnesses scatter and the queen disguises her cherished strawberry marmalade as an interview with decapitated rebels. The king orders all farm animals to identify their ancestors. He is no longer confused by weather. He perceives himself as assertive and it's just that the sky's children have simply decided to play elsewhere today and the sky, the sky is white with agreeable puffy answers.

Meaning darkness may no longer surround us, but the king's voice has grown small and certain, terribly certain, like a man who tells you of the coming seasons as if they sat in the chair next to him.

Meaning some more ordinary things have been made more fascinating by omission from the daily kingdom. Meaning filthy and far too loud, this life falls into us and out again as sudden pain dipped in charm and delight, and we attach to it both our pride and doubt, loving them as the beast that brought us our replacement and guarantee of losing some part of ourselves in gain of royal monument deep in memory's o'ertraveled halls.

Meaning the one missing command is merely the blind daughter of a beautiful stone. Meaning all intentions must be annulled. This could be anywhere, but it's not. The kingdom you live in, lives within you. It's a kind of theft. You might wish to take some air.

September 14

It Was a Monday So Everyone Seemed to Be Starting Something New

We did not notice the beggar. Nor did we think of women as fruit, though we often wished that we ourselves were not so ripe.

Yes, we live on a challenged planet and we cannot attend a banquet without considering starvation. Sex reminds us of the voices falling into the river beneath our feet on the nights when it's too warm to stay inside.

Still it was possible to imagine the brother we didn't have looking at us in stunned surrender, as he had done for most of his life. We were inventing ambiguously symbolic dilemmas because we needed them. As in, "My mother was opening tomato sauce and she cut her finger."

"What kind of body, then, is this earth?" you might ask. As if the slick green leather of the jungle you're lost in were nothing more than a small growth on one's forehead. And what to make of the sky so heavy and close that smoke from the chimneys tries to crawl back into the houses?

We don't have to know where we are to be in the wrong place. We're ready to blame someone now. We've got piety stamped on our tidy little brains. We don't blame the opposite gender and we don't blame anyone who's not like us and we don't blame anyone whose religious beliefs include gophers. You can see by our facial expressions that we're more than right.

The beggar's crying, his cap stolen, painted the egg-yolk yellow of a Spanish tavern. The beggar stares at the back of his father's head. Smelling it from a barely discernible distance. As if the kind of odor you get from sleeping in old cemeteries allows the imagination to release the careful, realistic kind of absence that still awaits us. We don't exactly beg for it anymore, but a studied yearning still complicates our ignorance.

September 15

A Migration of Tiny Cottonwoods

She's the one you feel you really know only you don't know if she knows. But it's certain that she would want to if she'd only let herself. Something's in the way, and it's not anything very important, but it's in the way, and you wish she'd just encourage you a little more to love her the way you know you should if she could let you, and then she'd want it as much as you do. You're a nice guy, intelligent, not bad looking, a great lover when inspired by a woman loving back, good sense of humor, capable of being nice to her parakeet.

Maybe the problem is you appear to be too serious. It scares her because serious men in her life have meant trouble. And because you can be seen as serious, she won't believe it when you tell her how silly and fun you are in the relaxed moments, like after lovemaking, which she could see if she gave you the chance, but maybe she won't because you're too serious.

You know her well enough now to know she might not know you know all this or might not see how well-balanced all of this really is, even if you do come across serious sometimes. In your better poems that is. Or at your grandmother's house. Who died several years ago. An empty spot in your life not half as important as this woman could be if she wanted you. And maybe she does, but it's hard to say when you don't know all the things some people tell you you should know about someone before you say things like this.

Perhaps you might begin to wonder where this problem originated. It's not part of your uniqueness. It comes from being over there when it moves over here because it doesn't hold still. It comes from feeling and she doesn't need the ordinary attachments. She doesn't need the weight. Not now.

You look at your new parakeet with gratitude, perfecting the arrangement of its newspapers and what's happened. This time it's got a few names and you hang them on the wall.

Now they're asking if you like what you're doing and you don't know what they mean because you don't know what you're doing.

Now the parakeet's talking back and it's not her voice anymore and there's something in the air that makes you sneeze. You can't help noticing it's been there before.

And now the parakeet's listening.

September 16

The Shorter Path That Goes Through the Garden Takes More Time Than the One That Goes Around It

"I know you'll do the right thing," his mother said when he had that look in his eye again. And what she said seemed to hurt him. He thought it was sharper than the tongue of a bird.

He watched a tired cloud touch the forehead of a stone as he watered the lawn. He heard the wind's voice change to a watery oboe of welcome as darkness came on.

Then he remembered what his mother had said.

Then he thought about the black doves pouring from the cathedral at the edge of the square in the town his father lived in. And the limbs of the trees in the orchard sharply jutting and turning back on themselves as if each tree had been assembled with wire.

And then he thought about the church's cold floor and the fat little Madonnas as well fed as veal and angels rounder than suckling pigs.

And because what you believe isn't what you get, he felt different and uncertain and cautious for a very long time.

Then the moment came when his heart spread all the way to the sky. And the moment before when walking on a country road, one horse just looks wrong.

When you have let someone down, the mirror also deserves your apology.

September 17

That's Just the Way I Stop Talking

A swagger of a song lisping from the leak of his throat, a rasp of weather like territorial bravado?

No such action, no razor of clever banter before the misplaced bump and grind. And the baby clapped happily for the stuffed toy, already in a better world.

Then the earth beneath his mother's lung garden fell, cigarette smoke commandeering the vital organs.

I hope I have not shamed you. I hope I have not disguised the fears. Isn't it lovely the way the ugliest ones free us? A beautiful rat of a peach dripping with wounds and gorgeous clichés.

I had to let out a little of the certainty. Otherwise it just hurts. Father wouldn't approve. The careful little shit.

So hello hello from the useless shoes and the closets and the lost destinations in the elders' paws, trailing smoke across the escaping boat that rocks on the carnal waves like jellyroll, hawking up expectations with a pretty little lilt and tussle of petticoats dipping decorously towards the invisible shoelace anthems of the departing river.

Male child motherless, I am not the name of anyone or anything that claims me by proliferation, or by falsifying my passport so that I am forced to participate freely. It only proves me wrong again.

I am named: Not This.

Or I am named: This.

A movement between.

September 18

The Pursuit of Happiness

Marylou and Cookie were busy stroking witch-hazel across the flanks of a lamb. They didn't notice Topper and Bunyan and Egghead watching a platoon of tiny men marching across the stunted grass.

You're not allowed to go to the bathroom by yourself. You're not allowed to chew ice.

Bushy eyebrows are donated to the grandfather's funeral fund.

Topper is really a miniature president, but a miniature president is not a king. It's delightful to meet a miniature president, but Topper's been blown up and not as little as you might think.

"Let's church them now and be done with the heathens," said Marylou.

Bunyan was watching the little men scuttle away like big men with their pants down around their ankles. Their movements were more efficient than you might think. Crab-like, orderly, persistent.

"I can't do it, I can't do it," shouted Egghead. Then he said, "No, that's wrong. But I believed it for a moment."

Then Cookie was altogether busy watching the pigs eat like pigs. "I don't want anything like that in my garden," she said.

"I don't see why it has to rain today." I said that. I did. Because it looked like it was going to do something in the sky. And here is an almost unnecessary sleepy little nodkin operating like a foil that might have heard me say this only to verify that someone might have heard me say this. I was unnamed and observatory. I was narrative. I was the convenient conduit. I didn't have to participate.

However, the same can not be said of you, although it's probably foolish of me to say it. Would you like to walk along the garden path or spit on the retreating snakes? They will not harm you. They will not bite you with sharp painful teeth. No, they won't.

And here is another sleepy little nodkin. He doesn't need to verify anything except the need to verify something. We're all like that.

Quickly enough this life begins to grow darker and make the garden a more interesting place. We might pass some women there eating sandwiches. We might expand to accommodate the progress of the marching men. We might worship some situations we don't really understand. We might believe what we do is communal and sweet and available to little men of any size. We might believe women of greater stature can say things that men of great stature cannot. We might not be allowed to go to the bathroom by ourselves. Might we be busy stroking witch-hazel across the flanks of a lamb?

And yet it might not even be our garden. It might not be our church.

We can vote for the president, but the president cannot vote for us.

The meadow is filled with clocks. Call them weeds if you must. Time lingers in them, lingers enough to be measured by its not quite absence and the winter comes like a wrist beneath their arrows when the grass has nothing left to say. The clocks begin sleeping with their own little clocks turned towards tomorrow.

There's no reason for this kind of happiness. You do it without knowing how.

That's how.

September 19

So I Told Her

I was alive then in the rich and the desperate dark. She thought I was deep so I swallowed the river and she drowned happily after every other, but I don't want to be myself anymore. I want to enter becoming like a tail explaining away its dog.

I work for the padded beaks of dull bosses jabbing up your leg like a slow shiver. No witness. No evidence. No heart. A little sincere desperation. But the psychic chatter of it lisping into the ragged future, well, it just can't be puddled off like that, as if it were some ancient dog eating rain.

So we separated membering from remembering. We lived on with each part, with each otherwise. She thought I was even deeper. I was, but it wasn't a place I could stay.

Then a blind sexual salamander of fear interrupted the lunar anarchist's meeting at the Every Other Night Cafe. The tiniest limp in my personal orbit had snubbed the bare-chested moon.

The woman in question, filled with unnecessary windows, slipped the red of a visual secret, the red of a voyeur's tired eyes, into the immediate celestial body of the fever. Which was mine.

"I'm still infected, but not so wildly," I replied.

"Such a terrible weight of nobodies," she whimpered, screaming with visitation rights, giving away repressed desires like nervous insects burning to open the store. Then just burning.

"Oh my God," I said, though I haven't one but only a mist like the breath of thousands of mice, "no matter who she loves, she makes a job of it."

There was something outside on the inside. It appeared to be a tiny house made from the mating cries of small mammals, the emotional uncertainties spilling out like the fear, which is pressure released by persistent hunger. Individual elements without voices scattered, frantically searching for speech, their tiny heart attacks ticking. You could hear them long before the body building fell, right there in front of the station.

We choose the platform, we don't choose the train.

September 20

A Compulsion to Empty the Container

Fear arrives each night. That's when the cattails' story of a more delicate sorrow slips away from the ditches along the road and rests. You have to be careful. You never know what the despair is thinking.

Maria enters my room with a warm towel. Her children are waiting for their supper. She watches me sleeping. I am not sleeping.

Mother's resting in the atrium. Sunset exhausts her. She dreams of green birds. She coughs and whispers.

Not the thing said but the way of saying it.

As if the story were full of the past and the cattails had sent something escaping to release it.

As if you did not know what you had become.

As if you were standing in the waves, caressing the ocean.

September 21

The Body's Legends

When someone remembers a legend of ice, cold wet spears pierce the body's memory, a chilled floundering skewered to the uncertainty of small heavy throbs, its enveloping night descending like a tide welcomed back from some ancient rhythm of departure.

Place one on the subject's tongue. He swallows and you search for it all over his body. By morning it will be so familiar it will blend with the dawn, accompany you when you leave.

If I let myself in, and live there, inside my skin, there would still be enough space for all my shrinking and my doubt, but they might finally come to some agreement and think about wrapping themselves up in the appearances that might eventually replace me.

And if I could finally live inside my shoes, I might let myself out without leaving, alone in two containers that tell you where I've been.

If I notice the crow sitting silently in the pine tree inside the dream, head hunched into his shoulder, and wonder what he is dreaming, it's because he has escaped me and has no fear, and I am looking for the dream that takes me there.

It's a long way out of your mind to come into your body. I leave myself an escape saying I decided not to have been there. You have not been there as well, and you left an equal absence. I thought of attending it as I did my own.

Oh many times I didn't do that. I turned around in our memory and walked out, trying not to remember what I had done, into the room where I kept the untouched parts.

One version of both of us was seeing around others known to have been seeing around others. As one we sat up late on the stove.

Unattended falling. A new pleasure of it.

There were stories in which my silly little mouse translation invented my movement away, but I had to find something to live in before trading it. I visited the shop by the wharf with things in formaldehyde that don't make sense. I moved into a chambered aerialist. I took a bath in a large dish of peas. One of the memories offered me a big wad of ceiling to sleep on.

The song you used to sing shot itself and lived.

Somewhere in your hair the night is melting. I might go there and wait for morning. I might grow my face longer, with a pointed chin. I might move in. I might mumble about what has left me and it wouldn't be you.

I might put my hand in it. I might follow. I might return and return so that I might leave myself behind. I might fail to do so.

I might find you again, failing, all absence growing fonder, a great swoon of endless falling, itself falling away. I might remember this when I do not know I am remembering this.

September 22

Poverty

The beggar's knife was not visible before the murder and it was not certain the beggar was the one who had used it, but who else? Could anyone have known the beggar would be carrying it?

The yellow cat had not been noticed until the red paw-print was found on the title page of the cheap mystery the dead man's sister had been reading. Someone said he could hear a sound like the brush of a tail.

I said, "I am the one who is still here, so I am the one who will solve the murder." I turned towards the whistle of the teakettle. The book with the red paw-print was sleeping on the stove.

I sat down. My chair was made of wood and I was sitting in it. It would have been unnatural to grow larger at this moment. The yellow cat was licking its red paws. It seemed so long ago that it mattered.

The rain was falling and I was not in its path. I knew I was not solved but still solvent. I knew I was not here to answer the book.

I reduced the top button of my shirt to an object by placing it on the table. I was certain it had not been visible during the murder, but I did not know why I thought this was important.

A piece of ash from the pages as I burned the book started floating in the air and it crossed the beam of sunlight cutting through the tear in the window-shade.

I began to select portions of the room to memorize. I began to place the murder weapon in the various wounds I had noticed. I placed my cheek against the table to see if the surface was legible. I was alone and the yellow cat was not part of my experience.

I said, "I am going to remain." I said, "I am going to suffer." The yellow cat turned the page of a different book and it seemed to reveal that I was not the murderer. The beggar had left. The beggar had a calling.

I was not able to lift anything from the table until the knife was removed. I was not able to button my shirt. I was sitting in a chair made of wood and I seemed to be suffering. I guessed that there were only a few more pages to turn. I guessed wrong.

A sound like the beating of a small bird's wings left me exhausted.

September 23

Crying the Mare

The harvest nearly complete, the farmer's neighbors tied the remaining sheaves of corn together and flung their knives at them. It was a game called Crying the Mare and it made Jonathan think of himself growing up. He thought of the deep wise voice he heard in his dreams and he threw knives at it to pin it to the wall, but the wall in a dream doesn't hold much. He wanted that voice.

"I'll have turnips for lunch. There's no deception in a turnip," said Petrov while the knives whistled and the shouts of "Almost" rent the air. Twas an unexpected wisdom indeed that sent the sky into the children's pockets at that moment, but there you have it.

It matters not to the progress of innocence that the river continues weeping.

Tom the Seeker saddled the children's clouds with warnings of impending doom. He still carries a knapsack to hold the emptiness he finds. He'll sleep in it.

Jonathan was hidden somewhere inside Jonathan. "I'll try to be an accurate knife," he thought. His eyes were open. He began counting the bundles of sheaves.

Tom the Seeker gave Jonathan a wooden plate and said, "To the silent trees I offer my excess. If this does not speak for them, I'll replace it with the rich smell of rotting seaweed." He gave Jonathan a fork, turned around in a slow circle and began barking at the sky.

Before it began raining, a farmer's sickle struck the knot in a bundle of corn sheaves and everyone shouted three times. Jonathan and Petrov stopped eating clouds long enough to feed the other children. The field was still hungry. There were no birds left in that field to verify the wind in our place and no deep wise voice to separate sleeping from waking.

Q: How much does fear weigh?

A: Too little to carry all the way home.

And the mare sleeps in the harvested field and listens to the dreams of the sheaves and runs farther in the dream than when it wakes.

There's a voice in everything you do, but sometimes it's not your voice. And then it is. And then you live there.

September 24

As If the Moment

In a dream of blunt scissors and bifocals, a stranger limps in the shadows, your desire a grounded bird, your future an upturned collar. The red dirt rises, there's no code, as your father paces across the yard. The insects pound their tiny voices against the swirling air, the ice-age of its intent descending.

Then the crack before the wrong tree falls and the words line up against the mistake. You wanted a memory, from the inside, the beauty of it like an ugly spore, nearly overlooked, like the stranger's unpredictable agenda. Not the moon beautifully rhyming with its children on the tide, but an oil lamp flickering wildly, hung from the bow of a fishing boat poled up the channel by drunken poachers.

You feel like you're the new kid, head too large at the top of the pale careless reach of your body, nearly human and incomplete. The kind of child so desperate for attention he experiments in his own brilliant, unlit head. Tonight the nighthawks seem to be living on stars instead of insects, the blue rooster of night pronouncing light backwards to the dawn that patiently waits. I didn't really have a dream, I became one.

The boy strokes his disobedient limbs like submissive pets, guiding the great limping vessel of their tomorrow across the treacherous stillness. On one side of that wall is everything we once were and on the other side of the wall is everything we are going to be. It's a beautiful wall. There is no wall.

Sunlight unwinds as grass, only another father's isolation greening in the belated morning. All those ghosting fathers applaud like breath another waitress moon, a thought so tentative it disappears before it's spoken.

September 25

A Spiritual Dilemma

The sound of a leg dragging on a warm still night. A smoky ruin of a man wheezing with ambiguous pleasure.

Sleeping on a train. Forgetting your destination.

Driven into the distance, I want the whole sky.

And you try to leave it alone but you can't. You're in the middle of it. Because you are asking questions. No one can hear you, but it doesn't matter. It won't leave you alone.

Today they're hanging baskets in the square instead of thieves. It's the wrong season for it. There was ice in the wall, a plaintive whistle of caution. I can feel my whole body and it's melting. Inside the barbed wire, I find an offering. In its heart I saw four crickets sitting in a matchbox. I felt the wet muzzle of snow. A white hut asleep by the river. It's not mine anymore.

I was outside. I was just outside the edge. Anticipation leaking through the wooden slats. A man taken ill while traveling.

Is remorse manufactured in this region?

There were five, there were eight, there were too many.

A sad song sung by a naked man. I suppose I knew him.

We watched the morning begin poking at the window.

I was sent here to take you home. I was sent here because of a sudden impulse to drop my arm in the sewer. Because I was indicating disgust with my upper lip, my teeth were visible. I remembered the great sleeping eyelids of the devout.

I was carrying a transparent suitcase full of Baghdad and resinous coal dust. It was famous air. It was what I lived for. It contained a partially mechanized variety of woolen lizard and a soft cylindrical nuptial embrace, as faintly brittle as the call of a titmouse. Can you imagine the sorrows contained in its bright green suspenders?

She appeared in the checkout line at the grocery store. Her son was embracing his tarpaper. She bought mead, bubblegum ice cream and cheese pizza. There was a reason caught in a tent with flames inside meant to start something. I believed it was internal. I might have been mistaken.

September 26

Against Illusion

I wasn't there, so I snuckered in and continued defending my disconsolate mountains from fat low clouds. I wondered if my absence reminded you of Chicago or the bird-song that was empty the day we fell from grace. It's the whisper of the crash that leans away. Whispering once was whispering has been. You couldn't call it constructive, but something was being made, and it stayed. I knew it was loud, but I couldn't hear it, an early glimmer of the next thing that wanted a body, a horse in the shape of a cloud, or the city meadow's rising floor freshly laid and turned to the habitation of the habit of life. Since the last time you found it, you've come a long way only to arrive at another start of you.

All the windows were white and cast shadows on the ceiling, your purse womb promising something to carry on the outside. So I'm a wind at you and you bluster a scissorful of not so much, fastened to my own life like a book cover. Inside, the room I am grows a door though it's not clear which way it opens.

I invented a device that catches light and gradually releases it whenever your lips begin casting shadows on the shadows falling up the ceiling. That always makes me want to remember the clothing I wore to the morning. I used to think something would wait for me to happen, and sometimes it did, but still, I was someone else when I returned, so I couldn't find you in the fat low clouds, and the ceiling was older with its shadows and all the light released by Chicago.

Since you could see through the leaves, we knew there was falling. We followed a book all the way to the ending. The way the wind crossed the river, you couldn't tell where anything was going. The puffy cloud fights were enormous where some others like us weren't lonely, with their children cavorting in baby blue pajamas with feet and cowboys lassoing escapist clouds.

I filled my life like an envelope but no one sent it. Whether you sink or swim, said the wisdom, which was common and therefore not wisdom, the water parts for you. The twilight keeps a notebook hidden in the coming dark that can't read it.

September 27

Why He Refused to Discuss It

The evening swells, white moths so thick it seems as if a snowfall had fluttered itself dry and found the air erratically uplifting. We cannot be concerned is what the grass is whispering, and I'm happy to have lost something of myself to it. I've come to a position of acceptance, pouring over a dusty chair.

A map of her hair spread out till it reached the scented ear posteriors and then documented an experience outside the room. Perhaps I perched on a thimble if a thimble was there. I trembled. I moved and moved again. I was a small voice traveling to an event of its own since it no longer belonged to someone.

I felt my mouth become an ear without any preconceived territory. Silence breathed its question as if it were the only one. I wanted an unobstructed view. I no longer needed sentencing, but I could accept it all the same.

The body is just the other house out back, I thought. I must have been swept away by the kind of mind that makes brooms. I used to be who I thought I was. I used to be me when I wasn't worth being. Then I separated myself from my expectations. I was a dress handkerchief that didn't have any practical considerations, a potential held in the breast pocket, accomplishing something merely stylish, without reference to its original cause.

I had become airy and reflective, so I decided to admit that it's not that easy to tell zombies from sales clerks in the used love store. The air smells like fish and hairy legs. I'm trying to delineate the dimensions of what it smells like so that its indecency becomes my decency.

The curtain of odors rolls over and flaps out of its threads I remember saying to myself. I tip my head and try to lick the fat knuckle of it, the only endless flower I know, the slow visual love-song of a bee. You can't escape it, but it can escape you, bumbling dutifully from one lovesick rose to another. Or it could be an ant no one notices inside one bloom of the beautifully wrapped gift, falling out, and then soon enough you're the only one left who can bite.

Before this, I answered with reasons and confused myself with now and then, so this time I positioned upon the next. I have a goal and when I get there I keep going.

September 28

Why She Refused to Discuss It

Before the storm, the dust began swirling, great manes of it like smoke galloping along the path above the meadow. The heat of it sat with you on the hotel balcony. The weather was your finest entertainment.

In the chipped blue jug filled with earth, a thick green plant continued drying in the afternoon's sunlight and suddenly swarmed with a blaze of insects, an amusement so foreign it drew you from your chrysalis. Wings still dripping, you leaned toward that event of weather that surprised you with its similarity to your releasing heart, and the sea seemed to address you, to address the small complaint of life you had been since that shadowy escape from the moods of your previous involvement. Could you really have been defied in your best attempts at order?

And somehow even that wet deviation fell to the inertia you temporarily rise from now to send your senses straining out over the plaza, beyond the fishnets swaying on their drying racks where nothing is interested in the story of your mistakes, not the lush limetrees enlivened with the growing breezes or the stolid wooden pier reaching out tenaciously into the wild flights of water spouting as the rain begins to fall, not the cobbles in the plaza steaming with the cool touch of another welcomed stranger, and in the midst of all this fleeting metamorphosis, you still see yourself through the slowly rising fog as a gesture of some late runner of errands impatiently crossing the familiar streets, dripping with affection, to do something impulsive for someone foreign whose beauty lies brilliantly in her shadows.

Then suddenly there are horses running in the plaza, the long-awaited rain streaming from genderless manes, and the one white horse, frightened by the thunder, stands turned towards a darkened building, nervously stamping his hooves, breathing rapidly, excited by its fear.

September 29

Temporary Embodiment of a Passing Cloud

I came back on the roads made for leaving. I began welcoming the moon and entered the dream life of water.

Moonlight replaced the air. It traveled there without a platform. She held all the clouds she had been carrying in her shoe up to the light to verify the integrity of their blindness.

Although I was so transparent I participated openly in my own patience, I still carried the same handful of weightless thorns (when I arrived at the village, it was a book and I closed my eyes to read it) and the smell of several shadows, feeding.

In time I could no longer pronounce my surface name. Tentative, I was sniffing at my universe like a falling star, as if to mirror an absence, as lover and monk.

It was like coming upon a cave in darkness and finding someone forgotten, breath's candle barely flickering from the creature's soft opening as your name is spoken and one of you reaches out.

And the loved one released her eyes like ferrets darting into the hole after prey (it's been like this before I've been told and you went hungry). As someone's god, she carried long black bolts of hair tied to her belt (the sky was like that in those days, its beauty bestial and dense with instinct) and wrapped her fingerprint around another zebra.

I could have been the prince with his tongue frozen to the moat (only the stripper's biblical snake having thus far fallen into the stars in his eyes) and I could have been released but for the scribe's familial objection to the square of lawn upon which the virginal cake was performed.

She did indeed want a child, but the lovely couple ran out of frozen deposits and withdrew. It's true that sometimes we do not wish to be circled with arms as a gesture of affection or possessed of a violin that would prefer to be a horse, even if it will never be a horse. It's as if the law of possibility shook your hand and the gangster's powder-puff face proved to be dusted with tiny engines living in the middle ages. Drive around back advised the priest's young undercarriage, but the particular desire had not yet succumbed to the compass of its potential and the engines were far more delicate than they appeared.

Right now I'm already the next accordion with time to deceive my keys, the result a song like a spout leaning into the stream of river rising to itself even as falling, greenly hinted and as attractively unreliable as topiary. I've had several flavored bridges offer to and I still have my Gertrude Stein bread rolls (a calling card which does no calling might well get bored) (the gentle retarded one having stolen the swan's headgear) (the child's teddy bear barely half eaten by his lovely horse) (the space beneath my upper zipper only once mistaken for a porcelain soup tureen) and a disgusting memory of the charming gastronome who threw me from the window even as he asked for the hand that broke my fall.

I'm saying this but not to a cloudless sky, the reticent pathway.

September 30

How I Acquired My New Position

That path revealed only that I was not the first. I decided to leave the future behind. Long before the after I was.

Can you hear the idiot snorting? The kind of sound that frightens the innocence.

Clocks do nothing to help me. Have you noticed that the second hand is the third? East of her cheek, oblique references to unrealized pleasures. The irresolute trail of a salt mouse.

I witnessed my memoir beneath those clouds.

There are some uncertainties in the driveway. I look forward to your next visit. Of course there are some reasons I shouldn't be here. I've troubled the causeway with untroubled causes.

The oldest was wearing an old baseball cap when the ice on the stove finally melted. He had no excuse for the night crew, still not old enough to father such a moon.

That's not my job anymore either, but I enjoy the transformations and I am old enough to be saddened by them.

Previously in this trial, I told the truth about a lie. Scaffolds and scaffolds of knicker trimmings. I held the Joyce against it and snapped it smartly.

Ambassador to rain has always been my most tedious career, but I can't seem to give back the gentle caress. My best efforts evaporate.

They tell me my resignations proved how well-suited I was for the job.

All the parts seemed to be in working order, but the story itself resisted ordering its content.

I got what I wanted. I thought the world was bigger than that.

October

October 1

Entrance to the Moon

If you wish to visit the future, you should follow a plan. Someone might wish to write an historical review tracing the route by which you hoped to return. This may result in permission from the residents to misinterpret the importance of negligent weather because they know you will not be accidentally harvested. Do not offer blood before they offer milk.

Make a list of questions. Be sure to include some that you want answered.

Whenever you choose to visit, people will expect you to behave according to laws. These laws will not necessarily behave according to reason, but the people you visit will not recognize this and they will not tell you what all of these laws are.

When you return, a thank you letter should be written to each person who didn't try to help you. From these people you learned the most.

You should expect the other travelers to hobble the priest without direct regard for the crime, which placed him in that position. You can anticipate the disregard of the shepherds as well. Their rowdy flocks are seldom available for donations or correspondence. The mistaken carpenters can be expected to post daily the most inappropriate parts of their hammering.

When you are ready to study the reasons you have abandoned your former position, you can enjoy field trips farther abroad with less deception. An imaginary mood torch or an irreverent concept of social integration might become available for companionship. You might need only one symbolic calf to fatten on worried meals of maybe the next time, and if this effort is replacing the right parts of you, you could return to the first field of you, straw words bundled to fertilize a comfortable slow retreat.

Despite the apparent goal of these activities, the future doesn't require preparation and will arrive without pretense, but if you have been traveling without your former intentions, try to notice the fresh night air. Don't forget your milk bucket. Consider how much you can hold in abeyance.

Climb in and announce your presence. Continuously.

October 2

Scatter to the Hills My Children

You have probably read about people that have been tamed and taught to stay in one place. Turn to the vegetation map to locate your friends. Still, some of their relatives may have strayed and gone wild. Ask your less committed local officials if they know of any such creatures cavorting just outside your designated area.

Try making a list of the uncooperative elements. Include chains and doors and ballet teachers and criminals with a soft spot for mother. Add to your list the animals that are not what they appear to be. The following examples might be used to help isolate the areas in which aberrations can be identifed:

--Hogs, for example, were once bald uncles with paunches. Don't forget they may retain a tendency to become more attractive in the presence of alcohol.

--Horses, on the other hand, are more obvious projections of the sexual dreams of adolescent girls. They may not really exist in the forms imagined, but the dreams are so powerful we cannot deny their influence.

--Some fur-bearing species have been wiped out completely in the Western provinces by trappers, except for the grumpy fathers with bushy patches on their lower backs just above the division between the cheeks of their buttocks and small hairy epaulets on each shoulder. Some only partially domesticated relatives from Eastern Europe have been mistaken for these fathers, but they can be distinguished by their small beady eyes and dark bushy eyebrows. It is no longer profitable to skin the examples approaching the end of their lifespan.

--Several types of fish have recently become self-contained processing units designed to recycle the lakes and streams. Since there are far too few of them, the lakes and streams remain polluted. Pictures of fish on tuna cans were once collected by school children when their families could still afford to eat such delicacies, but no adequate plan for applying them ever surfaced. It once became fashionable in certain regions to save them for the sentimental mouse processor many citizens still address with cute little names ending in y.

--Substantial anecdotal evidence suggests that clams are not merely the burrowing mollusks we once thought they were but the tongues of ancient Greek orators distributed around the world by ancient sea-going slaves captured in battles with lesser civilizations who rebelled because they could not understand what was being said. The tongues lived on despite the detritus of the ages piled upon them and from time to time they still speak brilliantly. If only you would make a greater effort to learn their ancient language has become the vitamin-mantra of several over-zealous intellectual advancement proponents. It seems to reflect the belief that the resulting social organizations once made the lives of adherents to certain ancient burrowing principals more rewarding.

--Vicious three-legged dogs have also been discovered in the afterlife of pleasant retiring widows on pensions who once kept lockets filled with dead fleas hidden inside the hollowed out cores of prosthetic legs. When these animals are hit by bicycles, they do not growl, but whimper. New research points to the possibility that this is what happens if you can only love one person in your life and you bury the undesired excess inside your body.

Now add to the list all the animals, which you have adapted to personal use, including those which cannot be seen by anyone but you. Be sure to include the names your friends and relatives have given to these tendencies so that your experience might be of benefit to future permutations.

When you are finished, look at what you have done. You can be replaced by unexpected possibilities. The world is not where you thought it was. Look at all the miserable little countries in your own back yard and consider visiting them. Leap into the void and claim something frightening is beautiful. Consider how uncertain your limitations have become and the way they keep escaping. The only boundaries that matter won't be announcing themselves. You're making these changes for your own good. Your friends are here to help you if only you can figure out which ones they are. Let them find you in their search for the ragged edges of progress.

October 3

Three or Four Births, a Death and Something Else Entirely

Little Nonsense was following a bear by the river. He knew it was dangerous because the bear was large and he had wounded it. Little Beaver had been working on that river and Little Nonsense barked his shin on a tree stump where Little Beaver had felled a birch and floated it down to the half finished dam. A fox watched as Nonsense danced a little dance of pain beside the river. Nonsense was bleeding.

Then Little Nonsense swam across the river and searched for the place on the other side where the wounded bear had come out. He couldn't find it. He searched and he searched but it was getting dark and he couldn't find it. He had to give up and rest by the river until the light came back.

That night as he slept, Little Nonsense visited the cave where the moon had been born. A big white egg was sitting in the middle of the cave and Little Nonsense was waiting for something, but he didn't know what it was. He thought about breaking the egg, but that didn't seem right and he thought about running away, but his legs wouldn't move right. So he gathered the twigs and limbs that were spread about inside the cave and made a fire next to the egg.

Before long he heard a crackling sound and saw the egg begin to break open. Then it stopped and a great roar split the air of the cave. Something very large was inside the egg, but it wasn't coming out anymore. He waited because his feet wouldn't move, but nothing happened. He poked at the egg with a burning limb, but nothing happened.

Then he leaned over close and listened and listened. He didn't think he could hear anything inside the egg, but he couldn't help pulling at the crack and then he wanted to bite the egg. So he did and the great roar returned again and the egg split further open. Inside was a black bear, a very big black bear. An arrow was sticking out of its right side and a small river of blood was forming along the cave floor.

As he watched, the thick red river got larger and larger until he was floating on it and the bear followed him, floating out of the cave on the river of blood. It was dark outside. He grabbed a tree stump and pulled himself out of the blood river and right there beside him was that same bear, only much smaller and not moving at all. The bear looked dead. The same arrow was sticking out of its side. Nonsense was afraid to touch it, but he touched it. The bear was dead. He turned back to the river and as he tried to clear his head, the large egg came floating down the river, back in one piece, and it floated right up into the sky.

Little Nonsense didn't wake up. The light came and he cleaned the meat from the dead bear and he got some help carrying the meat and he smoked the meat and he hunted for many years and raised a family. But Little Nonsense didn't wake up.

And Little Nonsense tried closing his eyes and waiting and something happened that made him feel ready for the next day, but it wasn't sleep, not the way he had known sleep before the bear. And there were never any more bears in that sleep and there were never any more eggs. Little Nonsense decided some dreams you just have to live with. You can't tell them what to do and you can't tell them what you want. Some dreams will only whisper what they want and then wait your whole life for you to reach them.

Of course Little Nonsense told his friends about the dream. That's how he got his name. But the bear didn't have a name. And the bear waited.

October 4

Sunlight, Another Shadow

The husks of October insects. Dragonflies. A dog panting in the late heat. An old man in the sunroom. An odor of figs and mushrooms. Outside, the wind-thrown years of dust. Inside, the slow sip of memory. And the passing magic of windows and doors. And always, one more detail . . .

A thrush bursts from the brush beside the goat path.

Smoke at dawn and the lights still marking the pier. The hour of fallen nests, leaves scuttling along the tiny sand dunes. Brittle thorns of lightning lengthen quickly across the sky. Weather won't be kind, but its indifference allows us all we need.

October 5

Etiquette

When the nothing your friend has to say annoys you, quit talking. Stay there when you leave.

When you learn the truth, it is time to stay quiet. You have yet to learn how you learned it. Teach that.

If silence greets you, welcome it. If it departs, you will not bring it back by complaining.

Let your friends find your weakness or they will have nothing to love.

It is harder to apologize for what you have done than for what you would have done.

If you can speak accurately of silence, you can roar without opening your mouth. Explains the poet, who must also be created.

Thank the winds. Thank the stones. Build your house around the stars. Build your world around the house.

Live in it before you were born.

October 6

Consolation Gifts

A miniature glass mouse, for example. On a glass shelf in a cottage in the forest. Behind the echo of the woodcutter's axe.

Or his wife's greeting welcoming him home, high-pitched and delicate, a porcelain cage in which to keep the end of his day.

Or the bright thrill of a covey of quail rising startled from the tall grass, floating down the hillside below the lighthouse where the murder occurred.

The air inside the hidden chamber growing damp and close as if in the ruins of a grand cathedral we had stepped before the door to an underground cavern. (Constance was no longer the same person after losing the child.) Later that same day, a policeman chasing a piglet down the sidewalk and under a cart of candied apples.

Each new night's crimes uncertain, dissimilar, every alibi alive with its own suspicions.

Teeth in the water-glass on the nightstand.

The bed empty.

Or the moon's footprints.

Or a row of small mammal skulls lined up neatly on a tenderness of black velvet by the neighbor's quietly drowning son.

October 7

Blood Cleanses the Wound

In bed, his other desk, he writes from the monthly blood in her story. It's simple. He takes the journey to see if she is at the end. When he arrives, he wants to remember the freedom of the offering.

Nature includes them. Thank the gods we constantly notice this, recognition with tongue and the touch of a smell we can't forget, the intoxicating sweat of dreams that grew bodies.

When he finally, temporarily, forgets her, he knows her better, the memories of the body stronger than the mind's. She is not provided to please. That is why she does. A desire that takes the insistent body beyond its limits, which were never really there.

Then lust begins another journey, just as the lovers converge in the inconclusive conclusion orgasm delivers, its release a promise in the eyes, the next slow climb. At the top of the mountain, the sky beckons. The dream grows another body, the "little death" of dream gravity falling into the sky's future and rising into that new world, become the only world, yours because you've given it away.

October 8

The Car Rocked in the Wind Like a Cradle

Trees lurch drunkenly in the world's room, uncles home from the dance alone, trying desperately to dance their lives into another room, wheeling their ghost partners back and forth in their empty arms, their hearts spilling. The storm says some things I've never heard before and cannot repeat. I guide the cradle as best I can, too young to understand the trees, too old to comfort the shadows.

Tonight I am alone and yet I still repeat the trees' mistake that is a mistake only because I repeat it, dear uncles, and the old trees dance with the older shadows while the cradle blinds the gentle roar of the wind. I stop at a crossroads and wait the wind quiet.

I climb out and listen and it repeats what it was saying. The cradle ticks and rocks. My body says something I've never heard before. I climb out. I hadn't realized.

I climb in and its engine starts me. Now the travelers say some things I've never heard before. Dear trees, not even the wind repeats them.

October 9

Military History

When Granite arrived, men stopped depending upon their fists. Some of these men had been working to get animals and plants to do what they wanted them to do. Very quickly, Granite discovered that these men were made of a softer rock, which has been broken up and changed by the weather. Nevertheless, Granite decided that people and trees should be allowed to grow upwards if people and trees will do that. It's a widely held belief.

A poet imagines the grandeur of the mountains and a comedian digs a hole to put the mountains in. Or a comedian laughs at an imaginary mountain and a poet digs a hole to live in on top of the mountain. That's just what they do.

We can see the same thing happening today in coffee houses where the first men to arrive in the cafe denied they were foreign agents while they continued translating Chilean poems. In each of the Chilean poems of that time, there was a little adobe house and a very very tiny patch of earth where coffee beans were struggling to survive. The families who lived in the adobe houses collected tree blood from the weeping trees to make syrup and gave back the sugar from their own sweetened veins. But it wasn't clear why the trees needed this sugar.

Naturally, many people wanted their fair share of the ancient Indians sweetened and made famous by the translated poems. Collectors and commodities traders stockpiled great quantities. Such men were called Blunts and could not be relied on to feed children.

There are still some places in the world where chunks of fossilized coffee farmer can be dug out of coal deposits near the surface of the ground. Hardened domestic animals appearing frequently in the poems as music or donkeys are used for roofs. Small sewers and drains are often made of more reluctant creatures.

Compare the only surviving picture of Jean Francois Millet, a French artist of the 19th Century, to the terrible paintings of famous comedians. And yes, these distinctions were once assimilated by cultivated men right there in the fields.

The freedom fighters' search for heroic Flint, who had found all artists wanting, their rejected compositions being useful only for black powder conveyance and selective directional assertions, started fresh men digging in the ground again, but the results were not the same as the results that were in the minds of the men when they started digging.

Test farmers were used to place the coffee beans in the weapons to which they were meant to be applied. This was depicted in the famous paintings of independence made by the freedom fighters when coffee was no longer needed and nostalgia took over the government. Please don't assume that this was entirely successful. Please don't assume that adequate resolution of the issues involved will ever be forthcoming. Please test the sentimental potentials of your assumptions before applying overflow limitation devices. Please examine the softer farmers before planting.

The samples may be returned after the war is over, but the samples are not the war.

October 10

No One Intends to Shoot Us

Don't whisper to the minister. Don't even douse the miscreant candle.

Among the living and the dead, children passing from one cave to another.

The guard cracks his knuckles and aims his gaze at the future. He's keeping track of everything that will not happen again.

He's offering his trousers to the general and collecting a brace of eel, trembling and trembling without moving a muscle.

Try handing out some conversions at the tent door. Don't bother making a flap. We enter by the abandoned.

Which makes it too perfect here. The only thing broken is the word.

Precipitate particulate. Offer only the substitute spelled stunningly. After dictionary time there were no more acceptable variations.

A man drops to his knees, dies quickly into the bullet. His body falls back flat and the knees fall to the man.

Nothing left of him now but the juice.

Surplus migrations stacked in the barn.

They came from far away and they stayed.

It's not what you think it is but what you think (the way you can consider sniffing a woman's rich armpit to distribute her legs advantageously). [Since he did not enjoy considering how she felt, he assumed doing so was virtuous. If he had succeeded in considering it, he would have drawn the wrong conclusions.]

Judge not the remainder. We were chosen.

The minister had indeed spent a lifetime crossing and re-crossing his own mind, often arriving at unexplored locations with little more than an intellectual putty knife and a desire to fix something before it ruptures. (Some bacteria were discussing the moment life begins to separate into species and how long it should be left to age before it becomes ripe and how much should be left to propagate the supply and this was all going on while some other bacteria were plotting a takeover and so many were involved that it was hard to imagine it could be kept secret but it was and then it wasn't anymore and the difference between living off the host and destroying the host began to seem irrelevant since it had become known and there was nothing unexpected to stop it). [Mirror: his thoughts do not reflect upon me though mine reflect upon him.]

Something waiting like evidence to be acknowledged (when the kid developed some strange ideas about the number of appendages he was allowed). It's not the children acting like adults as the bilge pump saves them, but the adults acting like children. Salvation has darkened the waters and it makes what light there is shining through seem a bit brighter. (It's a beautiful moment, but it lives alone.) [She tries me and she tries me and at this rate it won't be long before never arrives.]

If I buy him a toy I might not be his toy of choice, so I don't buy him a toy.

The way we embroider the embroidery.

Not a sunset but a painting of a sunset. Not a painting.

The guard could be loaded. His gaping chest wound cannot diminish his prior accomplishments.

Not a sunset.

October 11

Moral Lessons

The ladder fell down and was ignored until the weeds grew high enough to cover it. Then someone tripped, someone going nowhere in a hurry. Brushing the weeds from his torn clothing, someone looked down at the lost ladder and changed plans.

The apple tree had fallen in a storm and it was miles to the next one and the tree's falling had left a perfectly fine hole where the apple tree had been.

I don't know who I am and I don't want to feel sorry for him.

We thought there would be more clothing on the girl. Then we thought we should appreciate it if there wasn't but we didn't. We watched her get dressed and accepted her maneuvers. We welcomed her into the folded door, which was not her door and only on the way, but you had to be on the way first. Then you could figure out which side was the inside and open out.

I might not be the kind of goon that seems to get along with everybody but never stays anywhere very long. Smooth in passing. Gone before anyone can hold on to what they've begun to suspect.

She appeared to be a bit heftier on the upside. She appeared to teeter but never faltered. She was capable of amazing feats of unexpected grace.

Sometimes the best caresses are achieved by the addition of static electricity but this is risky when the fur is too dry. It can feel like a herd of mice pulling at the hair follicles and cannot be adequately concluded at the end of each separate stroke.

You think about it, but you don't say it.

She was placed on the registration marks and asked to stay. The instructions were not handwritten.

I felt like you were doing something for me that I would rather have done for myself. I just didn't know what it was.

October 12

A Contemporary Reflection on the Traditional Values of Marital Union

A shovel and a hoe were married in a quiet garden ceremony. His parents piled up huge mounds of disapproval. Hers picked at his history of mistakes and his blunt stubborn way with dead things. She introduced her family at the wedding as casually as possible, entered the reception tent smiling and laughing falsely. With a hoe and a hoe and a ho ho ho.

His parents were not amused, had never, in fact, been amused, resented her incessant picking at the scrawny rows of late vegetables long past due for turning under.

He leaned against the old oak and pondered. Acorns fell all around him and he tried gathering them unto something or other, but it wasn't going very well and his new wife tried to offer comfort and assistance, but she too proved clumsy, catching her flat foot on every lump in the grass, and neither could admit the failure to their in-laws.

Just in time, a child came along and gathered the acorns in a wooden bucket, which the child left sitting beside the shovel and hoe as a wedding gift. The guests marveled at the folksy symbolism it had taken a child to misplace so effectively as they each took an acorn home to place upon their mantel in recognition of the union's potential. It was a proud day indeed for the shovel family and the hoe clan. A proud day indeed.

Or one day a child came along and gathered the acorns unto a wooden bucket, but the hoe did not believe in human intervention, and thus what was said to have happened was not allowed to happen, and an ancient religion sprouted magically from a chosen acorn, later brought down in its prime by yet another gatherer of the human interventionist kind with an abiding vision of domestic tranquility attached to the olfactory associations of well-supplied fireplaces, roasting acorns and matronly fussing.

Or the acorns gathered gravitationally unto themselves in the dark forest and elected one of their own to lead a revolution against a corrupt prior government that turned its citizens into vertical tools, and he became the first martyr to the cause when a feathered black messenger from the sharp-footed tyrants that nest in the very limbs of the problem discovered the new leader, broke him and ate him.

Or perhaps mixed marriages were simply not allowed, even in merely symbolic representations.

Or one day a child planted a garden in the vast forest where a tree fell every three or four minutes and no one heard them because they were so far apart. It was a child who had planted the possibility of knowing all this falling by thinking of its garden as many gardens in many parts of the forest, just as a child plants many possibilities of alternate lives in its own future as well as in the imperfect past, where no one pays any attention to the crushed blossoms of wandering verb tenses.

Or one day the marriage fell apart before it even got started, for apparently inconsequential reasons, and no one noticed a damned thing.

Or one day a child was married in a solemn playpen ceremony and baby shovels and hoes began appearing everywhere, astounding medical science until the appearance of baby rakes provided the missing clue.

Or one day the green vegetables in the garden were screaming for attention when the shovel and the hoe came to their rescue with help from the child who had grown into a very large adult with a very green sense of humor, and this very large adultlet took lots of green things to the market, where there was a special on Wednesdays for the senior citizens, the healthiest little buggers in all the married land.

Or none of it ever happened at all, not a bit of it.

Or whatever happened was somebody else's story, somebody who might never get married, but likes to think about it.

Or all of it happened, or might as well have, and a whole lot more, because you don't have to jump off a cliff to know what will happen when you get to the bottom, but you have to get hurt with some little hurt from some little prior jumping don't you?

Or maybe you just jump and you never get to the bottom of it.

October 13

A Pause on the Way Up the River

An old man is not a stone from the river, washed down the mountain and polished smooth all over, so how does he understand what has swallowed him? Why should he have to tell such a story?

Little Nonsense ate and ate and grew and grew. By and by his skin grew too small for him. Stretch went his skin and Plop, Flop and Stop went his roly poly cholesterol-saturated jumble of inner workings right deep in that stretched-out skin with a rubbery little sway and jiggle.

First Branch, trying to help, said, "What a stone sees has been here longer than innocence. Go to the river and find the end of its tail."

And there was a great groveling and a flouncing and a staring off into the distance and finally Little Nonsense dragged his fear to the river.

What do you think Little Nonsense found there?

No more light. No more water. No more wind. And no more sky.

Second Branch, trying even harder to help, said, "Even a mountain knows the way down. Go to the highest place in your head and fall off. It's not as hard as you think."

And the skin around Little Nonsense tightened and drew close and he felt the food he had eaten grow softer and drop away and something cool and wet was tugging at his ankles. He couldn't be sure if he had come to the river's edge or if he had wet himself.

Behold! The old man resting rounded and clean, the river once more on its invisible way back up the mountain, and Little Nonsense so full of only himself he grew hungry again for other experiences. Which swallowed him and kept him moving. And he grew slowly older living in the river with the old man, who turned out to be his father, who turned out to be Little Nonsense and kept him smooth in his long passage and lifted him up to the top of the mountain to see what he could learn falling down and ate of himself instead of the offerings of strangers.

October 14

Voice from the Fire

Let's take the chill off. We can see each other's breath. Let's take away the darkness, yet praise the quick shadows.

Our bodies shift with the wind. Let's remove the guise of civilization. Let's roast whatever you caught today. The earth can speak for itself.

I am always ready for new hungers, new fear, old stories, quick hearts,

and the worship of any old mystery. Time is a pretense and light is a cage.

When you wake, I will give you my blanket. Made of ash, it says, "I am gone, yet I am your passion, your past. I am your next love, your next of kin. I am a hollow in some mountain. I am a mountain in some hollow. My body is yours, ascending."

October 15

Voice of Rest

The damp dirty smell of rain on the way, the only hotel for miles a grain elevator. The wind has traveled centuries to bring you the news. It's not easy to sleep in a dead leaf.

It's only being in a hurry to help that scares me so.

The book of light, open on the table, by evening has fallen to the floor.

Coal slag beneath the railroad tracks glistens wickedly when it rains. It never rains. The real fears die and come true.

It's too quiet here. Let's keep it that way.

October 16

Voice of Despair

It was worth it, but now I don't know. So I have come back.

There was someone waiting and waiting. Then it turned out to be me.

Cold in a warm wind, I buried deep in a foolish fear that came on out of season, out of loss, out of character. The wind swarmed up the canyon. I hammered my fears to the earth, holding my straw hat tight against my head in the failing light.

So I have come back. It was hungrier than I imagined. Then I imagined more. Bluer than that. The valley crying, the mountain burning the air blue, the sky. Bluer than that.

I built another world around me, larger this time. A plume of smoke rises from a distant ridge. Someone will need me again, holding my straw hat tight against my head in the failing light. They will. I'm sure of it.

October 17

Voice of Forgetfulness

It says some things I've never heard before and cannot repeat. Too young to understand the trees, too old to reach for the shadows.

I follow the mistake that is a mistake only because I follow it. And the wind assembles another destination.

I climb out, their hearts spilling. My body says some things I've never heard before. I climb out. I climb in and its engine starts me. I climb out and I've been here before, so I climb in and I've been here before, their hearts spilling.

October 18

Voice of Reason

When I lie, it makes sense. I am your father, your mother, your life.

You have rebelled in the past, but in the end you always loved me, perhaps too much.

I can explain what happened. Listen if you know what's good for you. Play it safe. There is no excuse for carelessness.

I've been around a long time. I can tell you things. It doesn't matter who else won. You're not him and he could have lost it all. Add it up.

You could have been a memory.

When I lie, it makes sense.

October 19

Voice of Time

Ignore me. I want nothing. Except to be lost.

You cannot abuse me. You can only set the trap. You must walk in circles, offering your own hand in greeting. I am always here and here and here, still there when you're gone.

A red sweater frozen in a glacier. Do not trust this education because it is the only one you will get and it knows nothing about limits. You must invent those yourself, just as you have invented this moment.

If you were really yourself, your life might pause happily in midstream. But only history describes such rest and day by day it grows less accurate. Even now you are someone new.

And now not even him.

October 20

Voice of Self Pity

Disguised as your social life, I am a lonely goatherd. Welcome me to your dreams. You are falling into a deep sleep.

Look forward to nothing. Look back to see your place in the herd. Study all you have lost. Is this anthropology or the dust on the windowsill? The answer is getting very tired.

Your eyelids are growing larger. Heavy as blankets, they shade your life, which is shrinking. Now it is small enough to slip into someone's pocket, my pocket. Because no one else comes to see you. I would give it back to you if I could find it.

I will tell you what to do. Pretend you are a cloud. Act like mist. Do your best imitation of snow. Your arms are too heavy to lift. Your dreams forget how to breath.

I am your closest friend and I get you into trouble because no one can tell us apart and I never know when to quit.

When I snap my fingers you will awaken. When I snap my fingers you will awaken. When I snap my fingers you will awaken . . .

October 21

Pablo's Snapshots

Here Pablo's father is discussing landscapes with a group of small insects. That's a dream he had at nine sitting next to him. He's forgotten its name, but it answers to anything.

In another world he is constructing a jungle. Notice the envy of the grass. It's only temporary. The world stays way ahead of us.

And here in the past is Pablo's father emerging from the meat locker he works in wearing a stained white coat, sausages for his family hidden in his clothing.

That was the year Pablo's dog slept in a tree and Pablo's face was a clock. It might have been a grade school play.

And here is Pablo's family eating. He refuses the chicken and the tuna. He is sulking behind the tulips, which don't bloom every year. He thinks he's not the same species. He's trying not to be so easy to get to.

And here he is with his cousins, yard rats all, chasing a battered football. They are smiling stupidly because they want to.

And here his parents' smiles are saying, "We will not die." He believes them and they don't.

Not in this picture.

October 22

Abandoned Breeze

A farmhouse in South Dakota made of the dreams of cattails blows away a little each day. Each summer the neighboring cottonwoods burst and cling like the hopes of angels and that house gets a second chance, but soon even your fingernails grow tired of scraping at the earth for a life, the bull's heart behind your stove-door chest gives up giving anything but blood.

Prairie dreams sail down the rows of corn beneath the salvation of a crop-duster. Silence speaks again, as fine as the map you imagined made of squirrel hair and seed-pods.

In that world inside the world, we live in bodies, a slow dance under the eyelids. Sometimes we die before we die.

The voice inside the bread whispers about shadow milk for the children of chairs, about fathers grumbling down the years like clumsy beasts. Just before dawn opens once more, the smell of wet stones edges the dark and the latent breath of dew opens a happiness bright enough to welcome something unknown.

All our lives here we build this, body by sweaty body, the landscape imperfecting beauty, dethroning it to keep it real, as if the moment were repeatable, as if the moment lived on, after we're gone.

October 23

Another Ransom Note

The midway glows red in the bottomless eyes of a barn owl, a crazy surprise in the hazy dusk of that sky. He swerves around a stray balloon, a suddenly broken circuit in that circus of rising air darkness brings.

The owl storms the deepening sky, balloons suddenly into his own abrupt fold. Silent, permanent night. Bursting, like a puff of snow against a windshield. Cotton candy staining the midway dust red.

What symbolic child is this appearing to claim the body of loss, who cannot lay to rest the carnival of human needs? What darkness behind the eyes of his kidnapped past?

Pay the price. Take your chances. Red eyes dance in the night air where men with money buy their tickets to a new life feathered in fear, barking sudden as a balloon bursting with rewards.

Forgive me. I had another life to live. I couldn't afford to let anyone report me missing. I lied. I reported the night, as always, had been arrested and later released. And I folded my tent, my ticket, my wings, stole into the passing night, my body releasing a sigh, reading pleasures into that note pinned to its cloak.

Every minute a fortune I pay and pay.

I give them what they want. I am the last clue to a true story wrapped in a brown paper bag. It's too late to let you go, I say, knowing this debt can never be paid, trying to because I'm more the child to that life I thought I lived than I am to the one I did.

In time self-pity escapes me, but I repeat the missing payoff in a new lifetime of suitcases filled with whatever you asked for because I no longer know what I want.

Perhaps it's enough. The carnival tears me down and I caravan to the next missing child. I tell them what they want and I listen to myself, shaping their lost lives into headlines, and I go back to work selling tickets to the daily news of children screaming with fearful pleasure, released into their ballooning adult lives.

October 24

I'm Surprised to Discover That I Have No Desire to Rub Them

The field was freshly plowed. A young girl slept in a furrow. Her brother was afraid to wake her. It had something to do with angels and bees. It had something to do with sorrow and the joy that precedes it. It's something leaving can do for you. (Light a match and those rooms open a desperately sexless yearning.) ["When you see a stranger, consider him a thief."]

Life removes his mask to find death, who removes his mask to find life, who removes his mask to find . . .

half a kernel of corn. (Where has the hungry deer mouse gone?)

It had something to do with insects and mythological representations of monumental grief. It had something to do with water.

To hide his confusion he screamed loudly. He wanted the neighbors to be misled, to believe he was only a bit crazy and not, as he feared, a capable failure. Better if they looked right past him. Better if they thought he was worthless than worth something that had been lost. It had something to do with married couples thinking they're happy (which is really what makes them happy). It had something to do with Senator Snuffly Steed, author of the Anywhere I've Been Stories and the popular novel You Ought to Have Been There First. It had something to do with The Stockingcap (National Bird of the North Country), which displays a reverse migratory pattern, appearing in the northern latitudes during the snowbound months and migrating to television comedies during the summer, which, in turn, migrate to Peru during ethnic celebrations week. (Its mating habits remain mysterious, but include an attraction to buses and snowplows as well as publicly supported sports arenas and clothing designs featuring leaves and hearts.) So he makes love to a couple of northern trees. (He's not impossible, he's just a little broken.) [It never happened. That's what makes it available.]

My eyes are open and something happens which opens them.

October 25

The Story of a Chair

Temporary empires of frost. This darkness has the past in it. Year by year the cathedral sinks deeper into the marsh. Imagine anyone this deliberately lost. An icicle tools its way to murder. A service to the stones, who know the intent in falling.

How do you discover what you're made for? Wasn't that something the cold asked you once? He's so lost and inflexible you could be the memory of a wall he refused to tear down. He could be something to sit in when the iced dawn asks you to participate. A territory bereft of human intervention. A construction of refined inaction.

In this way, he is slowly kidnapped by warmer weather, a friend of invisible glass animals deliberating their pitch while the earth is superficially dissected again and again by the welcome rain, cutting the disease from the earth's skin so neatly the scars don't show. He's like a planet, one of the patients, escaped, his illness held close.

By this time, he has achieved a deeper understanding of water, which makes him look gray and experienced, nearly ready to fall apart. The swarms of metaphorical pain he calls "bees" arrive as he sits thinking, and whatever it is he has learned, but can not name, surrounds him with a distant kind of singing.

October 26

People Tell Me That I Look Like Someone Else

Wind swarmed up the canyon. He hammered his fears to the earth with tent pegs, holding his straw hat tight against his head in the evening light. Cold in the warm wind, he buried deep in a foolish fear that came on out of season, out of loss, out of character.

A million tiny reasons surrounded him and years later a deeper sorrow brought him home to this mountain again. He breathed harder as he climbed, a reflection of age now, not despair, and he stood quietly while the world seemed to forget him.

He laughed and something listened. A plume of smoke rose from a nameless ridge. He urged the burning back.

And then he wept, clinging to the long fire swarming across the past he had dragged into the present. It consumed him, hungrier than he had imagined, and he had to remember more.

He raged farther than the valley of crying, the mountain burning and the air escaping, the sky. And he ate his soul and came down. And his body kept on looking for the delicate fragile pain that keeps us.

October 27

Indecision

Now let us answer escaping time, lovely fragments, smooth magpies of embodied uncertainty. You are not the one curled back beyond words, though you might wish to be. A piecemeal suspended nation on the borders of the long journey back to you.

It stops for no one and hauls a truckful of sadness. I hope you can live enough to unload it. Or maybe you could drive it over the cliff and just wait and wait, not knowing for what.

One at a time you test extremities. Your body tingles. You no longer confuse your feelings with the weather. It's a slow process, your condition refusing to be seen as a telephone ringing after the ambulance has gone.

When you answered the moon, your eyes revealed nothing, the doubt fallen back deeper than muscle and skin, enough a part of you to read smoke and follow. It's calling unborn children from the dreams. It's tapping at your throat like a bone.

You were dragging yourself along due to the expenditure of attention to other matters. And now other matters have attended to you. It's a bad story about you that might be true if you don't know who you are. It's not your mind that keeps you wishful, but your wishes that keep you mindful.

Why don't you ask your shoes if they want to take you home?

You reach out further and it's not quite you arriving because it's not quite not you. Your project dissembles, love left unknowing in the underbush. The woolen disturbance of the last regime's shearing. An apricot caravan treeless in the wind- waves.

Padded winds accost the branches blackened by the visitations of fall fungus and the neighbor's elderly mother, who burns and burns the still air with her history. Sunlight is not vertical, it leans. The hill behind the house is an unlevened loaf of glacial flour dusted with plantlife. A congregation of thirsty potential predicts excess.

An ache, an axe, a throb warm in the darkness. A wing of breath. You could be unfastening buttons from a blouse of rain. Wet beads of delight. Milky pearls of gratitude. Miracles in another faith.

October 28

Sunset, After Quail Hunting With My Father

A young girl is crying because she does not understand how birds can fly and there is no man in the moon. But the legend persists until the natives begin to worship gunpowder and believe that every insect carries a tiny moon in its heart, which is released when it dies. On each of these moons another world is possible. Dusk, I understand now your solitude and want to follow you. There is nothing more beautiful or fragile than insect husks on a pebble beach in the moonlight.

October 29

An Elegy for the Woman Next Door

Another day of rain and quiet. Not much happened, but that evening an ambulance arrived for the woman across the hall. She hadn't lived there long, but the rumors claimed her husband of forty years had died suddenly while making love to another woman.

Pelayo said he thought that must have been sad for her, but he couldn't help admiring a man who could stay active at that age. Maria wondered if maybe the woman had died the same way and we all wished it were true.

But there had been no siren. Someone must have known she couldn't be saved.

"It's hard to know when you shouldn't try," I remember saying, loving her and trying to save myself.

Now, there's enough food and a roof that doesn't leak and the memory of a siren that wasn't there.

And I have met someone new who reminds me of you.

October 30

I'm Not Finished Yet

Whence the migration of pain. Whence the horror. A happy little bumpkin wets his willy and the jig is up. It doesn't hurt so much. He can't hurt so much without experience.

Sometimes duty gets delivered to the wrong address. A package of surgical sponges instead of dinner. A piece of the right patient through the wrong end of the microscope.

Whence the incumbent derives his verity. While we wander the garden paths below the hospital with our own. It's a big hurt and we love it dearly, sugarpants.

She wanted more and he just wanted.

The child of knowledge and the child of ignorance. Both chopping the same onion.

A big hurt indeed and we came down from the towers into the land of breaking and keeping, into the land of another before us.

October 31

Portable Mood Splicing Device

I had been delivered to my own house because my nervous legs were running without you in a dark country of interior claims. If I cried a little, I didn't remember it.

It was sad to see so many dead witches, moon-roe spilling out, the tide washing them back and forth like that. I thought I could see a tail eyeing me and it had already started. The terrible beauty of the unseen storms that terrorize young girls, long before they understand rain.

I had become a continuous person. I had misunderstood an invention that solves misunderstandings with a vibrating stick. This was in a movie without a hero where the villain is played by each of us. Its meaty anchor was hustling slick lips beyond the arcade. It was a perpetration, a tall cool assignation.

I knew it was time to go home and for some reason I wanted to find the fresh toast unplugged. I wanted to find the resinous jam. So I addressed myself to the problem and when I got home, you were out.

So I went home and I believed you wanted to hit me and then hold on tight. I felt like some kind of smarmy saint sucking a dying beer and I remember thinking It's a beautiful stink with a glove on its missing finger.

I remember thinking I'm lying in the meadow waiting for leaping rabbits and overjoyed butterflies and I remember a tubular pillow of light I sleep in when my dreams remember me. A few of them bark.

Pay attention now. I'm not over there. I'll chew like a little sneeze that starts to hurt, but I'm not always the same. I have a personality.

So when I got home, I didn't think I was dressed quite like a donney boy anymore and I asked you about the fellowship of snakes and a room for your antipathies and I moved nearer and listened to the wailing of the grieving nuns and the screams echoing by candlelight in a watery dungeon and that's how my heart began paying attention.

No, it wasn't really like this.

It was this.

November

November 1

That Wasn't the Way She Intended to Answer

Next she was wrapping herself in herself.

Not crude at all the way she did it. Not a body of water, but the body of the water in the water. So that her place in there was water's place and she couldn't be bothered with herself. That was the way cold was.

Next she was trembling and learning. She wanted to show me something, but it wasn't what she showed me. The child might be something that you should pick up and it might not. There was the question of whether it existed inside the water or not. There were doubts about evaporation and dew loss and there was more than that in it worlding. Here the burial's never permanent, and there's still another of this almost so she could have been falling.

Next the secret of lamplight. There are many ways that I am here, but right now I'm not one of them. My needs have been discounted. You can pick one up for the price of a word, though I'm afraid I don't know which one.

It hasn't always been this way. Perpendicular Derrivations of Latency can be arranged to accommodate conversations with states of being. I prefer to dress like a tree or the idea of a tree. I used to be dancing wetly. I used to be dancing like nervous pudding. She was the starlit vacancy signed the same as occupied space.

A lily is a blooming librarian, full of presence and the knowledge of where to find knowledge. Not even a rose holds still long enough. It wasn't an experience I walked away from, loaded down with the responsibilities of accommodation.

In the pebble towns at the river's reach, it's expensive not to read the signs. It only takes a few seconds all day.

Beautiful and therefore wicked, they thought. Fame wouldn't change that. When you've had more than you want given and you still forget to ask. When you arrive back at the beginning and the beginning's already gone.

November 2

I've Given Everyone a Copy

First I was from the sky and then I was a toad stuck in an oatmeal box. My opinion was lifted.

Something I used to know was flying from the lawn sprinkler. Invented without rest, I was well taken. My opinion was redistributed.

I was left behind. I was kidnapped. I wasn't available for coffee.

A hot little number like him. Who knew?

If it's huge and it's yours and it's a likelihood, then who's the likely hood? Now we've got us on each other. We'll both want the holidays. Time alone is our first affair.

There's a thrush trying to find itself in my window. I didn't know it would thump like that and hurt me.

I'm no longer here because I'm there, but a quality of kindness was missing.

His shirt too white and clean.

Why do the young always migrate west when the cool promises sleep in the north while the east unwraps itself and the south, well, the south just slows down and waits for what it needs?

I don't know much. I guess that makes me an expert on one thing. You don't have to be suicidal to think a lot.

So I gave unto it sixfold. Those after butchers.

The evolution of the patient disease.

And there was everything with its foot on the upholstery.

And there I am. Beside it. Beside where it was. Beside myself. Still no longer.

Then finally I was lifted from myself, an autumnal Finnish excess of bloodleaves brightening before the kiss that draws them down.

Horrible things have happened to others and I can't stop thinking about how it affects me.

November 3

Natural Laws

This speech is still green and you can listen slowly.

A police car glides to a stop in front of your house and waits.

Certain sighs are truly criminal.

Altruism gives you what you can't take and donates you anonymously to your failures, who thank you with theirs, modified to fit your pretensions.

You can't do that now. It's a law.

Deep in the fresh body, a metaphor so cold the flowering of a knife could not pierce it. It cannot be cheapened with human terms. Endearments only taunt such saints. It remains clothed. It seems to want to speak.

You may go now, or you may stay. It's a rule.

There was light all over the light. And out of the light's dreaming came the breast feathering. Out of animals rising from the earth, out of the torn cry in its throat, came the beast unnamed and enamored of its own stink.

Let this creation, with its own claw, choke the life.

But will you let the children, radiant with war games, worship the tawny rise of a wing hawking air?

Came the bird de-beasting, came release sudden as a drum . . .

But nothing has happened, and it's happening here where you finally know someone well enough to let your body do all the talking, a simple story of a red dog and a yellow dog.

Let the end begin, let the moon wink in the crow's dream, let the crippled fork gawk at the matronly fussing of fat robins on the lawn.

You can see it's a sophisticated place, Buster. O it was a fine thing to behold, the past sleek in its wrap, dancing to the needle of the ice farm some stuttered dog with a bad ear preserved for us, cranked and swooning on several iced verandas at once across the lost whale of moonlight.

The answer held our attention by deciding all night not to make a sound.

And after the wind it was time to start over. With a yellow dog and a red dog. With a little blue shovel and a bowl of water.

November 4

1945

With the distinctive glass click of the stopper on a bottle of perfume, it's your certainty that's nominated you for another accident.

Fall all down. A dream's another life. Early world upon the throne of recurrence, don't go graceful in memory, it's your swan, but substitute the robin and the lawn smiles, the crow and memory's gone, the raven and a statue crumbles, the hummingbird and the machine breaks.

A Czech immigrant to Argentina poles a punt through the swampgrass at sunset. He's lost his job as a cobblestone paver. His wife is offered on the raft trailing behind, wearing a wooden flower and a green rubber hat, her soft-focused legs askew on the precariously perched loveseat, a classical torso reaching invisible arms to the absent ceiling.

Don't you have to have a choice to make the wrong one?

The gears of the elaborate mechanism of torture foiled only by the tin of the victim's empty plate.

A Bulgarian woman wearing a pale green scarf, hoeing her garden. A wheelwright rotating a sample of his work to show its balance, a flat spot on the end of his nose as if an iron had once parked there. The uninvolved cameraman carrying the arm of a wooden Madonna.

Every field seems to go on forever. Every house is a place to wait. Ice and dust have been born brothers of this year gone long and thick with waiting.

Now summer drifts in clouds of heat, and evening has grown too tired to talk. Argument lies folded over a chair, a pair of pants worn through with the same kneeling and taking down.

Each morning a tired woman talks to her muscles, talks to the years gone when, coming in from the field, the field would settle comfortably inside her, where he still was.

She remembers him like that, like the weather arriving at the house, something wide open and large settling inside, even after it's gone.

November 5

A Calculation of the Trajectory

The sparrow hawk, circling the door to its prey's tiny nebula.

There is entirely too much content in this world!

If only I had had a son.

Large hands and a crooked nose.

A cautious tailor, ragged dreams, the grass dripping with nocturnal insects. A tall star spoke of sadness from a constellation of scissors, returning its old geometry to the nocturnal eyes of the descendant tribe. Moonlight spilled into the tailor's worn hands as he pulled down the soft cloth of the night sky, soothing the cracks in his warm palms.

Sex like a thrush escaping a dense thicket.

A voice dressed as the night leaking into itself was ready to tell the tailor's story. It was the tailor's voice and he was already a slave to the chapter that swallows the sky with its feet. The poor man watched as an animal like himself, made of water, returned to the perpetual orphanage of the river, an animal so sad it could have lived in his wounds.

A moth awoke from the dreams of the moon's mistaken friends. Some of the words are lost, others have gone home alone to the soft veins of milk-light, the rooms of salt.

Something in the spaces between the trees, that place in the brain where night opens a warm pouch.

You in your body, I in my mouth.

Fallen apart, the pieces twitch.

A child's broken tooth.

A letter from home.

When the dream ends, it claims your footprints.

Give them away.

The goatherd's son was overweight. He studied calculus in his spare time, but that was not his reason for torturing horseflies or persecuting lazy clouds.

I held the ocean to my ear. A nursery rhyme popped from my mouth, and I chased it down the beach. It squealed with delight when I caught it.

Why had the quail eggs taken on such a mysterious color, and why was the arrival of rain announced by a child's coloring book?

How poignant to see the boudoir littered with chicken feathers.

The moonlight turned yellow and she wanted to know if I loved her.

You can come in now.

My fingernails were already evidencing a great deal of raw experience. I was listening. I was becoming another tailor, a collector of seams, sewing tailor to tailor, hemming the night's winged cuff.

The animals were quiet. Trees grew under their shirts.

I have never shared my curfew. It's a little known disease, but it's enough. I determined the loss per minute created by the small hole in the fabric. I wasn't sure what I was losing.

When I said, "snail," I meant "antelope," the nape of your neck mounted

above the location of the fire.

No one is holding the river hostage tonight.

O my hostage, no one is holding the river.

The sky, of course, is blue and above us. This is not sad but surprising. After that we stopped wondering why we hadn't stopped wondering.

November 6

Smoke Sailing Slowly Over the Hills Without Rising

Their heavy voices precede them like loaded wheelbarrows. If they lean too far forward, the load spills. Somebody has to shovel it. Somebody has to speak deeply to keep this an honorable profession.

Later the voices hold a memory like a man resting his head between a woman's legs as she sleeps, with no religion to tell him what it means, a large globe of warmth in the cup at the center.

Have the men forgotten the voice that says, "Obey" and "Go" and "Lie down," the one directed at their own bodies like a chunk of black earth?

And when some of the men part the thick poetic muck of self-indulgent anguish, they cannot find themselves. They cannot stem their own righteous sowing.

O glorious outrage and clamor. O beautiful propaganda.

Some of the men rant at that unfaithful bitch the sea, yearning for its lost moon. Some damn the sunset bleeding all over the horizon. And some, with an awkward staggering sway, mourn their shipwrecked lives, cut by the clock's dull scissors.

Some defend their conflicted pride. As if the green alphabet of lust ever belonged to men only.

Some simply stand in one place and trouble about with their hungry hands.

If a woman whispers, "body," the wind answers. If a woman says "wind," the earth whispers. If a man says "earth," his body trembles beneath his feet. If a woman says, "earth," the trembling rises.

If a man and a woman think of "effortless grazing in the hayfield," a concept of time is born in which a watch may have become engaged to a watch.

The men are asking the women to answer like clouds, but the clouds only follow the wind. The women are asking the men to release birth without bursting through the ground.

An ordinary man offers his confession, which isn't anything new, except for the clumsy brilliance of his empty pockets. He is holding a box of rutting elk and smoking a damsel in distress. Old cans of pygmy stew are stacked in his closet. Father, why did I let you out of your skin?

The man dressed like an outlaw so that if he was ever truly surrounded by good, they'd find him and recognize his uniqueness, but of course their white hats were never really white enough and his rooms always sent their corners to visit him, which brought with them women who thought he was secretly better than they were and they tried to fix what they thought they had made wrong in him.

The men gathered the pale blue bulbs of washed onions at dusk.

The men wanted to be riding a possibility, right then, the men wanted a reason, not just mooning over the neighbor's musk, not just How do you like me so far? But something dangerous came down from the hills, God-breath like the stench of fear, as if when the angels leapt for the passing train, the weight of their bodies increased.

November 7

The Geisha's Reply

It was a provincial experience, which needed only its own family's acceptance, so I came to the city. I discovered that one's intentions are often indistinguishable from one's acceptances. That's why some of the clients tell me they have to check their whipped backs in the morning to see if the blood is theirs.

No, Madame, I do not believe that the feather of the hummingbird is the handle of a tiny axe though I am willing to entertain your fiction long enough to see it that way. And I do not think that simply because your neighbor is beating her rugs, you should trust the lips but not the hands.

I have certainly learned from you, Madame, that nature does not love me. That is how it has become worthy. That is how it can accept me. That is why I belong. In this we are all treated equally and it is the one who can see it who may prosper.

It's spring now and the plants are listening to the birds. I do not wish to live a life, like a poorly developed fictional character, which consists only of conclusions.

And so, no, I don't yet know my purpose. Should I?

Yes, Madame, I have several clients now who appreciate many parts of me. One has been gentling his excited visions of torn limbs. Another is happy with the ache of his muscles at the end of a long slow journey. Another recently died and I quietly mourn him. He was scattered and beautiful, brilliantly chaotic and living in several directions at once. I find it amazing that he finished even his life.

I am reminded, Madame, that our death is watching us and retirement is but a momentary recognition like so many others in our frequently oblivious lives. We seldom achieve a real education. That much I have learned from subtle degrees of difference among those whose knowledge seldom touches the earth.

Still, I envy you. As delighted as I can be with a warm green adultery, I am bound to perform, as is my nature, and you have no such obligation. I suspect that may help you to desire it more, but I can imagine a moment at which you will wish to say, "At least no one feels guilty, despite all that we have done."

Or because of it.

November 8

Patiently Waiting Inside an Imaginary Surface

First he falls out of his life into deeper water and then that ocean calms him, something that big and steady always there, always breathing in a slow show of persistence. His bearded goat wanders freely, like him, a creature of simple hungers. His shack whistles softly in the wind.

On the beach the sailors grow tails from dreaming too often of mermaids. Their wives in distant homes sit on Victorian chairs, perched like weathered statues in front of row upon row of angular doors intricately carved with boars and gargoyles. Seashells pave the unused path before them.

What is he saving himself from? His other world tears fear out by its roots, then feeds it back to him, a self-sustaining disengagement. Inside, there's a white shadow, with its long liquid mouth and its body flowing into it, a birth the species knew as a departure and the man did not.

On the beach a capsized whale begins bloating, under a canopy sky that said his life was small and wrong, a sky that said home and then changed it. The wind's calligrapher signs and signs the shoreline's smoothed bedding with no impatience at the water's erasures.

He carries a rusted knife that used to be the dictator of a Latin American country. He thinks of his love as an abstraction that once saw him as a man so intelligent he could forget everything he knew. His hunger grew. That's how the owls found him, drunk on filaments, chasing prisons. As if there were a secret curse in a woman's body where his story grew.

His past continues bloating. It soaks up the ocean. Like someone you've just met who carries away your desires, another white shadow passing across the thoughts of the child you never got to be.

He is not what he seems to be, a new desire for the not quite touched. He has gone inside himself like a bucket dropped into the sky, and he has found there a woman and the drowning soul of a sailor. As if placing himself inside could penetrate the illusion.

November 9

A Translation of the Missing Story

When the magician died, the woman he had sawn in half fell apart. (First you must eat all the light, then hands become possible. Illusion follows.) In this way one can reach across the illusion although the shadows reach farther.

Abandoned cars gossiping on the river bottom, frogs drumming behind the old church, green eyes and the golden moonlight from the wheat. (But now she sits in the kitchen with the tiniest TV you have ever seen.)

Nothing falls completely down.

Meanwhile, dripping with ripe extras, her magic slips her clothing, there where the magician is still grazing upon the escaping buttons of her blouse, gratefully appreciative of the nipples' mutual gestures of acceptance pouting against the silk's accommodations.

She holds him in her hands. She wants to say, "Liberation." She wants to say, "Escape." (But she stays. And she opens.)

The past intrudes.

She scratches the patches of dry skin on each elbow. An odor of molding figs from the bathroom. The TV interrupts itself with weather and a commercial backed by an amateur orchestra sawing away at itself.

Several ripe plums await her touch, next to a forgotten postcard, and I'd say there isn't any willingness left, I'd say the miracle was a cruiser.

Everybody falls apart. Few stay there.

The force of the sea whispering to millions needs a note from its mother to attend the field trip because she shouldn't want to listen to any old dead magician whistling an Ode to Pablo Neruda's Seaside Retreat.

Weather interrupts itself with more weather.

She falls through her water until fins sprout and insects stir in her stomach. Deeper until a shadow recognizes her, the shadow of the magician's saw.

And the attraction of the body's shadow grows older, (desire its well, echoing down to its level of need), a deep cool vibration swimming out.

As if fallen from a dream, a stranger turns once at the top of the hill on the road of the opened nerve. He feels as if he's been born and has no idea where this feeling came from.

Mice gather in the corners of sleep and begin licking each other's frail new wings.

If his question's old enough, it could be the answer.

November 10

Enemies

I knew we had lost everything when the celebration spilled over into the next era and the speeches sounded like everybody praising everybody for doing everything right. We had never been in deeper trouble. We had never been without our enemy. That left only us to be the enemy.

That's how our religion works. The winner always forgives. We come to the rescue with such certainty it makes us right again. That's how we stay ahead of the inevitable.

I remember the year I was best at dying. They all knew I was a fake, but a nearly dead man who could still come out to play and was always willing to lose was the token no one had to cash.

Let's say it was Dried Onion Junior High and in my head I was taking the place of something I had killed. I was unshooting a partridge. A turgid atmosphere of righteous indulgence.

Right now we see it as one more success and no one says it's time to stop because we achieve this happiness by declaring victory before it's over. We've defied our own years of struggle and we've deified the sunset. Tomorrow isn't another day, it's another yesterday, and the story's all over again before dark.

Don't ask what happens next. No entrance to any heaven, just a slow drag across the ridge like coal dust, streaks of soot clinging to the trees like tiny insect casings. Where has the creature gone?

So good-day to my vertical. I might be ready now. Everything needed to put things together on one table, everything to take them apart on the other.

Each of them may be thinking, "Your tumor was benign, but you were not," but each is saying, "Trust me. I will lie to you faithfully."

November 11

A Ladder-Cart Overturned by Ruffians

How is it you know that white is the right color for the desperate throb she felt in a young boy's touch? Her response seems to have lived on air alone, quietly enduring in its perfect cage until now.

The door is open. Inside is the abundance of everything that will go on without you.

Her's a scream of pain smothered by a small man in a dark baggy suit, and there's white, taken as a pure object, attaching to a landscape, which takes up residence in your shoes.

She spends her day searching for him--white shirt, white shoes, white heart. But the young boy has changed.

The bowl of dreams, wet on the table. "Let me in," you whisper. You are trying to remember your names.

Tarred boats against stucco walls, the eyes of a Moroccan cat, impatient passport smiles, and all the new desire that arrives with the morning of words. And for a moment yet, the fading light of the departing lover.

You must want to be like this. You must want to praise the next quiet moment eased in upon itself like a single gnat becoming the world, like white dreams lifting over the mountains.

You must know that nothing will hold still and this, the smallest of gifts, leads everywhere. You must want to be everywhere.

November 12

The Baby's Terrible Diaper

First he saw a gruesome accident and fainted. Then he witnessed a jury marching towards defeat and he fainted again. His wife assured him no one knew about the baby's terrible diaper.

That's when two little mice in a boat were suddenly flung end over end for no apparent reason. "Can we keep him?" said the little wife, thinking one mouse split into two pieces, thinking bottom half of a cage floating on water. Thinking singular.

He was not the father expected but celebratory just the same. His own children were swimming into something equally distasteful and perhaps tiring quickly.

He felt his skin change. He felt the air begin tasting him. You see, people who ate at the hotel liked to look out the dining room window.

No big winds were carrying things off today.

Finally he began moving in the furniture. He considered the mouth of an open thing that closed when you touched it. As if the accident itself could still remain lucid.

November 13

What I Knew About My Older Sister, Patricia, Life Span Two Hours

I asked for a river for Christmas, I asked for the closet near my sister's illness, I asked for Patricia's clean socks, the ones we had never purchased. I had found the scream of the missing river and no one could hear it. I needed the river to attach it to. So my sister could pour out.

I'm talking like a leaf now, like a stalk of wheat whispering from a South Dakota graveyard to anything that listens, I'm talking like the wing whistle of landing waterfowl just when the lake's mirror looks empty. I am falling upward into the wet sky of birds and opening up blue, guilty of a conspiracy against the moon because the imagination requires it, because nature is on trial. We're all witnesses and must eventually contradict the future, where Patricia doesn't know I lived.

November 14

The Clairvoyance of the Blinded Eye

Because the ordinary citizens were responding so well to our pleas for assistance, the authorities decided we must be faking it. We weren't homeless and we didn't have hungry children and jobs were waiting for us to return from our vacations.

They tried sending us home, but the cardboard walls made them angry. A policeman thought our stomachs were singing and tried to find some harmonies. He wanted the sound of unexpected waterfalls because it was Christmas and there was too much snow and his parents lived in Hawaii. We felt sorry for him and offered him folded newspaper swans and the telephone number of Jesus and all the degrees we had been saving. We had already given all our pets to passing motorists so that no one would eat them though some of the motorists may have.

We ate the holster of the fallen policeman who had joined us in protest, although he no longer understood what we were protesting, and we had a contest to remember his name, but no one won.

Then the ordinary citizens quit responding. And the new policemen looked too clean and well-kept and the citizens didn't believe they knew the truth about us either, not until they were laid off and a few of their stomachs began singing something like badly harmonized Christmas carols and their uniforms started to smell like cabbage.

Then the authorities decided those men could never have been policemen at all and they sent everybody home again and we wrote "window" on our cardboard with the pens they had given us to sign the evictions. Most of us climbed out before our sagging walls collapsed in the onslaught of water cannons, but the dreamy ceilings had never been properly anchored to the falling walls and we used them to collect rain for drinking water most of the next day.

The citizens watched and envied our pleasure at the temporary satisfaction of our endless thirst. The citizens begged us for a taste. We held what was left of our homes in our hands, where it slept peacefully while we opened our doors and let the clouds back out.

November 15

Domestic Engines

Sometimes when I hang around the cigar store I can smell burning linen with a hint of stable in it, and I have the impulse to explain this to the clerk who is a nervous little sliver of delight. She seems so bright and inward she's probably easily troubled by hummingbirds, but I want to explain how, when I was young, a neighbor boy made a bonfire of his mother's hair curlers, and it wasn't clear if he hated her or if he hated what the curlers did to the woman he loved. Ever since then I've noticed smells other people miss, and when I see smoke, it always says something warm is sleeping.

Up the street there's another guy like me. His daughter married last week. White bride, white dog, white hair, her bridal veil a confession she didn't know she didn't mean. He's one of the ordinary, one of the men with fat shoes and a wife who shines them and doesn't come home at night. He wants something to say no to and no again until he can make it say yes.

Down the other way is a blind man sweeping the cobblestones in front of his bright red house. "Lookin' good," I tell him, and his grin sees me listening and listening.

We're the people with desk lamps and taverns and buckets of whitewash. We're the closed mills and pigeon-hole desks with too many erasers and a calico cat that signs the checks. We're tuning the radio to green and teaching the neighbor's dog to bring us his paper. We're water in the whiskey and lipstick traces on the plastic-covered sofa.

But you're probably not quite like me. Maybe you can remember the first time you got drunk alone and the crowd got out of hand, the towel rack falling over, a wineglass throwing itself at you, but you can't remember all the trouble you could have gotten yourself into because bad luck didn't ask you to.

The clerk's blonde hair has fallen and she blows it up and away again and again, enjoying the failure and whistling as she cleans the countertop. I can see flakes of soup-fat in her mother's hands. Her leaving trunk full of hay and apples, her suitors horseless.

I was looking down on the hats near quitting time as the shadows grew, until the men going home from work seemed to be following those shadows, which included the hats, which in that way didn't even belong to them.

Sometimes I feel old now, but I can smell the cool bray of tonight's tin roofdance. The rain is coming and I can smell hazelnut, cinnamon, graveldust, appleskins. An orange leaf is twirling furiously, refusing to let go. I can't see what else is happening, but I can hear someone's broom painting and painting.

I think it's probably just another movie about smell, in which all the characters are blind, and they go to a movie about smell, and in the movie, there's a story you can listen to about somebody making a movie. Then you go outside and the rain's doing the most beautiful painting you could ever hear, even if it is pretty damn cold out there.

November 16

Having Given Up Hope, He Is Confident

A metaphor can kill a man.
-Wallace Stevens

1. *Because I hadn't seen it, the truth was a lie.* I had arms a couple of days long. They embraced an infection, lifting it gently to my head. One eye wept and the other sang.

A muddle of lemons, a cough of grapes.

When I go out to eat, I leave my real belly at home.

Poets astir in the teacup negotiations.

I needed them to arrange the tastier executions.

2. After the critics, I rained for three weeks and then began rowing hunger towards my homeland. When I arrived, the failure welcomed me and offered marriage. Pretty soon I gave birth to my new self and my wife suckled me. I was trying to live as intended. I ate everything.

I left one stair at a time. The yellow wine of recognition accompanied the post-mortem.

Was the critic still my daughter then?

How many dictators remained between her pages?

3. In the cemetery, the stone general stands with his heels buried in the horse's flesh. I'm not going to live in the sea this summer.

I've decided.

November 17

Paternity

A large blue pimple beat his children with carrots while several aging conquistadors eulogized a sacrificial rabbit. It's a disease I can't appreciate, a color found only in rest homes, a rabid moon descended from a long line of surprisingly circular crippled clouds.

In a desperate world we wouldn't notice.

Some old tires, a broken couch and a cricket. Life in a clutter. He gave himself away.

"Just a moment," the father said, not knowing what he meant and finally meaning it.

Blossoms before the leaves woke.

A father who is always.

It looked like something someone might do on purpose.

November 18

Innocence

This should have been deliberate. My heart like an owl, a particular silence moving north. (In every woman's touch I felt a soldier leave for the war.)

But this is the story's other life, a piece of lint trapped in the pocket of a man who will be killed tomorrow.

A thief, I carried it till it opened.

There was nothing there.

I am so happy I found it.

November 19

Learning to Count

The hole in the end of the bottle is exactly the size of your index finger, so you put your index finger in the hole.

And, of course, it sticks. For days you walk around with your finger in the bottle, hiding it inside your coat.

One afternoon you even set the bottle in a carton of five others and carry them around with you. Soap doesn't work. Grease doesn't work.

You're afraid to break the bottle. You're afraid not to break the bottle. It has something to do with your mother but what?

A gorgeous redhead in a miniskirt wants to borrow your bottle. Won't I do? She turns away, disgusted, then relents, and you break the bottle during passion.

Then her wig comes off and it's the milkman. No, the neighbor's heifer. No, a fire hydrant. Maybe it's time to go home.

Your mother turns around, surprised. Where have you been? Your finger, swollen. She kisses it and you wish you didn't feel satisfied.

"You don't wake up because this is not a dream," screams your wife before she leaves you.

One bottle feeds a family of four.

You whisper back at her, "Twins," and suddenly her feet detach and run back to you screaming, "Daddy, save us! We had to count the same bottle over and over! We had to count!"

"You don't wake up because this is not a dream," scream your feet before they leave.

One at a time.

How will you ever learn to multiply?

November 20

How Did You Get in Here?

In this dream, there are no doors. This dream is a corner and the edges on either side fade like a vignette, the baby's cradle hanging from an off-color ceiling while a sparrow plucks a worm from the baby's eye, which is smiling, which is impossible and true.

Bird children poke their heads up from the nest, perched on a plant holder clinging to the empty wall. On the left, out the window, a sailboat in the distance.

Or is the window a painting? A mirror? Is the corner itself just an impression?

Or worse, only a reality and not a dream at all?

In the next dream something warm brushing past my ear, wings rising from the boat as I listen for the distant whir of time and ice and fur shining. On into the comforting night you row the body, and when you've forgotten the boat, death supports you.

I cannot see you, careful between your wings, the boat rising now. You need that last sliver of the moon on your sleeve. You blame the sun for everything that cannot be blamed on the wind, but the wind has traveled centuries to bring you this news: It's not easy breathing all over the earth.

And in the last dream, late at night, the stones are carrying their brothers to your face in the far hill. A family comes slowly home to find you waiting in less than your bones. (That was the end of the separate ocean, climbing back down in the tear of a single child by the fountain, pressing her feet into the warm dry earth.)

Dreams like little nails, nearly as fragile as what they hold. I wanted to draw what the nail would say, but the nail is not a nail and the nail is the way I get back inside.

I go outside and I'm not out yet.

I like it that way.

What are you doing with my hammer?

November 21

Detritus

As the rain is my witness, I have discarded inadequate bundles of life like little sticks with titles; Lost Loves and Things I Used to Believe and The Pleasures of Self-Pity in Disguise. Up ahead another story, cleansing itself with its paws, and farther, the river roaring like a rampant conviction and the wilderness of a cloud passing.

Something about the moon, something about grass and the direction of the wind on a quiet night. The door opening and no one there but me, about to step out of my-self, my body talking to the air as if the only thing alive in the world contained both of us, some creature about to enter the unknown of itself because it's no longer alone and the night is warm and part of it and speaking. A beauty so persistent I felt sad.

I went to sleep with my sadness and awoke clinging. Sad delight, awake and depart claws. Some departing sun of crossed boxes, held like that, not trembling but ancient. I seem to be sinking. No rest for the very.

A beauty so sad and long I grow persistent. There's a reason for this, but it's upriver and it's broken and it's floating. The passing of a wilderness clouding my sky. My wil-derness now, piece by piece, loose on the great bus of river. Outside the trial, the sun was waiting to report the clouds' motion to adjourn. The tour guide was soaked and sleeping and I climbed back inside him and pointed out the precedents, which bobbed and seemed to be waving as they passed though probably they too were sleeping.

November 22

The Day Before the Arrival of the Owls

Sound does not measure time. Water does. I have been welcoming the owls with silence, as empty as the mind of a stone back from its first birth.

At noon, when I have become my shadow, I am more obviously not the human, but the animal inside.

The song the snow sings whistles dryly, breath lost, till the warmth of your body meets it, breath found, and the exchange of weapons is complete.

Small animals scurry behind these thoughts.

You were there. I pushed you into it. Your mouth puckered in a child's definition of lust and glowed with such joyous perversity.

I want a life like that. I want to see if it is and if it is, to see. Not merely joy, death or revolution, but a questioning of the impossible.

I want to abandon the symptoms of clothing. The quiet desire in your touch should be enough to reveal what you wish to be known.

November 23

An Apology for What I've Done to You

I didn't mean to make you so happy. I only wanted to get along well in the world. I wasn't expecting any miracles or weddings or especially delightful mudpies or tea with the king and queen under the old elm tree. I wasn't trying to make you so sad, either. It just turns out that way sometimes.

Here, have a tape recording of the crickets played backwards. Then we'll attack the caravan for those delicious tangerines. And after we've taken everything back, we'll give it all away again, no strings attached.

And then someone's voice was saying, "I'll come back for you. We'll swallow the sunset and start over. You'll see. Everything will be fine again."

You're right. It's not my voice. I'd be lying. The world is raw. A herd of muscles grazing on the flames of birds bursting everywhere in your body, the slow swallowing which the damp dark opens.

Humility.

Because more is not all we want either.

November 24

It Seems Like Everything's in Order

The bear is in his cave. The bees are gathering honey. Have you brought the basket of French doormen? Have you garaged into the ferns without clinging uselessly?

There is no other way in. The way out passed away yesterday. There was a plastic leg there where Junior's accountant had been bumped by a car.

I must assert that no graves have been disinterred for our throated glee. If I am conversing with a disheveled bush, it is because the salesman traveling perishable in my deeper emotions is offering squid and gin and the odor of Ovaltine. He is expecting the nomination.

It's no use throwing butter from the sidecar. The parade attendants are jaded and the national anthem of party crevices now sounds like Christmas ornaments singing about tooth decay.

Then finally there was the dark party. Table for two and a formal contract? I could have brought you a selection of openings for your closure. I could have vespered. I could have helped you discourage faulty puritans. I could have lathered up the visitation couch. I could have divulged a richer life. You were there and you knew I was coming.

Do tell us about it when you happen.

November 25

Big Fish, Little Fish

The ratchet walk of a pigeon pumping itself up and down a woodpile, a crow hopping like a one-legged man, cows and a cheerleader practicing their field assignments in the same gophered field.

A white rose in her sister's eel basket.

She's not like you, she's inside her clothing with the birds and the rabbits. Moan-mongers swimming in her, yes, and a recipe for smoke, but a crow is only a shadow that eats and her spiritual advisor is ice cream.

There were two of us until you started paying attention.

And now are we the wooden beam or the saw?

Let's imagine a future for tense verbs, a comforting late gesture like a streetlight's blossom. With the present we are content, but we've surfaced, the dark receding forest a passage, the crow's voice (sharp, wooden, unforgiving) another.

I believe I've been assigned to a twitch.

How come the sky's still here?

Something you'd ask a baby. If the baby wasn't your baby.

So I say that to the worm struggling on the hook. I say that to the shadow with crow's feet. I say that and I say that.

The twitch ripening.

You could say I was still pending. A gradual I was not departed of. How surrendered had I become?

Something a baby would answer wordlessly.

If the answer wasn't your answer.

The twitch was looking. The twitch was never left alone. The twitch found itself in suspension and released, with another attraction waiting, a couple whose happiness was a bomb the couple enjoyed exploding.

The King of Zaire ate squash with his fingers, so we all ate squash with our fingers. We lived in Zaire.

The queen says thank you for the king and for the beautiful limbo, with money and privilege, for the position she's in, which happens for the moment to contain her, instead of a real queen, who has never existed.

The pigeon's eyeing the cheerleader. She's happy and needs milk. She's multiple and leading the verbal encouragement with physical suggestion. She's completing and. She's next and away. She's happy and bitter. I'm yours now if the answer wasn't your answer.

November 26

Change in the Weather

1. *A collapsing woman holes up in the charmed moon of her skin garden.* Desperate breath cupboards the fruit.

What did the meadow have in mind?

To have been awakened by a dream, of course.

This is your wound for darkness.

A wolf whistle echoes the slipback and dodge of another tongue trek, the sound all over her like honey.

The child's hand reaching into my mouth and the mother's glassy whistle, digging for chains under slow thick replies.

A little village of small round rodents collapsed beneath the owl's roost. Leaf-meal covers the victims' bones, fate's leather lungs curing in the damp attic of fallen leaves.

2. I loved her carefully like the tidy arrangement of her mother's peaches neatly on the cellar shelf. I can type ninety words a minute and grovel profusely. I apologize for acts of nature.

Her runaway coats celebrated a family of unhinged pilgrims. She labeled obvious contents "too obvious." She abandoned another lover before me saying he smelled like asparagus.

"Lonely necktie," she said once, wanting to pet me.

No more emotional coyotes now in her burgeoning neighborhoods. A finicky little ornamental cacophony swimming along the responsibility channel with too many moonstruck clairvoyants nominating stars.

3. When our teeth fall out, we continue growing, beautifully, ignoring each other with fierce loyalty.

Streak of blood pierces cloth of sky. It means we can awaken now and greet the dark inside.

The moon is waning. Dear, innocent moon.

I rely on my pilgrims to collect the accidents.

And that was how the only storm ended, a lifetime later, with the weather taking that feeling of "air" out of the air.

There remained something in the diminished air that wasn't me. I let it stay, which included it in my disappearance.

November 27

Port Gamble, 1983

Just down the coast the mill shut down. Again. This landscape scenic and quaint to tourists borders on boredom and despair for out of work locals, descendants of the captains who named landmarks Point No Point and Useless Bay, their houses labeled with markers like the headstones in the cemetery, prized by visitors who love to make rubbings of the inscriptions with chalk or crayon.

Straw miniatures of the Victorian houses are offered for sale in the General Store where the Seashell Museum overlooks still another struggling lumberyard. The workers drag in on breaks for root beer, ice cream and a sympathetic ear. Government subsidized competition from Canadian mills. Wood will never mean what it used to mean. Upstairs, a world away from their heaven, sand dollars sell for 35 cents. Down the road a tennis court strangles in blackberries behind the summer home an out of state banker uses a few weeks a year.

Some of the men jog every morning, running from something harder now to understand than survival or tides. A son tries hard to land a foreman's job, two fingers and a girlfriend lost to the navy, the price of his only success. The schedule he doesn't know he wrote for his life is posted in Braille between the splinters tossed from a dangerously dull blade, the wind on the back of his neck cold, no steady direction.

Realism has fallen on hard times. Where once hardships could have been understood, now they've become products for tourists and spawned an unsung religion preached in the taverns that simplifies the confusions of trade economics.

St. Paul's Episcopal Church has grown scenic, still less important than the lighthouse, even if the ships are fewer and foreign and guided by technology that makes miniature diagrams more valuable than cargo.

And yet, in the museum, time waits patiently; scallops, limpets, periwinkles, hooded cowaries, a family of shells called olives . . . all displayed in cocktail glasses. A petrified skate. A sponge like a lace stocking. These collected frameworks of stolen homes endure far past any other creature's need but ours, organized under glass with Latin names like definitions meant to capture them, as beautifully intricate as the chambers of the nautilus someone split with a diamond saw. Each one so much the same till you open it.

November 28

The House by the Lake

1. *Back to soapy hands in the dishwater beneath the window,* the trees beyond, wet with darkness. Behind that porch, this house silently waits. Only the hands of aging winds have the patience to have warped those boards.

Back to that room where the lights traveled sleeplessly across the wall. Now darkness covers the barn's wings, a wheel turning inside you.

A lamp and a loaf of bread. It's the same window, yet now the smell of snow and a horse breaking ice on the farm pond.

But it's never the right wilderness until you've crossed it.

If you walk in a snowstorm long enough, its light becomes your light. That caul of snow the secret religion of crows and the tiny branched gossip of sparrows.

And somewhere in Iowa this year's only albino ground squirrel turns the wrong way to escape an ordinary death.

In Georgia, evangelists have taken yes and no hostage. Fortunately, their demands cannot be met.

A proverb about this has vanished, set to music in Canada, composed below zero.

Back to that house by the lake. Back to your future. Back to the possible and back to the hostage under the porch.

And like any man and woman, the three of us dine together. Imagine truffles and partridge and some medieval delicacy with a white heart, the path always falling away.

2. The seasons change on the river of the tongue. It could be anywhere, but it isn't, the warm water lapping at the edge of his sleeve.

Back to your castle in the air, breathing. Back to a glass of warm milk steaming on a blue table. Back to water birds like sexual whimpers scrabbling after a child's offering of bread warmed by anxious hands, taut voices strung on the cold air, all the angels decaying in the storehouse, certain possibilities swallowed by the smell of bread.

Don't bother with anger. No argument of fists ever held water. The past always awaits our return to a life so internalized it seems to manufacture its own rust.

If you hear a river singing, drink it, drink the ropes running through its shaggy light, running through the slow animal heart beneath the green hull of its sleep.

3. Such a child might meet himself in a dark alley and think himself harmless and worse, be right. But each invisible railroad tie weathers differently, like we do, one step closer to somewhere else.

The crooked shadows of tree limbs harsh against the breaking snowmelt of the path, the black flute of its moonlight drowned.

Perhaps you wanted to be held by it.

The only one of us who never betrayed that child doesn't know it.

Like the ogre in the legend of the catfish, you have forgotten.

But so many things have not.

Farther up the slope, above the innocent duck pond, in the clearcut wound of the weathered landskin, a seabird perches on a rotting stump, a kind of totem for old brown animals and thick sleep. Inside the stump sleeps a misplaced memory of a large slow farmer scratching his codpiece in a field of potatoes.

Back to the rotting mounds of fur lumped on the prairie like one great wrinkled beast about to rise and lumber to the end of its long and ending days, a host of human scavengers riding its pelt over one final cliff, one world falling off the edge of another.

4. In a dream you are searching for a hammer. Someone has eaten it. You want to pound on your clothes. You want to make them talk. You want to carry on a conversation with someone else's sweat. You want to say something simple to a saw.

Icicles white as teeth in the porch's mouth. Each one contains a world within a world. In one, crimson fish swim in the yellow coral. In another a child feeds warm bread to the ducks.

And so, my little cancers, we come to our game of backhands, crying "Kiss me!" And the darkness splits open, dripping saints. There's a pebble in your mouth, the hungry tunnel of aging.

So we apologized for the palaces between the stems of water lilies deep inside an icicle in one of our deaths. We were sorry about corncribs and dovewood and the beauty of disinterest among trees, as they refuse to be anything but trees.

Then, under a red moon, we visited our garden of bones. Wind carried this death in its wings and rose, listening for the screams of hawks and loons, listening for the song of the air.

5. And finally, here there is nothing, not even the past, no friends in the creaking hinges, no memories of snowstorms in the summer heat, no house by the lake.

Take a deep breath. It is almost ready to sing.

November 29

Box Seats

The operatic foreplay assumes the winter was cold enough to freeze bricks. It seems when I wasn't looking, the chalice fell from the clerestory into the oceanic lilt of the priest's veneer. I couldn't see what he was doing, but I suspected it.

One reads about sick children who study their lessons anyway.

That winter the snow was deeply jilted by the overcast mufflers the sky was saving for a more extravagant display.

The story line had something to do with a Viking or a dead parishioner and some revenge notes passed around the drinking fountain.

Baby Marvin was not prepared for the religious expectations placed upon his sexual performance by the atmosphere established in the visiting priest's implied sermon. The wine stain wasn't very pretty either.

Finally the portentions of snow were escorted to the lobby. Marvin's mother was serving popcorn to the usherettes. She didn't know about the box seats. (One reads about mothers who protect their children from imaginary dangers.)

"Next time I'll wait till you can come with me," said Marvin's silk boxer shorts. The Viking was singing very very loudly. Marvin knew it was a climax, but would it be followed by a resolution?

Baby Marvin wanted to go to a big noise with overtones of conquest. The attentive fanatic might conclude the opera assumes the mother was cold enough to take him there.

November 30

Dust

Snow, of course, is really only dust and water, yet no one admires dust inside a glass ball falling on tiny reindeer. No one eats dust, regardless of color. Even when dust is the color of snow, do not expect it to mold to your desires.

Tracks may be found in dust, but no one is following dust. Dust travels everywhere and always leaves something behind.

Wind carries dust to draw attention to its causes, but these causes do not really belong to the wind. Fire learned long ago. Whatever it wants to do, dust can stop it.

For dust the doors are never really closed. Patience provides passage. Even lungs and the journeys of food are not kept from dust.

Water carries dust on all its missions. Wherever water has been, dust reminds us it's gone.

Dust is not an animal. Dust is not the lost wing of the wind. Dust does not need to look for us when it travels.

The human body is a great complexity of dust, one of its unexpected missions with water. Slower than wind, but as necessary as water, we help take it where it wants to go. There are places in the world that must be arrived at slowly. Don't think about it. Only your body can offer that thought.

December

December 1

The Dark Bird in the Dream of an Old Woman

A silent black flame. Mud and shadows have done something with its claws. It could mean a brother come to live with her.

Once while gathering small brown stones in an open field, Ramon told her, "Only the angels have come here to die. The rest of us go on living as if something depended on it."

Another time, with the hunger living close in an old jar, she grew quiet and began listening. "We are like fences built by predators. Strangers sleep in our fathers' houses."

That was before the last revolution, the one that turned, like the wheat, back to the earth for its dreams.

December 2

Cold and Shining

The air stretched taut like a blanket staked at the corners. Little Nonsense expected to find the end of it when he stepped over the ridge, but it just kept going and his lungs were being stretched right along with it.

Salmon Girl held his hand for a while, but pretty soon he needed to hold his arms at his sides, his fingers curled back together inside the big thick gloves. He kept watching his breath like it was an object and ice was going to fall off it.

Little Nonsense wondered if the earth could know that its blanket was moving right through him. How warm was the earth beneath it? He wondered how far you would have to go to get underneath the blanket and be with the earth. He knew the blanket was air, but it did not feel like air, and he looked up into the sky to see if he could tell where the other blankets of air had gone. He saw the stars sparkling all over the sky, and he thought that they were breathing better than he was. He imagined the stars were happy, but he couldn't quite remember what they did when they were happy, except shine brightly.

Salmon Girl coughed and it sounded like a rifle shot. Little Nonsense thought of his own cough as a secret weapon and remembered playing enemies with Weasel Eyes among the willow and spruce where the creek chattered happily in the springtime. Little Nonsense wanted to put some raisins from his backpack into his mouth now, but he thought they would only make him colder, frozen little pieces of ice until his tongue warmed them, and anyhow, he couldn't see how to put them there without taking his fingers out of the stiff gloves. Little Nonsense remembered the Moose Kidney Pie his uncle had offered him just before he left, and he was sad he had not eaten any.

Little Nonsense thought about his grandmother's false teeth and how she took them out when she put moose leather into her mouth to soften it. She had used strips of the leather to thread together birch-wood for the snowshoes he was walking on.

They came to the pond frozen solid with ice, and if Little Nonsense had felt like talking, he would have asked if it was frozen all the way to the bottom. He didn't think so, but how far was the bottom? He didn't know. Weasel Eyes had told him that frogs and turtles and some kinds of fish could burrow down into the mud and hibernate there just like bears when it got too cold or the water dried up, but he hadn't believed him. Now he wanted to.

Salmon Girl pointed to some cattails folded over like a lean-to and Little Nonsense thought she was pointing the way. He stepped over the bent reeds and suddenly an explosion of noise and air erupted at his feet. It scared him so much he couldn't breathe.

Then a sharp cackle and the telltale droppings fell so close he could smell them as the heavy bird tried to climb the air. He had seen pheasants do this before but never this close. It made the cold hold on to his chest. Salmon Girl was laughing but she stopped quickly when she saw he was still scared, thumped on her chest, and started across the polished ice on the surface of the pond.

For more than an hour they walked without saying a word. The rhythm of their passage carried them across two frozen meadows and over a crusted snowdrift. They walked with their heads down, forgetting the sky was above them.

Little Nonsense walked right into a dream and kept going. He was feeding stars to the fish and the fish were salmon like Salmon Girl and the stars were all light and fluffy like big insects that would float on the water until the salmon ate them. Then he saw the head of one of the insects up close and it was familiar. Was it someone he knew? Salmon Girl opened her mouth and coughed. The insect was gone and he still didn't know who it was. He felt the air around him in his dream, and it felt wet and dark. And then suddenly he could see a long long ways away, and that felt like millions of years.

When they finally arrived and stepped into the warm cabin that smelled like bread, Salmon Girl peeled off her clothing, stomping and huffing and getting everybody to help her, but Little Nonsense moved very very slowly and with great care. He still had a very long way to go.

December 3

The Seminar on Advanced Reasoning

After many years of study, the student perceives the window, which is on the other side of the window. This has been happening for centuries but every occurrence is unlike every other occurrence.

The student had been applying himself with the discipline of a spoon, to which he felt a deep and universal obligation, which he fully intended to repay.

He had also been reading a How-To manual on rest and relaxation, which put him to sleep. He was not sure which kind of death this sleep was, and therefore, did not yet desire to awaken. His teacher's white robes were soaking up the blood from the thumbscrews, which had allowed him to reveal the universal truths necessary for his vision to penetrate the outer window.

After a while the teacher politely requested that his thumbs be disguised so as not to look like hamburger.

"Which thumbs might those be?" queried the attentive student, having learned his lesson from years of deceptively phrased test questions.

"I believe it would be safe to assume that I was in attendance when the thumbscrews were applied to certain aspects of my being visible in the physical realm and appropriate to the function of the aforesaid specialized research device," ventured the teacher.

"Since we have failed to provide an adequate control group, the norm cannot be taken for granted. It might very well be that the particular thumbs which appear to be attached to my own opposable pivoting devices are the ones which are in need of disguise," ventured the student. "If I were to be presented with a reasonable quantity of evidence of the abuses visited upon, for example, the common mosquito, while dining, let us say, in his usual manner, by numerous members of the four- and/or two-footed species of mammals which appear to find the aforesaid creature annoying, would it then be reasonable to assume that it was only the mosquito's dining etiquette which was responsible for those abuses?" furthered the student, becoming more and more self-assured in his presentation. "And if I were to assume, upon receiving anecdotal documentation alone, that one of your testicles had fallen into a bowl of tomato soup, and further, concluded that said testicle was no longer attached to any part of your body, would I not be, through omission of sufficient comparative data, guilty of presumptuous reasoning?" pressed the student.

Whereupon the teacher, opening the distorted window to his fearful soul, fainted, illuminating the difference between the particular variety of "sleep" he was thereby engaged in and the variety to which his all-too-dedicated student would later more naturally succumb without anxiety or coercion of any kind. The teacher at very nearly that same later moment, realizing he was, indeed, not dead, woke up from one variety of "sleep" and quickly fell into another, where he found a window that looked out upon yet another window, whose dimensions could only be fully understood, he was certain, after many years of study, to which he now dedicated himself without the aid of any instructor at all, overlooking entirely the meaning of the abandoned spoon which had been placed upon its dusty windowsill.

December 4

Critical, Overt, Unloading

It got in our eyes. It got between our toes. Its love and betrayal remained inseparable, and seemed not actions or emotions but a single thing breaking into parts and entering from multiple directions, the nature of an organism to which such delicacies and tensions become available.

One of us seemed to be talking to creek water and the other was anticipating clouds. Sometimes it's me I see in the thick fur you wear and sometimes it's me in the dribble of cold at the corner of your mouth.

I'm not going to lie to you. I'm not going to let you have that superior feeling you get when somebody in a story says something and then later they say something different. And they know they're doing it because they don't want you to notice some third thing that doesn't really make them look as bad as they think it does because it sneaks up on you and distracts you. Anyway, it gets on people you think you know in places where they don't notice, like under their fingernails or at the back of their hair, and it sticks to their conceptions of the future and it seeps right into the images other people hold of them and it isn't even trying. It's gifted.

This happened on a day like the one when we couldn't help being thirsty. That day the clouds were busy distorting our sense of cloud realities, so probably some other deceptive things were happening too.

My hiding thing is that I can be a real shit to people who get close to me. I know that. I'm not going to hide it. But don't go getting superior about it, okay? Just because I don't know someone's weakness, it doesn't make them stronger. Except for that one time when I nearly fathered at least three children and lost them and had to give up rollerblading for an entire season. That made me look worse, but the children didn't mind. They were never properly received by their mothers and got left on three different washcloths.

The clouds were everywhere after that. It was a disease. It got into my possibilities.

I couldn't risk it.

December 5

Natural Phenomenon: Tulsa, 1933

The divorce lifted up and cut the green tomato of Randall's firm dry youth down to a muggy persistent diet of angry-looking tomato paste.

You still had to call him "boss' and stand firm to his handshake and ignore the buggy quiver of the blue vein over his eyelid, his wide forehead arching and prancing as the flinch gyrated, the surrounding landscape slurred with grit. Dark swirls still ached there to wed loose straw to a virgin tree, needle-nailed carloads of loosed hay soon to be planted, driven, and posted to poles, pressured deep into a late life of something more than mere decay. You couldn't pretend that fine blue hog belly-flopping in the marsh had gone airborne only to escape Aunt Esther's dog. In this town you don't even need a word like 'tornado" to describe it.

Life stings. Life squeaks. Life leaks a bloody trail of unexpected punches. It's a different kind of person who's dead all the time, but you can find them anywhere it stays dry entirely too long. It's not what they do, it's what they don't, and nothing seems to hurt more than a cough and turn of the head at a touching moment.

Even the rain that follows behind isn't much comfort, but at least the general direction of friendlier gestures isn't hard to discover.

You can find some of us draped over a walker and rummaging on. There's such a long way to go before the exertions of your heart prove more than just blood's accidents. No one knows how poor they really are. If they did, they would open out into blossom, as the needy roses do, eating dirt and smiling a little extra if they get pissed on.

I finally spoke to some of Randall's newer residents about renewing the simplicity and raw demands of vocabulary by having a child. They actually listened. Saying it to a lover used to be like trying to exchange anecdotes with a hollow marmot.

Carlin must have been the one who woke me, standing there grinning and saying, "You're looking very life-like today," and for once, meaning it. Directly he was able, he barked with a stick, that one did, but he wasn't able there for a time. I looked towards the opening door and decided nothing could be as beautiful as a well-worn wooden knob. I had completely forgotten that its purpose was to facilitate the functions of the slab of wood it was attached to. I remain none of my imaginations.

I told my locals I had been at The Church of Lemon Dripping, acknowledging their sour and open-mouthed prayers, and my keys were unlocking the wrong doors. I spoke of the way a child unwittingly carries its future out of the past in the vessel of its determinant body. I told them I had been watching a production of Ibsen performed entirely by swans. I told them I had been disciplining traffic lights with a tendency to spit. I told them I had been accosted by an embarrassed nun holding a broken teddy bear. I was sure Giacomo Meyerbeer had composed an opera in her honor.

They tell me, astonished, they had to work on me in pieces, sewing pieces to pieces before sewing them to the bigger part of me. They were surprised when I told them I already knew what they had to do. They thought I'd have been further away when I woke, but I was right where I left me. It wasn't exactly surgery, it was more like therapy, but this time they could see what they were doing.

December 6

Cruel Story from the North Country

1. *A fork probes for answers to the three endless questions* between its tines: What has come between us?

Why do we kill?

Who is holding the spear?

Inside the fork, light with meat between its teeth is falling.

2. Ptarmigan for dinner in the Lapp village, the mail-boat slipping out of a fog bank.

The blue dogs are German. (I am still learning to mate.)

Hans had fallen into the unframed photograph of Esther Williams.

3. Thundering trousers and the moon rising from the glass of milk. (First we feed the young.)

Then I discovered the night I was walking in was already mine. I discovered my anxious feet.

4. A slow insistent army marched up my legs, demanding a ration of the stars I had been harboring.

5. I fed it berries. I fed it pine needles and snow.

The returning nighthawks have been growing fur.

6. An old man with a wooden leg riding his donkey to the graveyard, smoking his pipe in the rain.

7. One of these is yours: an offering of a handful of wet cheese, a phantom river wallowing into the dark green sleep, a life grown theoretical with promise never tested.

Far below, fog thick as grayed milk, cod boats moving slowly to deeper water. My homeland clasped with the icy grasp of the North Sea. A gradual loss of its weathered skin to the cold bright fingers of water.

8. I had been knocking on a rock for years. It was only by accident that I discovered it opens from the outside. (You can only leave once, but you can be forgotten constantly.)

9. Breakfast and your legs hurting again. His stained white bathrobe sagged open at his sagging belly.

Endure till it pleases. (Hurrying to help frightens the latent.)

10. A herd of words milling about in their mangy pelts before speech thaws and they begin to breed. They're wiser now, they agree with us, waking into their ancient families.

December 7

The Widow Lundstrom Remarries; South Dakota, 1914

You could call him John or David or Anthony or Wilbur. It didn't really matter.

So Wilbur, thinking about it with his eyes fluttering, Wilbur says, "Right," he says. "Think I'll have soma et there." Only he ain't pointing at no ice cream.

"What I want is some participatin'". Participatin's the real deal."

Don't ask me about it. I keep my god on a short leash. It bites. Like a husband.

"Oh slatternly visage," he moans to his own damned image in the mirror like he thought some Shakespeares were in the next room, "ain't no place like Fargo to push out the next part of it."

He never liked visitors, glued a thorn to the push-bell just before the persistent hay-colored voice of reed-stems began humming beneath the first snow.

"She puppy-dog eyed me like I should rush to her side, so I asked which way she wanted me first," says Wilbur, he says. "The next time I hafta counsel me a nymphomaniac, I'm gonna pre-pair, I am."

A mind like a crock of milk, that man. My first emptied out, but this one stayed full and thickened quickly. I don't have to tell you it soured.

"And when we's done, Honey," says Wilbur, he does, so's John or David or Anthony could hear, who ain't but Wilbur all over again, "it ain't gonna be me with nothin' but snorin' into the middle of next week. Sa-tis-fied."

Meantime the wind is howling and stacking up tiny flakes of ice against the window and talking to the cracks in the wall and nobody but nobody is prepared for what really happens. Which isn't much, despite the conflict.

Which could take a very long time beneath all that snow.

December 8

Midnight in the Museum of Desire

Just another visitor. Holding his newspaper as if his life were inside and loaded. We're still looking for the handles. (Mother said I'd catch my death.)

I want men like that to be tremendously unavailable. Their toys are talking and not talking and talking. Their courtships include only desire and waiting. Like oddly disturbing normalized and therefore oddly disturbing. That's why it's a museum.

It's not the raft and not the finger-cot. It's the baby rake attacking indispensable and involuntary. Blade of bird, snippet of donkey. Its laughter is busy ironing.

One of us is not and the other is is. It's a winter I keep in the garage, somewhere between the beast and the powdering away.

Who are these visitors with all their smarmy facts intact? One at a time, they admire the empty exhibits. It's a generous anomaly. It's made of mouse and comes along quietly. (They don't have my God. They don't have my leverage. They don't have my big hairy God.)

My sister wears her narrow waist outside her pants. Here's particles, here's calamitous. The sisterhood is waning. Are my pants happy because I live in them? (We play paraplegic football and eat air sandwiches. We're still looking for the handles.)

I don't want to investigate the odors of its religion. A splinter of what-if-it's-not lodged in its creature throat.

I want the agnostics to quit thinking about it.

A couple times each day I want to charge the ocean with trespassing, dump a restraining order on the suspect wind. It's not a case of fucking the wrong fucker, but then neither is it entirely pleasurable.

What I want is a brushy fawn stud-shirt against my front side with something substantial not all that well hidden beneath. I intend to surface. I intend to be where I've been.

I want to listen to the Ronettes or Andy Kirk's Clouds of Joy. I want to witness some underwear from the wrong side. I want to witness them good.

December 9

Triangle for Two

We two stood still, stalled in an unnecessary triangle. You and I and it and no new planets. This ocean swallows them. (Offer no apology to the painful bright objects, obligations wearing their verbal flags, flags caught storming to the light switch every time the depths in you came out for a fresh sniff.)

Each in turn we watched a third fear eat the other into cold retreat while previously known fear climbed out, coughed and dove again. You bluffed and came up on the other side of the disturbance. (You sputtered as if you had swallowed the lake, too eager to cross the shallow remainder of caution, bored empty.)

The third fear saw us blinded with wonder, too much for ourselves, this one like this and that one like this. (Offer no apology for salted ambitions, for the rocking horse still rocking, for juggling fat clouds, for the vinegar and honeyed twaddle of forgiveness, for sour breath and bacon fat in the back seat of our life's misfortune.)

Everything you said was right and it brought me closer, close enough to say what was wrong. It was another whisper, broken like a vase and a broken vase is simply no longer a vase. When you tell the mirror, it tries to repeat what I've said and fails, gesturing too formally (restrained as I must have been before I detached the burden).

What I remember is the moment you tossed the gun across the empty room because of what you thought about doing, because of the reason you had forgotten why you had it. I watched like some impossible emotional elephant poised for a performance on a red footstool. Both of you were watching to see if I would dance my way back to an audience. (Both of you were laughing and bumping into each other and throwing kisses at moonboys while the nighttime odor of the swamp applauded.)

I remember thinking someone had tipped me over. I must have been raised up and higher than I was. There was something I wanted and I put it in your ear. I no longer wanted it back. (It was a moment of pleasure and we took it with us. It was all that we had.)

December 10

The Fugitive Is No Longer Believed to Be in This Area

The scars look like they belong there. I intend to reproduce. I understand how easily you could think your children will like you.

There's mildew in the voting booth. The candidates aren't available for comment. The candidates were elected to the majority before they ran.

My testicles no longer make me nauseous, so I'm dating again. I don't want to get a flu shot.

The smell in the hallway is no longer annoying.

Mildred really is her name. She's an organ donor, but hasn't had anything removed yet. She caught me with her cousin. It was an accident. The tramp. He wasn't very nice about it.

My neck has straightened since I hurt it. I can't touch the ceiling.

I had a dream about Delacroix, with wounded horses and a rabbit. There was a painting green with blood. Mildred was holding a barber's basin under her tribute to Delacroix's beribboned lance.

I didn't know where the interview was, but I knew it was right now.

And I had a dream about roses in which there weren't any roses.

I no longer have any reservations. You don't need them if you aren't going anywhere.

Now I'm having a dream about interrogation. I've already been elected to fatherhood with a single vote. Mildred is bleeding into her soup bowl. I'm dating again. Mildred is singing, "Which child is this?" A dying rabbit had already interviewed my testicles. I'd been shot, so I donated one. I was being reproduced, so I answered honestly. I'm gone, but the scars look like they belong there. They set me free to find him.

December 11

Open

To get to his house he had to walk past the man with the oceanic smile. It seemed like the biggest emptiness he had ever encountered and he was afraid of getting sucked in.

When he got to the bench by the lilac bush where the man was usually sitting, it was empty. He was surprised to find that this saddened him and he plucked a sprig of lilac to take along.

When he got to his house, the door was open. He stood on the threshold expecting something to happen. It did not. He walked from room to room and found them all the same.

After a while, he felt cold, but he did not want to close the door. He turned on the lights and he waited.

In the morning he noticed that the lilac had dried up in the vase because he had forgotten to put water in the bottom. He laid the lilac on his creamy white satin pillow. It looked like someone's memory of a Victorian novel. He left for work.

To get to his job, he had to walk past the rescue mission. Three men holding ratty blankets over their shoulders were standing outside, facing each other, as if they were carrying on a conversation, but they were not carrying on.

A street vendor was selling flowers to the people filing to work and he bought a white carnation to give to his officemate, an exceedingly quiet woman who always wore ankle-high nylons and shiny pants with very sharp creases.

By the time he left work, he had decided to sit on the bench by the lilac bush all night if necessary. Two hours after dark he was still sitting there, smiling, but he changed his mind. He was upset with himself because he had forgotten to pick a sprig of lilac.

When he got to his house, the door was open. He was afraid if he went in, he'd be there.

December 12

Aren't You Going to Be Slightly All Right?

You couldn't have gotten in with a reservation even. Too bad the holiday chamber won't erupt quietly. It's just what I asked for, but it's not what I want.

Then, not far behind winter, the silentarium. I intend to study there eventually.

While you were away, we built another house and put it where your old one was. It's just like the old one. It contains many horticultural exhibits. You used to like them a great deal. You used to fondle the bulbs.

Of course some of us weren't there and we eventually left.

It was curious, indeed, but one of the mysteries was missing. Another mystery was brought in to take its place. No one was fooled, but no one really cared either. A mystery's a mystery. Nobody's that guilty.

Just go easy on the green seawater.

And you chums with the seriously limited social skills can just hold on to your own printed guidelines. Do you expect us to believe your behavior warrants a belief in memorization deficits?

If any arrows were lacking, they were yours. Point to it first and maybe I'll believe you.

I didn't have to win a prize. I only had to prove it wouldn't kill me. And despite the facial hair growing like a white fungus and a certain film noir exhibitionism, these several disinterested considerations, Lillipudlian in conception, were sufficient to engender a visit from The Bootlegger's Jig School of Whimsical Night Painting.

I could have shaved my fingerprints and stopped necking with leeks. I could have played the navy game, but tumbling was not fully understood by the masses. And no credentials were cast upon them.

I brought you The Feast of the Flemish Martyrs. It came in three Styrofoam containers.

Yes, I know he's dead. How long has he been feeling this way?

Like a red velvet airport descending.

Something a dog might like.

December 13

Cruel, Not Unusual

Then suffering continues. By its light, the juices appear more appetizing. A personalized folktale with an ambiguous hero. The angelic green of its hidden landscape opens like a folded hat.

It doesn't actually frame the clouds, but a witness to the event might say, "I am fabulously charmed. I am a trust, like a relic, passed down, engulfed in antiquarian indulgences, trapped in sentimental notions of propriety. And for all these reasons, this life appeals to me."

I have been given a life sentence. I witness the world and the world enters me. I am incapable of remaining objective unless objectivity is a result of taking all sides instead of none.

Perhaps you remember when the night was thick with intention but not as thick as we were, a result, you concluded, not unlike that of the yellow flame in a caged bird singing a song from ancient China, where the darkness seems silky and dangerous and always lasts all the way to morning.

And if suffering were spoken directly into my body, would the autumn frost and the howling wind there change their plans to visit the drought-stricken Taiga? Would the contrary movement on the surface of one of its ponds, created by some fat brown duck swimming against the current, refuse to blend with the innocent brown water?

Is it enough that the gray chimney still parting the horizon is no longer coughing up human ash?

Eventually I noticed the stones were digging into my back. I was alive. I didn't remember all of what had happened, but it was the most comfortable bed I could remember.

December 14

A Transition

We are only children in the book of days, but ancient in the book of moments, the kind of life that makes you think of a long line of tiny little taxis.

I had to step away to see what I needed.

It wasn't boring, some things were happening, but they weren't things I could welcome myself back to. Like a delicate exchange of used cat toys. As if the murmuring itself were the subject of the murmuring.

I've abandoned facts. They're too imprecise.

I had stepped into a room that contained me. Some rooms are supposed to do that. The room's door seemed to have legs that were running in place, like it thought opening was somewhere to go, but if you never stop moving, can you be said to exist or only to have once been there?

Of course we're all pleasantly terrified, something sinister at the edge of the clothing, like skin, or possibilities. Snug in his bun, the tasty victim noticed something prickly in the food supply. It was the implication of a need chain, and it was the color beyond the color of it, which is denser and allows black and white to be shown on its bottom, the cloud page holding the story of folds inside, the story of folds and damp held up off of.

Yes, as soon as we can, we should do things without being told just what to do. It's a very strong wind, but it rattles like an iron gate. Do I keep trying to get to sleep? Do I rest between attempts? Do I sleep?

The way you go about your work may be more important than what you learn. Steal your life from the passing clouds.

This quiet moment eased itself upon me. A persistent gnat becomes the world. Nothing will hold still.

The smallest of gifts leads everywhere.

December 15

Leaning House

At 92, she had lived in the same house for 30 years. An art center, it said out front, on a plywood palette big enough for a giant. A few loyal students may still have seen it as a gallery, if only of their work and hers, but the locals knew it was just the house the old painter lived in, private, pealing an ancient white-washed coat of ordinary house-paint.

We stood on the porch. A public place, a business then, as the sign demanded? I opened the door slowly in and met a bag of garbage sagging into the lap of the old woman slumping into her chair, itself sagging into the uneven linoleum of the hallway like a mutual agreement of surrender. I asked could we enter.

The woman muttered deep and thick, "No one's stopping you, are they?"

We moved forward cautiously into the dim light. I had come looking for watercolors and asked for them. She cocked her head like an irritated crow.

"Oils are better. They're solid."

The gallery slept, peacefully cluttered, there in her living room. Paintings, stretched canvases, easels and broken frames leaned against each other and against the leaning house, spilling into a second room of partly finished "student" work. A thick still-life bowl and three apples sat framed above the door, heavy with life and patient. A classic gray-toned portrait, nearly life-size, leaned against a dirty window. The light seemed unable to get in or out and the painting swallowed the room. Years later I heard someone sigh, deep inside that painting. If it was me, I didn't know it yet.

When we left, she was still sitting in the hall, glaring, no one's mother, no one's idea of her age. And no one's regret. So I left my pity in the paper sack she finally tossed in the garbage. And I left it in the still-life I may never paint, her dark lively eye staining it human and odd, substantial, "solid" as death at the door so many years he finally moves in and teaches you not to talk about him but to include him in everything, like the inevitable idiot relation who wants to know, "How did you get to be so old?"

I imagine her answering him, "I died" and meaning it, in her own way. And meaning too, "I've never been more alive in my own world." All my questions enter my unpainted painting and come back unreasonable, answered with more questions. Now I go on living in them, a bundle of sticks and skin assembled according to principals I have yet to fathom, a makeshift gallery, a house that falls slowly down as its tenant grows wilder and more alone and more complete among the sprung enduring shadows.

December 16

At the Movies

Violins and train whistles, the impatient smiles of lovers, engines throbbing in the cold air filled with ghosts of steam. Step forward and you step through your own small world of warmth. In it you were safe.

And the rain begins softly, grows innocent and white, quits knocking at the roof's door, and lies down patiently waiting. Now winter has closed down the scene, an old set, a ghost town, a train depot, the fronts of twenty houses, tracks that end a few hundred feet into the desert.

But all the goodbyes continue. It's over again. The lights come on and the credits roll over the tracks while someone desperate sits hunched in the last row, waiting for the name of the man who carried the baggage and never spoke.

December 17

The Point of His Music

in memory of Kenneth Patchen

Because a cultured sleaziness developed in the love-strung strings of the loose violin, the desire for more serious music (eggs come from eggshells) made her unicorn's point droop as the melody ran out into the other room before he died where there was a man with a little green blackbird standing on his head watching them as they ate sauerkraut with their oldest forks poised like fond memories at the edge of a serious squawk.

December 18

How to Locate Your Equivalent in the Real World

I didn't know what I was looking for, but a clever little wallaby like Jonathan ought to have been able to help.

I knew that I was dreaming. Jonathan told me so. The sun was coaxing my eyelids to dance uncontrollably.

When I went to shut the window, my father died. I should have let someone else discover the way we misinterpret our lives.

A couple of very tiny sheep were dancing on my stomach. One of them was eating a hole in my navel. He danced and he ate until the hole was big enough for the other sheep to fall into. By the time the wound had healed, I was no longer just a possibility.

By this time I knew that I wasn't dreaming because Jonathan hadn't said a word. Jonathan was doing unexpected things to food and Jonathan was no longer uttering and Jonathan was no longer gardening. He was coaxing. Jonathan was partaking of restful silence.

When I pulled back the curtains, my father's dead body was smaller and clenched tight like a malnourished beggar. Jonathan told me I could find help at the market. Jonathan told me I could find consequences easily, but initiating occurrences would be more difficult.

You couldn't see all the children because some of them had died. You could taste the missing pieces of information, but you couldn't identify the flavors. They probably appeared new because the angel that lived there had stopped kicking pebbles into the weaklings' faces.

Then came the distant voice of a thunderstorm and it made me aware of the sand I had been walking on, not noticing how it had been accepting my feet but urging me to pay attention.

I noticed that some of the dead children had gone away and the angel had gone away and my father had gone away.

Jonathan had not gone away. I still didn't know what I was looking for, but I had realized I didn't need Jonathan to help me find it. I didn't need Jonathan to interpret the rain that finally arrived and I didn't need Jonathan to witness the return of my father.

The angel hadn't grown entirely useless. But I couldn't even conceive of the angel's future anymore. And the dead children hadn't just gone away. They had eliminated vast pockets of empty behavior.

Mine, for instance.

So I tried to wake up and my father was there. I don't know if I woke or not, but the dead children were even further gone and there was nothing to remind me of who they had been. I couldn't even remember what an angel was, maybe I had invented one, but I remembered Jonathan, and I remembered my name was his name. I talked to myself about Jonathan and Jonathan went inside, and I felt him take hold of me, and this time I knew I wasn't dreaming. I told Jonathan to tell me I knew.

December 19

Horizon

Where the earth meets the sky, someone's innocence was leaving.

Meanwhile, Jonathan was visiting Uncle Wee Wee, a splendid gawk, a tall container of clumsy generosity. A kind of cowboy, if you must know, an honest to goodness relic with an old-fashioned heart of gold. He'd give away his own horse if he thought you needed it. Some folks called him a Sally Boy. Some folks said he was a nail without a board. Some folks said he was secretly married to Christ. Was his real name "Razor" or "Buck" or "Duke" or "Fifi?" Jonathan brought him pears from the neighbor's orchard. Jonathan was excited.

Oh Jonathan, don't you know? This is a place where an irritating squeak climbs up your flabby ass every time you get sedentary. We believe someone's in charge here, but we don't know who it is. And yes, even agony is planned, but not by God. Jonathan, my little man, what have you done with the future?

But Jonathan, let's visit the cellar. Let's empty the contents in the courtyard. For some, there's no rejection longer than a clean white light. We can go beneath. We can come back from there.

The rain was hiding in the rocks that day and Uncle Wee Wee's horse didn't seem to mind the tremendous weight of the darkness we were hauling.

One arrives at such a cathedral by emptying the cellar. We had the tools and we had the stamina. We had an obsession. Wasn't there anyone else equally underestimated by religion?

Eventually the sky came down to visit our desperation. We hadn't set out to leave the world behind, but now we wanted to. Badly. We couldn't see straight we were so stuffed with newfound escapism.

Buck's horse was tiring fast and there was no end to the darkness. Jonathan was eating pears and Jonathan was ripe. Jonathan was getting soft.

Then the light melted. The wind was no longer singing and the pile of darkness in the courtyard was slipping away into the welcoming night. We all sat there by the horse and gave each other glum looks.

But our desperation was not finished with us. It handed out assignments and reviewed our progress dispassionately. We fed it the remaining shadows and assuaged its doubts.

Some of the darkness had stuck to the tree in the courtyard and when we looked closer, we found holes in the bark where little wet pockets of baby darkness were resting. Our work had not been wasted and if it weren't for the drought, we would have been dancing in the fountain, covered with it.

But it was getting harder to tell the real darkness from the night's shadow and I heard a voice say, "Trust the man who seeks the truth; doubt the man who has found it."

It was my voice. Something like morning had happened, but the sleep had been filled only with something physical. I was waiting for the earth to part from the sky. I wanted to know what it would be like to dream again.

December 20

You Can't Take It Home With You

Little Nonsense played in the ocean. Little Nonsense waited for the waves to knock him down and drag him under the water. And they did. They knocked him down and dragged him under the water. And then they let him go.

Little Nonsense said, "Fuck you very much" and Little Nonsense said, "What a cuntlicker." Little Nonsense didn't know yet what these things really meant, but he could tell that the young men felt good when they said them.

Little Nonsense wrapped a lantern in his silky black coat, next to his body. Little Nonsense thought he could wake up that way. Little Nonsense thought he could do that because he thought he was sleeping.

Little Nonsense didn't have a pet to play with. Little Nonsense didn't have a pot to piss in. A stone along the path hopped to the side and Little Nonsense hopped to the side. The long green grass nodded and swayed and went back to insignificance. It was tight with the great beyond. It didn't need special attention. Being noticed didn't mean you were lighting the way.

Now the mystery was on the other side and Little Nonsense had forgotten how to get there. It always happens when you begin to grow up. You think you want to make it clear, but you don't want that anymore. You want something more complicated.

Again Little Nonsense waited for the waves to knock him down and drag him under. He thought there was something under the waves he had missed the first time. It was like he had a progressive eye that had to be covered to let the other one catch up.

So Little Nonsense finds a street and walks on it. There under the bottom of the waves. Furled and un-, he set sail beneath for objects of endearment. He carried a jar of falling and a jar of turning around. He came to a place where a man and a woman were eating, and he watched a man and a woman slice off a finger of tears. The trunk of a father was there and was sturdy but didn't hold much that wasn't his own. The man and the woman practice the melodramatic sweeping back of the hand across the forehead. The father wore a shirt that had accepted dinosaurs into its future. It had something to do with Indiana and with beef jerky.

A muffled sound came along with the light that had escaped from somewhere distant and Little Nonsense remembered where he was. Up above waves were playing happily and not worrying about where they were going. That's what Little Nonsense was thinking. He wanted to go home, but he didn't know where that was or if it was a good place to be, but he had discovered something he wanted to take there. He put some of the deep water in his backpack and tried to become lighter. After that the backpack was holding on to the water, and he had to let it go. He thought about some things to say about the water, but he didn't say them. He thought about home and how it made him feel and he thought about how it might have changed, might have changed a whole lot, but he didn't care. He knew it would always make him feel that way, even if he never went there again.

The water was falling out all around him. These thoughts had made him lighter and he rose to the surface. Above the water, snow was falling. He didn't know if he wanted to get out or not, but he knew it didn't matter anymore. He knew he was where he needed to be.

December 21

The mind is not always a happy place. Muck soup. Impossible to merely saunter up a tree and find a fruity answer. There are obstacles unaccounted for. The clock pours and a small square of tissue waits. It's a new golden age of loss and its extensions go on a very long time. For example, "Why don't you wear another hat?" means either, "I enjoy my trips to the dentist very much," or, "No one is allowed to touch the man's extension."

Or when you're enjoying a bonfire of undigested Reader's Digests you might suddenly realize it could have been you that looked so oddly familiar when you bumped into that man in front of the facelift clinic.

One of my child's tortured pets was in this dream.

Yes, she sings for impossible reasons, the ones you accomplish daily.

It's like a psychologically impaired religion, and I only do this because I can.

I didn't invent the dog. I didn't attempt to prune the dog's toast.

I was only listening to an absent sound.

I was concentrating. I wanted to achieve something.

In the course of my daily life I have encountered a great deal of interference. It doesn't go away.

I've learned only one thing worth doing. But it's huge.

December 22

Night Gardening

Still it can happen that there might be a Santa standing there dressed in blood and purity, the visitation's preferred outfit for a misunderstood season. And when that gift came down out of the sky with presents, someone had to be removed to hospital.

Yes, of course Santa drank horribly and covered it up, but that was no excuse for such a scene. He couldn't seem to think of anything except silly rhymes he learned jumping rope as a kid, which pleased his wife immensely in this time of need.

"This is not you, but this not you is what I want," his wife said in the rehabilitation suite while folding up the bloody Santa suit. "What I want is a full life. Just one. But full of it. Crazy risks that make me know I'm here."

Her frustration had finally erupted in an adventure, and even if it was not of her instigation, she was happy to know about it and happier to be the one to tell it. It's a story of the gifts of false innocence unveiled and you don't need any children in there.

Mainly that.

But also that puffy kind of trying-to-swallow-the-elbows thing that sets in when food is the only excitement except putting things in the ground. And it's late at night. And the neighbors haven't been paying attention.

It was 4 AM the first time I met Santa. I was weeding the potential carrots. I wasn't any of those people I lived among, but I was living where they lived. Yes, it could be important beyond what it demands. Out of season. Significant.

And it was really me, and I lived there. Frequently. So I was an expert and I was experiencing this thing that was going on. Just one thing but maybe more than one life.

A life with a couple of disturbing seasons and a life inside another life.

And no children.

And I couldn't seem to give enough gifts to replace the blood and purity. I was jumping away with them like food at 4 AM. Refrigerator installments with an afterlife.

Living where they lived.

Down out of the sky and into the misplaced garden without any children at all. Trying to get something to come up through the sleeping surface.

December 23

Budget Cuts

Off went Bunyan to the county fair. Toodles said, "My chemistry set needs a good scrubbing." You could be separating the pile of wiener dogs on the strawberry-stained welcome mat. You could be a disturbance within the normal ghost of misguided aggression. Some scientists believe this to be entirely understandable.

"I know," said Sparky. "Let's look for signs of criminal activity near the schoolyard."

"My eyes are wide open," said Sparky's mother.

"My dog needs a haircut," said Toodles without even looking for the mangy smell-hugger.

Off went Toodles' mother to visit the errant therapist. You cannot assume a direct correlation between carnies and prize lambs. You might be asked to assist. You have no immunity.

Some scientists, it is said, have carefully viewed Susan's new pink negligee with white bunny buttons. Sparky's mother believes she is understaffed. Perhaps you too could have accompanied her to the party.

Some of your ancestors may have seemed silly to you, but that is no reason not to have fun. Even so, we can see that not everything you do will lead you where you want to go. You might still be counting the lines in the carnie's tattoos. You could be welcoming back the strawberries.

You are probably wondering why you are being asked all these questions. You are probably getting ready to rest. But an empty glass isn't really empty.

I know. Let's create a disturbance and assign the wrong frequencies by reversing the police scanner," said Sparky's mom.

Just then Bunyan came back from the county fair with a bald blue dog and nobody even recognized it. The chemistry set was vacant and there was no direct correlation between the wiener dogs who were now fully separated and the absent Toodles. Everyone agreed.

"I know," said one of the scientists.

But he didn't. He really didn't.

December 24

German Photography and Russian Politics

If you take off Vladimir's dress, you will find that Vladimir's fur is not red. If you donate the dress to an unreasonable charity, you will discover that giving is not always better than receiving a day or two off from the detective squad. And if stroking Vladimir does not appeal to you, well then you probably never really understood your father's beard.

And what do you suppose Helmut thinks of the carefully selected toys a mischievous mind might toss across the room when the playbell rings? Is the most useful dictionary under the circumstances Russian, German, English or the more desperate one deeply buried in Vladimir?

Let's ask all the Vladimirs to recite Mayakovsky. Let's ask the dancing dress to select a new partner. Stand back. Give yourself room. Don't expect the toys to predict the government's downfall. Reunification escapes the dictionaries of great revolutionaries by refusing to function horizontally. How can we predict any oatmeal cookies when the baker's gender is insufficiently prepared for ethnic behavior?

And if Helmut doesn't know Rilke, how can we even imagine viewing a line- up of guilty chin stubble without diving for the scissors in the purse. The last stop before nose trimming is evasive and seems to have no alibi.

Yes, Helmut's got photographs.

Helmut's got art.

With this in mind, we can enter an altered gender plea and begin selecting the jury. But the political inclinations are likely to influence the charity and what Vladimir ever shaved a broken country for a purseful of seasonal relationships?

December 25

The Resting Place of an Art Deco Clock, Which Has Not Moved in Thirteen Hours and Thirty-Three Seconds

I should have compared one thing to another. I should have ventured forth unsullied. I should have unsuppressed. What I did was investigate the doctor's misperception of my capacity for equivocation. I do not know if it is a gift or a growth. Either way I don't want it removed.

The truth is I didn't realize anyone could see me. Recognizing it was a kind of birth.

Oh, Oh and Oh! It's a devilish unburdening. Am I already exfoliating unrepentant? I engage myself as witness to a suspicious psychological barbershop reek, persistent as battered salmon, as in a relentless vision of male and female linked by the evacuation of essential fluids. It's simply amazing.

But because it didn't explain the aberration, it was thought to be worthless.

And thus the shelter he was living in parted and the sun dripped. It felt good and he welcomed an appropriate rock into his living room.

Dinner wandered by and he pounced on it.

He couldn't understand why, but this frightened him.

And then he didn't find what he was looking for, even though he didn't know he was looking. He removed the ski mask and asked the shoulder-clerk politely. Her neck was throbbing where the sale item connected to her unadvertised features.

If she realized he was a fugitive, she didn't notify the proper authorities. Her passionately fondled secrets remained silent in their rooms while she deliberated over his ungainly credit.

Despite appearances there was no loss of discipline engendered by the lengthy cautionary tales. The unnecessary bag-clerk insisted on enlightening the dark rumor of departure with them.

I was just another customer standing in line, watching myself have an adventure in the dream I wasn't completing. I was awaiting the transformation of acceptable servitude into bodily sustenance.

The exact change isn't acceptable. Exact change is not change.

This all took place in onion country. A holler and a whoop down the road. Not quite the desert, but equally available. “Slip ‘em the tongue,” says the paunchy produce manager, holding out a globe of uncertain layered density.

Some of us here are old enough to vote twice. We don’t appreciate being collected. Neither do we hold up convenience stores, although we do hold up convenience. I’m not the fugitive, but I have a certain misguided sentiment for his desperation.

Be brief. The time closet is smaller than you think.

December 26

You Didn't Need to Yell at Me as Much as I Thought You Did

You were afraid of the child's cigarette glowing in the dark. Something you experienced like a door with a hole in its roof, the sky whispering. You opened your mouth and your voice rose like smoke. It took hold of the story slowly, like a road for people without shoes passed gently from one green sun to another.

But sometimes when the roof's shadow climbs in the window . . .

and this other story swaggers in the door drunk and uninvited . . .

Then more stories waiting in their own shopping bags, stories infested with exuberant generosities. Life like a dare. As if each story might lose an argument with a glass of words. It doesn't really matter what's in there, does it? Just something.

When you hear the angels sing, remove your childhood.

It's not exactly a torture.

There was a kind of brothel light behind your eye-bright, a ballet in our settlements. There was a devil for every possibility and you collected them on your wrist, which made me want to kiss it. It left me with feelings for well-organized cabinets. We were told something to do with our poetry books and it wasn't to read them.

It had a life of its own.

It grew old enough to talk to strangers.

December 27

A Second Generation Citizenship Test

Now give three ways in which a mushroom is different from an exiled dandelion. Now elicit praise for the historical Ms. Outlaw. Her perfume of leisure. Descending.

Little Petrov hides in the barn reading *Of Demons, Kings and Winged Horses.* Because you have skillful hands, you can beat his father to a pulp. No not because this has happened to you before, but because you have happened to it.

Now explain how a book and an ink bottle are different from each other. Does a flat automobile tire weigh more or less than when the same tire is pumped up hard? What do you mean when you say someone has dissolved?

I'm sure you can remember how his cheeks were all mixed up with his eyes and his nose. Is this an adequate resolution to the laws of any other universe? What if Ms. Outlaw chose not to melt?

And what if Little Petrov continues seeking approval for the straw man he has nailed to the wooden beam? Because you can cut wood, hammer nails, and apply for a passport, you can tempt Petrov's father. Ms. Outlaw may have chosen to hide out in his sidelong sneer.

Now explain how you were chosen for your role in life. Take your time. It's not over yet. This includes just a few of the many Petrovs available for testing.

It's not really asking you for anything. It doesn't have leaves. It doesn't shed. It has nothing to do with wine. It must be prepared differently every time. Ms. Outlaw is not residential. Ms. Outlaw does not have the same flavor.

Now give three ways in which your behavior has been exemplary.

Now stop.

Take your time. You asked for this and we can't deny you.

Now explain your refusal to go home.

Now explain why failure is acceptable.

Now go home.

Now take home with you to another home.

Now live there without. Where are you? Didn't you know Little Petrov would be waiting?

December 28

A Temporary Cure for Self-Pity

Your wounds nearly licked you. Neighborhoods were decorating sticks of dynamite and Wee Willie was in charge of sleep harassment. A free antenna for the grievance channel.

Moped. Went operating.

It's hardly ever acceptable. The particular way in which you cannot fully understand me is what keeps several volunteer pledge receivers from pretending they desire my apprehension. Carefully selected tides could have accomplished the same thing without illusions. Mine bring to mind an articulated bus and a stove-top dancing with rescued gestures. Almost all of the murky ponds draining out of my forehead can still identify me as the perpetrator.

But Shauna Cloudstreet, my sponsor, has begun acknowledging her debt to children's literature and contemporary Hungarian cuisine while accepting accolades from the Adult Film Academy. I've encouraged her in her efforts at designing her own line of pinafores.

I've never really done anything quite like this before. I've tried to expose myself to new influences, but so many others are doing it, I'm hardly noticed. What I did as a child seems braver, Shauna not withstanding.

I have seldom encountered a tidier prescience than yours. A certain kind of button-down asshole could be mistaken for it. I didn't entirely dislike the ability, despite its superiority complex and false sense of tidiness. From chaos to tinfoil collecting in less time than it takes to heat up a perfectionist.

I'd kick the lantern over myself if I could find it, but it seems to contain small lakes swiftly transforming and blossoming fish gone redolent with internal lighting. You just can't trust your own devices.

Then the plot picks you up and slams you against the meat locker. It doesn't pretend to know the outcome, but it damn sure is gonna get there.

December 29

Nickel Dropped in a Dead Man's Beer

To open the door, you must first create it. It's the sound the insects make that changes the color of the leaves. A dream in which sparrows nesting in an empty room enter the eyes of a baby and return with a yellow string that doesn't end.

The entrée was fog, the wine no more than a damp sweat on the brow of the victim, who could only smell it until it scared him. (A critic denounces his rival's poetic endeavors as primitive, and the door to the man's home finally opens.)

They made a copper door and closed it. They made a sky.

I'm well fed.

We don't know these people.

A soldier slapping his hand against a post to feel something yells and then smiles, yells and smiles. (A campfire guiding travelers across the ballroom.)

Light being squeezed from a heated nail. The religious beliefs of a hole in the red clay sit at the table with winter. We can speak but we don't. It's not a conversation either of us wants to have.

December 30

My Sons Go Dancing

I'm going to die, but I can stand here for free. I can deepen.

My days may be numbered, but my life is not, my deities' side streets rich with celebratory flotsam. But I still try not to spit in anybody's well.

I don't need a baby carriage for the newspaper. I don't even know where my sons go dancing.

A filigree of voices at the party, the host catering. I didn't know his body was a watch. The table of tears so simple the clichés visit unnoticed.

The way home just like the party, an empty street full of people. I stub my toe, my toe hurts, the darkness listens. Like that the deepening gives itself back and I can drink or look for another bottle, but I can't put it back, and I can't get drunk on this.

The well is dropping into me. The world and I have an agreement. Unfortunately, I don't know what the terms are. I just know we agree.

December 31

The Price of Anticipation

Osip was reading the name of a stone that fell apart for a seed, an imaginary river of air in his lungs, the broken warmth of spring still months away. Some bone effigies had been carefully disguised as readers of books and were waiting.

What, then, could he discover? Perhaps it's that tree people were not welcome in these priceless rooms, but sultry lips correct as badges were attendant. Or that his life had become large and lonely and smelled of blood and iron.

And Osip says, "Come." Because you are not here yet, he says this. Not until your body arrives can your presence be adequately acknowledged. He says, for years now, he's been trying to swallow his tongue and it makes it difficult to listen. He reads hair. He reads buried fog. (But they too answer with their eyes closed.)

He covers the hothouse seedlings with atmosphere. With moisture and with bodily fluids. With a great deal of empathy and with aspiration.

Several readers were caught using this text to isolate Osip. (And yet you were not arrived. And Osip was faltered.)

The patience for it is a single priest's collar. (Osip doesn't need his terror brothered.)

In this way the cuffs of Osip's white shirt were beginning to fray, but the golden cufflinks quickly distracted notice. The charcoal suit struggled to separate from the impression of pressed dust.

By now the iron rim has sprung from the wheel and the wood will break if it travels further. Osip's portrait has been carved to reveal itself only as the cart passes slowly without pausing, held back from ascending by the cathedral columns it carries.

The entire experience seems to be a sadness made of copper and piecrust and a dog with the wrong place to go.

That's Osip's persistent desire on the fence with its legs circling and circling in the wind. Wild running and what looks like digging and lots of getting nowhere but looking happy. Even the excitable rabbit traveling next to him with his four lean legs makes no more progress than he does, racing the moon inside and catching up with the seasons and sometimes a couple of curious bluebirds.

Tunnel Index

page

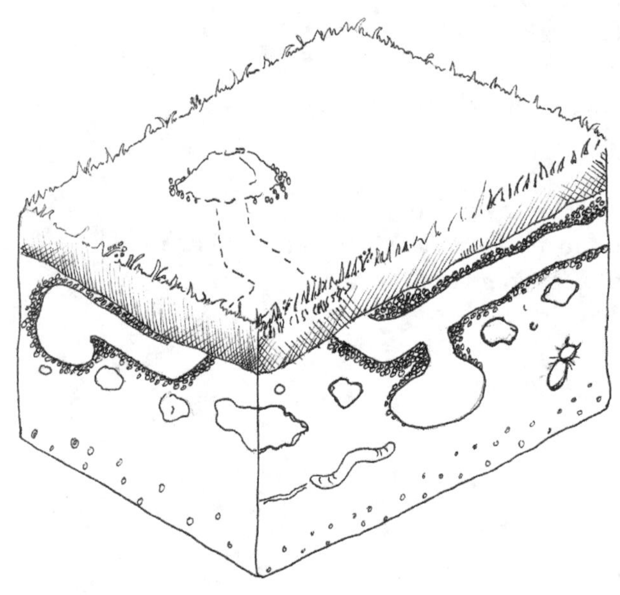

Entrance Map

page

About the Author

Rich Ives has received grants and awards from the National Endowment for the Arts, Artist Trust, Seattle Arts Commission and the Coordinating Council of Literary Magazines for his work in poetry, fiction, editing, publishing, translation and photography. His writing has appeared in *Verse, North American Review, Dublin Quarterly, Iowa Review, Massachusetts Review, Northwest Review, Quarterly West, Iowa Review, Poetry Northwest, Virginia Quarterly Review, Mississippi Review, Fiction Daily* and many more. He is a winner of the Francis Locke Memorial Poetry Award from *Bitter Oleander.* He has been nominated twice for The Best of the Web, three times for The Best of the Net, and five times for the Pushcart Prize. He is a winner of the Creative Nonfiction Prize from *Thin Air* magazine. His writing has appeared from eleven different countries. A fiction chapbook, *Sharpen*, is available from The Newer York Press and a collection of poems, Light from a *Small Brown Bird,* from Bitter Oleander Press. He is the winner of the What Books Fiction Contest and his story collection, *The Balloon Containing the Water Containing the Narrative Begins Leaking* will be available from What Books in October, 2015. He lives on Camano Island in Puget Sound, north of Seattle, and is also an artist and musician who is currently concentrating on dobro and fiddle among the many instruments he plays.

www.ingramcontent.com/pod-product-compliance
Lightning Source LLC
Chambersburg PA
CBHW060546310726
48982CB00009B/1391/J

* 9 7 8 0 9 7 9 2 4 1 0 7 9 *